THE DEVIL TO PAY

K. C. BATEMAN

KATE BATEMAN

Print ISBN: 978-1-7326378-1-8

E-Book ISBN-13: 978-1-7326378-0-1

"Love is a kind of warfare."
Ovid, 'Ars Amatoria'
- The Art of Love.

CHAPTER 1

 entral Italy, June 1492.

CARA DI MONTESSORI was sick of people trying to kill her.

As a child she'd trailed her father through some of the most godforsaken places in Christendom, so it had been a rare week that hadn't included a scimitar-wielding Saracen or bloodthirsty Moor trying to send her to the afterlife. Familiarity with the experience did not make it any more enjoyable. And besides, those instances had been impersonal, only to be expected of campaigning, whereas *this* attempt was personal in the extreme. 'Uncle' Lorenzo did not want her alive to dispute his seizure of Castelleon.

His men were proving annoyingly persistent. He must have offered a ransom to keep them on her tail, and though Cara doubted her life was worth a great deal, everyone had their price. In truth, she was staking her life on that very premise, about to make a pact with the Devil himself.

If she could reach him.

Alessandro del Sarto, 'Il Diavolo,' was the last person in Italy she would have chosen to ask for help, but engaging his dubious talents was her only hope of staying alive and regaining her home.

He was *condottiero*. A killer for hire.

Cara wrinkled her nose in distaste. Mercenary described both del Sarto's profession and his nature. Il Diavolo sold himself to the highest bidder. He didn't care which side won or lost, or whether the cause was worth fighting for, only whether the victor could pay his exorbitant fees. Every monarch in Europe wanted him. And now she needed him, too.

'Better to dance with the devil you know,' Father used to say. Well, she hadn't seen *this* particular devil in six long years, not since she was sixteen. He'd knocked her on her backside, then kissed her until she'd seen stars. She'd threatened to kill him in return. He'd haunted her dreams ever since.

Cara shivered. She hated being cold. At least if she ended up in hell for bartering her soul she'd be warm. She nudged her exhausted horse forward and wished—for perhaps the hundredth time—that she'd stolen a mount with a better saddle.

The urge to slump over the animal's scrawny neck was so strong. She hadn't eaten for two days, hadn't dared stop for more than an hour at most. Every jolt of the animal's hooves reopened the wound at her ribs and brought a fresh wave of dizziness and pain. Perchance the quick slash of an assassin's blade would be preferable to dying slowly of blood loss?

No. She would reach Il Diavolo. She had hundreds of things she wanted to do before leaving this world, and she'd hardly managed to achieve any of them. Quite apart from avenging her father's death and regaining her home, she planned on dying a wrinkled old crone in a nice warm bed, surrounded by a huge and loving family. A young, heroic death was all very well in principle, but it looked extremely unappealing now it was a distinct possibility.

Whirling lights crowded her vision like fireflies and Cara shook her head. The stumbling horse crested a rise, and she let out a breathless prayer of thanks. There it was, outlined against the deepening twilight; Torre di San Rocco, the fortified city stronghold of Italy's most infamous son.

Cara kicked the horse into an exhausted trot. She would reach Il Diavolo, or die trying.

CHAPTER 2

"*Y*ou've got to choose one of them. What about Lucrezia Borgia?"

Alessandro del Sarto, 'Il Diavolo', drummed his fingers on the armrest of his chair and briefly considered strangling his second-in-command. Not enough to kill him, of course. Just enough to stop this infernal listing of prospective brides.

He'd spent all day scaring the wits out of people and his head ached as if he'd been hit with a battle-axe. First, he'd dealt with a line of petitioners who'd flocked to the castle to beg him to settle their petty disputes. He didn't *care* who'd stolen whose goat. Then he'd spent a few hours thrashing the cockiness out of some raw recruits on the training field. That had been fun, admittedly, but now his shoulder hurt like the devil. Lastly, he'd overseen the flogging of a man convicted of assault. All that screaming and begging for mercy had made his ears ring.

Alessandro took a sip of wine and cast a simmering glance over the crowd milling before the dais. Even those brave enough to meet his eyes failed to hold his gaze for longer than a heartbeat. He smiled at a servant, baring his teeth in the merest hint of a snarl—and chuckled as the poor boy paled in fright and dropped his tray.

Francesco Neroni shot him a disapproving glance. "Stop ignoring me. You haven't lost your hearing as well as the use of your sword arm."

Alessandro's glower usually had the power to send brave men scurrying from the room. Sadly, it had no effect on the grizzled old soldier next to him.

"You look like a bulldog that's swallowed a wasp," Francesco continued calmly. "You forget, my lord, that I'm immune to your scowls." He pushed forward a small portrait. "What's wrong with the Borgia girl? She's pretty enough. And she's already buried her first husband, so you won't have to contend with a simpering virgin."

"I don't care if she speaks seventeen languages and plays the lute like an angel. I'm not marrying anyone, least of all Rodrigo Borgia's bastard."

"He *is* the Pope. No harm in getting on God's good side."

Alessandro snorted. "It's a sad outlook for Christians everywhere if that whoring, murdering tyrant is the Almighty's best representative on earth. And you've conveniently forgotten her brother. Cesare's a madman."

"Hardly the perfect brother-in-law, I'll admit. Rumor has it he's already killed one of his brothers." Francesco drew a line through the name at the top of his list. "Pity. You need all the divine blessing you can get."

"Your concern for my blackened soul is touching," Alessandro said dryly. "But the answer is still no."

"Fine. Forget an alliance with Rome. What about Naples? There's the sister of the king of Navarre . . ." The next portrait showed a buxom girl with a huge ruby nestled in her mountainous cleavage. "Fantastic breasts," Francesco coaxed. "It's like she's got two piglets wrestling in her bodice."

Alessandro glanced over. "She looks like a horse."

"You love horses."

"True enough. If you can find me a woman as brave and loyal as Saraceno I'll marry her on the spot, whatever she looks like."

It was Francesco's turn to snort. "Bollocks! You've an eye for beauty, Sandro, whether it's horseflesh or women." He sighed deeply. "I don't know why you're being so fussy. They're all the same with the lights out. You don't look at the fireplace when you're poking the fire, do you?"

Alessandro rolled his eyes. "I bet the ladies just love that silver tongue of yours."

"I do well enough, thank you," Francesco sniffed.

"Not with the only one you truly *want*. How *is* Renata?"

A flush reddened Francesco's neck at the mention of his unrequited love. "She's fine."

Alessandro shrugged. "You're probably the only man in the whole keep who hasn't had her. Just go to her room, slip her a few coins, and put yourself out of your misery."

"I will not! She doesn't do that sort of thing any more."

Alessandro raised his hands in surrender. "Eh, I admire her. At least she and the other camp followers are honest in their dealings." He nodded at Francesco's paper. "Those high-born girls on your list are no different, though they pretend otherwise. They're all willing to sell themselves. The only difference is the price."

Francesco deleted another name. "No to Principessa d'Albret then." He brushed the feathered end of his quill back and forth against his chin, where it caught against the short bristles of his beard. "You're not making this easy. How hard can it be to choose a wife from scores of rich, beautiful women?"

"Ah, yes, it is wonderful to be me." Alessandro spread his arms wide in a mocking, theatrical gesture that made the nearest candles flicker. "Behold, Il Diavolo," he lowered his voice so only Francesco could hear. "I couldn't even fight an old woman at the moment. Who *wouldn't* want me as a husband?"

"Stop being so dramatic. Your shoulder will be fine in a few weeks."

Alessandro growled. "We got back from Spain three months ago and it still hurts. Those same princes begging me to marry their daughters would all be challenging me to a fight if they knew I'd been injured." He glared at the room in general. "God, I hate sitting around doing nothing. I'd give anything to be to be spurring Saraceno into battle."

Francesco shrugged. "I'm not the only one who's grateful for a roof over my head and hot food in my belly. The men are glad to be taking a break, though they'd never admit it. Maybe it's a sign that you should think about settling down."

Alessandro didn't answer, so Francesco forged on. "You've rejected Florence, Naples, Rome, Milan, and Venice. There's hardly anywhere left." He pinched the bridge of his nose. "You haven't had a woman since we got back, Sandro. It's doing nothing to improve your temper, let me tell you."

"None of those girls would have me if they knew they were being bound to a cripple."

"Don't exaggerate. It's only temporary." Francesco inhaled sharply as a new thought struck him. "God, you haven't lost the use of *that* blade, have you?" He shot a meaningful glance at Alessandro's crotch.

Alessandro chuckled at his horrified expression. "No."

"Sure? Want me to send a girl up? Check everything's in working order? We've just got a new kitchen maid from Bologna. She's not a great looker, but I hear she's very enthusiastic."

"Not tonight. I'm in no mood for company."

"Your loss." Francesco studied his list again. "You know, you're going to have to choose one of these girls eventually, just to keep the peace."

Alessandro suppressed a howl of frustration. The scheming and machinations of court life bored him to tears. He hated the endless plotting and posturing, gossiping and backstabbing that

7

would accompany his guests when they arrived in a week's time. All those overdressed, slyly manipulating ladies with their not-so-subtle innuendoes and flirtations. Offers to grace his bed in return for a glittering trinket or a political favor.

It wasn't in his nature to pander and fawn. In his mind, action was always better than diplomacy. Bad enough that he was considering a pact of non-aggression with his neighbors so they could unite against the French. But to marry one of their spoilt, whining daughters as well, to sweeten the deal? That was too much.

"They'll never leave you alone until you're married," Francesco murmured.

"Don't you ever give up?"

The commander shook his head.

On the battlefield Francesco's refusal to admit defeat was a quality Alessandro truly appreciated. In this instance, however, it was just irritating. He stretched his hand forward with a resigned sigh. "Oh, give it here. I'll look at it again, but not tonight. I'm going to bed."

CHAPTER 3

*C*ara clutched the hilt of her dagger and pressed back into the shadows. A guard passed her hiding place and she waited a few minutes to make sure he'd gone, then flexed her fingers on the grip of her dagger. Her palm was sweaty. She could practically hear her father's chiding voice, echoing down the corridor.

A lady never mentions such things as sweaty palms, Cara.

Her heart twisted in her chest. Poor Father. He'd always wanted her to be a model of feminine respectability. Unfortunately, it seemed a little late to start now, at the ripe old age of twenty-two.

She inhaled a deep breath, crept forward, and pushed the heavy door inward. The room beyond was dark. Only a low fire glowed in the huge open fireplace and she could just make out the shape of a man slouched in a huge wing armchair. Her pulse pounded in her throat.

"Francesco sent you, didn't he?"

The voice, the one she remembered so well, was a gravelly purr, deep and forbidding. When this man spoke, he was obeyed. Without question.

What on earth was he talking about?

Cara edged closer, keeping her dagger hidden in the folds of her cloak.

* * *

ALESSANDRO LIFTED his head and scowled. He hadn't bothered to light the candles; the gloom suited his mood. He could barely see the cloaked figure that had entered.

Francesco must have sent a girl up anyway, the disobedient swine. She lingered uncertainly by the door—afraid of him, he supposed. Who wasn't? Still, for some reason her reluctance annoyed him. "Come forward."

The girl took a tentative step. A hood shielded her face and a dark cloak concealed her body, but she looked slim, beneath the folds. What had Francesco said about that kitchen maid? Ugly, but skilled.

She took another step closer and the firelight offered a brief glimpse of smooth jaw and pink lips beneath the hood. Skin the color of honey and cream.

An unexpected throb of desire shot to Alessandro's groin. He usually preferred well-rounded, experienced females who knew how to play the game. Women who understood that this was nothing more than a straightforward exchange, money for brief mutual gratification.

Still, perhaps he wasn't as tired as he'd thought. Maybe Francesco was right. A night in the arms of a willing wench might relieve the dissatisfaction that had plagued him for so long.

* * *

CARA TOOK an instinctive step back as Il Diavolo stood and straightened to his full, impressive height. Lord above, he was even larger than she remembered.

"You might as well come in, now you're here. And take off the cloak. We'll get to the rest later." He beckoned her forward with an imperious wave of his hand. "Closer. I won't bite." White teeth flashed. "Not unless you want me to, of course."

He must have seen her lips part in confusion because he shook his head and his low voice shimmered across the darkness. "No talking, sweeting. I'm not paying you for conversation."

Cara's brain took a few seconds to assimilate his words. And then her jaw dropped. *A whore.* He thought she was a whore! She almost laughed out loud. This was definitely the first time in her life anyone had made *that* mistake.

He cocked his head to one side, like a bird of prey eyeing its next meal. A log rolled down as the fire collapsed, sending up a flare of sparks, and the sudden orange glow showed his features in sharp relief. Flames danced over one high, angled cheekbone and a jaw faintly darkened with day-old beard.

Cara forgot to breathe.

No wonder he'd been dubbed 'Il Diavolo.' He truly resembled a sulky, brooding demon. She suppressed a growl. There was no justice in the world. A heartless mercenary shouldn't look like this. Years of remorseless killing should be etched upon his features, a visual map of his sins. He should be old and bloated, grotesque and jowled. He should look like the devil they called him.

She swallowed. Oh, he looked like the devil, all right. Tall and darkly beautiful. Languid and sulky—and unmistakably dangerous.

He's a murderer. A killer for hire. Absolutely not the kind of man to be attracted to.

And yet a strange heat uncurled in the pit of her stomach, a reaction she always associated with him; fear laced with . . . anticipation?

She forced herself to take another step forward, glad of the blade in the folds of her cloak, and kept her eyes downcast rather than look him full in the face. She took a steadying breath—and immediately regretted it when she inhaled his scent; a disturbingly appealing combination of leather, wood-smoke and man.

Do not *get distracted.*

He caught her hip with his big hand and tugged her the last remaining inches into his chest. Cara forced herself to remain passive, fought the urge to pull back from the searing, intimate contact. Her skin felt too hot, too tight. He bent his head, obscuring the light, and pushed back the hood from her hair.

She ducked her chin, hiding her face against his shirt as he pressed his face into her hair, then stroked the side of her neck. His breath warmed the sensitive skin behind her ear. Cara swayed, her senses reeling as she fought a fresh wave of dizziness.

Enough.

She slid her hand up his ribcage, feigning a caress, and her blade found the spot under his armpit where the artery throbbed close beneath his loose white shirt. She leaned into him, trying to ignore the press of her breasts against his rock-hard chest, and increased the pressure. Sharpened steel pricked flesh.

Il Diavolo froze.

And then, to her astonishment, she felt him smile; the faintest curve of his lips tightening against her throat.

"Put that away, sweeting. It's a little late to defend your virtue."

"I'm not here to defend my virtue."

His chuckle was soft against her skin. "Good thing, too. We both know it's a distant memory."

Cara pursed her lips. "You mistake my meaning. It's your attention I want, not your kisses."

"Believe me, my lady, you have my *undivided* attention." There was mockery in his tone, but whether it was aimed at her, or himself, she couldn't tell.

Cara pulled back, just a fraction, curiosity warring with pique. "Aren't you afraid I might kill you?"

He pushed aside her cloak and dropped a leisurely kiss onto her collarbone, still not looking at her face. "Plenty have tried, but none have succeeded. Give it your best, though. If you prevail, at least I'll die happy."

CHAPTER 4

Cara barely saw him move. One minute her knife was pressed against his ribs, the next he'd shoved her face-first against the wall. Hard.

The cloak whirled around her legs and her hair went flying out around her shoulders. Pain lanced along her side as her ribs cracked against the stone—and her blade went spinning beneath the vast bed that dominated the centre of the room.

Il Diavolo pinned her to the wall with ridiculous ease. He pressed himself full-length against her, using his weight to keep her there, effortlessly emphasizing his superior strength. One hand held her wrists together behind her back, trapped between their bodies. The other covered her mouth and nose.

Cara opened her mouth to protest and her lips moved against his palm. She tried to bite him. He chuckled. His warm breath fanned across the back of her neck. She bucked furiously, arching her body away from his and trying not to notice how they fitted together in the most interesting places. He was bigger in every possible way. Taller, wider, stronger. His thighs were rock-hard against her backside.

She felt very small, and suddenly very afraid. Despite his past loyalty to her father, this man was practically a stranger. She tried to scream but only managed a muffled murmur.

"Shhhh, sweeting." He eased his hand from her mouth.

"Let me go!"

"Now, now. Where are your manners? It's rude to pull knives on people you've just met. We haven't even been introduced. I'm Alessandro. And you are?"

She bucked against him again and he smiled at her rebellion. "Come on. You've just tried to kill me. That means we're acquainted well enough to use first names."

"Release me!"

"Tsk. Didn't your father teach you any manners?"

"My father's dead."

"You sound as if it's my fault. Did I kill him?"

"No. My father was Ercolo Montessori."

That got his attention. Every muscle in his body went taut. There was a pregnant silence, as if he weighed the truth of her words, and then he released her wrists, allowing her just enough room to turn within the confines of his arms. He caught her chin and angled her face toward the firelight. Coal-black eyes studied her features with a painful intensity.

Cara raised her eyebrows in what she hoped was a haughty manner.

"Cara di Montessori." His tone held more accusation than welcome. "Well, well. I didn't recognize you without the scowl. How long has it been? Four years? Five?"

"I don't remember."

Six years, three months, two days. Not that she'd been counting.

His lips quirked. "The last time we met, I knocked you on your arse."

And kissed me like the world was ending. Don't forget that, you beast.

His gaze dropped to her mouth as if he recalled it, too. Cara flushed and lifted her chin. Let him look. At twenty-two she'd come to accept she wasn't the kind of woman to ignite a man's lusts.

His grip tightened."You say Ercolo's dead? When? How?"

"My 'uncle', Lorenzo, murdered him three days ago."

He frowned down at her. "Your father never mentioned having a brother."

"Lorenzo is a half-brother, my grandfather's son by one of the maids. He arrived at the keep last week claiming kinship, and Father welcomed him. Three days ago we went hunting, and Lorenzo's men ambushed us."

Cara swallowed, reluctant to relive those awful memories. There was nothing she could do to bring him back; she had to focus on her current problem instead. "Lorenzo has seized control of my home. I'm Castelleon's rightful heir."

Del Sarto lifted his brows. "Your father intended for you to rule alone?"

She felt her cheeks heat. Actually, father had expected to have her married off long before she inherited, but that wasn't something she intended sharing with this arrogant brute. "Of course. My entire adult life has been spent managing that keep. I ran it single-handed while the two of you were off terrorizing Europe the past few years."

He narrowed his eyes, ignoring the jibe. "Why aren't you dead, too?"

Bile rose in her throat at the images that bombarded her brain but she forced herself to continue. "Father and his men gave their lives, fighting so I could escape. And Lorenzo only sent a couple of men after me. He thought I'd be easy to catch."

Del Sarto's lips twitched. "He obviously doesn't know you."

"They've been following me for three days."

His gaze sharpened. "Why did you come *here*?"

Because father sent me to you.

His last words had been shouted as he drew his sword and slapped her horse's rump. *Il Diavolo, Cara! Go!*

Cara took a deep breath. "I can't challenge Lorenzo on my own. His mercenaries outnumber the troops loyal to me. Castelleon might be small, but its location and harbor make it tactically important. It's in your best interest to help me get it back."

Del Sarto stayed silent, so she forged ahead. "I have a proposition."

He raised one black eyebrow. "Ah. Now you're beginning to interest me."

"You're a mercenary. That means you take orders for money, doesn't it?"

"Depends on what the orders are." His voice held a trace of laughter.

She ignored that. "I'll pay you to escort me back to Castelleon and expel my uncle. I assume all we need to do now is negotiate a price?"

He shook his head. "I don't negotiate. I demand a fee. The other person pays it. Or not."

Cara restrained the urge to stamp her foot. She crossed her arms instead. "Name your terms."

The subsequent silence jangled her nerves and she held her breath, wishing she knew what the fiend was thinking.

"Hmm. It's a thorny problem. What price your life, eh?" His voice was pure devilry. "How are you going to pay me? You don't exactly look weighted down with coin."

She didn't have anything *with* her. She'd barely escaped with her life. All her money was hidden back at Castelleon—which was under her uncle's control. The sum should have been her dowry, but she had no intention getting married any time soon. If ever. She didn't need a husband to rule Castelleon. She wasn't going to accept some miserable dynastic marriage just because it was expected of her. She would have what her parents had shared; a union of mutual love and respect, or nothing at all.

K. C. BATEMAN & KATE BATEMAN

She attempted a nonchalant shrug. "I have enough to pay a blackguard like you."

"I doubt it. Professional blackguards don't come cheap. Not with my level of expertise."

The way he said it, laden with innuendo, made her shiver. He paused, as if considering, then named a price so outrageous it made her gasp.

"Believe me, I'm worth every florin."

Her stomach dropped. It was more than she had in the world. And he knew it, the beast.

His deep voice was honeyed with amusement. "You can't afford me. Besides, I've already got more money than I know what to do with."

"You can't refuse! You're a mercenary. Everyone has a price."

"Interesting you should say that. I made the same point to my captain earlier this evening. But I'm taking a break from fighting at the moment. Sorry."

He didn't sound sorry. And she didn't have any other options. Like it or not, she *needed* him. "For my father's sake, then," Cara said desperately. "You fought by his side for years. You were friends. Doesn't that mean anything?"

Il Diavolo shrugged. "Your father's dead. I can't help him. And I make it a rule never to support lost causes, which is what you are. Forget about your home and move on. Go and throw yourself on the mercy of a kindly relative."

"I can't do that! My people need me. I can't abandon them. Besides, the only relative I have is trying to kill me. Have you no honor?"

"Mercenary, remember? The two are mutually exclusive."

"A mercenary's what I need."

"No, you want an *assassin*."

"There's a difference?" she sneered, thoroughly annoyed. She tried to pull away from the disturbing closeness of his body but he stopped her with an impatient move that only pressed him closer.

"Of course. An assassin only kills one or two people at once—"

"—whereas you kill hundreds in one fell swoop," she finished bitterly. "I see. But a murderer's a murderer, surely?"

His eyes flashed. "Killing a man in the heat of battle's very different from dispatching someone in cold blood. And might I remind you that it's unwise to insult me when my murderous ways are exactly the reason you're here."

She flushed. "I don't want Lorenzo dead. Just gone."

He shook his head. "You want him dead. Whatever action you take has to be final." He studied her closely. "You know, paying to have someone killed is almost as bad as wielding the blade yourself."

"No it's not."

"Ah. So it's all right if *my* eternal soul's damned, but you're loath to jeopardize your own, is that it?"

"I doubt the state of your soul is something that keeps you awake at night," Cara snapped, goaded beyond endurance.

His lips quivered. "Quite true. I have far more interesting things to keep me awake at night."

Her face heated at the suggestion in his tone. He chuckled and flicked his finger across her cheek in a casual, devastating caress. "You should blush more. It suits you. You're too pale."

She wasn't too pale now—her cheeks were burning. She suddenly remembered why he thought she'd come to his room; he'd been expecting a courtesan. "If you won't help me, I won't keep you from your . . . evening activities any longer. Let go of me!"

He clicked his tongue. "You shouldn't give up so easily. As you said, every man has his price. Including me. Make me another offer. One I might be more inclined to accept."

K. C. BATEMAN & KATE BATEMAN

Renewed hope and anger clenched her stomach. What game was he playing now? "You just said you never negotiate."

He gave a shrug of his muscled shoulders. "There's always a first time."

"Fine. What *else* do you want?"

"Something money can't buy, of course." His lower body still kept her pinned against the wall. The raw heat emanating from him contrasted sharply with the chill of the night air.

Cara gave an impatient sigh, feigning boredom, but her whole body tingled. "Get on with it, del Sarto."

"It's been ages since I had a woman."

She snorted. "Money can buy you *that* kind of favor, as I'm sure you're well aware."

"That's not the sort of woman I want."

She began running through all the impossibly hard-to-come-by criteria he could ask for. He'd probably demand a Nubian princess, or an Oriental concubine. Or a whole harem of them. "What, then?"

He dipped his head, and for a heart-stopping second she thought he was going to kiss her, but he paused a hairs-breadth away. Those gorgeous lips framed just one word.

"You."

CHAPTER 5

*C*ara blinked. "What?"

His lips curled upwards. "My fee is a fortnight of your life. Plus the money, of course. It's a fair exchange. You can't pay me in coin unless I complete the task and I don't work for free. All you have to do is live here and act as my hostess for two short weeks."

"You've got hundreds of servants, paid to do your bidding."

"I need someone well-bred and educated. You're the answer to my prayers."

"I doubt that very much."

"Some of the most important families in Italy are coming here in a few days to discuss an alliance against France. I need a chatelaine. Someone to perform all the functions of a wife. You can grace my hall and attend to my guests. It makes perfect sense."

Cara narrowed her eyes, sensing a catch. "Exactly how far would these wifely duties stretch?"

His gaze never left her face. "I said '*all* the functions of a wife,' did I not? That includes sharing my bed. You asked my price —that's it."

Her brain froze before pounding back into life. "Why *me?*"

"You're here, you're suitable, and you're desperate."

Well, that was hardly the most flattering declaration! "You hardly know me."

"Now that's not true. I know you've survived an assassination attempt, ridden a hundred miles without getting yourself killed, pulled a knife on me, and want your uncle's blood in revenge. In fact, you're probably my perfect woman," he mocked gently.

She stared up at his shadowed features in dismay. "You're no better than an animal. I'd rather die."

He chuckled, a rich, dark sound, and placed an index finger over her parted lips. "That's a bit dramatic isn't it? What's two weeks with me when weighed against a lifetime of freedom?" His voice dropped to a whisper. "I guarantee you'll enjoy it."

Cara fought the urge to bang her head against the wall. Or— even worse—rest it against the broad chest in front of her. His scandalous offer went round and round in her head like some bizarre dream. He was a devil for even making her *consider* it. "You're asking me to whore myself out in order to save my people."

"If you want to cast yourself as a martyr, go ahead." He angled her face towards the firelight and studied her, his own features impassive. "Although I have to say, you don't have the look of a martyr."

His touch sent firebrands arcing across her skin.

"No," he murmured, repositioning her face at another angle. "You're no Joan of Arc. Looks like yours have started wars."

He compared her to Helen of Troy? Her temper rose. "Don't mock me. I know I'm no beauty. "

His dark eyebrows shot up. "You think not?" He turned her towards a mirror suspended by the fire and positioned himself behind her.

Cara barely recognized herself. The flames gave her face a flattering, peachy glow. Her skin was flushed and her eyes looked luminous. He trailed his fingers along her jaw in a leisurely caress she felt all the way down to her toes. Alarmed, she pulled from his grasp and stepped away, creating a cool gap between them, but her body still burned from the contact. She whirled around to face him. "*You* won't go to war for me, though, will you?"

His lips gave a bitter quirk. "Not for *any* woman. At least, not without payment."

"Money," she said hollowly, "and sex."

"Both excellent motivations."

Cara's mind whirled. She had no other options; she needed his protection. "All right. I accept your terms."

She had the gratifying sense that she'd surprised him, though his expression didn't change.

"You give me your word?" Disbelief fairly dripped from his tone.

"You'd trust the word of a mere woman?" she countered.

"Rarely. But yours? Yes, if you gave it. Your father was the most honorable man I've ever known. He'd have taught you to keep your vows."

His words, surprisingly serious, made her wince. She certainly didn't intend to keep her promise to sleep with him, even though it meant breaking her own moral code. But a promise to a liar like him didn't mean anything. *He* wouldn't hesitate to renege on a bargain. She crossed her fingers behind her back and promised an extra fifteen minutes of prayers at bedtime for a whole year for what she was about to do. "Fine. I give you my word."

He chuckled and flicked her cheek. "Oh, sweeting, you're a terrible liar. I can practically hear the cogs turning in your brain as you try to think of a way out. Don't bother. I'll hold you to your word." He held his arms out to the sides. "So, I'm all yours. Let's seal our bargain, shall we?"

She glanced up, alarmed, and found his strange, blacker-than-black eyes staring down at her, intense and unfathomable. He slipped one hand under her hair and cradled the back of her

K. C. BATEMAN & KATE BATEMAN

head. Cara held herself completely still. Slowly, achingly slowly, he drew her closer.

He was going to kiss her! Alessandro del Sarto, her hero, her nemesis, was going to kiss her! She'd been waiting for this moment for six long years.

Cara closed her eyes, determined to savor the sensation, to see if it really was as good as she remembered. His lips were warm and slightly rough but annoying little swirling pinpricks began to dance behind her eyelids. She tried to ignore them, to concentrate on the kiss, but her knees began to buckle. She barely managed to stop herself from groaning in frustration as she sagged back against his supporting arm.

Del Sarto frowned down at her. "What's the matter? God, you're not going to faint, are you?"

She managed a scornful frown. "Don't be ridiculous. I've never fainted in my entire life."

A tunnel was narrowing her vision; she tried to blink it away. This was just typical. Here she was, *finally* getting the kiss of her dreams, and she was making a mess of it.

The darkness was irresistible. Cara surrendered to it with a resigned sigh.

24

CHAPTER 6

*A*lessandro caught Cara's limp figure in his arms, amazed at how little she weighed. He swept one arm under her knees and bellowed for Francesco, then stood still, afraid to move in case he somehow hurt her even further. He hadn't pushed her against the wall *that* hard, but then, he usually fought against fully-grown men. He was twice her size. Maybe he'd broken something.

"Francesco!"

She didn't stir at his shout, which worried him further. He shifted her to get a better grip and his fingers slipped on a patch of sticky warmth under her arm. He didn't need to look to know it was blood. "Francesco!" he bellowed again, depositing her gently on his huge bed.

She looked angelic, unconscious. Not cherubic, exactly. She was too dark and too dirty, her face too angled for mere prettiness. Mud and dust caked her skin and clothes. A filthy angel, then.

Alessandro made a swift search of her small frame and smiled. His filthy angel was armed to the teeth. In addition to that dagger he'd sent under the bed, she had a blade strapped to the inside of her wrist and another one tied to her thigh. *Good girl.*

He pushed back her rough cloak and stopped in surprise. She was wearing the clothes of a stable boy; a rough pair of hose and a tie-neck linen shirt. Sandro tested the material between his fingers, identifying its quality, before he grasped the neck and ripped. Her clothes wouldn't matter if she bled to death.

Another layer lay beneath, a cotton shift, apparently her only concession to feminine attire. Alessandro ignored the tantalizing swell of her breasts just below his palms and swore at the amount of blood that stained the white fabric.

Francesco barely blinked when he saw her on the bed. "Changed your mind, did you? That was fast. Want me to send up another one?"

"She's not a whore, you idiot. She's Ercolo Montessori's daughter."

Francesco raised his brows. "You sure?"

"It's her."

It had been six long years, but the instant he'd seen her eyes Alessandro had known the truth. And he'd been as stunned as if he'd fallen from his horse wearing full body armor. No one else had eyes that color. Her father used to dismiss them as 'dirty mossy green,' but they changed depending on her mood and the color she wore. Alessandro knew them as well as he knew his own blackened soul.

Francesco stepped closer and peered at the bed. "Not dead is she?"

"She will be, if we don't fix this cut on her side. Fetch Renata. And tell her to bring a needle."

A moment later Renata da Mosta bustled into the room. The woman took one look at Cara, then glared at Alessandro with all the familiarity of a long-time retainer. "What did you do to her?"

Alessandro held up both hands. "Nothing, I swear. Why does everyone assume I did something to her? I just disarmed her."

And kissed her.

He'd never had a woman *swoon* from one of his kisses before, although he probably couldn't take all the credit. He'd barely touched her lips with his, although even that scant touch had been enough to heat his blood. "She was hurt before she came in here."

Renata placed her hand on Cara's forehead. "Poor little thing, what happened?"

Alessandro snorted. "Don't feel too sorry for her. That 'poor little thing' pulled a knife on me not five minutes ago."

Francesco's eyebrows disappeared into his hairline.

"Stay with her," Alessandro ordered Renata. "Bind up her wounds and then let her sleep. When she wakes, feed her. And bathe her." He wrinkled his nose at the filthy, disheveled clothes. "Then send for me. And Renata?" His eyes never left the bed. "Don't let her out of your sight."

Renata frowned. "I've seen that look before, Sandro. Usually just before you trick someone into surrendering. What are you going to do with her?"

Alessandro shot her an innocent look. "Why, keep her, of course. She's fallen into my lap like an offering from the gods. Who am I to overlook a gift like that?"

Several hours later Alessandro stood at the foot of the bed and watched his captive sleep. She was a brave little thing, and bravery and loyalty were qualities he valued above almost everything. He believed her when she said she'd never fainted before; her stubbornness was just one of the things he remembered about her.

His huge bed dwarfed her. She'd curled up in one corner, clutching the coverlet as if afraid it would be pulled from her. A primitive satisfaction warmed his belly. He liked seeing her wrapped in material that usually covered his skin.

She looked so small, so vulnerable. He rubbed the sore spot under his arm with a smile. Hardly defenseless, though. She'd done what hundreds of grown men had tried and failed to do; drawn a blade on him while close enough to inflict some damage.

He took a step nearer, inhaling the faint perfume that rolled off her skin. A hint of rose petal soap from her hair mingled with the warm scent of her body, barely discernible under the layer of dust from the road. Intoxicating.

Her desperate scheming amused him. It was clear she had no intention of completing their deal, but it would be interesting to see how far she'd go to get her birthright back. Alessandro shook his head. She was such an innocent. All he had to do was keep her eyes glazed with a little of the passion he'd glimpsed tonight and she'd be easy to control.

Cara di Montessori was going to make the perfect wife. Not for *him*, of course. But his guests were expecting a marriage to cement the forthcoming peace negotiations and *she* would be the sacrificial lamb. The idea was blinding in its rightness. He'd be helping the daughter of his old friend, too. It was charitable, really.

She'd grace his bed first, of course. She was exactly what he needed to take the edge off his current restlessness. Fate had sent her to him. Why should he deny himself so much temptation when it was right here, under his nose?

Was she still a virgin? All her reactions pointed to it. Blood throbbed in his temples as he imagined introducing her to the intricacies of sex. He'd enjoy her as a mistress for a couple of diverting weeks, then hand her over to some dull, worthy burgher to live a life of pampered luxury. It would kill two birds with one stone.

Alessandro glanced over to where Francesco waited patiently

by the door. "Send word to all those coming next week. Tell them Cara di Montessori, chatelaine of Castelleon, will marry whoever I deem the most suitable. Say her father left her in my care. It's close enough to the truth."

Francesco placed a heavy hand on his shoulder. "I'm sorry about Ercolo."

Alessandro nodded. "He was like a father to me. He took me in when I was sixteen and taught me how to fight. I'd probably be dead by now, if not for him."

Cara sighed and turned over in her sleep and Alessandro shook his head at the vagaries of fate that had brought her to his door. His eyes swept from her soft lips, pouted in slumber, over the sweep of her throat to the silky skin of her shoulder, exposed to the cool night air and his hot gaze. He could just make out the tantalizing shadows between her breasts, and cursed his immediate arousal. He had women falling over themselves to grace his bed, women far more beautiful than her. His attraction to this stormy waif was—and always had been—inexplicable.

She'd be horrified if she realized how much of her history he knew. While he'd been away on campaign with her father, her tutor had sent regular letters to inform Ercolo of the progress of her education. Barely a month had gone by without some missive detailing Cara's latest lapse in behavior.

Ercolo had loved reading the letters aloud and Alessandro had listened intently. Lacking any family of his own, he'd been fascinated by those glimpses into her pleasant, if somewhat chaotic, domestic life. Those letters had been the highlight of his days.

"Who'd have thought one small girl could wind an entire monastery round her little finger?" Ercolo had chuckled, not without a degree of paternal pride.

Cara had hated her enforced inactivity back at Castelleon. Her lively nature had always been searching for small but significant ways to rebel. Alessandro smiled in memory. The good brothers at the Monastery of St. John, where she'd received her lessons, had obviously failed to quell the feisty spirit he'd come to appreciate.

Part of him was amazed that he hadn't recognized her immediately. The girl had plagued him for years, flitting in and out of his thoughts, always lurking at the back of his mind. Somewhere along the way, Cara di Montessori had become his fantasy woman.

For a soldier between engagements there wasn't much to do except sit around and think. He'd had plenty of opportunities; long, restless nights where the men would gather around the campfires and the topics of conversation would revolve around the universal male interests of wine, women and song. But while some argued over the first meal they'd have when they got home, or the best type of horse to take into battle, he'd lain awake, thinking of her.

He'd been cursed with a fiendishly vivid imagination.

He only wanted her because he couldn't have her. She was forbidden, unattainable. And therefore all the more desirable. That was the *only* reason his fevered brain had conjured up literally hundreds of scenarios in which he was making love to Cara di Montessori.

Alessandro laughed in self-directed irony. He'd lost count of how many times over the past six years he'd caught himself imagining the kind of woman she'd grown into. And now here she was. The woman of his dreams; not only real, but in his home, in his *bed.*

His imagination hadn't even begun to do her justice.

He toyed—briefly—with the idea of taking her as his own wife, instead of giving her to someone else, then discarded that plan. Marrying her would certainly be a delightful challenge, but the fictional Cara di Montessori had haunted his dreams for so long that reality would, no doubt, be a pale disappointment. He'd tire of her soon enough.

And besides, she was a high-born lady, a sheltered innocent, whereas he was a violent, cynical bastard, too hardened by war to be a fit mate for anyone. She deserved better than him. However much he might wish it were different, all he could offer was his strength and cunning—for a price.

CHAPTER 7

*C*ara cracked her eyelids, blinking against a shaft of sunshine that filtered through a high glazed window. She drifted on the fringes of consciousness, enjoying the softness of sheets against her skin.

The bed was warm, and her ribs ached. Something tugged at the back of her mind, annoyingly insistent. She'd been sleeping on hard ground and soggy leaves for the past few nights, not silken sheets and down-filled velvet pillows. Memory came flooding back with unpleasant speed. A swift glance beneath the covers confirmed her worst fears. She was naked. In the Devil's own bed.

Panicked, she checked her throat for the necklace she always wore and breathed a sigh of relief when she touched its familiar weight. The small compass pendant had been a gift from her father.

How had she ended up here? The last thing she remembered was being in del Sarto's arms, about to kiss him. And then—nothing. She must have fainted. How humiliating. Someone had tended to her wound; a tight bandage wrapped her ribs. Who had undressed her? Please God it hadn't been *him*.

"Good morning, my lady. I'm Renata."

The speaker was an attractive older woman, perhaps fifty years old. Her suntanned face and sparkling dark eyes gave her a youthful, cheeky appearance and her long black hair, threaded through with a few silver strands, had been left loose and unstyled.

Cara tried to sit up, groaned, and slumped back down again.

"You'll feel as right as rain in a day or two, I promise," the woman smiled.

A knock on the door made Cara jump. Her heart pounded at the thought of seeing del Sarto again, but instead two kitchen boys entered laden with buckets of steaming water. Renata directed them through another doorway and Cara heard splashing.

Renata beckoned. "Come on, while it's hot."

Cara gaped at the huge copper bath that dominated the room. How decadent! Her own tub was half the size of this one. She winced as Renata unwound the fabric bandages then bent to inspect the neat row of stitches.

The servant nodded, satisfied. "I've been patching people up for years, both on and off the battlefield. This just needs a good soak."

Cara sank into the water. The heat made every muscle ache, but it felt wonderful. Renata handed her a bar of soap and she ducked under the water to wash her hair.

"There's linen over there, on the chest. I'll just let him know you're awake."

No need to ask who 'he' was. Cara sat up, sloshing water over the edge of the tub. "Wait! Where are my clothes?"

Renata gestured to a dress laid out on the trunk.

"That isn't mine."

"I know. One of his mistresses left it here last year."

"I won't wear some strumpet's cast offs."

The servant smiled. "I think that one belonged to a duchess.

He said you'd probably refuse. He *also* said that if you weren't dressed in fifteen minutes, he'd come and get you himself. Dressed or not."

Cara leapt out of the tub, all plans for a lengthy soak forgotten.

Renata chuckled as she handed her a bath sheet. "Come on. One dress isn't going to sap your virtue."

Cara scowled at the beautiful garment. She'd never worn anything so luxurious. She stroked the deep red velvet, then ran her fingers over the gilt thread embroidered at the cuffs, waist and bodice. It was so soft, so heavy. *So expensive.*

Renata helped her into a silk chemise, underskirt, and then the dress itself. Cara tugged at the low-cut bodice, which exposed an unseemly expanse of breast, and gasped as the garment was laced tight at her back. She'd grown so used to wearing her boys clothes she'd forgotten how uncomfortable dresses were. When she turned to face the mirror she gazed open-mouthed at her own reflection. The bodice pinched in her waist and pushed up her breasts. For once in her life she had something resembling cleavage.

"There," Renata said, pinching her cheeks to add some color. "As soon as your hair is dry, you'll be ready to face him. Come sit by the fire."

* * *

CARA COULDN'T HELP but be impressed by the luxury of her surroundings as she followed the servant down several long hall-ways. She hadn't been looking at the furnishings when she'd sneaked in to the castle last night, but this was no Spartan soldiers' abode. The walls were hung with rich tapestries and arms, paintings, and gilt sconces. Her own home was comfort-able, but this was the abode of someone who appreciated quality and had the means to acquire it.

They descended a wide flight of stairs and Renata ushered her into a room that clearly served as a study and library. A wide desk stood near a bay window and rows of shelves held books and scrolls. Maps and drawings hung on the walls, but Cara's attention was drawn to the man seated in a huge carved chair behind the desk, his long legs stretched out in front of him.

She took a moment to study her host in daylight. That fascinating mouth was the same as she remembered it; with a scornful curl to the corners and a full bottom lip which made him look both cynical and sensuous. Sunlight flashed off his thick gold signet ring as he rested his elbows on the arms of the chair and steepled his fingers in front of him.

He reminded her of a wolf, wild and unpredictable. *Predatory.* Cara grew uncomfortable with his unblinking stare. A show of hesitancy now would be fatal. She strode forward and took the seat opposite him, placed her hands in her lap, and raised her eyebrows in polite enquiry.

At last he spoke. "It's past eventide. I trust you're feeling better?"

She'd slept almost the whole day away! "Much better, thank you."

His eyes never left her face. Cara struggled to hold his gaze.

"I want to know about your father's death. How was he killed? How can you be sure your uncle was responsible?"

She glared at him. "I was there." Her stomach twisted and a wave of impotent rage threatened to overwhelm her as the scene reformed in her mind with horrifying clarity. Her father and his loyal men, holding off the attackers so she could flee. Guilt suffused her. She should have stayed. Fought.

No. She would have died, too. It had been her duty to survive. To avenge their deaths.

Del Sarto sat in silence, patiently awaiting her explanation like a spider at the centre of his web.

"Lorenzo ambushed us while we were hunting in the forest.

His men killed my father and three of our men. They died giving me time to escape." Del Sarto made no reply, so she cleared her throat and continued. "I wasn't thinking clearly last night. I cannot accept your proposal. I'll find another way to regain my home without your help. Return my clothes and I'll be on my way."

"I can't do that. I've had them burned."

"What?"

"They were filthy."

"What will I wear?"

"If you'll reconsider my offer, sweeting, you won't need anything at all."

She gasped. "You're shameless!"

"Hardly. If I were as barbaric as you claim, I'd have taken you while you were insensible last night."

"How civilized! To prefer your conquests *conscious* when you rape them."

He ignored her sarcasm. "Why were you wearing boy's clothing?"

That answered the question of who'd undressed her. Cara was annoyed to feel a blush steal across her cheeks. Awful man. "I'd joined father on the hunt. I could hardly ride in my skirts, could I?" The thought gave her an idea. "Last night you said you wanted someone refined and used to socializing, to act as your hostess. Believe me, I have no feminine accomplishments whatsoever. I'm honestly the last woman you need."

"Ah, yes. You're 'The Girl Who Blew Up The Monastery.'"

Cara suppressed a groan. It would have been too much to hope that he hadn't heard of that particular incident.

"Your father often regaled me with tales of your antics," he said, as if reading her mind. "I always enjoyed hearing what new catastrophe you'd masterminded."

She flushed, mortified that her childish rebellions should have been exposed to this man's ridicule.

"In one letter, I remember, you'd diverted water onto the monastery vegetable patch and flooded the cloisters."

"St. John's needed a new irrigation system. We had an excellent crop that year."

"And the injured fox cub?"

"How was I to know it would scale the organ pipes in a bid for freedom?"

"It pissed against the lectern, I recall." Del Sarto's mouth looked on the verge of breaking into a smile, but never quite did. Despite her embarrassment, Cara bit her own lip. That *had* been quite funny.

"My favorite, though, was the time you declared Castelleon's moat too narrow to deter invaders and tried to prove it by jumping it yourself. How many bones did you break?"

She clenched her right hand in memory. "Only three fingers. And I cleared it on my second attempt."

He leaned across the desk and took her hand, feeling along the knuckles for signs of the injury. His touch sent tongues of heat racing up her arm. "You were lucky you didn't break your neck."

She snatched her hand from his.

"I always wondered why you weren't sent to a nunnery. Nuns wouldn't have you, eh?" he prodded.

She winced at the truth of his words. "There weren't any nunneries nearby," she lied. "The monastery was very convenient."

In truth, Father had hoped that some of the piety and calm of St. John's would rub off on her. *Hah.*

Pain stabbed her heart. Though he'd never have admitted it, she suspected that Father had always longed for a son, rather than a daughter. She'd spent her whole life trying to make him proud, to prove that she was not only worthy of his love, but of inheriting Castelleon too.

It was too late now. All those hours studying subjects she'd known would impress him—military tactics, ancient history, languages—all for naught.

Contrary to what she'd told del Sarto, she *had* learned some feminine skills too, albeit under duress. Her old nurse-turned-housekeeper, Bianca, had been given the task of instructing her, but Bianca's 's ideas of a fitting education had been diametrically opposed to Cara's own. Bianca favored tasks like starching bed linen, sewing, flower arranging, and curtseying. She'd ignored Cara's protests that the kitchens functioned far more efficiently *without* her interference.

"So what happened at the monastery?" del Sarto's deep voice interrupted her recollections.

"I'm surprised you didn't get a full account of that, too," Cara sighed. "I was helping brother Domenico make an explosive powder we'd found mentioned in an Oriental text and a slight accident occurred, that's all."

In truth, she'd doubled the quantities when Fra Domenico had turned his back. The results had been surprisingly incendiary. Who'd have thought such a small amount of black powder could do such a huge amount of damage?

"Only the west tower actually *collapsed,*" she muttered. "And it was practically rubble to begin with. That's why we were using it for our studies."

There was no need to mention the smoke damage to the refectory, or the scorched statue of the Virgin Mary in the vestry.

"In the event, we discovered the most efficient way to evacuate the monastery," she said piously. Inspiration struck. "See, this just shows how unsuited I am to be anyone's hostess. I know fortifications and tactics far better than gossip and small-talk. I can't sew or cook or do *anything* remotely feminine. I only sing when I want to make the dogs howl. I can barely even dance."

"We'll arrange for a few lessons, to refresh your memory."

Cara set her teeth. "I can be remarkably difficult to teach when I don't want to learn."

CHAPTER 8

Del Sarto's gaze flicked to the huge carved letters behind her on the fireplace. "Do you know what that says?"

She glanced over her shoulder and then back at him. "Of course," she said haughtily. "*Quis est mei ego servo.* What's mine I keep."

"Right. And I've decided to keep you. At least for the next few weeks."

She narrowed her eyes and he chuckled. "Why the outraged virtue? Not to be accused of false modesty, but plenty of women would kill to be in your position right now."

"I will *not* lie with you."

"Don't you want to?" He sounded only mildly interested, as if they were discussing the weather, but his smile was wicked. "You will."

He said it with the absolute certainty of a man who always got his own way. Cara laughed to cover her fear. "What conceit! Do you think you're irresistible?"

He gave a negligent shrug. "We'll see."

"The only way you'll have me is by force."

"Now, that's not true. I've never raped a woman in my life. But you're welcome to try to resist me. It will add a challenge to the next few weeks, while you're my guest."

"Guest? You mean hostage. I will not be your whore."

"Why not? We all sell ourselves, Cara. I've done it myself since I was sixteen years old." His mouth gave a cynical twitch. "Only instead of hiring myself out for love, I did it for war. For some reason I thought I'd weary of lying on my back all day and chose fighting over whoring. Either way, it's using your body to provide a service for money."

He was being deliberately crude to shock her. She hadn't even known that there *were* such things as male whores, but she could quite believe that someone might pay for his remarkable body. The idea left her breathless and uncomfortably hot. What woman wouldn't want such strength and beauty at her command?

You could order him to do things. Anything.

Her ideas about what those things might be were rather nebulous, but still, just the thought brought her out in a hot-cold sweat.

His lips twitched.

"Something amuses you, my lord?" she snapped.

"Yes, you. I'm rarely entertained by my fellow man. You are indeed a novelty."

The man was infuriating. She could withstand him, despite his sinful good looks. "What about my reputation? I'll be ruined! Even if I *don't* lie with you everyone will think I have."

"Damned if you do and damned if you don't," he agreed cheerfully. "You might as well enjoy yourself."

Cara ground her teeth. So much for appealing to his conscience. "Don't you care?"

"What other people think of me? Never. Of what they'll think of you? No. Be honest, will *you* care when you're back in your beloved Castelleon? Is your pride so great a price to pay?"

He sounded so reasonable, but it was more than mere pride.

More than just her virginity, even. He wanted her integrity, her honor. Her soul.

As if he'd read her mind he said, "Stop being so dramatic, sweeting. It's only sex."

"So I'm a prisoner here?"

He made an elegant gesture towards the door. "You can go anywhere you like within the city walls. With an escort, of course."

"How kind," she said witheringly.

A servant entered bearing a steaming tray of food, followed by another bearing crockery and silverware.

"Let's not quarrel. You must be hungry."

She was about to deny it, but her treacherous stomach rumbled in anticipation. Perhaps if she grabbed a chicken leg and ate like a ravenous dog he'd have second thoughts about her suitability as lady of the keep.

The twinkle in his eye suggested he knew exactly the direction of her thoughts.

She shot him a honey-sweet smile. "I'm surprised you're letting me near a knife again so soon."

"It's not sharp. Besides, if you were a competent assassin you could kill me with anything. Your spoon, perhaps. Or your bare hands."

Without thought, she glanced down at his hands. They were strong and tanned and certainly looked capable of murder.

"I prefer a sword," he said, reading her mind again like some black magician. "Do try some wine." He poured the deep red liquid into her waiting glass.

Every item on the table was of the highest quality. The cutlery was silver, the glasses exquisite—Venetian, no doubt—with an enameled design under a gilt rim. Murder was obviously a lucrative business.

Much as she would have loved to refuse his hospitality, the aromas wafting from the food were impossible to resist. Cara took a mouthful and almost groaned in pleasure. She hadn't eaten properly for days. She took another sip of the wine, an excellent red, and made a point of ignoring him while she consumed her meal in silence. As soon as she finished she pushed her chair back and rose. He did the same.

"Thank you for dinner," she said, her effort at politeness straining her voice.

He smiled, as if he knew how much it galled her to thank him, her gaoler, for anything. "Are you going to bed?"

"I'm extremely tired."

"Shall I come with you?" The corners of his lips turned upwards as her mouth fell open. "You *have* been sleeping in my bed. But perhaps you'd prefer your own room? At least for tonight."

Cara didn't know what to say. He stepped around the table, took her hand, and kissed it. A jolt of heat shot from her throat to her stomach. "Goodnight, my lord," she said firmly.

THE TWO GUARDS stopped barely ten paces further down the hall from Il Diavolo's chambers and Cara suppressed a growl. He'd put her in the room adjoining his own. Nodding to her escort, she went inside and sank onto the bed.

What had she got herself into?

She'd been surrounded by men her entire life but del Sarto was the only one who'd ever had this bizarre effect on her senses. It had been bad enough six years ago, when she'd succumbed to his unexpected kiss, but she'd put that down to the inexperience of youth and temporary insanity on her part.

She had no such excuse now.

It was animal attraction, pure and simple. She'd heard the servants and soldiers gossiping about it often enough. It was just so annoying that she should feel it toward this obnoxious, unsuitable man, of all people.

She glanced around the room. A single candle had been left burning on a table by the bed. Like the rest of the castle, the chamber was furnished in the height of luxury. A dressing table with an ornate gilt mirror above it had been placed against the wall next to the window. A set of silver-backed brushes and a bar of perfumed soap rested on it. An X-framed chair with lions carved on the armrests held a stack of fresh linen, and her bed was a rather grand four-poster—although smaller than the one she'd slept in next door.

Two further doors led off the main room. The first housed a bathing room with a tub big enough to wallow in. The second door refused to budge and had no key. From its position she deduced that it opened directly into del Sarto's rooms. No doubt the fiend imagined he could come and go into her bedchamber at whim. She dragged the dressing table across the room and set it squarely in front of the door. There.

A tall cupboard stood against one wall. Opening it, Cara suppressed a little squeak of triumph. A dozen shirts and hose were folded neatly upon the shelves. The room's previous occupant had left some of his clothing behind. Or perhaps it was a store cupboard for unexpected guests? Either way, she'd found the perfect outfit for an escape.

She crossed to the window, climbed up onto the seat, and peered through the diamond-shaped panes of glass. The wall below was in annoyingly good repair; all smooth stonework, with not a helpful toehold in sight. No ivy to climb down. Typical. In the troubadour's songs the hero always rescued the heroine thanks to some strategically placed trellis or a convenient balcony. No such luck here.

Cara had always privately wondered why the heroine never rescued herself. She loved reading stories of courtly romances, but the women were always depressingly apathetic.

Salvation came in the form of a huge chestnut tree growing just beyond the window. She gauged the distance carefully. The larger branches would easily hold her weight but it was a good thirty feet down if she fell. Certainly high enough to break her neck. She hadn't climbed a tree in years, but the alternative—staying here with the insufferable del Sarto—was far worse. She had erred, thinking she could deal with him.

It was too dark to escape tonight. Cara stripped off her heavy gown and crawled into bed, luxuriating in the softness of the mattress. Gilded it might be, but a cage was a cage, nonetheless. Come the morning, she'd be gone.

CHAPTER 9

*C*ara woke at first light. The shirt she'd donned hung down past her knees and she had to roll the waist of the breeches over three times to get them to stay put, but it was still a better outfit for tree-climbing than a dress.

The window was small—but she was smaller. She squeezed through and gripped the metal frame with white knuckles as she balanced precariously on the outer stone sill. Two servants crossed the courtyard below leading a huge black horse, and she froze, but they were too busy trying to control the snorting, skittish beast to notice her.

She sent a swift prayer heavenward, and jumped. For a timeless second she hung in mid-air, then hit the tree with a crash that knocked the breath from her lungs. She clutched the nearest branch as tightly as she could and pressed her cheek to the rough bark as it swayed and shook.

A flurry of leaves and horse chestnuts rained down onto the ground below, startling a wood pigeon into flight, and she waited, her heart hammering, for a cry of alarm, but none came.

There. Easy!

Her position wasn't exactly dignified. She was hugging one

large, nearly horizontal branch like a bear, with both arms and legs wrapped around it. At least it hadn't snapped under her weight. She pried one hand free, spat out a leaf, and inched towards the trunk. The branch creaked but held. Her injured side ached in protest. Her inner thighs were going to be black and blue, but it was a small price to pay for freedom.

Another servant crossed the yard, whistling, but hurried on without noticing her.

Damnation. The lowest branch was still about ten feet from the ground and the trunk below was smooth. Cara was just wondering how to lower herself down when the doors at the far end of the courtyard opened again. There followed a clatter of hooves and then a laughter-tinged voice that filtered through the large green leaves.

"Morning, Signorina. Having fun?"

Cara cursed—in five different languages. It was del Sarto, the swine, mounted on the same beautiful black horse she'd seen moments before. The animal pranced, eager to be off on its morning canter.

"Now what does this say about my hospitality when guests throw themselves out of the windows? Has something displeased you, my lady? An uncomfortable bed? Insufficient hot water? Unaired linens?"

Cara looked down in exasperation. "Go away!"

"And let you escape? I don't think so. How were you going to get down? It's too high to jump, although you seem foolish enough to try it."

He dismounted in one fluid movement and dropped the reins. The horse simply waited for him, despite not being tied up. No doubt the man was used to blind obedience. Well, he wasn't going to get it from *her*!

"Lower yourself down and I'll catch you."

"No!"

"I won't drop you. You weigh less than a starved sparrow. I've already carried you, remember?"

She flushed at his casual reminder. He approached the foot of the tree and stood looking up at her, hands on hips.

"Leave me alone!" Cara grabbed one of the horse chestnuts and threw it as hard as she could at the smug figure below. She missed; it struck him on the shoulder, instead of the centre of the forehead. He leapt backwards, but her satisfaction was short-lived. He bent down and swept up a handful of the hard, prickly spheres at his feet. Her eyes widened in disbelief as he aimed. "Don't you *dare*!"

"Why not?"

Cara howled as one hit her on the arm—hard. He wasn't even throwing them *softly*. "Ow! Stop!"

One hit her thigh. Another whacked the top of her head and tangled in her hair. She ducked for cover behind the trunk, lost her balance, and let out a horrified shriek as she plunged head-first towards the ground.

Del Sarto caught her effortlessly.

Cara kicked her legs and pummeled him with her fists. Laughing, he lowered her to the ground, unmoved by her attempts to get free. "You're welcome, milady."

She pushed him away and tried to tame her hair into some semblance of order.

His too-perceptive gaze ran over her. "Why, you look a little flushed. Will you join me inside for a drink? Saraceno and I were about to ride, but it can wait."

"Oh, please don't let me keep you," she said with forced sweetness.

Her fury throbbed between them, a palpable force. Del Sarto reached towards her face and she flinched, but his fingers detoured at the last moment. He tugged a leaf out of her hair and let it flutter to the ground.

"Come."

Cara bristled at his tone—then realized he was talking to the horse. The animal trotted forward and nuzzled his outstretched hand. The sardonic glint in del Sarto's eye told her he knew exactly what she'd been thinking.

Glad of the distraction as the horse's head came between them, Cara stroked the beast's neck, sleek and shining in the early morning sun. "Hello, handsome."

The horse wiggled its ears and huffed in ecstasy.

"Another conquest," del Sarto addressed the horse. The animal nodded its head in agreement, gazing at Cara with huge intelligent eyes. It lipped her softly on the nose and he swatted it aside playfully. "You're pathetic. Anything for a pretty face. Well then, where are your manners? Bow to the lady."

Cara couldn't repress a charmed smile as the horse backed up three paces and extended its front leg. It lowered its head and executed a perfect bow. The foolish antics dissipated some of her anger and she shot a rueful glance at her captor. "Very impressive. Is that a useful skill on the battlefield?"

"You'd be surprised." His idle gaze flicked down her body. "You've ruined that shirt. I'll add it to the list of things you owe me."

Her anger returned in a flash. "I've got nothing to wear."

"The lament of every woman I've ever known," he mocked.

"In my case it's *literally* true. You burned my clothes."

"Well, we can't have you running around dressed like that. You'll incite a riot. Were the dresses I provided not to your taste?"

"I won't wear some other woman's cast-offs."

"You're in no position to choose. You'll wear them, or walk around naked. Believe me, I don't care which." His wicked gaze belied his words. It was no secret which *he'd* prefer. He turned to go, then swung back to her. "Seriously, don't try this again. You could have been killed. I want your word."

Cara crossed her arms. "No! You can't expect me to sit around and accept what you're doing to me."

"It's for your own good."

"My welfare is not your concern."

"You made it my concern when you turned up here, alone and injured, and placed yourself under my protection."

"'Protection?' You've taken me hostage! I demand to be released immediately."

He caught her chin in his fingers. "Or what?"

Cara ground her teeth but stayed silent.

"Exactly," he said, with infuriating calm. "There's nothing you can do. That's what chafes the most, isn't it? You've placed yourself in this predicament."

"I *assumed* you'd be a man of honor!"

He shrugged. "Others have made the same mistake. A few even lived to regret it."

Damn him! She was a toy, an amusement to him, nothing more.

His fingers tightened. "Your word."

She gazed up at him. "All right. I promise I will never try to escape out of the window again." Their eyes clashed, battled. She lowered her gaze first.

He released her chin and beckoned to a hovering servant. "Massimo, be so kind as to escort Signorina di Montessori back to her rooms." He glanced back at her. "When you've dressed in something more appropriate, perhaps you'll do me the honor of attending me in the warehouse?"

CHAPTER 10

ifteen minutes later, and back in a borrowed dress, Cara followed the servant across the bailey. Il Diavolo was lurking at the entrance to a large stone building. He stood aside and ushered her into the cool darkness.

She stepped past him, careful not to let any parts of their bodies touch. Just being near him made her nerve endings jump in the most alarming way. She squinted, taking a moment to adjust from the bright sunlight outside. Only a row of narrow, slit-like windows high up near the rafters allowed any light to enter. Rows of shelves reaching from floor to ceiling ran along the length of the room. The air was heavy with a mix of spices and other enticing aromas.

"What is this place? A store room?"

He nodded. "One of my warehouses. My ships trade around the world. Goods are stored here before they're sent to market in Venice and Rome."

Cara walked forward, astounded by the sheer quantity of stock in this one storeroom alone. Why, the man must make an absolute fortune!

As if he'd read her mind, he said, "We poor mercenaries barely earn enough to put food on the table. We have to scratch out a living as best we can."

"Hah! Your 'services' cost enough to keep the whole country in silk slippers. Merchant, tradesman, kidnapper *and* extortionist. Is there no end to your talents?"

He ignored her sarcasm. "I have many business interests. Your food, for example, was flavored by spices brought here from the East."

"If you're showing me this to prove how little you need my money, you're wasting your time." She slanted him an arch look. "All I see is how much you need Castelleon's harbor to get these luxuries here. Think of the revenue you'll lose if you have to unload them elsewhere."

He failed to rise to her baiting and Cara's inquisitive nature got the better of her. She strode ahead, inspecting the contents of each shelf they passed, recognizing all the standard herbs used in the kitchens. Some, however, were unidentifiable. She picked up a jar that held a dark, resin-like substance and unscrewed the lid. It smelled vaguely like incense. "What's this?"

He took it from her hand. "Trust you to go straight for the dangerous substances. That's opium, made from white Persian poppies."

Intrigued, she peered more closely.

"It can be used to ease pain or to make an injured man sleep so he can be treated for his wounds. Some take it just to lose themselves in the daydreams it brings on."

"Have you ever tried it?"

"Once. It gave me the worst headache I've ever had in my life. And considering I've attended several of the Borgia's parties, that's saying something."

"I'd like to try it. I think you should try everything once, don't you?"

"I don't recommend murder," he said dryly.

She grimaced. "Well, granted, *some* things you can live without. But I'd be interested to see what effect it has. I used to help Father John, the monastery doctor. He used hemlock juice to make his patients sleep."

Cara knew she was chattering, but she was uncomfortably aware of del Sarto's proximity. Her nerves hummed. Her stomach somersaulted. How could she be both hopeful and terrified that he might touch her? To distract herself she picked up a handful of cloves from a tray, letting the fragrant black seeds run through her fingers. "You could get drunk just on the smell in here!"

"It is rather overwhelming." He selected a glass jar and held it in front of her nose.

Cara dutifully inhaled. "Ah, I know this! It keeps the moths away from clothes. It's camphor."

"Very good. Here's another."

"Rosemary. Your servants use it on the floor to scent the hall."

"Very observant, Miss Montessori." He guided her further along the row of shelves. "Now we come to those used for perfume." His voice had grown lower, more intimate. "The scents used to seduce the senses." He selected another glass bottle. The aroma was sweet and heady.

"Mmm, Jasmine."

"And this?"

"Orange blossom. I've always imagined this is what Spain smells like."

"It smells like dust. And donkeys."

She frowned at him. "Don't ruin my illusions! Can't you be more romantic?"

"No."

"And here I was," she teased, "imagining your rough exterior might secretly harbor a sensitive soul."

"Should I lie and tell you that Spain smells exactly like orange blossom?"

"And lemons and almonds."

"Faerie dust too, I suppose?"

She smiled, enchanted by his playful, mocking tone. "Much better." His arm brushed her sleeve as he offered another jar and her heart stuttered.

"This?"

She wrinkled her forehead, trying to identify the strange scent. "I don't know."

"Sandalwood. It comes from the Indies."

Cara inhaled deeply. It smelled like him, spicy and fragrant. Addictive. An unsettling warmth spread through her stomach.

"Unfortunately, my little romantic, most of the alluring scents have less than alluring sources." He chose another jar. "Take this, for example. Musk."

She took a tentative sniff.

"It comes from the reproductive sacs of a deer," he said, straight-faced.

Cara recoiled in horror. "Ugh!"

"And this one," he selected another, "is ambergris, which comes from the fatty excretions of whales."

"How revolting!"

"Yes, but extremely lucrative. As are the poisons." He gestured towards the next shelf.

Intrigued, Cara removed the lid from the nearest pot and sniffed warily. She looked at him in question.

"The assassin's favorite," he said, obliging her. "Cantarella. In tiny amounts it induces a deep sleep. Sometimes it looks like the person's dead because they have no detectable pulse. Too much, though, and it's a lethal poison. It's called the 'liquor of succession.'" He smiled thinly. "It's one of the Pope's favorites. There's an old joke in Rome; lots of people say 'I'm dining with the Borgias tonight' but hardly anyone says 'I *dined* with the Borgias last night.'"

Cara chuckled. "Because so few live to boast of the experience?"

"Exactly. We Italians have turned poisoning into a fine art.

Have you heard of a man named Da Vinci? He's an artist working for the Duke of Milan. He's injected the bark of fruit trees with cyanide. The resulting fruits are poisonous, but they contain such small amounts of poison that it's almost undetectable. They need to be consumed for a long period to have an effect."

Cara pretended to note something down in an invisible book. "Stay away from the fruit."

He smiled. "Apparently sending someone a series of poisoned letters is all the rage now."

She added to her imaginary list. "Don't open any correspondence."

He shook his head at her foolery. "Poison's a coward's weapon. It takes a special hatred to poison someone."

"You don't hate any of the people *you* kill?"

He raised his brows in surprise. "Of course not! I don't feel anything for them. They choose to fight me. It's not my fault if they lack the talent to stay alive. It's nothing personal. A poisoner, on the other hand, kills his victim in cold blood after carefully planning his crime. Far more women resort to poison than men."

"Worried I might try to finish you off?" she asked sweetly.

He smiled. "I doubt you'd lower yourself to poison. You'd prefer a good clean stab through the heart."

She smiled at the backhanded compliment. "Why, thank you."

He strode forward. "Here's my favorite section. The aphrodisiacs. An extremely lucrative part of my shipments. Pepper. Artichokes. Oysters." He handed her a jar filled with strange black lumps. "Truffles."

Cara wrinkled her nose at the small, wizened pieces. Suddenly, on the next shelf, she recognized the distinctive root of the mandrake and her heart gave an excited flip. The lumpy, knobbled tuber had offshoots that made it look like a man, with arms and legs protruding from the trunk—and it spelled another chance of freedom. Mandrake was the main ingredients of a sleeping draught she knew how to make. She turned away quickly, afraid he'd note the direction of her gaze.

"What else did your tutor use to ease pain?" del Sarto asked, reclaiming her attention.

Cara frowned, trying to order her racing thoughts. "Willow bark, feverfew, and meadowsweet are all good. And arnica for aching joints. You soak the flowers in oil, let it cool, and rub it into sore muscles."

"I'll try that. My shoulder is giving me trouble."

She blinked, surprised he'd admit to such a human failing. And then she spied an opportunity. "If you'll let me take some of these herbs, I'll make you some . . ."

He brushed past her without answering and she quelled a stab of disappointment as he rounded the end of the aisle. "Ah. Here's the reason I brought you in here."

Rolls and rolls of material were stored end-on, each bolt of cloth wound tightly around a central wooden pole. Every possible hue was represented, from dusky peach to shimmering gold.

Del Sarto pulled some out and unfurled the uppermost along the table. Yards of jade silk shimmered in the shafts of light. "The Orient's finest for milady." He unrolled another and Cara reached out to touch the deep midnight-blue velvet. The luxurious knap rubbed against her fingers like the pelt of an exotic animal.

He looked at her sideways, assessing. "Those two will suit you. One of the women will measure you up. We can't have you dressed in castoffs, now can we?"

"I wouldn't have thought a mercenary would be interested in ladies fashion," she taunted.

"Oh, I have many talents." The merriment in his eyes gave a teasing hint of what those other talents might be and Cara felt herself heat up again.

Del Sarto turned. "I have things to do. You may return with

Renata and choose some more fabrics. And take what you need to make me that salve."

Cara couldn't believe her luck. The man was handing her the keys to her prison! She tried not to let her excitement show in her face. "Thank you. You're very kind." On impulse she sketched him a curtsey.

"That's not my reputation. One more thing."

"Yes?"

"I thought you'd like this back." He pulled her dagger from the folds of his shirt and tossed the blade end-over-end with casual assurance. Cara narrowed her eyes. If she'd tried that, she'd have lost a finger. The cold steel flashed as he stepped closer. "I've had it sharpened."

She snatched it from his hand. "Not worried I might try to stab you again?"

"You're welcome to try."

His diabolic chuckle followed her from the room.

CHAPTER 11

Cara frowned down at the ingredients in front of her and wished she could combine the muscle salve with a sleeping draught. Nothing would make her happier than rendering his Satanic Lordship unconscious for a day or two.

Unfortunately, the only sleeping potion she could remember how to make had to be administered in a drink. She'd probably never get close enough to doctor del Sarto's wine without him noticing, but still, it was better to be prepared.

A servant had been waiting to measure her for her new dresses when she and Renata had returned to her rooms with the fabrics. She was a pretty, plump girl dressed in a gown so low-cut that her mountainous cleavage looked to be in constant danger of falling out. A white apron tied over her dress did little to provide either cover or support.

The girl clapped her hands with a gasp of delight when she saw Cara. She bobbed a hurried curtsey, talking all the while.

"Oh, my lady, let me look at you! I could hardly believe it when my Lord told me I was to have the task of dressing you!" She made a slow circle around Cara, assessing her task. "Don't you worry, my lady. I only do a few things really well in this world, but sewing's one of them!" She winked suggestively and Cara couldn't help smiling back. "Oh, I'm so excited I can barely think!"

Renata rolled her eyes. "This is Pia. One of our seamstresses."

The girl pounced on the rolls of fabric, her blue eyes as round as saucers. "Ooh! Look at these! You're going to look like a princess!"

Cara closed her eyes. If Pia was going to make something in her own inimitable style, she was doomed.

"His lordship wants her in something simple and understated," Renata said firmly, and Cara shot her a grateful glance.

"I've brought my pins and needle, my lady." Pia cast a disdainful glance at the ill-fitting dress Cara had been forced to wear. "Let's get that thing off you. Just step up here on the chair and we can get started."

As the girl pinned the blue velvet in place Cara tried to tug the neckline of the emerging dress higher. "This is a bit lower than I usually wear," she protested.

The servant chuckled. "Heavens, if you think *this* is low, you haven't been keeping up with the fashions in Venice and Rome. This'd be modest there, believe me!"

"But I don't have anything to show off—"

"Nonsense! You've got a handful, which is all most lads want!" Pia giggled and tugged the fabric lower still. "I'd give you some of mine, if I could. I've got more than enough to go around."

"You can almost see my—"

"Bubbies?" Pia finished, unabashed. "The important word is *almost*. There's nothing better to get a man's attention than a dress that promises a flash of something naughty when you move."

"I don't want to get anyone's attention!"

Pia snorted. The concept of not wanting to appeal to a man was clearly ridiculous. Cara envied the other woman's cheerful lack of morals. Buxom, flirtatious and cheekily confident, Pia was everything she herself was not.

"Do you want a square neckline or rounded?"

"It's entirely up to you."

Pia looked like she'd been handed the keys to paradise. She carefully peeled the pinned dress over Cara's head. "I'll have the first one finished by tomorrow," she promised. "I *was* supposed to be meeting one of the blacksmith's boys tonight." Her eyes took on a faraway look. "Big strapping lad, that Marco, huge hands—" She blinked, coming out of her daze. "Still, he'll keep 'till tomorrow." Gathering the rolls of silk and velvet from the bed she bustled out, full of new importance.

Cara turned to Renata and found her studying her critically. "Now what?"

"Hair." Renata pulled the chair out for her and gestured for her to sit. "His lordship said if you cooperate you can use his solar and borrow some of his books."

Cara plopped herself down in the chair. "I know I should be immune to such blatant bribery, but it's too tempting. Get your comb."

Five minutes later Renata stepped back with the flourish of a magician.

Cara glanced in the mirror and gasped. Her erratic tangles had been tamed into something actually resembling a *style*. An ivory comb pulled back each side. Pretty tendrils framed her face. She'd never seen herself look so feminine. It was a miracle.

Renata gave a satisfied nod. "Now, if there's nothing else you need, I'm going to make sure Pia's not creating anything too outrageous."

When she was finally alone, Cara mixed the promised salve and the sleeping potion too. Ever hopeful, she pushed aside the dressing table, put her ear to the interconnecting door, and gave it an experimental push, but it refused to budge. Clearly one of the reasons his Satanic Lordship had survived thus far was because he took no chances with his personal safety.

Opening the door to the corridor instead, she came face to face with her two guards, who snapped to attention. One was around her father's age, with a lined face and greying beard, the other a few years younger than herself.

She gave the younger one her most winning smile and held forward the small bowl of salve. "Would you deliver this to my lord del Sarto with my compliments?"

A blush crept up the boy's smooth cheeks. "He isn't in the castle, my lady."

"Do you know where he is? When he'll be back?"

The boy nodded, like a puppy eager to please. "He's overseeing arms practice in the bailey."

Her spirits dropped. There would be no chance of sneaking away with half an army assembled outside. Still, it was a good opportunity to take a peek at the defenses. "Take me there, please. I wish to see him. I take it I *can* leave my rooms?"

The older guard looked both surprised and offended by her question. "Of course, my lady! You're our honored guest."

She felt ashamed for asking. "All right, let's go."

"Don't you want to change into something else first, milady?" the younger guard asked incredulously.

Cara glanced down at the shirt and hose she'd donned to make her medicines and smiled. "No, I don't think so."

Anything to annoy her host.

The guards positioned themselves on either side of her as they walked along the corridor. It was like being led to her own execution. "I'm sure I can find my own way."

"Il Diavolo's orders. We're here for your personal protection, my lady."

Cara snorted under her breath. *Hah! Here to see she didn't make another run for it, more like.*

After a bewildering series of twists and turns she abandoned any hope of being able to find her own way back to her room. They descended the main staircase, crossed the great hall, and stepped out into the bright sunlight of the bailey. The noise that greeted them was instantly familiar—the sound of fighting. Over a hundred men were practicing their skill at arms in the grassy area between the castle's encircling curtain walls.

"Captain Neroni." The guards saluted as they approached.

The captain at arms was observing the training from one side of the field. He turned to Cara with a welcoming smile.

"My lady. Can I help you with something?"

"I was looking for my lord del Sarto."

Neroni nodded toward the centre of the field. "You've found him."

Il Diavolo was right in the middle of the fray, demonstrating some complicated-looking move to a group of soldiers. Cara couldn't take her eyes off him, the sleek economy of his movements as he fought. Compared to the less-experienced soldiers, whose arms were flailing about all over the place, he hardly seemed to move. Every action was smooth and deliberate, with a controlled grace that was a pleasure to behold.

There was no obvious sign of any injury to his shoulder, but she lifted the bowl of salve. "I made some salve for him. For his shoulder."

The captain shot her a surprised glance. "He told you about that, did he? Huh."

The clash of metal drew their attention back to the field and Cara winced at the ferocity of the fighting. "It looks like quite a punishing regime," she ventured. A young recruit limped off to the side, a trickle of red dripping from his jaw, only to be called back. "Don't they stop when blood's drawn?"

"Not for something as minor as a broken nose," the captain scoffed. "In a real battle your opponent's not going to wait while you wipe the sweat from your eyes."

"I suppose not. Still, it looks a bit . . . brutal. My father never worked his troops so hard."

"Your father wasn't as good as Il Diavolo." The captain said bluntly. "It's hard, but necessary. Those who can't meet the standard are found other roles. There's no room in the ranks for weaklings and cowards."

Across the bailey a great bear of a man was being escorted by two of the castle guards. He wore a leather breastplate over his shirt and scuffed brown boots and he looked fearsome, with huge shoulders and a bristling black beard that obscured most of his face. His hands were manacled at the wrists.

"Now we'll have some sport," the captain grinned. "We captured that one in a recent skirmish."

Cara frowned as the guards released the prisoner's manacles and handed him a sword. The man swung the weapon in a few wide arcs to test its weight. "You're letting him go? Why have they given him a weapon?"

"We challenge all our enemy prisoners so we can learn their fighting tricks. If they can best one of us in hand-to-hand combat, they're released with the guarantee of safe passage home. If not, they have to swear allegiance to my lord and join us."

Del Sarto detached himself from the group and approached the stranger. His long legs closed the distance with cocky, confident strides.

"Del Sarto's going to fight him?"

The captain nodded. "He won't let anyone else do it."

"Has anyone ever beaten him?"

He gave her a 'what-do-you-think?' look and turned back to the field.

The prisoner unbuckled his breastplate and stripped off his undershirt in preparation. Del Sarto did the same, removing his own shirt to reveal a set of muscled shoulders and a tawny, rippled torso. There wasn't an ounce of extraneous fat on him. Unlike his opponent, whose chest was covered in a thick mat of dark hair, *his* body was smooth and tanned and far too appealing. Cara's mouth went dry.

The two men shook hands then assumed a readying stance.

Francesco continued. "He says he has to prove to the men that he's worthy of leading them."

The two men circled each other slowly and she jumped as they came together with a terrible clash of swords.

"We train our men for the worst possible scenario. That way, the real battles are easier than they expect." Neroni said.

Sunlight flashed off the blades. The two men fought with a level of dexterity that far surpassed any she'd seen. Cara felt herself growing hot—which was a troubling reaction, considering it wasn't unseasonably warm in the bailey. Her body seemed to have a will of its own. It was stirring to life in the most alarming ways. And it was all *his* fault.

She prayed His Dark Imperiousness would be knocked flat on his perfect arse.

CHAPTER 12

"*H*ere comes trouble," the captain growled under his breath.

Cara glanced round to see Renata sauntering up to them with a twinkle of mischief in her dark eyes.

"Now there's a sight to gladden the heart!" Renata wiggled her eyebrows. "This is my favorite part of the week."

The captain frowned. "Get a hold of yourself, woman. You've seen enough naked men to last you a lifetime."

"No harm in looking," Renata laughed, unoffended by his tone. "And it's not just me. Haven't you noticed how many of the serving girls just happen to find an urgent errand in the bailey whenever it's skill-at-arms practice?" She nodded at a cluster of kitchen maids, huddled and giggling near the doorway.

The captain sent them a disdainful glance.

"Not practicing yourself, Neroni?" Renata cast him a saucy look, raking him from head to toe. "Why don't you strip off and join them? Show us what you've got. I tell you, you'll forget how to do it if you don't practice. Or are you too old for all that now?" There was a wealth of innuendo in her words.

Francesco's neck reddened. "I could best any of those saplings, and they're half my age."

Renata chuckled. "I'll take two boys of twenty-five over one man of fifty, any day!" She nudged Cara in the ribs.

"Only because you can't handle a *real* man." Francesco turned on his heel and stomped away.

"Like you?" Renata called at his retreating back. "Any time you want *handling*, Neroni, just let me know!" She noted Cara's questioning look and sighed. "We've a long history, Francesco and I."

Her tone indicated it wasn't something she wanted to discuss so Cara changed the subject. "We were talking about how the men are trained."

"I know it looks harsh, but Il Diavolo's a good leader." Renata glanced sideways at Cara. "You shouldn't believe *everything* you hear about him. He works hard to maintain his reputation, but it's mainly for effect. If the enemy doesn't think there's a chance of beating him, half the battle's won before a sword's even been drawn. He's a brilliant tactician, too. If he finds out where the enemy's troops are gathering, he'll cut off their supply line. If they plan to ford a river, he'll ambush while they're halfway across."

Cara sniffed. "Those aren't very honorable tactics."

Renata shrugged, her eyes on the fight. "Better a bloodless surrender than facing your enemy 'honorably' across a battlefield and losing half your men in the process. I've seen too many good men killed not to appreciate his methods, underhand or not."

The prisoner swung his sword in a huge arc. Del Sarto sidestepped and used the man's imbalance to deliver a punishing blow to his side.

Cara shivered, pricklingly aware of del Sarto's body, the deadly strength apparent in the play of muscles across his back. Each strike was precise, calculated to inflict the maximum damage, but there was a poetry, a lethal grace in the economy of his movements. He was like a wild animal at the peak of its fitness. What would it be like to touch those hard planes and flexed muscles? She balled her hands into fists.

What was wrong with her? Castelleon was littered with strong, good-looking men. She could barely turn a corner without seeing an attractive shirtless blacksmith or handsome foot soldier honing his muscles on the practice field. This man teased her. Mocked her. Was doubtless using her for his own devious ends.

So why did the sight of *his* body affect her as no one else's ever had? Her fascination with him was ridiculous. It was just a body. Just a collection of muscles and bones.

Renata fanned herself with her hand. "I don't know about you, but just watching them makes me hot!" She grinned. "All that sweaty flesh . . ."

Cara's cheeks flamed. Was she *that* obvious?

"He's not *just* a fabulous lump of muscles, you know," Renata inclined her head. "Watch how he fights. It's not always orthodox, but it's effective."

As if on cue, the two men engaged again. Del Sarto forced his opponent back with a punishing series of blows then used the hilt of his sword to land a brutal punch on the man's face. Cara winced at the sound of bone crunching.

A roar of appreciation went up from the crowd. The prisoner howled and staggered back, blood streaming from his nose, but he recovered to attack with a fresh assault.

"Well done, my lord!" Renata shouted, cupping her hands around her mouth.

The two men were still raining blows upon each other, each one bone-jarring. Neither showed any inclination to stop.

"It looks like they're actually trying to kill each other," Cara remarked.

"Don't worry about Il Diavolo. He'll be fine."

"I'm not worried."

"Oh really? Then why are you wringing the front of your shirt like that?"

Cara released her clenched fists. "I'm wishing it was his neck."

Renata laughed.

"I'm merely concerned about what will happen to *me* if he gets himself killed, that's all," Cara said.

"No chance of that, look."

Sure enough, del Sarto had disarmed his opponent. The prisoner's sword flew harmlessly to the turf. When the man tried to attack using his bare hands, del Sarto delivered a blow to his side with the flat of his sword and threw him to the ground. The prisoner flung both arms out in surrender as the blade pressed against his throat.

Del Sarto stepped back and extended his arm. The prisoner allowed himself to be hauled up and the two men clapped each other on the back in a display of respect and admiration.

Renata chuckled at Cara's surprised expression. "I know. Men. Murdering each other one minute, sharing a pitcher of ale the next. And they say *women* are incomprehensible."

"Now what?"

"The loser swears fealty to my lord."

Cara was well acquainted with the ceremony of allegiance. She'd seen it performed many times for her father as he received new men into his forces. She always enjoyed the formality of it, the solemnity of the Oath of Fealty. The vassal knelt before his lord in an act of homage. Clasping his hands together as if in prayer, he would swear the oath, promising faithful service. The lord would take the man's outstretched hands and announce his acceptance.

Both men replaced their shirts. The defeated soldier approached del Sarto and kneeled before him on the grass. Apparently they weren't going to organize a specific ceremony inside the hall.

Del Sarto looked completely at ease, every inch the disreputable prince. A lock of dark hair fell over his forehead and his tanned face was inscrutable as he surveyed his vanquished opponent. There was no hint of gloating at his victory, merely the certainty that this was his due, the natural order of things. That this man *should* bow to him in deference.

The prisoner spoke his words clearly, for all to hear, and Cara let them wash over her, a flood of memories assailing her with the familiar cadences. She experienced a sharp stab of longing for her father, for everything she'd lost. Her throat ached with tears she refused to shed so she bit the inside of her cheek and concentrated on the pain instead.

Del Sarto nodded his acceptance and clapped the man on the shoulder, signaling him to rise. The assembled crowd applauded and closed around to welcome the newcomer. Cara turned to go inside, but jumped at the sound of that rich, deep voice calling her name across the bailey.

"Signorina Montessori!"

She turned back. Del Sarto curled one finger at her. She hadn't realized he'd known she was there, but he'd probably been aware of her presence from the moment she'd set foot in the bailey.

"Yes?" she called out cautiously.

His lips twitched in a diabolic half smile. "Now it's *your* turn."

CHAPTER 13

"I beg your pardon?"

"Come here and kneel to me."

His deep tones carried across the bailey. There was no mistaking the command. Or the challenge. Every head in the keep turned to look at her. The air buzzed with whispers. Cara shook her head and tried to turn, but a hand at the small of her back stopped her.

Renata shoved her forward with a cheerful grin. "Better go. He hates to be kept waiting."

Escape was impossible, given the number of witnesses. Cara approached on shaking legs, eyeing del Sarto warily as he wiped sweat out of his eyes with his forearm. At least he'd put his shirt back on.

She stopped several feet away. "I don't believe I heard you correctly, my lord. Did you wish to speak to me?"

"You heard me." He gestured to the ground with the tip of his sword. "On your knees."

"You want *me* to kneel to *you*?" She gave him her most disdainful look and lowered her voice so only he could hear. "In your dreams!"

His smile made her stomach somersault. "Oh, I've certainly dreamed of you kneeling in front of me, Signorina Montessori. Ready to serve my every whim." His eyes danced with unholy amusement and his hot gaze promised untold delights. He raked her from head to toe with an insolent, leisurely inspection that had her flushing to the roots of her hair.

Cara raised her chin. "If you think I'm going to bow and scrape to you, you're sadly mistaken."

"You'll kneel to me, your new lord and master." His voice was steel, implacable, and her cheeks burned with anger and humiliation. How *dare* he? She wasn't some lowly foot soldier! She was the daughter of an Earl. Fury raced through her veins. She took a quick step forward and without really knowing what she was going to do, slapped him on the cheek. Hard.

An audible gasp went up around the bailey as the crowd witnessed her rebellion. Cara was amazed herself. She snatched her hand down, wincing at the tingling in her palm. She'd never slapped anyone before. She watched with horrified fascination as the pink imprint of her hand slowly appeared across his tanned cheek. A pulse ticked in his jaw and she tensed, fully expecting him to backhand her across the bailey. Instead he gave her a chilling smile.

"You want to fight me? Is *that* what it will take to prove you're truly beaten?"

She gazed at him, astonished.

"I'm not known for being merciful, but I'll give you one last chance. A new bargain, if you will."

She narrowed her eyes. "I'm listening."

His eyes raked her masculine clothes. "You seem determined to be treated as a man, so I'll extend to you the same offer I give *all* my prisoners. If you can beat me in single combat, you can go free." She opened her mouth to argue but he held up a hand to stop her. "If you lose, you belong to me, body and soul. You'll swear unconditional fealty. No more arguments, no more escapes."

Cara's mind was churning. Part of her was amazed that he was offering her this chance. He was treating her as an equal worthy of respect, something not even her father had ever done before. The other half of her was furious. She couldn't possibly beat him, and he knew it, the monster. He just wanted to humiliate her in front of everyone.

She curled her lip. "It's a worthless offer. You're risking nothing. You know I'm no match for you physically."

"Come on. I never thought you'd back down from a challenge. You might even have the advantage. I've been training for over an hour and I've just fought an extremely grueling fight with our hairy friend over there. *And* I have an injured shoulder."

He sounded so reasonable, but she could hear the underlying amusement in his lazy drawl. He was relishing making her squirm.

"Now, do you want to fight, or do you want to just kneel and get it over with?"

She scowled, fully aware she'd been backed into a corner. "I'll fight, curse you."

He smiled. "A brave choice. Stupid, but brave. Your choice of weapons. Not that it will make any difference."

"Swords," Cara said immediately. Even if she couldn't beat him, she'd make him regret taunting her.

He turned his wrist and offered her the hilt of his own sword and she repressed a shiver of awareness as their fingers touched over the warmed metal. He shot her a lazy, devastating grin and she stepped back, already regretting her impetuosity. *Why* did she always let her temper get her into these situations?

* * *

FRANCESCO REAPPEARED at Renata's side and she shot him a sidelong glance.

"What did I miss?" he demanded, aware of the heightened tension in the bailey, the air of excitement humming through the crowd.

"Sandro's challenged her to a fight."

"What?"

Renata shrugged. "He told her to kneel and pay homage and she refused."

Francesco raised his eyebrows. "Interesting."

Renata's eyes narrowed. "If he hurts one hair on her head I'll have his hide. That poor girl's been through enough."

Cara shot them a helpless glance across the field. Renata sent her a supportive wink and a wave.

Francesco chuckled. "She can hold her own. He just needs to show her who's wearing the breeches in this castle, that's all."

"They're *both* wearing breeches."

"That's precisely the problem," Francesco grunted. "Still, he won't hurt her. He wants to run her through, all right," he chuckled, "but not with his sword!"

Renata rolled her eyes. "You have a one-track mind, Neroni."

"You wish, da Mosta."

* * *

DEL SARTO ACCEPTED a new sword from one of his men. He paced to the centre of the field and stood facing her, legs apart, arms hanging loosely at his sides, and raised one black eyebrow in challenging invitation for her to do her worst.

Cara gritted her teeth. The man was far too self-confident for his own good. Where was a friendly bolt of lightning when she needed it? She'd done more than her fair share of praying at the monastery. Maybe not always with her complete attention, but still, it had to count for something. Surely a little divine intervention wasn't too much to ask for? She was *clearly* the more deserving party here. Anything would do; a freak hailstorm, flash flood, plague of locusts. She glanced upward. The sky remained stubbornly cloud-free.

His sword was heavy in her hand, far weightier than those she was used to handling. He'd probably known she'd find it difficult to use when he offered it to her, the fiend.

Cara circled, looking for an opening. She'd never actually engaged in a *real* fight before. She'd sparred with the knights and squires of Castelleon, of course, despite her father's disapproval, but she suspected they'd always held back because she was a girl.

Holding the sword with both hands, Cara swung it high, trying to catch del Sarto's neck. He parried easily. The impact of metal against metal jarred her wrists and she staggered back. *He* wasn't softening his blows just because she was a woman. Well, he might be stronger, but she was fast and clever.

She wrinkled her brow and tried to remember the location of the fighting points; the weak spots on the body that were best places for striking an opponent. She got in two or three good hots, meeting his sword, then swung her leg behind him and kicked him in the back of the knee. The crowd cheered, relishing the display like spectators at a Roman gladiatorial contest scenting blood.

Del Sarto's leg buckled, but he righted himself immediately and caught her arms in a punishing grip. He lifted her right off her feet and a second later they were both on the ground, his body lying half on top of hers. The crowd roared.

All the air left her lungs in a painful rush. Oh, God, not *again*! He'd beaten her in less than a minute. The iron weight of his thighs crushed hers, her breasts were plastered against his chest, and the heat of him pulsed through the thin layer of her shirt.

Cara closed her eyes in humiliation, both at his easy victory and her own body's traitorous reaction. Such aggression. Such attraction. How could she want to kiss him and kill him at exactly the same time?

Her chest was heaving with exertion and her heart was hammering in her throat, but del Sarto hadn't even broken a sweat. Cara gulped in air, opened her eyes, and glared at him.

The cocky bastard was smiling! His insolent gaze dropped to her trembling mouth, then lower, to her breasts, and Cara flushed as she realized how immodest the thin shirt was. Her nipples were visible where the material was stretched taut.

"We've been here before," he murmured.

Trust him to bring that up. He was referring to The Kiss.

Six years ago she'd been impatiently awaiting her father's return from the Holy Land. When she'd heard that he was barely a day's ride away, she'd ridden out from Castelleon to surprise him. Cara had just been ducking through his tent flap when del Sarto, the great oaf, had wrestled her to the ground.

He *claimed* he'd mistaken her for a would-be assassin, but he was far too good at his job for such an error. He'd known exactly who she was before he'd touched her, and he'd done it anyway, just for fun. They'd ended up in this position then, too. Right before he'd placed that wicked mouth on hers and stolen a kiss she'd never been able to forget.

Purely for comparison's sake she'd allowed Castelleon's resident lothario, Giulio Pescari, to corner her in the dairy a few weeks later in order to prove that del Sarto's kiss hadn't been as earth-shattering as she'd thought, but it hadn't worked out quite as she'd planned. Giulio's kiss had been wet and slobbery, like being lipped by a horse. And when he'd ignored Cara's command to stop, she'd crippled him with an unladylike move she'd learned from the stable lads. Castelleon's men had given her a wide berth after that.

So del Sarto was still the only man who'd ever properly kissed her. And, damn it, she'd been dreaming of a rematch ever since.

"I'm so glad you came dressed ready to fight," he teased, jolting her back to the present. "Ready to give up yet?"

"No." Cara pushed against him with all her might.

He rolled off her with an agile move and she was humiliatingly aware that he'd chosen to let her go. She ignored his outstretched hand and rose by herself, stumbling away, her sides heaving as she drew in shaky breaths. Her lungs ached and her injured side was agony. She'd probably just undone most of Renata's handiwork. The thought of her injury reminded her of his; she changed the angle of her attack and battered his shoulder with a series of stinging blows.

"I'm sorry I made you that salve!" she panted between hits.

His teeth flashed white as he laughed. He was so smug, so superior. She prayed for the strength to hurt him as he deserved. She charged again but he swatted her away as easily as he would an annoying fly, then ducked under her sword and stepped in close, catching her around the waist and crushing her in a brutal bear hug. His hipbone pressed into her stomach. Cara squirmed, managed to free one arm, and punched him as hard as she could in the kidneys. He barely grunted in reaction. Grabbing a handful of her hair, he pulled it back so her face tipped up to his.

"Yield, woman!" he growled.

She bared her teeth at him. "No!"

His gaze dropped to her lips again and she had the awful thought that he really *was* going to kiss her, right there, in front of everyone. Panicked, she raised her knee and tried to catch him in the groin but he anticipated the move and she hit the inside of his rock-hard thigh instead.

A shout echoed from the side. "Don't hurt him, my lady!" Francesco clapped his hands in glee, ignoring the black look his master sent his way.

Taking advantage of del Sarto's inattention, Cara pulled her head forward and bit him hard on the shoulder. With a surprised yelp he dropped her back onto her feet. She scurried back, shooting him a smile of triumph as she swiped a tendril of hair from her cheek but her smile faded when she saw the evil look he shot her. He stepped back and very deliberately tossed his sword from his left hand into his right.

Her stomach dropped in horrified realization. He'd been using his weaker hand this whole time! Playing with her, like a cat with an injured bird.

CHAPTER 14

*W*hen he advanced again, Cara closed her eyes, pulled back her fist, and punched him as hard as she could in the face. Pain shot through her knuckles at the contact. Sweet Lord! She'd just broken every bone in her hand!

The crowd bayed with delight. She opened her eyes to see him clap one hand to his nose. The pain was worth it; blood dripped from between his fingers. She shook her wrist to try to restore some feeling and treated him to her finest smirk. "Do *you* yield, my lord?"

He gave the smear of red a disbelieving glance before wiping his upper lip on the sleeve of his shirt. A dangerous smile hovered at the corners of his mouth as he sketched her a mocking bow. "Nice move. We'll make a mercenary of you yet."

"No thank you," she panted, bracing her hands on her knees as she struggled for breath. "I have better things to do with my time."

He swung his sword so fast she barely had time to block it; the blow shuddered all the way up to her shoulder blades. Cara staggered backwards, her ankle turned on an uneven patch of ground, and with a yelp of dismay she landed flat on her backside. Del Sarto knocked her blade aside and she watched in mute horror as it tumbled point-first into the soft ground, just out of reach. He grabbed her arm and hauled her upright.

They were both panting hard. He was hot and sweaty, covered in dust, and as she looked up into his hooded gaze she felt hot too. Hot and restless and violent.

"*Now* do you yield?" His eyes were dancing with laughter and something else she didn't dare identify.

She shook her head.

He pressed his mouth to hers. It could hardly be called a kiss; it was swift and punishing, a symbol of dominance and possession. A cheer went up and Cara belatedly realized that almost everyone in the castle had gathered to witness her humiliation.

"Do. You. Yield?" He enunciated each word.

She still had her knife in her boot. She could stab him in his injured shoulder. But if she did that, he would lose face in front of his men, and she needed his deadly reputation—and his sword arm—intact if he was to beat her uncle.

He interpreted her silence as another refusal. His mouth lowered to hers once more and Cara braced herself for another assault, but this kiss was nothing like the first. His breath shimmered over her lips like ripples over the surface of a pond and then his lips brushed hers, petal-soft.

Her heart stilled. Such gentleness from a man with so much physical strength was glorious. Unexpected. Irresistible.

A sudden urgency seized her. He might never kiss her again. She would escape, and he'd probably go and die in some stupid battle somewhere and never come back to haunt her.

Not acceptable. Cara bunched her hands in the front of his shirt, opened her mouth, and kissed him back.

His inarticulate growl, deep in his throat, turned her knees to water. The hand on her arm tightened, and his tongue swept inside her mouth, dancing in and out in some strange, erotic rhythm that was new and yet, somehow, achingly familiar. Cara gasped. He was claiming her. Branding her.

Well, she'd claim him right back.

The kiss became a battle for supremacy. The whole world dissolved and narrowed to his lips, his tongue, his breath in her mouth. It was darkness and sin, promise and fulfillment, all rolled into one swirling red-black vortex. The whole world tilted on its axis.

Then, as suddenly as it had started, del Sarto pulled away and Cara's wits returned with the dash of cold air. The sound of the crowd intruded and the reality of their public position made her cringe in embarrassment. She glanced at the sky for impending thunderbolts, this time aimed at *her*, for being so monumentally stupid.

The corner of his lips curled upwards into that irritating half-smile. "Well, that *was* interesting."

She wiped the back of her hand across her mouth, then raised it to hit him again, just for good measure. "I hate you!"

He caught her fist and kissed her knuckles in a parody of a courtly greeting—which elicited more cheers from the crowd at his tomfoolery. Cara dragged the hand back and hid it behind her. The spot he'd touched throbbed as though burned.

"You don't hate me," he taunted. "You hate what I do to you."

Her heart missed a beat as he wiped the pad of his thumb over her lower lip and she watched in horrified fascination as a bright smear of blood stained his fingertip. He brought it up to his mouth and licked it clean, his eyes brimming with secrets and complicity. Heat pooled between her legs. It was barbaric, what he did.

"I find fighting with you strangely arousing," he murmured. "Next time you draw my blood, in fact, next time you show me *any* act of aggression, I'll treat it as an invitation. Clearly the way to subdue you is through kisses rather than blows." He raised his voice so all those present could hear. "Do you yield?"

Cara bit back her instinctive denial. Her submission now was the most politic option if she wanted to regain her home. She let out a disgusted sigh. "Yes."

He gave a satisfied nod, placed his hands on his hips, and glanced pointedly at the grass in front of him. She knew what he wanted. On shaking legs she bent and kneeled, her gaze fixed on his boots. Then pride kicked in and she raised her eyes to his. She would not be cowed. He might have won this battle, but the war was far from over.

"Repeat after me," he murmured, thoroughly enjoying her discomfiture. "I promise on my faith that I will in the future be faithful to my lord—"

With trembling lips, she copied his words, hating him for inflicting this humiliation on her.

"Nice and loud, so everyone can hear," he taunted.

Cara raised her voice. "—never cause him harm and will observe my homage to him against all persons in good faith and without deceit. I become your liege man of life and limb and truth and earthly honors, bearing to you against all men that love, or move or die, so help me God and the Holy Dame." She almost choked on the words.

His eyes blazed with triumph. "Now you belong to me."

She blanched at the satisfaction in his tone.

He turned away. "Renata? Take her away and make her presentable. Next time I see her, make sure she's wearing a dress and behaving as a woman should. If she gives you any trouble—" his eyes flashed briefly back to Cara in warning, "—inform me at once and I shall deal with her as I see fit."

He turned on his heel and strode away, leaving Cara kneeling in the dirt.

* * *

ALESSANDRO TURNED to the assembled crowd. "Anyone else?" he bellowed.

The foremost line of men took a step back, accurately interpreting his coiled, watchful stance. Deprived of another fight, he strode off the field and glared at Francesco while he dabbed a fresh trickle of blood from his nose.

"I thought she had you there a few times!" Francesco chuckled. "You want a cloth for that?"

"No."

"For everyone's sake, just bed her and get it over with. It's painful to watch."

Alessandro winced as pain lanced down his arm. His shoulder still hurt. The little vixen had landed a few solid blows there, too. Fighting her was like trying to tame an unbroken horse—exciting and wholly unpredictable.

He'd meant to taunt her with that kiss, and had fully expected a slap in the face in response. But what had started as a brief, mocking punishment had changed into something else completely when she'd kissed him back.

He prided himself on his rigid self-control. Kissing her had been the most stupid thing he'd ever done. What the hell had he been thinking? He *hadn't* been thinking. At least, not with his brain. God, he wanted her. His body hardened in reaction as he remembered her beneath him, panting and sweaty. He'd been shaking with the need to mould his hands to her breasts, her hips, her pert backside. Thank God he'd had the strength to pull away before he did something *truly* idiotic. Like drag her off to the nearest bed, or stable, or hayrick to assuage the burning fever she'd ignited.

Alessandro shook his head. He'd developed an insane curiosity to know what it would be like to have all that fire and fury in his bed. He wanted Cara di Montessori more than he'd ever wanted a woman in his life.

He couldn't erase the image of her kneeling at his feet,

defeated but still defiant. *Magnificent.* He'd been so distracted by the vision she'd presented in her ridiculous boy's outfit, with a pink flush staining her cheeks and her eyes flashing daggers at him, that he'd struggled to remember the words to bind her to him.

A flash of undiluted satisfaction shot through him. *She was his.*

Francesco slapped him on his injured shoulder, interrupting his mental self-flagellation. "Seriously, man. Go and have a cold bath!"

* * *

CARA BARELY REMEMBERED WALKING BACK to her room. Her whole body was shaking with delayed reaction.

"I've never heard of a woman taking the oath of fealty before," Renata ventured.

Tears stung Cara's eyes. "He humiliated me. In front of everyone!"

Renata sounded puzzled. "I don't think that was his aim, my lady. In fact, he's shown you a great honor. He made a public declaration that you're equal to one of his men."

Cara sank on the bed and buried her head in her hands. "He tricked me! Don't you know what I've done? I'm *bonded* to him. It's a promise before God. As solemn as marriage vows!"

She should have put something nasty in his salve, like mustard or itching powder. Something to cause him the same woeful discomfort she felt—this burning ache of frustration and anger.

And the worst thing was, the arrogant bastard had been right. She *hated* what he did to her. The memory of his kiss mocked her. Her hand still tingled where he'd touched it. She glanced down and noticed a smear of red on her knuckles—he'd left a bloody streak there, like a brand. She rubbed it away with her fingertips.

The man was impossible to deal with. Her sanity disappeared in direct correlation to his nearness.

CHAPTER 15

*C*ara didn't see del Sarto for the rest of the day, for which she was profoundly grateful. She was still brooding that evening when she was requested—no, ordered—to dine with him. Recalling his comments about her clothes, she decided that sometimes discretion was the better part of valor, and dressed in the new gown Pia had delivered to her rooms.

As her guards escorted her through the labyrinthine corridors she reminded herself she was poised, unshakeable. The sort of woman who dealt with men like del Sarto every day. Her self-assurance flagged when she was shown into a small solar and she realized that they would be eating alone, instead of in the great hall with the rest of the household.

Del Sarto rose to his feet, his simmering gaze taking in her new dress and Cara waited for some sarcastic jibe about finally doing his bidding, but he forbore to comment. "I take it you spent a restful afternoon?"

"I was bored."

His lips twitched. "Knowing your preference for violent activity, that doesn't surprise me. How shall we amuse you? I can think of any number of interesting ways to pass the time."

She ignored the suggestion in his tone. "I'm sure none of them would interest me."

"A game of chess perhaps?" He gestured to a handsome red and white ivory set, laid out on an oak side table. "Do you play?"

Cara suppressed a smile, remembering the countless times she'd bested her father. She gave a nonchalant shrug. "A little."

He shot her an amused glance. "Your eyes give you away. I bet you play quite well, don't you?"

"Care to try me?"

* * *

ALESSANDRO'S GROIN hardened in immediate response to her innocent words. Try her? *God, yes. In every conceivable position.*

She took the seat opposite him; the enormous wing chair dwarfed her as she folded her legs and tucked her feet beneath her. So prim and proper.

But she would need to be ruthless to deal with the guests who would be arriving at the castle. He could teach her that lesson.

He turned the board so the white pieces were in front of her. "Ladies first."

"Trying to throw me off-balance with a display of chivalry?"

His mouth twitched at her cheekiness. Few dared speak to him this way. He loved the way she constantly challenged him. "Is it working?"

"No."

* * *

DEL SARTO STEEPLED his hands on the chair arms. "Pay attention, you'll be in check in three moves time."

Cara narrowed her eyes at the board but it took her a full minute to discover the fiendish trap he'd laid. She swore under her breath and moved her rook.

Del Sarto gave an exaggerated sigh. "If only life were as straightforward as the chessboard."

"What do you mean?"

He gestured at the squares. "Here it's clear-cut, black against white. Real life is never so defined." He glanced at her from beneath sinfully dark eyelashes. "No man is wholly good or wholly bad. One never knows who to trust." His hand hovered over his knight. "Often it's simpler to trust nobody." He swooped the knight and toppled her king—a blatantly illegal move.

"Hey! You can't do that!"

He smiled, white teeth flashing. "Why not?"

"It's against the rules!"

"*So?* Life is rarely played by the rules. Why should chess be any different? I've taken your king. Does it matter how it came about?"

Cara pursed her lips. "Of course it matters."

"I'm a ruthless mercenary. You should expect me to win by any means." His hot gaze flicked down to her lips. "Let me use another example, one closer to your own heart. What's to stop me taking you to bed right now and claiming Castelleon as my own?"

Her heart lodged in her throat. "Honor? Chivalry?"

"Chivalry's for fools."

"Basic decency, then?"

"What makes you think I have any?"

His wolfish grin made her hot and sick at once. "We made a bargain," she reminded him.

"So we did." He held her gaze for a breathless moment, then leaned back, dispelling the sudden tension. He reached inside his doublet and pulled out a folded piece if parchment. "Speaking of Castelleon, I've had a letter from your uncle."

"Sent here?"

He nodded. "He knows you're alive. And here with me. He's 'concerned for your safety' and demands that you return to

Castelleon." He smiled at her horrified expression. "I declined on your behalf."

Cara wasn't sure whether to be relieved or annoyed by his high-handed behavior. His amused expression suggested he understood her feelings perfectly.

"You might also be pleased to know that I rejected his suggestion that you marry your cousin—" he consulted the letter, "—a youth named Piero."

"How kind."

Her sarcasm bounced right off him. "I thought so. It must have caught me in a rare moment of charitable weakness. I have other plans for you."

She raised her brows. "Oh really? Am I permitted to know what they are?"

"Of course. You will be married. Just not to your cousin."

"If that's a proposal, I decline."

He sent her a mocking smile. "Contrary to popular opinion, I neither need nor desire a wife at the moment."

Heat scalded her cheeks. It went without saying that she'd be a long way down the list of potential brides. "And I don't need a husband! I can do a perfectly good job of running Castelleon on my own."

"That's probably true. But I've seen hundreds of well-run keeps—and captured them shortly afterwards. You're far too trusting. Everyone's corruptible. It's not about the strength of the walls or who has the most men. All it takes is one traitor and hundreds of innocents die. Your father didn't want you to live that way."

"No one at Castelleon would betray me."

"Don't be so naïve. You just need little blackmail, the right leverage to turn someone. Money, threats, promises, torture. You must suspect everyone. Then you'll never be surprised by the inevitable betrayal."

"That's not much of a life."

"No." He fixed her with a bleak look, his eyes dark and bottomless. "It's not. And it's why people like you pay people like me to do your dirty work. No blood on *your* hands, milady."

"Do you think I'm so sheltered that I can't fight my own battles?"

She froze as he reached across the table and stroked her cheek.

"That's exactly what I think. It does someone like me good to know that there are still things in this world worth fighting for." His eyes held hers for a moment before he let his hand fall and she glimpsed sincerity in his gaze before it faded to his usual cynicism. "Every court is full of backstabbing and intrigue. The men are ruthless and hungry for power. The women are petty, vindictive gossips. A whispered word or a misinterpreted glance can cost you your life."

Cara winced at the bitterness in his tone. "Surely it's not *that* bad."

He shrugged. "Maybe not at Castelleon, but most other places. You'll need a strong man by your side if you intend to rule Castelleon. Someone wealthy and politically astute. I owe it to your father's memory to arrange such a match for you."

She glared at him. "I see what you're doing; you're just trying to weasel out of our bargain. You want to make me someone else's problem."

"Far from it. Life without you here will be far duller, I promise you."

"That's what abbot Andreo said when I left the monastery," Cara said darkly. "But your plan to marry me off is flawed. You'll never find me a husband if everyone thinks I'm your mistress."

He ran an assessing glance over her face and figure, like a market trader sizing up a pig. "Oh, I think they will."

She sighed. Del Sarto's determination to find her a husband was ridiculous. If she were wed, the moment she regained Castelleon it would become her husband's property, to dispose of at his will. She would lose not only her cherished independence, but her beloved home too.

Her father's faith in del Sarto's integrity had clearly been misplaced. It pained her to break the vow of fealty she'd given, but there was nothing for it but to remove herself from this situation. She would make her way back to the monastery of St John and find some other way to reclaim her birthright.

One which didn't include irritatingly attractive mercenaries who thought they had the right to play God with her life.

"I'm tired of arguing with you, my lord. I'm going to bed."

"Not until I claim my prize for winning our chess match."

He hadn't moved from his chair, but he was suddenly too close, too intimidating. Too tempting.

She should leave. But the wicked part of her made her stay right there, gazing into his harsh, handsome face. Where was her pride? She ought to be grabbing the nearest candlestick and defending her virtue, not enjoying the heady thrill of this verbal sparring. "By unfair means," she said.

"It doesn't matter *how* I won. I'll have my prize." He rose and stepped around the table.

Cara stayed where she was, determined to show no weakness. He took her hand and raised it to his lips; his kiss warmed the back of her fingers. She snatched them away, her breath coming too fast, and headed for the door.

She was *not* disappointed that he hadn't kissed her lips.

CHAPTER 16

ara dreamed of a wolf. She was sitting in a wood with the huge black animal curled around her. She'd been stroking its belly, enjoying the silky-soft texture of its fur between her fingers. The wolf's head had been resting in her lap, pink tongue lolling, and she'd laughed as it licked her wrist with its rough wetness.

And then the dream changed. The woods darkened into a place of menacing shadows and nameless dread. She was running, tripping in her haste, whimpering in fright. Her wolf was tracking her, stalking her through the nightmare forest on silent paws and she knew, without a doubt, that she'd been marked for death.

She couldn't run fast enough. Panting, terrified, she turned just as the animal leapt from the darkness, fangs bared, grey eyes glittering with malevolent intent. She threw her arms in front of her face to shield herself, screaming a denial—and awoke with a jolt, her heart pounding, sweat beading on her forehead and sliding between her breasts.

No need for a soothsayer to interpret *that.*

Morning brought Francesco, dressed for riding. "His lordship says I'm to accompany you if you wish to ride. I thought you might like a tour of the city."

Cara beamed. "Oh, yes, please! I'll be just one minute."

She donned a riding cloak and, out of Francesco's line of sight, retrieved her dagger from under her pillow and secured it in her boot. As she followed him down to the stables, she tried to quell the burst of hope in her chest. This outing might reveal a new avenue of escape.

Saraceno's black face appeared over a half door as they passed along the row of stalls and he gave a whicker of welcome as she stopped to stroke his velvety nose. He waggled his ears in ecstasy when she scratched the side of his face.

Francesco looked amazed. "He likes you!"

"Doesn't he like everyone?"

"Are you joking? That is the meanest-tempered horse I have ever encountered."

Cara smiled into the horse's cheek. "Just like your owner, hmm?"

Right on cue, the horse lunged past her and tried to take a bite out of Francesco's shoulder. He cuffed it affectionately across the nose. "Get off me, you unsociable bastar—I mean, er, brute," he amended, flushing. "He won't let anyone ride him except my lord."

"Oh, I'm sure that's not true!" Cara crooned. "You'd let me ride you, wouldn't you, handsome?" The beast nodded its head as if in complete agreement. "There, you see! He would!"

Francesco shook his head. "Not a chance. It's more than my life's worth to let you near that widow-maker. Come on." He stopped next to a stable lad who was tightening the girth on a dun mare. "This is Pandolfo."

Cara took one glance at the animal and abandoned any hope of escape.

Pandolfo was ancient. Sway-backed, knock-kneed, the pathetic thing was half the size of Saraceno and stood placidly chewing a mouthful of hay and regarding her out of huge, cow-like eyes. Sighing, she patted its greying nose. "Let me guess," she said dryly. "Unlike Saraceno, Pandolfo's the slowest, oldest and most even-tempered horse you have in your stables?"

Francesco chuckled. "The children train on her when they're learning to ride. Sorry. Master's orders. He said not to give you anything that might go faster than a trot."

Pandolfo looked as though anything more than breathing might be too strenuous. She might as well try to escape on one of the castle goats. She led the painfully slow animal into the court-yard, where no fewer than twenty fully-armed men were lined up on horseback, waiting for her. "Oh, for heaven's sake! I don't need an armed guard!"

Francesco gave her an 'it's-out-of-my-hands' shrug. "You can go anywhere within the city walls. Pandolfo tires easily, though, so we'd best not go too far. Is there anywhere in particular you'd like to go? Something you'd like to buy, perhaps?"

Cara smiled, a little devil inside her prompting her to tease the gruff soldier. She gave a feminine sigh of excitement. "Ooh, I'd *love* to go shopping. Why, I could visit every dress shop and jewelry vendor in the city and never tire of it! And that's not even *considering* all the underclothes and personal items a lady needs." She shot him a meaningful glance and thoroughly enjoyed his look of dawning horror.

A giggle escaped her as she took pity on him. "You should see your face!" She patted his arm. "Don't worry. Much as I'd love to bankrupt His Annoying Highness, I have no interest in that sort of thing. I would like to feel the sun on my face, though. A tour of the city would be wonderful."

Francesco gave a relieved nod. "Of course, my lady! This way."

Despite the escort—which she did her best to ignore—and her useless mount, Cara began to enjoy her ride. Soon they were immersed in the bustle of the narrow streets within the walls and she discarded the idea of trying to lose herself in the crowd. Even if she escaped her escort, she'd never be able to get past the castle walls; a quick glance at the gates they passed confirmed that they were all far too well guarded.

She soon became distracted by the hum of activity. All manner of wares were being traded from small shops and stalls. She inhaled the smell of leather from a shoemaker, caught a glimpse of a blacksmith hammering a piece of armor over a glowing forge. A small boy pumped the bellows to keep the fire red hot, his sweaty mop of hair sticking to his forehead.

"I bet he does a good trade."

"Who? The armorer? He's never out of work," Francesco nodded. "With a standing army as large as ours, there's always a broken shield or a cracked breastplate that needs attention." Noting her interest in a bakery stall, he stopped and bought a small twisted bun studded with raisins.

Cara sank her teeth into it, savoring the taste of spices and cinnamon. "Lord, that tastes good!" she moaned. "The one thing about being on campaign is that you really appreciate all the things you don't have. Like sweetmeats."

"And a soft bed," Francesco chuckled, nodding. "I hear you. Come on."

They crossed a shell-shaped piazza where a group of women gossiped around a central stone well. Francesco dismounted and gestured for Cara to do the same. Leaving their escort outside, he ushered her through the studded door of a large red brick building.

The interior was cool and quiet and Cara experienced an instant sense of recognition. The place radiated serenity, like the monastery. "Is this a church?" she whispered.

Francesco's laugh echoed off the vaulted ceiling. "No, my lady. It's a hospital. For those who've been injured in battle. Il Diavolo's got some of the best doctors in Europe working here."

The entrance opened into a central courtyard garden with pillared walkways leading off each side and Cara gazed around in wonder. If anywhere on earth could come close to matching her idea of the Garden of Eden, this was it. Raised flowerbeds held a profusion of plants and herbs. Flowers bloomed over trellises and covered walkways. Fruit trees scattered their pink and white confetti with each gust of wind. A long, rectangular pond filled with waterlilies reflected the sky overhead. It was a complete contrast to the bustle of the city, a surreally perfect haven.

Several figures were tending to the garden; some kneeling to weed the borders, others gathering fruit with a sense of calm purpose. All the workers had some form of disability. Some had obvious injuries, like missing limbs, while others seemed less seriously hurt, at least physically. Not every wound was visible from the outside. Mental scars, Cara knew from experience, were often harder to heal than physical ones.

A row of chairs had been set in the shade of one of the arched porticos. Four or five less able invalids reclined in cushioned comfort, watching the others.

"This is like the garden at St. John's," Cara smiled at the memory. "Father Giovanni has a passion for gardening. He's the one who taught me all about healing plants. Together we improved the vegetable patch and added a rose garden in the middle of the cloisters."

After the flood she'd caused had drained, that was.

"Then you'll recognize the herbs they grow here." Francesco snapped the head from a dried flower.

Cara glanced sideways at him. "I assume you're showing me this to prove del Sarto isn't *all* bad?"

"He's a hard man to know, my lady."

She raised her eyebrows at the understatement. She'd never met anyone more infuriatingly guarded than Il Diavolo.

"He's loyal." Francesco continued. "He never leaves an injured man to fend for himself. Those who can't work, he supports here, in the hospital. The men love him because he's a 'come on' kind of commander."

At her frown, he explained. "The kind who says 'come on' and gallops forward into battle, instead of ordering 'go on' and staying safe at the back of the line. He's always the first into—and last out of—a fight. He drinks the same water, eats the same food, sleeps on the same hard ground. They'd die for him, if he asked them to."

Cara was touched by this impassioned speech. Her father's men had felt the same way about him.

Francesco took her silence as a sign to continue. He turned and caught her eye. "Don't judge him too harshly. If he's done something you don't like, you can be sure he has good reasons." Clearly deciding he'd said enough on the subject, he bent to pick a silvery sage leaf from the nearest border. He crushed it in his fingers and inhaled the scent. "That salve you made for him worked wonders. His shoulder has definitely improved."

She smiled at the compliment.

"Perhaps you could find time to take a look at some of the injuries here? Just seeing your face would be enough to lift the spirits of most of them." Francesco flushed as he realized he'd complimented her.

Guilt crushed her. If she were staying at Torre di San Rocco she'd relish the chance to use her healing skills. She'd been nursing the cuts and bruises at Castelleon for as long as she could remember. But she wasn't going to be chatelaine here. She wasn't staying around long enough to help anyone. She gave Francesco a noncommittal smile as she followed him out of the courtyard and up a narrow spiral staircase. "Now where are we going?"

"The bell tower," he explained over his shoulder. "It's the best view of the city from up here."

Cara blinked as they emerged into the bright sunlight and when her eyes adjusted she studied the countryside laid out below her. Fields of still-green barley undulated like shimmering seas in the wind, punctuated by lines of darker cypress pointing skywards. She turned her eyes west, towards Castelleon. How was it faring without her? What atrocities was her uncle subjecting her people to? How on earth was she going to get home?

Her worries distracted her all the way back to the keep. As they re-entered the courtyard, however, she roused herself enough to notice a group of laborers had erected scaffolding around the horse chestnut tree and were pruning it.

Francesco noted the direction of her gaze. "His lordship thought it was growing too close to your window. He was worried the tapping of the branches might disturb your sleep."

His innocent expression and laughing eyes belied his words. He must have been told of her ignominious escape attempt.

Cara managed a strained smile. "How kind. He thinks of everything, doesn't he?"

CHAPTER 17

*T*hat afternoon Cara entered the study, prepared to leave if *he* was there, but the room was empty save for a crackling fire. She bypassed the imposing desk that dominated the centre of the room and crossed to the large bay window, which claimed a view over the main entrance and the bailey beyond. Choosing a few books at random, she settled herself against the plush velvet pillows and began to read.

Some time later she jumped at the sound of the door. It was her gaoler.

"Renata said I could come in here," she said, starting to rise. "I'll leave if you want."

Del Sarto strode forward, darkly handsome in white shirt and leather doublet, as if he'd been riding. He settled his narrow hips against the desk and crossed his arms and Cara had the unnerving sensation of being trapped in a cage with some wild beast; tame for now, but likely to strike at any moment. Idiot that she was, she found it thrilling rather than terrifying. Unable to sit still under his cool scrutiny, she got up and started to walk about the room. "You have a wonderful library. Thank you for letting me use it."

He inclined his head. "Think of it as a reward for your continued good behavior."

"Must *everything* be an exchange?"

He shrugged. "It's the basic principle of commerce."

She refused to get into a discussion on the subject. Having perused the shelves earlier, she'd begrudgingly realized that he was far from the ill-read boor she'd imagined. "This is a far greater selection than the library at St. John's. Have you read every one?"

"Only the ones with pictures," he mocked. "Too many words give a poor soldier like me a headache."

She ignored his sarcasm. "I've heard accounts of the Medici library in Florence. People say it's astonishing."

"It is, I've seen it. Lorenzo used to send agents out to retrieve books from all over the world, especially the East. My ships brought them back."

Cara ran her fingertips over the spines, impressed by the scope of subjects. Military history, maps, medical tomes. A large section concerned with warfare, naturally. She drifted to the far wall, where drawings of different castles had been hung. "Where's this?"

"A place called Crac de Chevalier. In Syria."

"Have you been there?"

"No, but studying fortifications is an interest of mine."

She glanced at him over her shoulder. "Mine too."

"What an unusual young lady you are." Somehow he made it sound more like an insult than a compliment. "I expect you've already made a thorough study of San Rocco's defenses?"

She shot him a jaunty smile. "Of course."

"I'm also assuming—since you're still here—that you've found no weaknesses. Care to suggest any improvements?"

"And help fortify my prison?" she snorted. "I think not. If I do find an escape route, you'll be the last to know."

His lips twitched. "I stand forewarned."

She returned to the window seat and plopped onto the pillows.

"What are you reading?" he asked.

She turned a book over so he could see the cover. "Chrétien de Troyes. It's a courtly romance. A concept I doubt you're familiar with."

He made a face. "Did you find that in here? It must be Renata's. She loves all that nonsense."

"You should read it. It's very instructive. Full of examples of how to behave towards a lady."

He laughed. "I wouldn't go as far as to call you a lady, sweeting. Female you might be, *lady* you are not." He pushed away from the desk and stalked forward. Snatching the volume from her fingers, he flicked it open at random and began to read aloud.

"'Through their kisses and caresses they experienced a joy and wonder the equal of which has never been known or heard of. But I shall be silent . . . for the rarest and most delectable pleasures are those which are hinted at, but never told.' God, how nauseating!" He crossed the room and drew a different volume from the shelves. "This is better." He handed the book to her.

"Machiavelli? I found him fawning and pompous." In truth, she found the man's witty, acerbic commentaries on court life most entertaining, but she wasn't about to admit it. "He advocates winning at any cost."

Del Sarto rolled his eyes. "I bet you're one of those idiots who think warfare should be conducted honorably."

"And why shouldn't it be?"

"A chivalrous man on the battlefield is a *dead* man. There's no fair play involved. Remember our chess match?"

Cara sniffed. "I do. And I still believe brains are preferable to brawn." She shot his lean, muscular form a scathing glance.

He shook his head. "Brute strength is *always* preferable. Your brains didn't get you very far in the bailey, did they?" His eyes dropped to her mouth, as if she needed to be reminded of her humiliating defeat. "But if you'd care to try again, I'd be happy to oblige." His slow smile was knowing, cynical. Her lips tingled in awareness.

He searched the shelves again, prowling around with the fluid grace that characterized him, then selected four or five volumes and placed them on the desk in front of her. They had odd, exotic sounding titles, like 'The Ananga Ranga', and 'The Perfumed Garden for the Soul's Recreation'—obviously an Arabic work— by someone called Sheikh Nefzaoui. Cara wrinkled her forehead. Perhaps they were about horticulture?

"You want something instructive? Read those," he said.

Intrigued, she drew the topmost book towards her. It seemed to be from the Orient. Vertical lines of incomprehensible script ran down from the top edge next to a beautifully painted image of a man and a woman seated together under a flowering pagoda in a garden.

The wicked twinkle in his eye should have alerted her, but she opened it without thinking. At first she was so engrossed by the intricate, detailed brushwork of the illustrations that she failed to notice the actual subject matter. As soon as she did, however, she blushed beetroot-red. Painted on thin paper, with a silk border, each of the Chinese pictures were extremely explicit images of lovers, engaged in all manner of sexual positions. Absolutely every inch of their anatomy was depicted in graphic detail.

She slammed the book closed.

He chuckled. "What? I'm only broadening your education. I doubt the monks were particularly instructive in this matter. Did you see the one with the fruit? Feel free to take them to your room, if you want a closer look in private."

Cara knew her face was burning. "You're disgraceful!"

He shrugged, unabashed. "Everyone does it. Well, maybe not the monks. I bet they never had anything like *that* at St. John's. At least, not out in the open. Don't look so shocked. You've spent half your life around soldiers. Didn't you ever talk about it with the camp followers or the servant girls?"

She couldn't believe they'd got on to the one subject she never wished to discuss with him. "No!"

He sighed. "Pity. You might have learned something useful."

* * *

ALESSANDRO CHUCKLED at Cara's obvious mortification. *She was so much fun to tease.* The thought made him pause. *Fun.* He couldn't remember the last time he'd used the word. Since his return from Spain he'd almost forgotten what it was like to interact with the world and enjoy it. She brought out the playful devil in him, made him laugh, without even trying. He enjoyed her company, her quick wit and her unexpected reactions.

He wanted to reach over the table and kiss that frown of disapproval from her lips. To hear her sigh with pleasure. Ah, the things he was going to teach her.

She deserved more than the few nights' pleasure he could offer her, of course, but that was all he had to give. To any woman.

"So, if it's not erotic manuals, what *do* you like to read?" he asked.

She folded her hands primly in her lap, as if even touching the offending books might be contaminating. "I prefer the classics."

He tilted his head to read the spines of the books she'd piled next to her. "Ah. Ovid's Metamorphoses."

"You've read it?"

"Absolutely. It's full of women escaping the nefarious clutches of the gods. Like that girl Daphne who turns herself into a tree instead of making love with Apollo. That was a bit drastic, if you ask me. What's so bad about being loved by a god?" He caught her gaze again, unwavering, and enjoyed the jolt to his pulse he experienced whenever she looked at him directly. "If she just stopped running, she'd find she enjoyed it."

As predicted, she flushed, and Alessandro cursed the effect it had on him. He couldn't recall a time when he'd been so innocent. Perhaps never. He'd killed his first man and had his first woman before he'd turned fifteen. Things had been going downhill ever since. And yet even when he was with Cara he felt more alive, more lighthearted, than ever before.

The strength of his desire for her intrigued him. He'd had far more experienced, sophisticated women. Women more beautiful than her. But he'd never been interested in much more than their bodies, in the pleasure they could give and receive. He'd certainly never wanted to spend much time with them fully clothed.

He smiled. "Even your saintly Ovid writes smut. There's a copy of his Ars Amatoria around here somewhere." He crossed back to the shelves, found the slim volume on the shelf, and tossed it to her. "Here you are."

She caught it automatically, along with the next one he sent sailing towards her, and frowned down at the title. "Lysistrata? Never heard of it."

"The Greeks are usually deadly dull, but that's hilarious, I promise you. A bunch of Greek women hate that their men are always away on campaign. So they stage a revolt and refuse to have sex until the men promise to come home for good. It's a brilliant strategy."

Cara set the Aristophanes down on the table and lifted Chrétien de Troyes. "I'd like to borrow this one, please."

Alessandro rolled his eyes but gave a permissive wave of the hand.

"And this." She picked up the Metamorphoses.

"Fine. But you have to take the others too. In the spirit of broad-mindedness." He crossed back to the table and swept up the naughty books along with her other choices and before she could offer any resistance he preceded her out the door and handed the pile to a nearby servant. "I shall be chivalrous enough to have them carried up for you, milady."

CHAPTER 18

Cara couldn't help looking at the awful books, of course, once she was alone in her room.

Ovid's 'Ars Amatoria' seemed to be advice to women on how to deal with men. The author wryly suggested taking both young and old lovers, and exhorted women to make the most of their best bodily feature when making love by choosing the most suitable position. Her face flamed as she read about the various sexual positions he described—most of which she'd never even considered. And naturally she couldn't help wondering what position *she'd* have to adopt to make the best of herself. Her breasts were small. Her hair was a disaster. Her skin would never be the porcelain-white favored by the fashionable women of court. Her legs weren't so bad, though, even if they were muscled from riding.

There was no harm in reading about these things. Ignorance was something she deplored, after all. And reading about a battle was not the same as being in one, just as reading about love-making was no substitute for, well, practical first-hand knowledge.

It wasn't as though she was *never* going to have sex. She might

K. C. BATEMAN & KATE BATEMAN

as well have all the relevant information to hand. The problem was, she kept imagining del Sarto as her partner.

When she reached Ovid's discourse on a man's fingers pleasuring a woman, she threw the book aside in dismay and picked up his 'Metamorphoses' instead. This was guaranteed to be far more soothing. Except she kept thinking about what *he'd* said about it. His damned argument made a warped kind of sense. She was running from him like Daphne from Apollo.

Would it really be so bad? To be loved so fiercely and so well? Surely, if one were going to have a lover, he might as well be the one you wanted. Even if it was only for a limited time.

Her stomach gave a funny little quiver.

She had to stop thinking about it. About him.

About *Him* in relation to *It*.

She frowned down at the page before her. Del Sarto was ruining everything, making her question her own ingrained sense of right and wrong. The man had enough charm and guile to seduce a nun—and she'd never even made it to novice.

He was her nemesis, the most irritating man she'd ever encountered. She disagreed with everything he stood for. Everything he was. And unlike her father, or the soldiers or the monks, he was the only man she'd ever met she couldn't meddle with. He was impervious to her demands and tricks, her wheedling and cleverness.

It was, admittedly, gratifying to have found such a worthy opponent, but del Sarto was simply too dangerous for her peace of mind. The sooner she left Torre di San Rocco the better.

Cara glanced up guiltily as the door opened, but Renata was too busy with what she was carrying to notice her shamefaced flush. Cara slid the offending copy of Lysistrata under Chrétien de Troyes. She was *not* going give into her near-insatiable curiosity and ask what the author meant by a sexual position called 'the lion-on-a-cheese-grater.'

Renata was carrying yet another gown. She laid it on the bed and stroked it lovingly, as one might a favorite pet. "Look at this! Pia's done a wonderful job." She noted Cara's flushed cheeks and placed a hand on her forehead. "You look a bit feverish. I *told* him it's not good for an energetic girl like you to be cooped up inside." She bustled over to the casement and opened the window.

"I'm well," Cara protested weakly.

Renata handed her a small, inlaid wooden box. "He sent you these, to wear with the dress. Look."

Cara's mouth formed a silent O of surprise as she lifted the lid. Inside, nestled on a bed of silk, was a set of the most exquisite bracelet and earrings she'd ever seen. "I can't wear these!"

"He said to remind you about swearing allegiance—"

Cara growled and inspected an earring. A pendant of finely wrought gold surrounded a red stone like a polished pebble. Ruby, she supposed. It caught the light and flashed with a fire that was breathtaking. She'd never owned anything so fine.

Why would he bedeck her in such finery? What game was he playing? Reluctantly, she put the bracelet on, turning her wrist this way and that to admire the effect. She hadn't worn earrings in so long that the holes in her ears had almost closed up; her earlobe throbbed as she pushed the drops into place. They hit the side of her jaw when she moved her head.

Renata helped her into the dress and deftly fastened her hair with a comb, but when Cara tried to leave the room the servant caught her shoulders and steered her towards the door that led to del Sarto's chambers instead of the hallway.

"You're dining in his rooms tonight," Renata said airily.

* * *

CARA STEPPED through the door and narrowed her eyes at the scene before her. Dinner had been set on the table. Candles glowed in the sconces. Compared to the bustle of the great hall, or even his study, it was intimate, private, a scene set for seduction.

It was a battlefield. And as his home territory, she was immediately disadvantaged.

He was waiting. He'd changed into a doublet of navy velvet, so dark it seemed to absorb the light. His thoughtful gaze swept from her head to her feet and Cara felt a tingle run through her. Did he think she was beautiful? It would be better if he didn't.

He waved her over to the table. "Come. Sit down. I'd like your opinion on something."

She noted the wicked twinkle in his eye with suspicion as he reached forward, uncovered a plate, and offered it to her with a blandly innocent look on his face. She glanced down at the offering and just *knew* her face was reddening with embarrassment.

The tray contained a collection of what could only be described as pale white breasts, each with a puffy red nipple standing pertly to attention on top.

"Our discussion on foods the other day got me thinking. I asked chef to conjure up something to amuse our guests. These are called 'minni di virgini,'—virgin breasts. First baked by Sicilian nuns. They're marzipan covered in custard and finished with a cherry. Quite realistic, don't you think?"

The monster was clearly relishing her embarrassment. Refusing to be outdone, Cara lifted one to her mouth, took a tentative bite, and had to suppress a moan of pleasure. She'd always had a soft spot for desserts and these were tooth-achingly sweet. Del Sarto's lips quirked at her enthusiasm. He chose one himself and bit into the rounded curve. Her own breasts tingled. She licked a patch of icing off her bottom lip and his eyes followed the move hungrily. When she'd finished, he pushed forward another plate and she smiled. "I'm sensing a theme."

"'Capezzoli di Venere.' Nipples of Venus," he said. "Roman

chestnuts in brandied sugar, toasted almonds, and grated nutmeg."

Cara closed her eyes, savoring the delicious sweetness. Oh good Lord! These things were so good they should be outlawed.

"I don't know how you stay so thin if you eat like that all the time," he teased.

"Sweets are my weakness. Everyone at Castelleon knows I'd give my right arm for a slice of cook's lemon cake."

Bianca, her maid, swore the only thing better than cook's lemon cake was making love. Cara didn't have any experience of the latter, of course, but she secretly doubted *anything* could give more pleasure than the cake—however accomplished the lover. She met del Sarto's stare. "You're trying to shock me, my Lord."

He didn't bother to deny it. "I find it amusing. I see you're wearing the earrings I sent you." He reached out and touched one, making the bauble swing, then rose and padded over to a side table. He picked up a velvet-covered box and opened it with a careless flick. "I want you to wear this too."

Cara's breath caught. A huge ruby swung from an intricate golden latticework of chains to form a necklace.

He pulled her to her feet and stepped behind her. "This is known as the Black Prince's ruby. Although, technically, it's a spinel." The hair on the back of her neck rose as his fingers brushed a wisp of hair aside to fasten the clasp.

The central stone nestled like a pigeon's egg between her breasts and she shivered at its coolness even as it warmed, absorbing the heat of her skin. Her gaze met his in the mirror on the opposite wall and she watched transfixed as he skimmed one finger idly along her collarbone, then lower still, tracing the neckline of her dress, skating over the top of her breasts. Soft as snowfall, hot as hellfire.

"This once belonged to a Moorish Prince of Granada. He was stabbed to death while negotiating a truce with Don Pedro of Castile."

She murmured a wordless exclamation of protest, both at the gruesome story, and his feather-light touch. His fingers stroked back and forth, their subtle magic at odds with the history-tutor dryness of his tone. The gems in the necklace glistened against her skin like little drops of blood. Flustered, she raised her hands to undo the clasp, but his fingers stilled hers at the nape of her neck.

"Leave it." His voice was low and hypnotic. "Don Pedro made an alliance with an English knight known as the Black Prince, who demanded the stone in exchange for his services."

"All your stories contain mercenaries," she managed weakly. "How did *you* get it?"

"The Black Prince took it to England where it was added to the crown jewels. When Henry Tudor won the crown in battle he gave it to *me* for services I rendered him in France."

"Such a violent history."

He smiled and dipped his head. "Perfect for such a violent woman." His lips grazed the bare flesh of her shoulder.

For the briefest of moments Cara closed her eyes and savored the sensation, then she jerked away. "Stop that! You only do it to control me."

He dropped his hands and stepped back, releasing her from the sensual haze he'd woven so effortlessly. Air rushed back into her lungs.

"But of course. It's much easier than having you clapped in manacles, although the idea holds a certain appeal." The twinkle in his eyes was wicked.

"I don't like being manipulated," she said coldly.

"I enjoy it too much to stop." He gestured to her neckline. "Wear those tomorrow evening. As my hostess, you should reflect my magnificence." The self-mockery in his tone was evident.

"We are both to be paraded in public as your prized possessions?"

He laughed at her cynicism. "Precisely. You'll also be expected to start the dancing. I need to know you won't embarrass me."

Cara frowned. "I can dance."

He held his hand out. "Prove it."

She studied his long, elegant fingers and shook her head.

"Afraid?" he taunted.

"No," she lied. "There's no music."

"That doesn't matter. Follow my lead."

He caught her hand in his and raised them to shoulder height. His free hand settled on the curve at the bottom of her spine; his touch burned all the way through the thick fabric of her dress.

Where were the hundreds of servants when you needed them?

She kept her gaze on his tanned throat as he moved, guiding them both through the intricate patterns of a tessera, and marveled at the way they floated together so effortlessly. She was usually a stumbling mess on the dance floor, but his lithe ability transferred itself to her as if by magic. The only sound was the whisper of their feet on the wooden floor.

She felt oddly safe in his embrace, despite the undeniable thrill of danger, as if her body recognized that he was strong enough to shield her from the worst the world could throw at her. A haven in a storm.

But his protection came at a hefty price.

"Look at me," he commanded softly.

She raised her eyes and the air between them thrummed, tight as a bow string.

"Will you be coming to my bed tonight?"

He'd stopped. They stood, their bodies touching, her breasts to his chest, his hard thighs against hers. Blood pounded in her ears. She felt as if she were hovering on the edge of an abyss, and desperate to fall. She'd wanted him for years. All she had to do was say yes—

Sanity came to her rescue. She stepped back from his hold.

"No. You don't truly want me. This 'bargain' is just a game for you, a diversion."

His eyes glittered. He grabbed her wrist, drew it downward, and placed her hand directly onto the throbbing bulge at the front of his breeches. She gasped as she felt the hardness of him through the material.

"No game." He rocked his hips, pushing himself against her palm. "Will you honor your part of the bargain?"

She was drowning in his eyes. "No!" Her voice was a mere croak. "I—"

He stepped away, and the loss of his body against hers was like a physical ache. He crossed to the door, opened it, and gestured for her to leave. He seemed neither surprised nor disappointed at her refusal. "Then I'll bid you goodnight."

Cara let out a shaky breath at the unexpected reprieve. She swept past him as quickly as her shaking limbs would allow.

Back in her own room she glanced in the mirror and barely recognized herself. The gems of the necklace sent shimmers of red across her heated skin. With fumbling fingers she unfastened the catch and let it fall onto the table, pulling off the bracelet too with a sense of relief. She tried to remove the earrings, but they hurt her ears and she gave up in frustration. It hardly mattered if she left them in. She'd barely sleep a wink anyway.

CHAPTER 19

*T*he first guests began arriving just after breakfast. Cara watched from her window as a seemingly endless procession of horses and carriages wound their way over the city bridge and up to the front gates.

Each of the great houses appeared to be vying to outdo the others with the extravagance and number of their party. Richly clad couples were helped out of the carriages and ushered into the hall, attended by scores of servants and luggage. Her stomach dropped. They were all so polished and sophisticated. She'd rarely entertained guests, save those military friends of her father's who'd visited Castelleon. She was woefully ill-equipped for tonight.

A new gown had been laid out on the bed. It was midnight-blue velvet, so dark it was almost black, with a squared neckline and a narrow waist that flared out into a full skirt at the hips. A thin silk under-dress with a ruched bodice provided a little extra modesty, but not much.

She fidgeted as Renata fussed with her hair, weaving a thin gold ribbon into her braid, then suffered through the application of eyeliner and sneezed when Renata whisked a hare's foot covered in powder over her nose. Finally, Renata fastened the ruby necklace around her throat, pushed the bracelet over her wrist, and stepped back to admire her handiwork.

Cara risked a glance in the mirror. Her eyes glittered with excitement, their odd color turned to a haunting, mossy green by the darkness of the dress. Her hair didn't look like its usual bird's-nest, either. She gave Renata's arm a little squeeze of gratitude.

The older woman glanced out of the window to see the latest arrivals and sniffed. "Oh, wonderful. The Canozzis."

Cara peered over her shoulder. A beautiful woman descended from a coach, closely followed by a much older man. They were both dressed in the height of fashion. Cara caught the briefest glimpse of pale blonde hair and alabaster skin before the woman hastened up the steps, leaving the gentleman in her wake to order the outriders and oversee the unloading of numerous traveling trunks.

"Is that her husband?" she asked, surprised.

Renata snorted. "Yes, poor devil. A word of warning, my lady; Vanessa Canozzi is nothing but trouble." She turned away before Cara could ask more. "I'll see you later."

When Cara made her way to the festivities she found del Sarto hovering at the bottom of the staircase, looking as darkly elegant as usual in a black velvet doublet with high collar and slashed sleeves. His eyes never left her as she descended the steps, and Cara bit her lip as she waited for his verdict.

"You'll do."

She let out the breath she'd been holding. "Such flattery!" she chuckled. "Remind me not to let it go to my head."

He ignored her sarcasm and led her into the great hall, which was already crowded. Her fingers tingled at the contact. She tried to pull away but he held her fast and bent his head toward her ear so as to be heard over the din of conversation.

"Let me tell you about some of our guests, before you start a war. The Sforzas of Milan, over there, are the traditional enemies of the Medici of Florence, to your left."

"And you've put them in the same room? That's either very brave or very stupid."

"They'll behave. We all play the game when we have to."

"Who's that weaselly man over there?" Cara indicated a tall, well-dressed gentleman surveying the assembled crowd with an alert air. "He's been watching me since we arrived."

"Don Michelotto, Cesare Borgia's right-hand man. He's one of the most lethal assassins in Italy. We should be honored he's left Cesare's side to come spy on us." He caught the man's eye, bowed, and received a polite nod in return.

"Aren't you worried, having him here?" Cara said.

"I'd rather have him as an invited guest than loitering around, uninvited, in the shadows. 'Keep your friends close, and your enemies closer,' they say." He pressed up against her, sending a hot thrill through her body. "Don't worry. You'll be perfectly safe with me."

She almost snorted at that blatant untruth. Safe was the last thing he was.

"Now, who else is interesting?" he asked. "Some of the Borghese family are here, from Siena. That's Niccolò over there." He indicated a man of around sixty, deep in conversation, as he guided Cara smoothly through the throng, his hand pressing the small of her back.

A well-dressed, slightly older woman approached them. "Ah, now here's someone you'll be interested to meet," he murmured. "Caterina Sforza, Lady of Imola and Countess of Forlì. Since her first husband was murdered she's ruled as regent for her first-born son, Ottaviano." He bowed low as the woman reached them. "Caterina! Let me introduce my honored guest, Signorina Cara di Montessori."

Cara curtseyed. The woman smiled. "Enchanted! You are

Ercolo di Montessori's daughter, are you not? I heard about his passing. I'm so sorry for your loss."

Cara inclined her head. "Thank you."

The woman's forehead wrinkled. "Aren't you the— "

"—girl who blew up the monastery?" Cara finished with a rueful smile. "Yes, my lady." She held her hands up. "Guilty as charged. That's going to be on my gravestone, I think: 'Cara di Montessori. Destroyer of holy places.'"

Del Sarto's lips quirked. "You'll be thrilled to learn that you share many of the same interests. Caterina's intrigued by experiments in alchemy."

The older woman nodded. "Absolutely! Alessandro, leave us alone. Stop hovering like some dreadful bird of prey."

He bowed again. "If you'll excuse me, ladies."

The Countess drew Cara gently away by the arm. "My, my. He does seem very protective of you, my dear!"

"Believe me, he's just as possessive of his horse," Cara sniffed. "More so, in fact."

"Nonsense! I've seen the way he looks at you." The older lady winked. "As if he'd like to eat you up!" She laughed at Cara's expression. "Forgive me, I've embarrassed you. I'm told I'm too outspoken, but I'm far too old to be subtle. Now tell me, what *exactly* did you use to bring down a monastery wall? I'm compiling a record of all sorts of alchemical experiments. It's a little hobby of mine." She regarded Cara's nose with a dubious eye. "I'll give you a wonderful recipe for improving those freckles of yours in exchange."

Cara couldn't take offense; the woman was trying to be helpful. "I made Chinese black powder, which is a mixture of sulphur, charcoal and saltpeter," she said. "You grind each ingredient separately then add just enough boiling water to wet it and mix. Let it dry, wrap it in paper, and store it until you need it. And—obviously—*don't* keep it near heat or flames!"

"What a remarkable education you've had my dear!" the

Countess said approvingly. "So much more interesting than some of these empty-headed geese one meets nowadays who only think of the cut of their gowns." She waved a hand, dismissing a cluster of giggling young women by the fire. "Now if you'll excuse me, I see Borgia's odious little lackey, Don Michelotto, is here. Much as I hate to talk to *anyone* connected with the Borgias, I know he'll have the recipes for several new poisons I can include in my little book of secrets."

CHAPTER 20

*V*anessa Canozzi was furious.

As was her custom, within half an hour of her arrival her loyal servants had apprised her of all the important gossip. And the only subject on everyone's lips was Il Diavolo's female 'houseguest'.

Vanessa checked her reflection in the mirror, searching for imperfections. She smoothed one pale blonde hair back into place and peered closely. No, still no wrinkles to blemish her perfect skin. Her pale blue eyes hardened. How could Il Diavolo possibly prefer anyone else? It was inexplicable. She glanced down at her perfect, soft creamy breasts swelling indignantly above her bodice. It just didn't make sense. By all accounts, the little mouse barely had any breasts to speak of, and Il Diavolo had made it abundantly clear how much he enjoyed *her* ample bosom.

She'd been his lover for several months, encouraged by her toad of a husband, who saw no reason why she shouldn't use her obvious charms to stay on the good side of one of the most powerful players on the Italian political stage.

It hadn't been a hardship. Vanessa sighed, remembering the feel of his luscious body and the raw sensuality of his passion.

She knew she shared his favors with other women, but that was a small price to pay for such a masterful lover. She smiled. He'd never before refused her his bed and she hadn't seen him in months. No reason he'd be immune to her charms now. Still, the presence of little Miss Mouse was an annoyance.

She'd watched the two of them covertly from across the room and her gut had twisted in envy. Del Sarto's hot gaze devoured the girl whenever she wasn't looking his way. Vanessa knew that look of pure, possessive lust. She'd thrown it at Il Diavolo herself on more than one occasion. If he hadn't already got the girl in his bed then it was only a matter of time.

Vanessa ground her teeth, furious that such a naïve little nobody might have usurped her position. Still, she had no fears that the girl was anything more than a temporary conquest. Sandro would tire of her soon enough, but still, it was annoying. She'd thrown him her best lures and inviting glances all evening, but so far he'd proved completely immune. He'd been icily polite. And he'd failed to show up at her rooms, despite her prettily worded note.

Well, she wasn't just going to sit around and accept it. Time to show Miss Mouse she had a rival.

Vanessa beckoned her maid and handed her two slips of folded paper. "See that this is delivered to My Lord del Sarto. Wait ten minutes then give *this* one to that little brown mouse he's escorting around. Be sure she doesn't see you, though."

"Yes, Signora."

Vanessa pinched her cheeks to add some extra color and debated whether she had time to change her dress, then decided against it. This brocade was fetching enough, and besides, Il Diavolo rarely took much note of her clothes when he was removing them. Slipping from her rooms, she headed outside.

Gratifyingly, she heard his entry into the stables less than five minutes later and her heart fluttered with anticipation as he stalked towards her down the row of stables. Undaunted by his disinterested expression, she placed her finger to her lips and beckoned him into one of the furthest stalls.

"Well, Vanessa, what is this news of the utmost importance?"

Vanessa pouted. She knew it was a captivating trick—it showed her mouth to its most kissable advantage. "Oh, darling, don't be like that. You know I don't have any news, important or otherwise. It's just that I've missed you these past few months." She pressed herself full-length against him. "It's been so long since I last saw you."

He barely flicked her a second glance as he took her upper arms and pushed her away. "Not now. I'm busy. I must get back to my guests."

"Oh come, you know what they say about all work and no play—" Vanessa slid her hand down the front of his shirt, enjoying the ridges of taut muscle under the cotton. Her hand went lower and she cupped him boldly, licking her lips and gazing into his eyes.

She felt a flicker of annoyance as she raised herself on tiptoe to kiss his mouth, only to have him turn his head so she grazed his cheek instead. She gave him a seductive smile. "I know how much you like it when I do this—" She pushed him against the wall and slid down his body so she was kneeling before him in the straw. Her nimble fingers began to unlace the ties at the front of his breeches.

CARA FROWNED AT THE NOTE. Someone had slipped it into her palm while she watched the dancing, but when she'd turned the messenger had already melted into the crowd. The note requested that she go to the stables.

Obviously, anyone who signed themselves 'a friend' was unlikely to be so. She had no friends here. It could be a trick from her uncle. Another of his assassins? But what if it was someone with genuine news from Castelleon? She had her dagger. She'd be careful.

The crowded room gave her the perfect chance to slip away unnoticed. She glanced around, sure that del Sarto would take one look at her face and immediately suspect something, but luck was on her side—she couldn't see him anywhere. Avoiding Francesco and Renata, who'd stationed themselves on either side of the main door and were pretending to ignore one another, she slipped out of a side door and crossed the darkened yard towards the stables with her senses on full alert.

The doorway was in darkness but over the row of half-height stalls she could see a lantern glowing at the far end. The horses whickered and stamped their feet in the straw as she passed. Pandolfo's ugly nose pushed at her skirts through the wooden slats but Cara ignored his greeting and tiptoed forward with her dagger drawn.

Soft, muffled sounds were coming from the end stall. She rounded the corner, tensed for a confrontation, but instead, her mouth dropped open in shocked disbelief. Vanessa Canozzi was in the stall, and so was Il Diavolo.

And they were paying no attention *whatsoever* to the horses.

Cara stilled, rooted to the spot like a rabbit caught in the fox's stare. Vanessa was on her knees. Del Sarto was standing braced against the wall, his head thrown back, his eyes closed. His hands held either side of Vanessa's head as she fumbled to release him from his clothing.

Cara might have been gently reared but she wasn't stupid— and she'd read those awful books. There was no mistaking what service Vanessa was about to provide. She was appalled and yet strangely fascinated by the sight. Reading about something and actually *seeing* it were two entirely different things.

Determined not to disturb them, she started to withdraw, but something—some perverse, battle-honed instinct—made del Sarto's head snap up. Her heart stilled. His gaze found hers unerringly and for one brief moment she registered shock in his gaze, which quickly turned to taunting amusement. She turned and ran, heedless of the noise.

God, she was so stupid! How could she ever have thought him attractive? How *dare* he look at her in that hot, hungry way over the head of another woman! Of *course* he was having sex, the rutting pig. He was a typical man. That's all they ever thought about. That, and filling their stomachs. She'd been right to refuse him last night. It wasn't her he wanted; any willing female body would do.

Holding her hands to her flaming cheeks she raced up the spiral staircase to her room and flung herself down onto the bed. She buried her head under the feather bolster with a groan of mortification then punched the pillows a few times for good measure.

What she was feeling was not in the *slightest bit* jealousy. That Canozzi woman was welcome to him.

ALESSANDRO SWORE SILENTLY. He'd wondered what Vanessa was up to when she'd summoned him to the stables. She *always* had an ulterior motive. "Happy now?" he murmured, grasping her wrists to prevent her from unfastening his breeches any further.

She glanced up from her position at his feet. "What do you mean?" Her blue eyes were all innocence.

"You've made your point. Signorina di Montessori got the message, but there was no need for this little scene, I assure you."

"I don't know what you're talking about. Don't stop me, darling. Let me do this for you. I want to."

The worst of it was, he'd barely been aroused by Vanessa's practiced touch, but now he was rock hard against her hand, and it was nothing to do with her and everything to do with the little vixen who'd just left. It wasn't Vanessa he wanted between his legs; this was exactly how he'd imagined Cara as she'd knelt to swear him fealty. Her hand on his hot flesh, her tantalizing mouth closing around him. His shaft throbbed in response and Vanessa smirked, sensing victory, but he pulled her to her feet and pushed her away.

Vanessa was panting, enjoying the rough handling, and he suddenly lost his patience. He turned her, pressing her against the wall so he couldn't see her face. She laughed quietly and rested her forehead against the wall, expecting him to continue, but he pushed away and stepped back.

"But darling, we haven't finished!" she whined. "Don't tell me you don't want me!"

Alessandro met her gaze. "I told you, I'm not in the mood."

She cast a mocking glance down at the bulging evidence between his legs. "Really? It doesn't look that way."

"It's over, Vanessa. Find someone else. Or better still, go back to your husband." He strode out of the stables without a second look.

Alessandro returned to the hall but a swift glance told him Cara wasn't there. He tensed, alert for one of her tricks, but relaxed when Francesco reported that she'd retreated to her room. Alessandro grimaced. She was probably dying of mortification. Or planning to stab him in his sleep.

She'd done well tonight. He'd been impressed at how well she'd hidden her nerves at appearing in public with him. They'd set tongues wagging, too. Speculation was rife as to the exact nature of their relationship, but no one had the guts to ask him outright.

A little mystery was all to the good. There was no harm in letting the others believe he'd bedded her. For some, it would only make her more interesting. He'd have no difficulty finding her a husband who'd turn a blind eye to the fact that his new bride might not be a virgin on her wedding night.

Alessandro frowned. No, the difficulty would be finding a

man who could handle her. Protect her. Cherish her, as her father had done.

A man worthy of her.

He massaged the back of his neck and sighed. It was going to be a Herculean task.

CHAPTER 21

*C*ara glanced up and down the hallway then knocked on Vanessa Canozzi's door. When it was opened by a sour-faced maid, she placed her foot in the gap to prevent it being closed in her face.

"Who is it?" Vanessa Canozzi's querulous voice came from behind the servant.

"Cara di Montessori." Cara pushed past the maid without waiting to be invited in.

Vanessa was sitting on the bed. The woman was perfectly dressed, not a hair out of place to show what she'd so recently been doing in the stables. Her eyes traveled the length of Cara's body and her lips curled in distain. "What do you want?"

"To leave this place," Cara said, equally blunt.

Vanessa tittered. "I'm not surprised. The whole castle's gossiping about you climbing a tree to escape Alessandro's evil clutches." Hard blue eyes raked Cara from head to toe with a critical gaze that managed to convey total incredulity. "Rumor says he's become fixated with bedding you." Her laugh had a brittle, bitter edge. "It's the novelty, I expect. I doubt he's ever had a virgin, and he probably thinks it will be entertaining. Or perhaps he sees you as a challenge? Men like him can't resist those, whether it's on the battlefield or in the bedroom." She inspected one dainty fingernail. "Either way, he'll tire of you soon enough, once he gets what he wants."

Cara tried not to wince at the older woman's scathing verdict and nodded. "I agree. Which is why I refuse to stay here and play his games. I need you to help me escape."

Vanessa flicked a strand of pale hair over her shoulder. "And why would I do that?"

"So you can have him all to yourself."

The older woman raised her brows and let out a sharp burst of laughter. "Ah. Straight to the point. A woman after my own heart."

Cara shrugged. "You want me gone, and I'm keen to leave. We both want the same thing."

"What do you suggest?"

"I can saddle a horse in the stables, but I need you to create a diversion so I can leave undetected."

Vanessa smirked. "I believe most of the stable boys have been dismissed for the night." Her knowing tone made it clear she'd been aware of Cara's presence there earlier.

Cara tried not to flush. Hateful woman. "I also need to get past the guards at the end of the corridor." She tilted her head at the maid. "If I wear your servant's cloak and pretend to be her, I can follow you out of here. When I have a horse saddled, you can distract the guards at the gatehouse long enough for me to ride out."

Vanessa narrowed her eyes in thought, then nodded. "Very well."

Cara hoisted the bundle containing her pitifully few belongings. She wished she still had her breeches, but the velvet gown she had on was warm enough to spend a night in the open. The maid handed over her hooded cloak, and Cara pulled it up to shield her face.

Vanessa tugged the front of her gown lower to expose more of her cleavage, pinned a bright smile on her face, and opened the door with a breezy laugh. Cara followed, keeping her face down, and as they neared the two guards at the end of the corridor Vanessa 'tripped' on the hem of her gown. Both men instinctively reached forward to assist her.

"Oh, how silly of me!" Vanessa gasped breathlessly, squeezing the nearest soldier's bicep to steady herself while managing to plaster herself onto his chest at the same time. A flush crept up the guard's cheeks. Vanessa rubbed herself against him like an affectionate cat and shot him a look full of indecent promise from under her lashes. "I must be getting back to the party," she breathed. "Come, Julia."

The guards barely glanced at Cara as she fell into place behind her 'mistress.' Their eyes were too busy following Vanessa's swaying derrière, like honey bees drawn to a field full of clover.

Once they were outside Vanesa slipped away with a curt nod. "Make haste."

Cara entered the stables cautiously and made her way to Saraceno's stall. The horse whinnied in pleasure as she stroked his sleek neck. "There now, handsome," she crooned. "Will you let me ride you?"

Del Sarto would be livid if she stole his horse, but he was going to be furious anyway, so what did it matter? Saraceno was the fastest mount for hundreds of miles. He was her best chance of escape.

The beast was enormous; she had to climb onto the metal hayrack in the corner of the stall just to get onto his back. Saraceno shifted as she settled on him but thankfully didn't try to unseat her. Clucking her tongue, she urged him forward. His dark coat blended perfectly into the shadows.

"Stop thief!"

Cara jumped, certain she'd been discovered, but it was Vanessa at the main entrance, clutching her throat and screeching like an enraged fishwife. Cara had to admire her performance. The woman should have been on the stage.

"Guards! Don't just stand there! After him! A man—he stole my pearls and ran off! Quickly—that way!" She pointed in the opposite direction to the stables.

Cara slipped past the gatehouse unchallenged but she hardly dared to breathe until she'd made her way down through the town, passed under the city walls, and reached the safety of the fields beyond. Then she let out a gusty breath of delight.

"Come on then, handsome." Saraceno pricked up his ears. "Let's see if you're as fast as everyone says."

* * *

"What do you mean, 'she's not in her room'?"

Alessandro's tone, practically a whisper, made the trembling page take an inadvertent step backward. Two of the castle hounds whimpered and slinked outside.

"Exactly that, sir. Renata went to check that she was asleep, as you ordered, but she was gone."

Alessandro was already striding down the corridor towards Cara's rooms. The hapless servant scurried after him.

"Are you sure she isn't hiding somewhere? Did anyone see her leave?"

Good God. A short break from campaigning and his men couldn't even manage to contain one unruly female. The whole place was going soft. He needed to bash a few heads together. Still, the little baggage couldn't have got far. She was alone, and on foot. God help her when he caught up with her. "Have Saraceno saddled. I'll go after her myself."

"Want me to come with you?" Francesco asked, catching up with him.

"No, I'll be quicker alone." Alessandro frowned when another page appeared. "What is it now?"

The boy quailed. "Ah, sir? It seems she's . . . taken your horse."

Francesco's lips quirked. "You've got to hand it to her, she's a plucky little devil— "

"One more word and I'll strangle you!" Alessandro took the front steps three at a time.

Francesco struggled to keep his face straight. "Any idea where she might be going? Not back to Castelleon, surely?"

"She's not *that* stupid." Alessandro reached the stables and mounted a ready-saddled bay. He glanced down at his second-in-command. "She'll head for the one place she thinks is safe; the monastery of St. John."

"Take it easy on her, Alessandro. You'd do exactly the same in her place."

Alessandro scowled, mainly because Francesco was right. "That doesn't make me want to strangle her any less."

The thought of Cara, alone and unprotected, made his stomach knot. What if she encountered her murderous bastard of an uncle? Or bandits? He spurred the horse into a gallop. His pounding heart matched the beat of the horse's hooves. If anything happened to her he would never forgive himself.

CHAPTER 22

*I*t had been going so well.

Cara had ridden for hours, enjoying the magnificent animal she'd stolen. She hadn't dared give Saraceno full rein in the darkness in case he was injured, and the leisurely pace had given plenty of time to replay the scene she'd witnessed in the stables. What would it be like to touch a man that way? To have him in her power, at her mercy? She'd always imagined it would be repulsive, but thinking about it in connection with del Sarto was anything but. The thought of it made her flushed and achy.

Dawn was turning the sky salmon pink when she reached the river and eyed the water with distaste. She'd forgotten this particular obstacle, and she'd deliberately avoided roads and bridges. She could swim well, but it was wide and fast running.

She rode upstream until she found a place that looked shallow enough for Saraceno to cross. Even so, the deepest part still looked as though it would come up to his belly, so she started unlacing the ties of her heavy velvet gown. If she ended up in the water, she didn't want to be bogged down by the weight of her skirts. She pulled off her dress and bundled the expensive material into one of the saddlebags. The early morning air was cool against her exposed skin and she shivered in just the thin cotton shift. She hitched her underskirts over her knees and bunched them around her waist so they wouldn't get wet.

A twig snapped and she jumped, then let out a relieved sigh as a bird fluttered low over the water. No reason to be so nervous. There was no one to see her for miles. She urged Saraceno into the shallow water and the stallion moved forward, stepping carefully on the sandy shingle that lined the bottom. The water rose, first to the horse's knees, then to its belly. At the centre of the stream the water lapped the horse's chest.

Cara had just taken her feet out of the stirrups and balanced them up on the saddle to stop them getting wet when she heard the most horrifying sound she'd ever heard in her life.

It was laughter, deep and rich—accompanied by slow, sarcastic applause.

She cursed in every single language she could think of.

A shrill whistle sounded from the undergrowth. Saraceno stopped dead.

Cara turned and of course, it was *him*. Her worst nightmare. Waiting on the bank behind her, as if he had all the time in the world.

Another whistle, and the traitorous horse turned around. No amount of kicking or tugging on the reins could make it turn back. Cara shrieked in frustration.

"Miss me?" Del Sarto called.

"No!"

"I was talking to the horse," he said dryly. "Congratulations on getting so far, though."

Cara ignored him. It wasn't easy; she was facing him, on an uncontrollable mount, in the middle of a freezing cold river. She tried to turn Saraceno's head again, but the stubborn thing stood still as a statue.

Del Sarto laughed. "Don't waste your energy. He's too well trained to ignore my commands."

Too late, Cara recalled the perfectly executed bow the horse had made the day she'd climbed down the tree. *Damn and Blast and Bloody Hellfire.*

"You realize stealing a horse is an offense punishable by death?"

"I was only borrowing him! I'd have sent him straight back, when I'd reached—"

"St. John's? Your uncle will be having it watched."

"I know that! I wasn't going to ride up to the front gates. I know plenty of ways to get in and out without being seen."

"Of course you do. Still, I can't let this crime go unpunished. It's the principle of the thing."

"You don't *have* any principles!"

He held up one hand to silence her. "Can you swim?"

Cara narrowed her eyes at the innocuous question. "Of course. "

He whistled again. Saraceno began to sink down into the water. "Take a deep breath!" he shouted cheerfully.

"Don't you dare—!"

Her shriek of outrage was cut short as the devil horse sat right down in the icy current, fully immersing them both. She gasped in shock. Her hands slipped on the wet leather as Saraceno rolled sideways, neatly dislodging her from his back. Submerged in the frigid water, she made a desperate grab for the pommel, but the fast-flowing current snatched it from her fingers and she went under. She resurfaced, coughing and spluttering, only to hear del Sarto whistle again. Saraceno, the deceitful beast, stood up, splashed past her, mounted the bank and shook himself vigorously.

Del Sarto patted his wet neck and the horse snorted in plea-sure. "Good boy! That will teach the bad lady to steal you away."

Her bare feet found purchase on the rocky bottom as she belatedly realized the water was only up to her chest. She consid-ered pretending that she couldn't swim, just to make him jump in and rescue her, but discarded the idea. Del Sarto wouldn't get himself wet to stop her from drowning. He'd just watch and laugh.

Snarling, she glanced at the opposite bank, weighing her chances. She couldn't get far without a horse, but any plan that annoyed him seemed like a good one.

"Don't even think about it," he called, reading her mind. "You don't want to know what I'll do if you make me come after you. I promise you won't like it."

She gritted her teeth and set out towards him. "I am going to kill you, del Sarto," she said sweetly. "Maybe not today, but soon. And I'm going to enjoy every minute of it. You should watch your back."

He grinned, utterly unrepentant. "Brave words, coming from someone looking like a drowned rat. Have you forgotten your vows to me so soon? I distinctly remember there being something in that oath of allegiance about safeguarding my life and limb. That includes from yourself."

Cara swallowed another mouthful of water.

* * *

"THEY DOWSE WITCHES AROUND HERE, you know," Alessandro said cheerfully. "The innocents always drown. Only the guilty float back to the surface. *You* must be a witch."

As he said the words, he realized how true they were. Cara was an enchantress. She made him crave her company. Made him want her in his life.

The dawn light outlined her body with a glowing halo; the wet cotton of her shift was practically transparent and the cloth clung to her feminine curves. She might as well have been completely naked. Alessandro shifted uncomfortably in the saddle. He couldn't have looked away if the sky had fallen down.

Her long hair dripped over her shoulders, stopping just short of covering her breasts, which were outlined in all their pert glory. They were small, perfectly formed, just right for his hands. The peaks of her nipples pressed against the fabric. His gaze dropped lower, to her narrow waist and flared hips, the dark mysteries barely revealed at the junction of her thighs, and a fantastic length of slim thigh. He took a sharp breath in as she rose from the water like some mythical water nymph surrounded by the silvery haze of morning.

She glared at him. With a look of defiance she pushed her wet hair back over her shoulders then lowered her hands to her sides, facing him like a condemned prisoner going to the gallows. Shoulders back, head held high, she splashed towards the bank.

She was the most wonderful sight he'd ever seen. He should drop to his knees, grasp the hem of her robe, and beg forgiveness from this glittering, heavenly creature. It was all he could do not to jump from his horse, pull her down onto the riverbank and kiss her senseless, everlasting torment be damned.

CARA SCOWLED up at him as she slipped on the muddy riverbank. "You could help!"

"I'm enjoying the view."

She frowned. Del Sarto was looking at her with the oddest expression on his face. The best way she could describe it was . . . awestruck. Reverent, even. It was the same look she'd sometimes noticed on the faces of the monks as they gazed at the statue of the holy virgin, except there was nothing remotely holy about del Sarto.

She looked down—and gasped in horror. *Holy Mother of God!* The man could see *everything*!

She clapped her hands over her breasts and sank back down into the freezing water. The useless shift billowed up around her legs, puffed with air, and she had to use one hand to drag it back down again. "Turn around this minute!" Her cheeks burned in mortification. "Have you no shame? No honor?"

"None." He crossed his arms over his chest. "I can stay here all day, but that water looks pretty bracing. You don't want to catch a chill."

She swore through her chattering teeth. "I'm not coming out unless you give me something to cover myself with. Hand me your cloak."

He shook his head. "I'm not ruining a perfectly good cloak. This is lined with sable."

"Your doublet, then."

Another shake of the head. "Leather. Too heavy when it's wet. You'll never stand up. Now come out and stop being such a prim little virgin. Believe me, yours is not the first naked female body I've ever seen in my life."

Cara was mortified at his casual dismissal. Then anger came to her rescue. Damn him! Let him look. She had nothing to be ashamed of. It was his fault she was wet anyway. She stood up, gathered her hair, wrung it out, and marched right up to him. Since he was still mounted, the top of her head barely came to his knee, but she tilted her head and looked him straight in the eye. "Your cloak."

"Not until you've taken that wet thing off."

"I will *not*. I'll be naked."

"You're nearly there now," he said, with irrefutable logic. "Rest assured, I have no designs on your person at present. I prefer my women warm and dry." He unfastened his cape and handed it down to her. "Put this around you, but take off your shift. You'll catch your death."

The cloak was ankle length black velvet and the inside was lined with the softest fur Cara had ever encountered. It still retained his body heat and she savored the feel of it against her chilled skin as she tried to stop the shivers that racked her body.

He leaned over and rummaged in his saddlebags. "Lucky for

you, I always travel with a change of clothes." He threw something white at her, and she made a grab for it while maintaining her death-grip on the cloak. "It's one of my shirts. Stealing them seems to be quite a habit for you."

She took advantage of his dismounting to struggle out of her wet shift.

"You expected me to try to escape again, didn't you?"

He chuckled. "I'd have been disappointed if you hadn't." He swapped Saraceno's wet saddle with the one from the bay, then tied the bay behind. Cara expected him to order her to take the wet saddle, but he picked her up, threw her up onto Saraceno, and swung himself up behind her.

Cara squirmed and tried to drop back to the ground, but his fingers squeezed her thigh.

"Hold still. Saracen's over eighteen hands. If you fall off you'll probably break an ankle."

CHAPTER 23

They rode all day. When the light began to fade they stopped in a tree-lined clearing but Cara had no idea where they were. She was still trying to decide on the most satisfying form of revenge. It was a tie between having del Sarto's entrails eaten by wolves or having him dragged behind a team of stampeding horses.

Only when he dismounted did she become aware of just how quiet it was in the forest. A few birds could be heard, the faint ripple of the wind in the leaves high above. "Why aren't we back at San Rocco?"

He grasped her waist to help her down and her body slipped down his in a slow, tantalizing slide. The bunched muscles of his arms flexed with the effort of lowering her and her breasts brushed against his chest. Her feet touched the ground. His hands were still at her hips, their bodies touching down the full length, and she allowed herself the briefest of moments to savor the sensation. He smelled wonderful; a combination of leather and earth that made her stomach somersault as if there were butter-flies trapped inside.

She gave him her sweetest smile. He narrowed his eyes. She

K. C. BATEMAN & KATE BATEMAN

tried to make her voice all honey-sweet and cloying, like the serving girls when they talked to him, all fluttery giggles, but it didn't come naturally. "Oh, *thank you*, my lord," she simpered, batting her eyelashes.

He looked like he wanted to smack her backside.

She tried to knee him in the groin.

He was too quick; he dodged and her knee struck his inner thigh. "Temper, temper," he chided, laughing. "That's a vital part of my anatomy."

"Ha! I'd hate to deprive every serving wench and harlot within a fifty-mile radius of your dubious services."

"Don't mock what you haven't tried. In fact, perhaps we should see if you've succeeded in ruining my manhood." He placed his hand suggestively on his belt and she flushed as the meaning of his words sank in.

She gave him a quelling stare and tugged his cloak more securely around her. "You are despicable, underhand, dishonorable—"

"Spare my blushes. I'm sure you've stored up a whole host of names for me, but wait until I've lit a fire and made us some dinner before you get started. Think how much more energy you'll have to curse me once you've had a hot drink."

He turned his attention to the horses. The second his back was turned, she edged toward the cover of the trees.

"I wouldn't, if I were you," he said, without even turning round. "For one thing you won't get far on foot and I'm in no mood to go stumbling about the forest in the dark after you. And for another thing, there are wolves around. You don't want to meet one of them. Or a boar. They're grumpy this time of year. It's rutting season."

Cara had never considered the reproductive cycles of boars or wolves, but the forest suddenly looked a lot less appealing. And a hot drink *did* sound inviting. With a huff she withdrew the wet bundle of her belongings from Saraceno's saddlebag. Her velvet

136

dress, which had been on the outside of the bundle, was soaked through. She draped it over a bush to dry. Her boots were only a little damp, however, so she put them on, along with a linen underskirt, and felt marginally better protected.

Del Sarto caught her sliding her dagger into her boot and chuckled. "Still armed to the teeth? You are a violent little thing. What are you going to do with that? Prick me full of holes like a sieve and wait for me to bleed to death?"

Her knife was a paltry weapon against someone like him, true, but it was comforting to know it was within reach. "I can defend myself if necessary," she sniffed.

"I don't doubt it. Your father once told me how you crippled some unfortunate bugger who dared to kiss you."

Her cheeks flamed. Father had clearly regaled him with all her most embarrassing exploits.

He removed a wineskin, a small pan, and a tin cup from the saddlebag. "Make yourself useful and gather some dry wood, there's a good girl."

Cara bristled at his assumption that she'd obey his orders without question, but she was cold and hungry and desperate for a drink so she complied. Muttering as she snatched up fallen branches, she stifled a yelp as a thorn stabbed her finger. She sucked the pinprick of blood and glanced up to see if he'd noticed her ineptitude.

He was watching her with a faint smile curving his lips and she flushed, discomfited by his gaze.

"Amazing the aggravation such a tiny thing can cause, isn't it?" His cynical inflection left her in no doubt he was referring to more than just the thorn.

Within minutes he'd lit a fire and had the pan suspended on a stick above the flames, warming some wine. Cara stood with her arms wrapped around her body, just beyond the glow of the fire-light, watching him as he worked. He moved with such economy of movement, a grace born of familiarity with this routine. How many hundreds of times had he performed the same basic rituals?

He unearthed a dead rabbit from his saddlebag and skinned it with astonishing dexterity. Soon it was roasting over the embers, sending delicious aromas into the night sky. Her mouth watered in anticipation. Accepting defeat—temporarily—she unclasped her hands from her elbows and deigned to drag a log to within sitting distance of the fire. No reason he should get all the warmth, the beast.

* * *

ALESSANDRO RAISED his eyes from the rabbit and caught Cara studying him across the fire. She averted her gaze, staring down at her hands, away at the trees, anywhere but his face. He poured some wine, took a sip, then offered it to her, reaching over the fire. The little vixen made a point of wiping the beaker with her sleeve and turning it around so that she wouldn't have to touch the same spot his lips had contaminated. She wrinkled her nose at the taste, but took a healthy swallow.

He smiled at her antics. She was like a fairy princess in a royal sulk, infuriated with her lowly subjects because they weren't doing as they were ordered.

The fire showed her features clearly and his chest contracted as he studied the curve of her face. She had a smooth forehead, slanting cheekbones, rounded chin. Her nose was small and straight, with the slightest tilt upward at the end, just begging to be kissed.

He reminded himself to breathe out. *Slowly.*

It was too dark to see the extraordinary color of her eyes, but that didn't matter. He knew their shade from his dreams; an indefinable grey-green-blue. They were currently glaring at him as though she were laying a curse on him. The little witch was probably muttering incantations under her breath. Little did she know, it was already too late. He'd been under her spell for years.

Her dark hair was disheveled, with little wisps escaping from the braid she'd tied for night-time practicality. He loved her hair. It was always messy, despite her constant attempts to tame it. She looked delightfully tousled, as if she'd just been for a roll in the hay. It undermined that stern-as-a-nun expression she was trying to maintain. He could just imagine new and exciting ways to ruffle it even further.

She licked at a drop of wine with her tongue and he saw a flash of fear in her eyes as she caught the hunger in his gaze. She tried to hide it behind a haughty stare, but he'd seen it, all the same.

Good God, surely she wasn't *really* frightened of him? The last thing he'd ever do was hurt her. He'd kill any man who tried. Hadn't he shown last night that he would never force her to do anything? Did she honestly think he was going to take her, like an animal, here on the forest floor? Judging by the way her hand hovered close to that pitifully small knife, she really did.

He could have the weapon before she noticed it was missing, of course, but he loved the fact that she carried it, naïvely certain of her effectiveness. She reminded him of a cornered kitten, hissing and scratching with her tiny needle claws. He'd ruffle her hair, except she'd probably try to slice his arm off if he tried.

Alessandro stifled a brief spurt of self-directed humor. Signorina di Montessori's opinion of him could only go in one direction—upwards. He'd become so accustomed to the women at court propositioning him that it made a nice change to be so studiously ignored. Maybe that was part of her attraction.

"Oh, come on, don't look at me like that," he coaxed.

"Like what?"

"Like I'm going to eat you alive. You're safe from my nefarious clutches tonight."

"You mean you're releasing me from our stupid bargain?"

The eagerness in her voice made him smile. "Not a chance, my love. Our bargain stands. But I wouldn't complete it *here*, even if you were begging me."

"Your kindness and nobility astound me."

He grinned at her withering sarcasm. "Nothing to do with kindness. As delightful as a roll in the pine needles would be, I think we should hold out for a nice comfortable bed."

Her flush was charming. She took another long gulp of the drink and breathed in at the same time, which started an unladylike fit of spluttering. He shot her a knowing glance and carried on eating. "Sit down. The rabbit's ready."

He ripped the carcass apart and handed her a portion.

She sunk her small even teeth into the meat, closed her eyes, and heaved a blissful sigh. "Ohhh. That tastes heavenly!"

Alessandro barely suppressed a moan of his own. *Heavenly was the word.* She had no idea how provocative he found her. *Thank God.* He adjusted the uncomfortable bulge in the front of his breeches, grateful for the concealing darkness.

They settled into a companionable silence for a few minutes, but as soon as the meal was finished the wariness reappeared in her eyes. He rose and cleared away the food, packing everything away in the saddlebags. So many years as a soldier had ingrained in him the need to be ready to leave at the slightest notice. He checked Saraceno's tether, then padded back to the fire, kicking the embers back to life with his boot.

She was pale, with shadows under her eyes. The poor little thing was tired out. In fact, he'd wager the only thing still keeping her upright was stubborn determination. She reminded him of his new recruits after their first taste of battle, numb with exhaustion but desperately trying to appear unaffected.

A wave of tenderness washed over him. He wanted to gather her in his arms and hold her as she slept. "Time to sleep. Relax, I won't touch you tonight, on my honor."

"Is that supposed to reassure me? You don't *have* any honor, del Sarto."

"Fine. On my life, then. How's that?"

"It'll do," she sniffed. "Not that it's worth much, either. Now if you don't mind, I'd like a few moments of privacy."

She picked up the small bundle of her belongings and Alessandro frowned, realizing he'd have to let her out of his sight.

"Go ahead. There's a small stream just over there, behind those trees. Enough to wash in. Just don't forget the boars," he called after her. "And the wolves. Great big, hungry, fearsome wolves."

* * *

CARA BREATHED a sigh of relief as she ducked behind a tree, glad to be out from under his penetrating gaze. She was fairly certain the only thing remotely wolf-like in the vicinity was *him*.

Pale moonbeams barely penetrated the canopy of leaves above her head and ominous rustling sounds took on new significance. Terrified that he would come looking for her if she took too long, she washed her hands in the trickle of water then unrolled the bundle of things she'd brought from San Rocco. The small glass vial containing the sleeping draught she'd made fell into her hand. If she could find a way to slip it into the wine she might still escape him yet.

She returned to the clearing. He'd unrolled a blanket next to the fire and sprawled at his ease, propped on one elbow, using the saddle as a pillow. He looked like a Roman senator after an orgy, the very image of relaxed animal power.

"Only one blanket, I'm afraid." He crooked a finger at her, beckoning her forward. "We'll have to use my cloak to cover us."

"How cozy."

"And here I was, thinking you'd admire my chivalry in offering to share."

"If you were truly chivalrous you'd give it to me and sleep without it."

He slanted her an enigmatic smile. "Give me your wrist."

"Why?"

He picked up a thin skein of rope from his side. "So I can tie it to mine."

She rolled her eyes. "I swear I won't try to escape."

"Forgive me if I doubt you," he said. "I'm cautious, if not chivalric. It's what's kept me alive all these years." His unwavering gaze assured her that obedience was the only option.

Cara shrugged. She had her dagger in her boot—she could cut the rope if she wanted—but she was too tired to try to escape tonight. She would drug his wine in the morning. "Go ahead." She offered one wrist like a queen awarding a knighthood to a courtier.

His thumb stroked the sensitive skin of her inner wrist as he tied some complicated-looking knot, then he stretched out his arm and tied the other end around his own wrist. His deft fingers looped and twisted the rope around his tawny skin and when he pulled it tight with his teeth she felt a corresponding tug somewhere in the region of her stomach.

"There. Long enough for you to turn over and sleep. But I'll know the minute you try to escape. Remember that."

She folded herself down next to him on the blanket, noticing that he'd placed her on the side closest to the fire. He might deny all claim to chivalry, but the small gesture belied those claims. She stretched out on her side with her back to him, careful not to make contact, and tugged the cloak around her. The rope trailed loosely over her shoulder. He settled behind her, not touching, but she could feel the warmth radiating from his body. It was surprisingly comforting.

She believed his promise not to touch her. Scoundrel he might be, but if he said he wouldn't do so until she came to him willingly—then he wouldn't. Besides, she must look entirely unappealing. Even when she *wasn't* dirty and unkempt, she was hardly the sort to inspire uncontrollable lust in a man. She was too much the hellion, too unfeminine. He was used to taking his pick of the beautiful women of the Italian courts. He was probably as attracted to her as to a case of the plague.

Suspended halfway between wakefulness and sleep, Cara closed her eyes and allowed herself a smile. Of all the positions she'd imagined she'd be in when she'd risen yesterday morning, lying on the forest floor with her nemesis less than a few feet away, physically *tied* to her, for heaven's sake, was not one she'd imagined in her wildest dreams.

Well, perhaps in her very *wildest* dreams . . .

* * *

ALESSANDRO LISTENED PATIENTLY until Cara's breathing evened out and when he was sure she slept, he raised himself onto one elbow to watch her.

It was torture. No other word for it. Pleasure and pain all in one. He pondered the irony of having the woman of his dreams less than a foot away and being utterly unable to touch her. It was worse than being ten thousand miles away.

He permitted himself the slightest brush of one fingertip against her cheek. They could have been back at San Rocco by now if he'd taken a less circuitous route. But he'd been enjoying his time with her, and he hadn't wanted to share her with his guests. Soon he would force himself to hand her over to some dull, worthy burgher, someone who could love her as she deserved. But just for a few more nights, she was his. And he would savor whatever time they had left together.

He reached over and pulled the end of the blanket over her body. It was going to be another bloody uncomfortable night. Staring up at the stars, he began naming constellations.

CHAPTER 24

A low, inhuman moan and a tug on the rope roused Cara. Her heart hammering in alarm, she rolled over and encountered del Sarto's huge, shadowed back. His shoulder twitched. Then he flung out an arm with a yell as though trying to brush off an invisible insect. His movement made her own wrist jerk awkwardly in response.

She sat up. "Del Sarto?"

"From the flank! Now!" he murmured, rolling over onto his back, almost squashing her.

His features were lit by the dull embers of the fire. His beautiful face was fierce. A muscle ticked in his jaw, as though his teeth were ground together, and his eyes were squeezed tightly shut. She shuffled her body closer, watching as his right hand made a fist.

His head thrashed as if he had a fever. "No! You're not going to bloody die. Come back!" he snarled.

Silence.

Her hand hovered close to his taut shoulder; his muscles strained against the fabric of his shirt. Then his eyes snapped open, staring and wild and he sat bolt upright. "Hold! Hold the line!" He ducked a blow from an unseen enemy.

Cara touched him gently on the bicep. "Wake up! You're dreaming."

He threw his full weight upon her, slamming her onto the ground so hard that every ounce of breath was forced from her lungs. He straddled her thighs, trapping her legs between his. The moonlight outlined his powerful shoulders and sleep-mussed hair. His eyes were wide, their dark glitter unfocused. He snarled something incoherent and closed his battle-roughened hand around her throat.

Cara struggled for breath. "Stop!"

His black, merciless stare held no glimmer of recognition. His face grew dim. At the periphery of her vision, little lights began flashing black and white, dancing and circling like snowflakes. Cara fastened her hands around his wrists and dug her fingernails into the corded tendons, desperate to break his grip on her throat. When that failed, she hit blindly at his head and ribs, raining blows wherever she could reach. It had no effect whatsoever.

Then she remembered her dagger. She scrabbled for her boot, found the handle, and with a strength born of desperation, slashed the point towards his arm.

* * *

COLD STEEL CUTTING his flesh cleared Alessandro's vision. He deflected the blade in a reflex action that sent it skittering into the undergrowth and as the red mist dissolved he came to the horrifying realization of where he was. Cara—not some imaginary foe—was crushed beneath him. He was on top of her, his thighs straddling her hips. And one of his huge, murderous hands was around her throat.

"Christ Almighty!" Bile rose in his throat and he let her go abruptly, sickened by the red marks his fingers had made on her pale skin.

She lay where she was, gasping for air like a landed fish, and he pushed a shaking hand through his hair and risked a glance down at her. The moonlight showed her face all too clearly. Her magnificent eyes were huge in her pale face, staring up at him in fear and astonishment. He felt as though he'd been kicked in the gut.

How had he lost control so completely? He'd been within a hair's breadth of choking the life out of her. *Oh God, he'd hurt her.*

What the hell was happening to him?

He'd been dreaming of a battlefield, naturally. Bodies piled high, rivers full of corpses. And so much blood that it soaked him; on his hands, on his body, his face. He'd been wading through it, thigh-high, sticky, every movement an effort, like walking through treacle. His enemies had been all around, cutting him off from his men. He had to kill, survive, lead them out of danger—

It frightened *him*, the savagery of his response, that blinding-hot flash of violence. God, she must think him deranged. It wasn't far from the truth, but still, to have it revealed so openly, to have his charred and broken soul laid bare in front of her was the utmost humiliation.

He rolled off her in one swift move, onto his back, suppressing a groan of despair as he covered his eyes with his forearm. He should apologize, explain, but he had no idea where to begin. Why the *hell* had he allowed her to sleep so close to him? He knew better than that.

"What's wrong with you?" she croaked.

Alessandro wiped the trickle of blood from his arm. She'd made a shallow gash with her dagger, nothing more. "It'll take more than that to finish me off."

"Well, I'm sorry," she said. "But it was your own fault. I was only defending myself." She sat up and brushed the leaves from her hair. "Are you all right?"

Her concern for him—the very man who'd almost strangled her—made him want to kill himself.

"How long have these nightmares plagued you?"

"I don't want to talk about it," he growled.

"What were you dreaming of? Tell me. Maybe I can help."

"I told you, I don't want to talk about it."

This was *exactly* the reason he'd always made his squire sleep outside his tent rather than share with him, as was usual. Marco had thought it singular, as had his men, but at least they'd never uncovered the humiliating truth; that their fearless, untouchable leader regularly woke to find himself shaking and bathed in sweat, as confused and terrified as a stray dog in a thunderstorm.

He'd managed to keep the galling truth from them for years. Even Francesco had no idea how bad it was. And yet in Cara's company he'd managed to expose himself completely. What was it about this woman? Just being near her was enough to set his defenses crumbling.

He wasn't fit to be near her.

He was a trained killer. He could have snapped her neck with his bare hands just now. Grown men cowered from him. But she, tiny slip of a girl, looked up at him with little more than surprise and confusion. And pity.

The pity made his anger mount. He met her gaze and held it menacingly, watching as wariness crept into her expression. *Good.* She *should* be afraid. If she had one iota of self-preservation she'd run screaming into the forest. She needed to be taught to stay away from him.

In a lightning move, he rolled back on top of her and pinned her wrists, pushing them flat against the blanket over her head, holding them easily in one of his hands. She gasped in alarm. The bones of her wrists were so fragile beneath his fingers, and the ease with which he could hurt her only increased his fury. "What the hell were you thinking?" he snarled. "I could have killed you!"

Her eyes flashed. "What else should I have done?"

"Left me alone."

"I was trying to help!"

He gave her his best sneer. "This isn't something you can doctor with your herbs and potions. Or were you going to offer a distraction?"

Color flooded her face as she caught his meaning.

"It's not a bad idea," he continued silkily. "Maybe the best way for me to sleep easy at night is to go to bed so exhausted I don't have the energy to dream. A good fuck might do the trick."

Her eyes widened. "Don't speak to me like that!"

"I'll speak to you any way I please, m*y lady.*"

He was acutely aware of his position. The ridges of his stomach pressed against her belly and his hard, aching groin was pressed between her thighs. Only a few layers of cloth separated them. His cock throbbed painfully and he ground his teeth. *Christ alive, he wanted her.*

"Let me up!"

"Oh, I don't think so." He gave her the smile he used to strike the fear of God into new recruits. It was equally effective on her. She paled and swallowed. "You've never had to deal with a real man before, have you sweeting?"

"Of course I have. I deal with men every day of my life."

"Monks!" he sneered. "And servants. They don't count. They left you alone because they respected your father, or because they feared him. They treated you like a Madonna, remote and untouchable." She froze as he caressed her cheek. "*I* dare touch you. Now. Here. Whenever I like. Out here in the real world, courtly manners mean nothing. It all boils down to simple, savage things like which of us is stronger. Brawn wins again, Cara. I'm stronger than you. That makes you mine. To do with as I please."

CHAPTER 25

Cara scowled up at him, her heart thudding painfully against her ribs. "All right. You've made your point. The next time you have a bad dream I'll leave you to suffer. Now get off." She bucked her hips and tried to roll over, but he didn't move an inch. She was crushed by his weight, suffocated by his hot, hungry stare. She could only get up if he chose to let her go. And he did not choose.

"I could take you now," he growled. "You know my reputation. I plunder without mercy and give no quarter to the vanquished. What's one more violated innocent to me?"

She held his gaze. "You won't force me." For all his threats and bluster, she was sure of that. He was only lashing out because he was embarrassed at having shown any sort of vulnerability. Typical man. "Where would the challenge be in that?"

His brows drew together, as if he were trying to come up with a counter-argument, and then all the tension left his frame. He sighed and released her wrists. "You're right."

He sounded disgusted with himself. He shifted his weight, about to roll off her, and she was seized with the need to banish that bleak, defeated look from his eyes. Before she could think better of it, she caught his shirtfront, tugged him down, and pressed her lips to his.

* * *

FOR A BRIEF, stunned moment Alessandro's mind went blank. And then Cara opened her mouth, inviting him in, and he was lost. With a groan of defeat he slid his tongue against hers.

He'd meant to frighten her away, to scare her into never coming near him again. God, this was madness. Any minute she would come to her senses. She'd probably try to stab him again.

He wouldn't give her time to think.

He kissed her again and again, long, drugging kisses that barely gave her enough time to breathe, let alone reason, lost in a desperate, driving rhythm that made his blood thicken and sing.

He pressed his mouth to her cheeks, her closed eyelids, feathered kisses over her poor bruised throat in silent apology. He made a sound, somewhere between a sob and a groan, at the damage he'd done, but she just tilted her head back to grant him better access.

Her simple trust decimated him. He raked a shaking hand down her body, from shoulder to the curve of her waist, then back up. She still wore his shirt. He traced the tie opening, pushed aside the fabric and cupped her breast. It fitted into his palm; a perfect handful. Like the cakes he'd watched her eat.

She gasped and slid her fingers through his hair.

He ducked his head, fastened his lips over the peak and sucked, using his tongue to flick and tease, and her hands tightened on his scalp. He breathed in her scent as though he were a man drowning. *God, her skin.* His senses reeled. He was dizzy with desire. He applied himself to the other breast, lavishing it with the same attention, and watched in satisfaction as her nipple beaded in the cold night air. *Madness. Heaven. Sin.*

When his fingers found the soft, bare skin of her knee he

nearly groaned aloud. And then his hand was on the back of her thigh, then higher still, on the warm curve of bare buttock. No undergarments barred his way. Her skin was soft, *so soft*, like a sun-warmed peach.

His clouded brain clamored for him to unlace his breeches and lose himself inside her, to take and take and take until they were both spent and thoroughly exhausted. To forget himself in the pounding, glorious, mindless rhythm of sex. *Do it! Claim her! Now.*

* * *

DEL SARTO'S hand on her bare bottom jolted Cara back to reality. How had things got so out of control? She'd only meant to comfort him. Good Lord, his mouth had been on her breasts! He was halfway to *taking* her, here, on the forest floor!

Shocked to the core, she used both hands to push him away. "Stop!"

Mercifully, he did as she commanded. He raised his head, stared at her for a breathless moment, then with a harsh exhalation he rolled off her and onto his back and gazed sullenly at the sky. She tugged the edges of the shirt together, covering her still-tender breasts. After a few agonizing moments he turned his head and watched as she shuffled backwards in the leaves and rearranged her clothing.

"Go to sleep," he grated harshly.

Cara turned her back on him and squeezed her eyes closed, willing her heart to slow its frantic pace.

* * *

WHEN HE WAS certain she slept, Alessandro let out a long, shuddering breath. Thank God she'd pulled away. He'd been seconds away from losing his mind.

K. C. BATEMAN & KATE BATEMAN

She alone made him lose control, challenged him at every turn. And that made her dangerous—to his sanity, his pride. His heart. No matter that she filled the empty spaces inside him, that she made him forget his nightmares in the sheer joy of sparring with her. There was no room in his life for a girl who was nothing but trouble.

This little interlude hadn't changed anything. If anything, it had shown how important it was to get her married off as quickly as possible. He'd send her away, somewhere safe, with someone good.

"I'm sorry I frightened you," he whispered at the stars.

His tortured confession was met with a tiny, ladylike snore.

CHAPTER 26

The sun was breaking through the early morning mist when Cara surfaced from a dream in which she'd been Ariadne, tied by a silken string to the Minotaur, waiting for heroic Theseus to save her. Only, somewhere in the dream the two had become confused until she didn't know which was which, hero or monster. Her bleary gaze followed the rope along the ground to where it ended in . . . nothing.

Startled, she sat up and looked around. There was no sign of del Sarto, but a rustling in the distance indicated he'd gone to the stream to wash.

Now was her chance! She scrambled over to her bundle of clothes and unearthed the bottle of sleeping draught. With a quick glance over her shoulder, she took the wineskin from the saddlebag, uncorked it, poured a cup of untainted wine for herself, then tipped the sleeping draught into the wineskin. She swirled the wine to mix it up, and replaced the cork.

By the time she heard del Sarto returning, she was on her hands and knees, searching for her dagger. It was somewhere in the shrubbery, where he'd thrown it last night.

He reappeared, pulling his shirt over his head and she caught a brief, tantalizing glimpse of tawny, sculpted torso, all intriguing ripples and shadowy planes, before it was hidden by opaque white linen. Her stomach clenched at the way it had felt against her own.

He gave an exaggerated yawn and stretched his arms over his head. "Now there's a sight to behold! The high-and-mighty Signorina di Montessori on her knees before me. Finally recognizing me as your new lord and master?"

She gave him a hard stare. "Never. Enjoy this moment. It's the last time you will ever get this view." She located her blade and tucked it securely back into her boot. "If you think I'm going to bow and scrape and call you 'your highness,' you can think again."

She watched him from the corner of her eye as he shrugged into his leather hauberk. He hadn't shaved, and his cheeks and chin were covered in dark stubble. It only made him more attractive. The man had no right to look so good at this ungodly hour of the morning.

Her velvet gown was still damp. Excusing herself, she pushed through the bushes to the stream and shivered as she donned the thick cloth. Heat rose in her cheeks as she recalled him kissing her breasts. She shook her head. She would pretend that both his nightmare—and what had followed—had never happened.

He'd kicked the fire into life when she retuned to the clearing. He threw her a stale chunk of bread, and she picked up the cup of undoctored wine from where she'd balanced it on a rock, took a deep draught, and watched in satisfaction as he lifted the wineskin to his lips. His Adam's apple bobbed as he swallowed.

Depending on how strong she'd made the sleeping draught he'd be asleep—or too drowsy to stop her escape—in a matter of minutes.

He tilted his chin at her. "Drink up. We have to get back to San Rocco. More guests will be arriving today."

Cara downed the rest of her wine, savoring the burn in her belly, if not the bitter taste. He replaced the empty cup in the saddlebag, mounted Saraceno in one fluid movement, and offered her his gloved hand.

She ignored it; she might need to catch him if he started to slip from the saddle. She wouldn't be able to support his full weight, of course, but she could break his fall and prevent him from hurting himself too badly. A beast he might be, but she didn't want him cracking his skull open on a rock.

"I'd rather walk." She stalked off into the woods.

"The castle's that way."

He pointed in the opposite direction and she quelled the strong desire to scratch his eyes out. With as much dignity as she could muster, she turned around and began walking again.

His voice, annoyingly smug, sounded behind her. "It's still several miles to San Rocco. Ride with me."

"No thank you."

She could practically *hear* him shrug. Reaching into her bodice, she withdrew the locket she always wore; the small circular case of brassy metal suspended on a thin chain.

"What *is* that? A lock of your beloved's hair?"

"Nothing so romantic." Cara stared at the mechanism in her hands. The hinged lid opened to reveal a thin needle floating on a bronze disk. "It's a compass, a present from Father." She smiled in bittersweet memory. "He used to call *me* his compass. The thing that kept him turning towards home. The point by which he set his course."

"New-fangled wizardry."

"You've never used one?"

"Never needed one. Any idiot can tell which way is north." He pointed a gloved finger.

She glanced down to check. He was right, damn his eyes.

He nodded at the rising sun. "That's *east*," he spoke slowly, as if schooling a simple child. "And where it sets, in the evening . . . that way is *west*."

"What about when it's dark?"

"You have the stars."

"What if it's cloudy?"

"Well, then I'd give up and cry like a baby. By the Saints, woman! I've never met anyone as argumentative as you!"

Delighted to have riled him, she marched on, then bit back a curse when she stumbled over a rock. Hooves thudded behind her. Without warning, he scooped her up in front of him as though she weighed no more than a sack of grain and deposited her sideways on his lap.

"Don't argue!" he growled.

His voice was rough by her temple, and her stomach contracted as his iron-hard forearm clamped around her waist, just under her breasts. She grasped Saraceno's mane and pulled away from him.

"Hold still!" He tugged her back against his chest. "I can't ride with you leaning forward. Sit back and don't struggle."

To her silent mortification, struggling was the last thing on Cara's mind. Everywhere he touched tingled with awareness. She shook her head. She'd developed a fever, that would explain it. She'd caught a chill in the river and was becoming delirious.

Her hair was blowing in his face. He smoothed it back with his gloved hand and she bit the inside of her lip and fought the urge to turn her cheek into his palm. She was an idiot.

After a while it began to drizzle and he pulled his cloak over them both, cocooning her in darkness and warmth. Cara slipped her arms around his waist and tucked her head beneath his chin. Del Sarto made her feel safe, just as her father had done.

Her eyes misted with unexpected tears. She missed her father. It had been easy to pretend that he was still away on campaign, that he might ride over the horizon at any moment and come galloping towards her, his arms outstretched in welcome. But he was never coming back. She'd never see his patient, exasperated smile again. Never have him hold her close like this again. She was a twenty-two year old orphan.

Cara kept her eyes closed. The rain had stopped, but she felt drowsy and oddly content. A strange lassitude had taken hold of her limbs. She pressed her cheek against del Sarto's chest and breathed him in.

This was wrong. She shouldn't be snuggling up to him like some pathetic stray, desperate for a shred of affection. But it was hard to find her pride when he smelled so wonderful. She yawned.

He lowered his chin to look at her. "Sleepy?"

"A little. Are you?" Surely enough time had passed for him to be feeling the effects of the sleeping draught? He was a large man, true, but—Cara groaned as the true reason for her tiredness became clear. "You monster! You swapped the wine, didn't you?"

His chuckle reverberated against her ear. "I certainly did."

ALESSANDRO BRACED himself for Cara's righteous fury, but after a few seconds of silence, she simply sighed. He raised his brows in astonishment. "What? You're not going to stab me?"

She wriggled in his lap to get more comfortable. "As if that would do any good. You're unkillable." Her eyelids were drooping as she fought the somnolent effects of the drug. "It serves me right, I suppose," she murmured. "I meant to do the same to you."

Alessandro smiled at her innate sense of fair play—something he completely lacked.

"How did you know?" she asked.

"I'm used to people trying to poison me. It's second nature to sniff my wine before I drink it. The stuff in the wineskin smelled odd. When I realized the wine in the cup smelled fine, I knew you were up to something. So I threw away the wine in the cup and refilled it from the wineskin. And I only pretended to drink."

"You watched me drink a whole cup! What if I *had* been trying to poison you!"

He chuckled at her righteous indignation. "I recognized the scent of mandrake—like red apples. And while I've never heard of anyone being poisoned with a concoction of mandrake, I have seen it used to make injured men sleep. I know you're devious enough to give me something like that."

"You can't blame me for trying." She shrugged against his chest. "You know, I've never actually tried it myself. It's a strange sensation."

"Afraid you'll spill your deepest, darkest secrets?" he teased.

She gave an unladylike snort. "Hardly! I don't have any."

"Oh, I'm sure *that's* not true. Everyone has secrets. Things you dream about in the dark of night. Like *me*," he added wickedly. "Surely you've dreamed of me, Cara?"

"The only dreams I've had of *you* are of murdering you," she said sweetly. "They're lovely dreams."

And yet her actions belied her words. She snuggled closer, like a kitten curling up in front of the fire.

Alessandro scowled, cursing the fact that he wasn't immune to her closeness. He hadn't let her ride her own mount because in her drugged state she would have fallen off. And because he'd take any excuse to be near her. His body responded to hers as if they were old friends. Having her draped all over him, molded to him—as if she'd suddenly lost any sense of where her body left off and his began—was a side-effect he hadn't anticipated.

He stared straight ahead and began to recall every minor skirmish he'd ever fought, every wound he'd ever received, analyzing the tactics he'd used. It failed to take his mind off the fact that Cara was pressed painfully close to him. Every time she breathed out he could feel the exhalation against his neck. It was agony. And always a glutton for punishment, he was enjoying the slow torture, in a perverse sort of way. Her fingers toyed absently with his collar and he ground his teeth against the exquisite torment until his jaw ached.

She raised her hand and stroked his cheek, petting him as if he were Saraceno. "This muscle tenses, here on the side, when you do that, you know. You should try to relax. *I'm* relaxed."

"Yes, I can see that," he drawled, but his fine sarcastic tone was completely lost on her. Her fingers trailed down his jaw and he froze, unwilling to stop her, silently praying she'd continue her torturous exploration.

He was pathetic! He craved her touch like a man in a desert confronted by a lagoon full of water.

She traced his lips, frowning at him in intense scrutiny. "When you smile the corner of your lips curl up, just here." She touched the place she described, then slid her finger over his lower lip. It was all he could do not to take it inside his mouth and suck. *Christ.*

"You went to the Holy Land with my father didn't you?"

Alessandro blinked at the sudden change of topic, then gave a wry half-smile. *Her* mind was obviously on other things.

"I was always so jealous of the years you spent with him," she admitted quietly. "What was it like?"

He frowned. "Damascus? Hot. And full of people trying to kill me."

"You're very good at rousing murderous instincts in people."

"I'm a mercenary. People are *supposed* to want to kill me. It's my job."

"What about Spain? I know you've been to Granada. Did you see the Moorish palace there?"

"I fought in its shadow for three weeks."

"I've heard it's beautiful."

The last time he'd seen the place the dusty plain had been

strewn with bodies. Most of the dead had been Spaniards, fighting for King Ferdinand and his wife Isabella, who'd been fierce in their determination to drive the Moors back to North Africa. They'd paid well for his military expertise.

Appalling images seared his mind. A cluster of dead Moors heaped together like discarded toys as crows picked over the unburied bodies. They'd fought bravely, defending their beliefs against insurmountable odds. He'd admired their passion, envied it, even, but emotion made a man weak. His detachment was the reason he was still alive—an improbable feat after eighteen years of constant warfare.

He hadn't emerged completely unscathed, however. His nightmares were the proof. They were frequent, vivid. As if his mind had seen so many different visions of hell that it was filled to overflowing. He was so tired of seeing good men die. Tired of fighting other men's wars.

He shook his head to dispel his brooding thoughts and brought his awareness back to the far more pleasant sensation of the woman in his lap.

"The palace is at the top of a high ridge, with a view over the land around it," he said. "If you look out over the plains, the mountains beyond it shimmer in the heat. It can only be reached by a steep hill and the entrance is a huge stone gate with a Moorish arch. It's deliberately dark inside, so enemies are blind for a few seconds, after the dazzling sun. It's cooler too—enough to raise the hairs on your arms—and the walls are covered with tiles, too many to count, in dizzying patterns, blue and white. The ceilings look like honeycombs."

"It sounds wonderful," Cara sighed. "And the gardens?"

"Smell of pine resin. You can hear running water, but it's always hidden by a wall or by a hedge, just out of reach. It's harsh, but beautiful." Alessandro halted, embarrassed.

"Thank you for describing it to me." She smoothed her fingers over the crease between his brows. "You shouldn't frown, you know. You'll get a headache. Maybe I could give you a massage? I used to give them to my father. I'm very good with my hands."

He rolled his eyes at her innocent double-entendre. "I can imagine."

He tried to banish the splendid, sinful images her words produced and failed miserably. Those small, pale hands on his chest, his thighs. His cock. *Oh, Hell.* Saraceno gave a snort of indignant protest as he spurred him on with unnecessary force. Mercifully, the sudden jolt dislodged her fingers.

She was burbling on about something else now. Alessandro listened to her talk, barely absorbing the words, just letting the sounds trickle into his ears. The soft cadences pattered around him like drops of rain, restful and calming. She had a lovely voice —when she wasn't berating him—low and slightly husky. Her passion for her subject, her interest in the driest and most mundane of topics, rendered them fascinating. He could listen to her for hours.

Her father had been right. She was like a lodestone, or the pole star. Only instead of pointing to north, she pointed to truth. She was bright and sweet and glowing. And for someone like him, who'd spent his entire life in darkness and intrigue, listening to her was as refreshing as the first sip of water to a parched throat after years in the wilderness. He craved her youthful optimism to purify his soul and wash the bloodstains from his hands.

When she finally fell asleep Alessandro took a relieved breath and shifted uncomfortably on the saddle. All that soft skin, just inches away. He adjusted his throbbing, insistent erection, which seemed to be his permanent state around this aggravating woman. No chance his cock would drop off from insufficient blood flow, was there?

She hadn't said anything about his rock-hard state, despite practically sitting on top of it for an hour, and he quelled a surge of righteous indignation. How could any female be so ignorantly naïve at her age? Still, it was probably a blessing. If she ever discovered the devastating power she had over him he'd be in serious trouble.

She wriggled her backside in her sleep and he prayed for patience. The Almighty had obviously decided not to wait until he was dead to consign him to the torments of hell. He'd sent him Cara di Montessori, to murder him by degrees.

CHAPTER 27

Cara opened her eyes and frowned at the dark red bed hangings that swirled above her. She was back in her bedroom at San Rocco. She groaned and struggled to sit up but only managed to raise herself onto her elbows. Her body felt like lead; even holding her head up seemed too difficult so she let it fall back onto the coverlet just as del Sarto appeared in the doorway between their two rooms.

He'd removed his shirt. His hips were still slung with his belt and daggers and the hard lines of his long legs were clearly delineated beneath his black leather breeches. She smiled at his bare chest in sleepy appreciation. The man really was beautiful to look at.

He moved to the end of the bed and stood looking down at her, his expression unreadable. He'd clearly made use of the wash basin. A drop of water trickled down the angle of his collarbone then raced lower, over the ridges of his stomach, past his navel, and into the intriguing line of dark hair that disappeared beneath his waistband.

Her mouth went dry.

"Looked your fill, my lady?" he asked dryly.

Cara tried to think of something—anything—to say, but her brain was dull and sluggish. "I can see why all the women fawn over you."

Good Lord! Had she really said that out loud? From the stunned expression on his face, she must have done. And yet she couldn't quite bring herself to care. Clearly the effects of the drug had yet to wear off.

Her gaze fell to a pale ridge of skin over one of his ribs. "I thought you'd never been wounded in battle."

He glanced down and shrugged. "I bleed, like any man. Each scar is a reminder of a mistake I made."

She gazed up at him. The hint of imperfection only made him more human, more approachable.

I wish you really wanted me.

The plaintive thought echoed sadly in her head. Thank God she hadn't said that aloud.

And then, to her absolute horror, she realized she *had*.

Del Sarto's brows disappeared into his hairline and for a brief moment stunned silence reigned. Cara wanted to bite off her own tongue. And then the coverlet dipped as he fisted both hands next to her head and leaned down.

ALESSANDRO FELT like he'd been coshed around the head with one of cook's saucepans. This was no woman's ploy for flattery: Cara genuinely believed he wasn't attracted to her. God, for an intelligent woman she had the most idiotic notions.

He should leave her alone. She was still experiencing the effects of the sleeping draught. He was just a hazy apparition she'd conjured up in her delirium. Some fever-sent combination of romantic childhood dreams and faceless demon lover.

But the idea that he wasn't attracted to her was so ridiculous it *had* to be remedied. He sat down near her hip. The bed sagged under his weight and rolled her towards him. "I want you, Cara di Montessori," he whispered near her ear.

"You do?"

Her eyes were drowsy, already closing. He stroked a tendril of hair from her forehead and she turned into the touch like a cat.

"Very much." *More than life itself.* "So much I'm nigh mad with it. But you know our bargain. You have to come to me willingly. That means without any wine or potions that might mar your judgement." He brushed his thumb over the pulse fluttering at her throat and she arched up into the caress. Blood pooled in his groin. "I want you fully conscious. Fully compliant. Because you're going to want to remember every single thing we do."

* * *

CARA SUPPRESSED a shiver as he lifted her hand and set his lips to the soft hollow on the inside of her elbow. She held her breath as he trailed kisses along the inside of her forearm until he reached the sensitive skin at the inside of her wrist. He laved it with this tongue and she jerked in shock.

The fighting points, she realized dazedly.

He was kissing the fighting points—those sensitive places where the veins ran closest to the surface of the skin. She'd studied them, practiced to target them as the places to inflict maximum hurt on an enemy in combat.

She'd never imagined they could be used this way; for pleasure, not for pain. She felt light-headed with the discovery. A whole new world existed. How strange, that del Sarto—this dealer of death and destruction—should be the one to show her *life.*

* * *

ALESSANDRO SLID his hand over her throat, relishing the creamy softness of her skin, the supple play of muscle and flesh beneath his fingers.

She was biting her lower lip, trembling at his caress, and he realized he'd never wanted anything more in his entire life; not the surrender of a castle, nor the capitulation of a foe. It took every ounce of his self-control not to strip off his own clothing and show her exactly what pleasure could be had between a man and a woman. But if he took her now he'd never know if it was because of the sleeping potion or her own desire.

He forced his hand away from her skin, pulled the cool linen coverlet up over her body, and brushed a chaste kiss on her temple. Her sigh could have been disappointment—or merely exhaustion. She turned on her side and snuggled down into the sheets.

"Sleep well, Cara mia," he said.

Alessandro stalked to the door and closed it quietly behind him.

CHAPTER 28

"I've compiled that list of suitors you asked for."

Alessandro nodded for Francesco to continue. "Let's hear it, then."

"Well, first there's The Medici of Florence. Lorenzo's eldest is already married. And his second son, Giovanni—" Francesco nodded across the hall toward a young man deep in conversation with his brother, "—has been promised to the church."

"Any other brothers?"

"Giuliano." Francesco indicated a youth with brown hair and a thin face who was playing with two of the castle dogs. "But he's only thirteen."

Alessandro dismissed him with an imperious flick of the hand. "Who's that flirting with Catherine Sforza?"

"Lorenzo's adopted son Giulio. He's really his nephew, the bastard son of his murdered brother."

"Giulio, Giuliano, Giovanni. Can't the Medici choose any different names?"

Francesco chuckled. "Confusing, isn't it? Anyway, he's still only fourteen."

"Fine. What about the Este brothers? The eldest one's here, I see."

Francesco shook his head. "Married Anna Sforza last year. The others are too young."

Alessandro frowned. "Cara's too spirited for anyone younger than herself. She'd ride roughshod over the poor bastard within a fortnight."

"I have older," Francesco consulted his list. "There's Francesco Gonzaga—"

"He's condottiere!"

Francesco's brows lifted. "A soldier would be just right for her. Strong enough to keep her in line."

"Absolutely not. No mercenaries."

"Vitelli, then?"

"Too old."

"He's thirty-four! Same age as you."

"Cara might be old in years, but she lacks a world of experience."

"All the more reason to pair her with someone older then. Farnesi?"

"Pier Luigi? Christ! Even *she* doesn't deserve to be shackled to him. He's just been tried for molesting the bishop of Fano. You might as well tell me you've got Cesare Borgia on the list."

Francesco surreptitiously crossed a name from his paper. "I do not! What about Urbino then? Rumor has it the impotent duke plans to leave it all to his brother, Giovanni. *He'd* be good."

"Is he still a mercenary?"

"Well, technically, yes. But that rule gets rid of almost everyone except the Pope. The Baglioni—"

"—are pursuing vendetta against everyone," Alessandro interrupted. "I'm amazed there's any of them left."

A muscle ticked in Francesco's jaw. "This is Italy. Revenge is our country's lifeblood. *Everyone's* pursuing a vendetta."

"I want her married, not murdered."

THE DEVIL TO PAY

Francesco gave a long-suffering sigh and made a great show of crossing yet another name off his list. "All right, what about Jacopo Petrucci of Siena? I've never heard a bad thing said about him."

"Siena's less than fifty miles away."

"Too close for comfort, eh?" Francesco said slyly.

Alessandro shot him a dark look.

Francesco gulped. "Nowhere within a hundred miles. Got it. Is Venice far enough? Leonardo Loredan's tipped to be the next Doge."

Alessandro shook his head. "Too dull. My lady hates to be bored, remember."

"Luca Orsini?"

"Too fat."

Francesco buried his head in his hands with a groan. "Let's just get this clear; I'm trying to find an unmarried nobleman, aged between twenty-five and thirty-five—" he ticked off the attributes on his thick fingers "—who's *not* a mercenary. He must be rich enough to keep her, strong enough to tame her, and *thin* enough not to *squash* her? Is that about it?"

Alessandro smiled. "Precisely."

Francesco dropped his forehead onto the table in front of him with a thump. "It's impossible. Even if you discount your stupid 'no mercenaries' rule, there's probably *still* only one man in the whole of Italy who fits your description."

His tone made Alessandro narrow his gaze. "And who's that?"

Francesco looked up and grinned. "*You*, my lord."

"Francesco," Alessandro made his voice very soft, and therefore all the more menacing. "Go away."

Francesco rose and bowed irreverently. "Yes, sire. Immediately."

CHAPTER 29

Cara remained in her rooms with a pounding headache all morning, but the pain had diminished by the time Renata brought her a tray of food.

"His lordship thought you might have an appetite, after all your adventures." The servant's eye held a wicked twinkle.

Cara knew her face was suffused with guilty heat, but she gave a resigned sigh as Renata coaxed her into one of Pia's extraordinary new dresses and arranged her hair. She would have to show her face downstairs sometime this evening; she couldn't ignore del Sarto forever.

"More guests arrived yesterday while you were gone," Renata said. "The whole place is packed to the rafters."

Cara gave a wan smile as Renata deftly fastened the rubies at her throat. The stones warmed to her skin like a caress. "Oh, good."

She found del Sarto at the bottom of the the main staircase. Her step faltered and a shiver of awareness swept over her skin. She'd had some embarrassingly erotic dreams of him last night— doubtless an unwanted side effect of the sleeping draught.

He extended his hand and escorted her down the last few

steps, stepping back to admire her outfit. "You're looking well tonight, my lady." His gaze devoured her. "All that galloping around the countryside has put some color in your cheeks."

Beast. He knew exactly what caused her blushes, and it had nothing to do with bucolic landscapes and everything to do with remembering his mouth on her breasts. Her skin warmed. She was spared having to answer as they stepped into the great hall and were immediately surrounded by a horde of people, all clamoring for introductions. He extricated them and deftly guided her up onto the dais so she could have a better view of the proceedings.

Cara grabbed a goblet of wine from a passing servant and gulped down the contents, desperate for a little liquid courage, then glanced at his profile. He seemed to be watching the crowd with a mixture of amusement and disgust. She tried not to react as he lowered his head to her ear but a shiver of awareness skittered along her spine, raising the hairs on her arms.

"Italy's most powerful men and women are in this room tonight. Pay attention. Feel the currents in the air. Who's talking to whom? Who's avoiding one another? Who's flirting? Who's plotting? If you're to survive at court you need to know these things."

She pulled away from him. "I don't need to survive at court. I'm going back to Castelleon."

His exasperated sigh was audible.

To give the devil his due, the hall looked magnificent. The ladies' gowns were a swirl of sumptuous color, a kaleidoscope of claret and burgundy, amber and teal. Fur glistened. Candlelight glimmered on gold hairnets and an obscene over-abundance of jewels. It was exactly as Cara had dreamed court would be; lavish, extravagant and hedonistic. The air was warm and heady with the mingled perfumes.

Del Sarto was certainly making a statement with the magnificence of his hospitality. Wine was flowing freely and the food tables practically groaned, laden to overflowing with roast meats, sweets and pastries and serving bowls piled high with exotic fruits. The serving dishes were solid silver. Just one of them would feed a family at Castelleon for a month.

He seemed to read her mind. "People are always impressed by appearances. It's all pomp and show. Everything hinges on my showing no weakness. If any of the other city states suspect I'm weak—even temporarily—they'll descend like carrion crows after a battle to feast on my corpse."

"What lovely imagery."

He ignored her sarcasm. "San Rocco lies between the feuding states of Milan and Venice. I've got the French to the north and Rome and Florence to the south. I'm surrounded by jackals. I must ever be vigilant." He caught her eye. "Sometimes one does not have the luxury of being kind."

That was probably as close to an apology for his behavior as she was ever going to get. She accepted a cup of wine from a passing servant. "I see your erotic food is going down well."

He glanced over at two elderly matrons giggling like naughty schoolgirls over the nipple cakes. "Mmm. Sex and scandal are universally popular, whatever the occasion."

Cara fanned herself with her hand. The crush of bodies was almost overwhelming. Or perhaps it was the proximity of just the one body she found so disconcerting.

It was easy to imagine plots and conspiracies, assignations and intrigues being whispered in the buzz of conversation. She had to admit, there was definitely a piquancy to the danger.

His warm breath fanned her bare shoulder. "That's Lorenzobaldo, the Duke of Urbino and his wife Elisabetta." He directed her attention towards an older man by the door, deep in conversation with one of the Sforzas. The man looked rather sickly, with a yellowish tinge to his skin. The woman hovering next to him wore a mantle of brown velvet, slashed at the sleeves and caught up with huge chains of gold. "He's rumored to be impotent, but his long-suffering wife refuses to divorce him."

Cara frowned. "A wife should be loyal to her husband, whatever his faults. And he should be loyal to her. Perhaps she loves him?"

He snorted. "Perhaps she loves being the Duchess of Urbino." He indicated another man. "That's Ludo Sforza, the Duke of Milan. He changes political allegiance as often as he changes his shirt. Don't let him fool you; he's an unscrupulous intriguer. Come, I'll introduce you."

Cara determined to make up her own mind about the man. Almost despite herself she found him a charming companion, with a droll, sly wit. She couldn't help but laugh as he entertained her with gossip on almost everyone in the room.

After a while del Sarto returned to her side. "You enjoyed talking with Il Moro?"

"He's extremely amusing."

His smile was cynical. "He can be, when he chooses. Did he proposition you? A word of warning; both his wife and his mistress are already here. I doubt he has time for you, too."

"*Both* of them?"

Her shock seemed to amuse him. "That's his mistress over there, Cecilia Gallerani. She gave birth to his son last year, a boy named Cesare."

"His poor wife! Does she know?" She followed his gaze to a pretty young woman on the other side of the room.

"Beatrice? Of course she knows. These things are commonplace."

Cara shook her head, covertly studying the two women. "How can they bear to be in the same room?"

"Politics. They tolerate each other because they must. Watch how studiously they ignore one another. It's quite an art."

The mistress was blonde and beautiful, with a thin, clever face. Her dress was deep blue, the upper arms folded back to reveal a dark red inner sleeve. Deceptively simple, it enhanced the seductive sway of her body. Instead of dazzling, it insinuated. A long row of perfect pearls wound around her swan-like neck.

"She's dressed as finely as his wife," Cara said disapprovingly.

"It's a measure of Il Moro's prowess that he can afford to keep such an expensive mistress as well as a beautiful wife." His gaze skimmed over her body, making her nerve endings hum. "A man likes to look at a woman and know he's paid for the clothes she's wearing. It gives him the right to remove them."

Her blood heated. He'd paid for every stitch of clothing she had on. "That's yet another reason I never want to marry," she said firmly. "I'd want my husband to be faithful only to me."

"How novel!"

"Il Moro didn't proposition me, anyway. We were discussing ways to develop Milanese agriculture."

Del Sarto rolled his eyes.

"Not everyone spends their time waging war on their neighbors," she scolded. "Some people grow things, make things. I found it most interesting."

"Have you met his wife yet? Beatrice is d'Este's youngest daughter. She's only sixteen."

Cara shot him a sideways glance, amused by his unflattering inference. "Whereas I'm twenty-two and still unwed."

"Oh, I haven't lost all hope for you. I'm sure we'll find someone to overlook your over-educated brain and bloodthirsty ways."

"I don't want or need a husband. How many times must I tell you?"

He ignored her continued rebellion. "There are plenty of eligible men here. Would you care to enlighten me as to your criteria?"

She feigned surprise. "You're interested in my opinion? Good Lord!"

He raised one brow and gestured for her to continue.

"Very well. If I ever *did* marry, I'd want my husband to treat me as a partner, an equal. I would not want some tyrant who'd dominate me, override me, and treat me like an imbecile."

"Is that all?" It was his turn for sarcasm.

"Well, it would be nice if he wasn't hideous to look at," she added mischievously. "I'd like to have relatively attractive children."

"You forgot to mention rich and powerful."

"Money can't make you happy."

"Of course it can. This is *exactly* why you need me. Left to your own devices you'd choose some weak, peace-loving scholar and Castelleon would fall to the first strong-armed invader who came your way."

Cara didn't have time to argue that point. A handsome youth was approaching them with a determined expression on his face. He stopped in front of them and shot a nervous glance at del Sarto, even as he addressed her.

"May I have the honor of this dance, Signorina di Montessori?"

"Oh, no. I really . . . that is, I don't dance—"

"Of course she does," del Sarto supplied smoothly, pushing her forward. "She'd *love* to."

Cara shot him a filthy look over her shoulder as she was dragged into a newly-forming line of dancers.

Del Sarto's gaze burned her skin as she whirled and stepped around the floor. No doubt he was watching to see if she embarrassed herself—and therefore him, by association. But the steps were easy to follow and she quickly relaxed. It was far less nerve-wracking than dancing with *him*. Her partner made some amusing comments on the fashions of another couple and she laughed, beginning to enjoy herself.

* * *

ALESSANDRO IGNORED a scalding stab of jealousy as he watched Cara move to the intricate dance, flushed and smiling at her besotted partner. This was exactly what he'd wanted, was it not? To find her a husband and cement a peaceful alliance in the region.

The young buck she was dancing with was handsome, in a flashy, overconfident way. He was smiling at her like he wanted to eat her up. Half the men in the room were watching her, too. Alessandro made a conscious effort not to bare his teeth and snarl.

Cara was naively unaware of her own attractiveness, which made her a breath of fresh air amongst the practiced coquetries of the courtiers. Her dress shimmered as she moved with unconscious grace and the jewels at her neck caught the light.

He'd given jewelry to previous lovers, of course, generous trinkets that meant nothing. But he'd kept the spinel locked away. In truth, Cara was the only one he'd ever imagined wearing it. In his dreams she was usually wearing nothing else; blood-red gems for the woman who'd wormed her way into his blood. He frowned. The thought of allowing another man to have her made his chest hurt.

CHAPTER 30

Cara's partner returned her to a scowling del Sarto and scurried off.

"That's Il Moro's wife, Beatrice, over there," he said.

She followed his gaze. The younger woman seemed to be in her element, laughing and confident. Her dark hair was parted in the centre and tied back in a golden net that glittered with pearls. Her gown's neckline was so low that the smock beneath only just managed to preserve her modesty. The dress itself was striped black and gold, embroidered with metallic thread that caught the light. The effect was sumptuous and utterly bewitching.

The woman noticed their attention; she excused herself from her companions, crossed the room, and bobbed a curtsey to Il Diavolo, who bowed low over her hand.

"My lord, thank you for inviting us to your magnificent home." Her voice was low and melodic, and held a trace of laughter.

"You're welcome. Beatrice, may I present Cara di Montessori, my honored guest. If you'll excuse me, ladies, I'll leave you to talk."

He withdrew as the brunette gave Cara a dazzling smile. Her very poise made Cara nervous. What on earth could she have in common with such a stunning creature? "Your dress is amazing," she blurted out desperately.

"Oh, do you like it?" The girl beamed and smoothed the fabric of one sleeve, then lowered her voice and shot Cara a conspiratorial smile. "This is the first time I've worn it in public. Be honest, do you think the sleeves are too much? The slashes are copied from a dress I saw in Germany. I'm trying to set a new fashion, but I'm not sure Italy's quite ready for it yet!"

Her brown eyes sparkled and Cara had to smile. The girl's sense of fun was infectious; she clearly didn't take herself too seriously. "Don't ask me. I know *nothing* about fashion. I grew up surrounded by men."

"So I heard," Beatrice chuckled. "Everyone's talking about you. Did you *really* blow up a monastery?"

"Only part of one. It was an accident."

"How exciting! I do hope you'll tell me all about it sometime. So, you're staying with Il Diavolo?"

Cara grimaced. "That's one way of putting it. I'm effectively his hostage."

This revelation failed to get the sympathetic reaction she expected. Beatrice grinned. "Ooh, you lucky thing! No wonder Vanessa Canozzi's in such a bad mood." She chuckled. "Odious woman. That's her over there, flirting with him now. He finished with her months ago, but she hasn't taken the hint. That little man behind her is her long-suffering husband."

Cara narrowed her eyes. "We've met."

Beatrice raised an eyebrow, scenting intrigue. "Then you already know she's awful. I won't have her at *my* court. Still, she's a lucky woman. Del Sarto's extremely attractive, don't you think?"

"I suppose so."

Beatrice shot her a mischievous look. "What's not to like about tall, dark, and dangerously handsome?"

Cara glanced across the room. The blasted man looked devastating, as usual. Her gaze dropped to his lips and her blood heated as she recalled the feel of them against her skin. He looked up and caught her studying him, and her heart lurched as their gazes locked. He raised his wine glass in a mocking toast.

Beatrice followed her gaze. "Uh-oh. He's talking to my father. I bet Papa's offering up one of my brothers as a potential husband for you."

Cara felt the blood drain from her face.

"What's the matter?" Beatrice touched her arm in a comforting gesture.

"I don't want to get married. Ever." Cara bit her tongue and savored the sting. She was an idiot, to be mooning over a man who was doing everything he could to get rid of her.

Beatrice interrupted her self-flagellation. "Marriage isn't *that* bad, you know. Even men have their occasional uses. Still, I'll try and put Papa off the idea. I'd love to have you as a sister in law, but no-one deserves one of my brothers. They're too young for you, anyway. Experience is *always* preferable in a husband." She gave a knowing smile. "How old is my lord del Sarto?"

Cara rolled her eyes. "I don't know. At least thirty."

For one, brief moment, she imagined herself married to him, and her heart skipped a beat. The vision was both unnerving and strangely compelling.

"Are you honestly saying you've never thought about it?" Beatrice teased. "I know *I* have! There's not a woman here who hasn't imagined herself with him."

"He's not thinking of marriage. To me or anyone else. In fact, I can't think of anyone worse suited to being a husband. All he cares about is fighting and making money."

Beatrice looked sympathetic. "Well, you'll be lucky to avoid marrying *someone.*" She glanced across the room and sighed. "Oh dear. I should go and drag my husband away from the Medici. They can't be in the same room without arguing." She gave Cara's hand a squeeze. "It was nice to meet you. I hope we'll have a chance to talk again soon." She was quickly swallowed up by the crowd.

Cara had just turned to look for del Sarto when he reappeared soundlessly at her shoulder. She jumped. "Stop creeping up on people like that!"

He sent her a diabolical smile. "Force of habit. Did you enjoy gossiping with Beatrice?"

"I did indeed."

"Her sister's wedding to the Duke of Mantua was a good alliance. The ceremony alone cost over twenty thousand ducats."

"Must you think of everything in terms of money and power?"

"Yes. That's the way the world works." He sounded bored. "Have you chosen a husband yet?"

"No."

He withdrew a folded paper from his surcoat and Cara stared at it suspiciously. "What's that?"

"Despite your lack of feminine accomplishments and your complete inability to take orders, I've received eight separate offers for you. These are the names. You will choose one by the morning. If not, I will make the decision for you."

Shock and fury warred with disappointment in her chest. She felt brittle, like a glass goblet that might shatter into a thousand pieces at any moment. She couldn't look at him. She took the paper and scanned the list instead.

"I doubt any of them meet your exacting standards," he said darkly. "None of them will ride to your rescue on a dazzling white charger or serenade you with flowers and sonnets."

She blanched. His mocking description was uncannily accurate to the daydreams she *had* spun when she was a little girl, still naively hopeful for a happy future. She raised her chin and forced words past her aching throat.

"If that is all, my lord, I think I'll go to bed."

He nodded coolly. "I bid you goodnight."

CHAPTER 31

*C*ara sat on the window seat in her room and stared out at the darkness beyond. Del Sarto was a brute and his insistence on a dynastic marriage for her was infuriating.

Her own parents had married for love, not land or power. She'd been both proud and slightly envious of what they'd shared; she wanted what they'd had, that no-one-else-will-do conviction. And if she couldn't have it, she wouldn't settle for less. Even the prospect of living alone for the rest of her days was better than a loveless marriage.

At least del Sarto, the miserable cur, had finally provided her with a means to escape. She would accept one of these infernal suitors and leave San Rocco. She'd use the man's forces to recapture Castelleon, break off her engagement, and return home. Alone.

It was hardly the most honorable plan, to be sure, but it was the best she could come up with under the circumstances. And at least she'd be free of del Sarto and their ridiculous bargain.

She studied the list again. None of the men were remotely appealing, but the most logical choice was the elderly Duke of Parma. He had the largest number of standing troops, after del

Sarto. He was a widower, around sixty years old, with a tanned face and kind eyes. It would be cruel to mislead him, but he would recover. He could live without a wife, but she couldn't live without avenging her father and regaining her home. Her primary duty was to the people of Castelleon, to free them from the tyranny of her uncle.

Cara gave a frustrated sigh. But what of her own needs? Her own desires? She'd done what others wanted her whole life. The most annoying part of all this was that, of all the traits she desired in a husband, Il Diavolo possessed more of them than any other man she'd ever met.

He was undeniably handsome. Protective. Strong. He encouraged her reading and appreciated her military knowledge. He found her lack of feminine accomplishments amusing, instead of repellent. He made her laugh, made her feel safe. She'd even appreciate his fiendishly clever mind if it were working *with* her, instead of against her, and she loved butting heads with him. The thrill of their verbal sparring, the challenge of testing her wit against his own, was thoroughly invigorating. The thought of leaving him, of never seeing him again, made her feel oddly wretched.

Cara stared at her reflection, distorted by the wavy imperfections of the diamond-paned glass, and the awful, irrefutable truth hit her in the face like a low-hanging branch.

Good God. She was in love with del Sarto!

She sat completely still, stunned. How *could* she have fallen in love with such an undeserving, black-hearted, conniving, arrogant . . . the list just went on and on.

He didn't want her, or anyone, to wife. He was using her for his own political ends. All he'd ever offered was a few nights of pleasure.

Cara stripped off her dress and jewels and slipped on the sheer silk nightdress that Pia had provided—so insubstantial she might as well have worn nothing at all. She unwound the tight braids from her hair and sat on the edge of the bed to brush it out, then tossed the brush aside, flopped backwards, and stared sightlessly at the canopy above.

She would be leaving soon. She didn't need to lie with him for the sake of their bargain.

But that didn't mean she couldn't lie with him if she *wanted* to.

Her heart began to pound. Livy, the Greek historian, said "temerity is not always successful." She'd never been good at sitting around, waiting for things to happen. Was she going to be like Ovid's Daphne, always running away? No. She wanted del Sarto. He wanted her.

So why not take what he was offering? Why not allow herself one night of sin, of pleasure, before the rest of her life without him?

She glanced at the connecting door. It was well past midnight, but she'd heard him come to bed only moments ago, heard him moving around the chamber; the splash of water, the scrape of a chair.

Without giving herself time to think, she crossed the room, her bare feet soundless on the cool flagstones, and shoved aside the table that stood in front of the door. She experienced a moment of blind panic as she pushed it open. *What was she doing?* This was madness! She should turn around and go straight to bed. Already regretting her foolish impetuosity, she glanced around his room, suddenly willing it to be empty.

"Looking for something to kill me with?" del Sarto drawled.

Hellfire and Damnation.

He was lying in bed, propped up by the pillows like a lazy sultan, watching her by the embers of the fire. His chest, visible above the coverlet, was bare. Her heart caught in her throat.

His narrowed gaze took in what she was wearing. Or, rather, what she *wasn't* wearing. The sheer silk was a scandalous piece of clothing, utterly impractical for anything other than seduction. It was the most revealing thing she'd ever worn, and Cara suddenly felt ridiculous, like a child caught trying on her mother's clothing.

"Where did you get that gown?"

She glanced down stupidly. "Pia gave it to me."

"A definite improvement on my shirts. Dare I ask why you're here?"

She stepped forward and adopted a cool, businesslike expression. "I've chosen a suitor. The Duke of Parma."

He raised one eyebrow. "An interesting choice. But couldn't it have waited until morning?"

Temerity is not always successful.

She strove to keep her voice cool, as though charging into a man's bedroom and propositioning him was a regular nightly occurrence. "I've changed my mind."

His gaze grew alert. *Predatory.* "About what, specifically?"

She quaked under his intense regard. "You said I had to come to you willingly." She spread her arms out in a gesture of both challenge and acceptance, and lifted her chin. "So here I am. Willing. I want you to teach me."

He narrowed his eyes, obviously suspecting a catch. "Teach you?"

"Everything there is to know between a man and a woman." She looked him square in the eye. "I want to go into my marriage prepared."

His reaction was impossible to gauge; if she'd surprised him he gave no outward sign. He merely raised his hand in an imperious gesture and crooked one finger. It took all of her courage not to turn on her heel and run.

"Come here."

She took one tiny step forward.

"Closer."

Another step.

He watched her with a slumberous, hooded gaze, a wolf assessing her for weakness. The children of Castelleon played a game called *Lupo del'ore*. Players taunted the 'wolf' until the call of midnight, at which point he turned and gave chase until someone was caught. Eaten for dinner.

What's the time, Mr Wolf? One o'clock.
What's the time, Mr Wolf? Two o'clock.
What's the time, Mr Wolf?
Dinner Time!

The ludicrous thought brought a smile to Cara's lips. It was clear she was on the menu, but suddenly the idea was less terrifying than exciting. She'd chosen her wolf; she wouldn't back out now, however unnerving he appeared.

She walked to the bed and stopped when her shins hit the wooden frame. Her gaze roamed over his biceps, ribs, the intriguing ridges of his stomach. Most of the men she knew had tanned necks and forearms but pale chests. Even when unclothed they appeared to be wearing shirts. Not him. He was golden all over, all sculpted planes and interesting shadows that made her fingers itch to touch.

She tensed when he moved, but he only rolled over onto his stomach. The sheet exposed his back right down to the indentations at the top of his buttocks.

Cara swallowed. *Oh Lord. He was naked under there.*

He rested his head on his folded arms and turned his face towards her.

"What would you like me to do?" she managed, her mouth dry.

"Give me a massage. You did offer, if you recall. In the forest."

Had she? Her memories of what they'd discussed were vague, at best. Still, she was intrigued. "All right."

She leaned over him, extended her hands, and placed them tentatively on his shoulders.

His skin was warm, and the muscles twitched like those of a skittish stallion. She flattened her palms and stroked outwards, then, growing bolder, ran them down the hard ridges of muscle that bracketed his spine. She stopped when she reached the top of the sheet and slid back up, over his ribs, back to his shoulders, in a rhythmic, mesmerizing pattern.

The room was quiet, save for his breathing and the crackle of the fire. He lay completely at ease, eyes closed. His eyelashes were ridiculously long, fanned against his cheeks. She'd kill for eyelashes like that. They were wasted on a man.

Gaining confidence, she alternated firm strokes with a lighter, feather touch, and was gratified to see goose-bumps rise on his skin. The healer in her was pleased that she could make him relax. The woman in her just enjoyed touching him.

He gave a deep groan of appreciation and she took a moment to admire the landscape of his back. Purely from a detached, scholarly perspective, of course. He was as well-proportioned as the warriors of Homer's Iliad; Achilles maybe, or Hector, her secret literary heroes. She could just imagine him storming the walls of Troy or stealing another man's wife.

With one finger she rubbed the pale ridge of an old scar, as if her touch could erase the pain it must have caused. How hard and violent his life had been. A mistake, he'd called it. He was human, after all. Just a man.

But what a man.

She splayed her fingers wide. They didn't even reach half way around his bicep. He tensed as she pressed a tender spot on his shoulder; presumably the injury that was still causing him trouble.

A shiver of awe at his strength ran through her. There was such banked power in his frame. Even at rest he seemed ready to explode into action. His fingers twitched on the pillow. Holding her breath, she swept her hands lower, edging under the sheet.

CHAPTER 32

*A*lessandro suppressed a soul-deep groan as Cara's fingers skated toward the base of his spine. The bloody woman had done it again; surprised him, when he'd cynically imagined that nothing could surprise him ever again.

Whatever had made her change her mind about sleeping with him—and he was sure she had some complicated, convoluted reason—he wasn't about to question her decision, nor fail to take advantage of what she was offering. He'd wanted her for far too long.

"Enough," he growled, rougher than he'd intended. He flipped over and she leapt backwards as if she thought he was going to bite her. The idea only made him harder. "Take that off." He nodded at the flimsy nightdress, privately amused at the catch in his voice. He'd told her to remove her clothes the first time she'd visited his room, too.

She wouldn't go through with it. Any second now she'd come to her senses and bolt.

She grasped the hem of her gown.

Alessandro watched, outwardly impassive, inwardly incredulous, as she raised the thin garment over her thighs. Past gently flaring hips, the dark triangle between her legs, the pale skin of her stomach.

His mouth went dry as she exposed her small, perfect breasts, pink nipples beading in the cool air. His breath caught as she pulled the material over her head and her hair settled around her shoulders in a dark cloud.

For a moment she clutched the bundled silk to her chest, then she gathered her courage and slowly extended her arm away from her body. Opening her hand, she dropped the nightgown defiantly to the floor as if throwing down a gauntlet to challenge him to a fight.

Her bravery was costing her; he could see her nervousness in the tightness of her shoulders and his heart gave a jolt of admiration. Firelight flickered over her body as she faced him, an Amazon queen, haughty and proud. His blood thundered in his ears. *Bravo Signorina Montessori.*

An unwelcome glimmer of unease assailed him. She was offering exactly what he'd demanded; total surrender. Complete trust. He wasn't worthy of either of those things. But he wasn't above taking them.

"What now?" she whispered uncertainly.

"What do you think we should do?"

Her small white teeth bit her lower lip in indecision and his cock twitched in response. God, she was killing him.

"Kiss?" she ventured.

"A good start. Come here then."

She didn't move.

He refused to make it easy for her. The decision had to be hers and hers alone. "If you want it, you have to come and take it."

* * *

ACUTELY AWARE OF HER NAKEDNESS, Cara drank in the sight of him, long and lean, stretched out on the bed. Terror and excitement roiled inside her and his hot gaze turned her bones to water. She bent her knee on the bed near his hip, playing for time.

His lower half was barely covered by the sheet; she could feel the heat of his thigh through the thin barrier. She placed one hand on either side of his face and bent forward so that her lips hovered a scant inch above his own. Her breasts brushed against his chest and she paused, terrified of the momentous step she was about to take.

"My education didn't include seduction," she admitted. "Father Andreo used to blush just reading the Song of Songs. Especially the bit where it says 'my lover's breasts are like the twin fawns of a gazelle.'"

"Ah, the only good part of the bible."

She gasped at his nonchalant blasphemy, and he chuckled. "I've read it. 'Set me as a seal upon thine heart, as a seal upon thine arm. For love is strong as death and jealousy is cruel as the grave.'"

She shivered at the intensity of his gaze.

"Kiss me." His voice was like woodsmoke, curling around her. His breath teased her lightly parted lips. "Just put your mouth on mine. Is it so difficult?" There was laughter in his eyes. And challenge. "Don't back out now, Cara. I never took you for a coward."

That did it! She lowered her mouth to his and flicked her tongue across the seam of his lips, tasting him, coaxing a response.

His lips stayed firmly closed.

She raised her head in annoyance. His eyes were still open, frankly assessing. His hands were exactly where they had been, on the pillows behind his head. He hadn't grabbed her hair to hold her in place, hadn't thrown her down onto the covers in impatience. How could he not be affected? Was she really that bad?

"You have to kiss me back!" she scolded.

His smile was slow and impossibly sexy. "Is that how it works?" He slid his hands up her arms and over her shoulders, raising goose-bumps, then threaded his fingers through her hair and tugged her forward. He bit her lower lip, teething gently. Her stomach flipped. "Let me show you," he said.

His lips claimed hers, and for a few seconds Cara was simply content to marvel at his artistry. *Lord Above*, the man knew how to kiss. He tormented, teased, and soothed in the same breath. She kissed him back, clumsily, inexpertly, wholeheartedly, and she must have done something right, because he made a low, growling noise in the back of his throat and tightened his grip on her hair. The sound was one of sheer, animal arousal.

The tenor of the kiss changed. It became a competition, each of them vying for supremacy, pleasure the only goal. Their tongues tangled and fought, an endless game of advance and retreat. Shivers raced over her skin.

Minutes, or perhaps hours later, she reared back, gasping for breath. His lips were wet and glistening. Her heart was racing as if she had a pack of wolves after her.

"You're definitely improving."

His words were taunting, but there was a roughness in his voice that betrayed him. He wasn't unaffected.

"I still don't like you," she whispered against his mouth. "You're still a Devil."

His lips quirked. "I know."

In a lightning quick move he tugged her down onto the bed beside him and rolled her over so she was lying beneath him, as they'd been in the forest. He trapped her hands against the rumpled covers. She gasped as his chest pressed her into the softness of the mattress and then stilled, intensely aware of his size, his strength, his sheer domination.

"Don't give me the timid virgin Cara," he whispered, sensing her uncertainty. "Give me the girl who bloodied my nose in the bailey. The girl who stabbed me in the forest."

"You deserved it," she whispered. "Show me what to do."

His smile was pure wickedness. "You don't need to do anything. Just lie there and enjoy it."

He kissed his way down her body as if he had all the time in the world. First her neck, then her collarbone, then the upper slope of her breasts.

Cara struggled to breathe. Until recently she'd barely given her breasts a second thought. They were just, well, *there*. Annoying things that bounced painfully when she rode and got in the way when she practiced archery. She'd never dreamed they could be so incredibly sensitive.

He flicked one nipple with his tongue then circled it with a lazy swirl. And when he put his mouth over the peak and suckled her, she arched off the bed with a gasp. His fingers traced the healing scratch on her ribs and his dark bows lowered in a frown, as if he were angry that she'd been hurt, then he feathered kisses down her stomach and she tensed, suddenly ticklish. He traced his way up her legs, fingers skating over her calves and the weak spot behind her knees, and she jerked as he nipped the tender skin of her thigh with his teeth. Her blood pulsed thickly in her veins as she grasped his shoulders. She felt light-headed, over-warm.

"What are you doing?!"

"Relax, Carissima. Enjoy."

His tongue traced the crease where hip met leg. She grabbed his hair with both hands and tried to pull him back up, but he ignored her and dipped lower.

Embarrassed beyond anything, Cara felt herself wet, there, where he was.

Oh, Holy Mother! He was kissing her *there*! In places she couldn't even name. She closed her legs around the sides of his head just as he touched her with his tongue.

Cara closed her eyes, certain she was about to die of mortification. Ovid hadn't mentioned *this*. A bolt of pure energy shot through her. "Good Lord!"

His upward glance was entirely wicked. "I doubt He has much to do with this."

He was right; the feelings he was producing were sinful indeed. This was the Devil's touch—she was burning and desperate, like Satan's Inferno itself. Del Sarto fanned the flames with his tongue then blew on her gently, sending icy shivers all over her body.

She yanked on his hair in wild desperation. "Don't stop! Don't you dare stop!"

He laughed darkly against her skin. He kissed and licked, teased and tormented, and Cara nearly jerked off the bed. Maybe it *was* heavenly, after all. Her heart felt as if it would burst out of her chest.

When he pulled back she moaned in wordless denial, aching and somehow bereft. Why had he stopped? She could have howled in frustration. If she'd had her dagger she would have stabbed him, without a moment's hesitation. She was restless. Fevered. Incomplete.

"Turn over," he murmured. "It's your turn for a massage."

Cara frowned but complied unquestioningly. The man clearly knew what he was doing. His hands settled on her back, rough and smooth at the same time. She could feel the skin on his palms, sections coarsened by constant weapons practice. They moved over her, kneading the tense muscles of her shoulders and she bit back a groan. It felt so good.

He stroked the ridges bracketing her spine over and over again in a mesmerizing rhythm, then smoothed the indents at the top of her buttocks, and moved lower, onto the curves of her bottom. Cara floated, her body strangely languorous, both relaxed and increasingly excited at the same time. The place between her legs throbbed.

His hands moved over her buttocks onto the top of her thighs, then reversed direction, gliding upwards again. The V made by his splayed thumbs and forefingers pushed her cheeks upwards before he returned to her lower back. She buried her head in the coverlet and held her breath. And then his fingers dipped down and she gasped as he parted her slick folds and rubbed the spot where his mouth had been.

Cara had never experienced anything like it in her life. It was glorious.

Then he pushed the tip of one finger *inside* her. She squirmed, but he rested his other palm on the small of her back, pressed her gently back down onto the bedclothes. His voice at her ear was velvet-rough.

"Enjoy it, Cara. Let it happen."

She didn't know what he was talking about. She shifted on the bed, aching for his touch. His finger pushed deeper, then withdrew and pushed in again. It was a monstrous invasion, but it felt so *good*. Each slide seemed to hit a spot just inside her that made her desperate for something out of reach.

She fisted her hands in the bedclothes, suddenly reluctant to cede all power to him. She resented the way her body surrendered so easily to his wicked, clever hands. She tried to resist the feelings building inside her, but it was no use; she was shaking, gasping—almost there, reaching for some end to the exquisite torture—

The world exploded. Pinpricks of silver lightning exploded behind her eyelids like one of Fra Domenico's fireworks and her body was clenching, contracting. Splintering apart and reforming. For an instant nothing existed but darkness and pleasure. And then, slowly, slowly, she returned to earth and lay stunned and panting.

What a wicked, magical thing.

CHAPTER 33

*W*hen Cara finally found the energy to roll over she found del Sarto, half propped against the headboard, watching her. Her face flamed at the liberties he'd taken with her body but he gave her an amused smile, and brushed her hair away from her neck. "Beautiful."

He'd tugged a sheet across his lap but her eyes were immediately drawn to the disturbing bulge that was ruining the contours of the bedclothes. Her body was still warm and tingling but it suddenly occurred to her that they weren't finished. He hadn't taken his own pleasure.

He lay there like a sultan awaiting the ministrations of one of his harem, the planes of his chest muscled and hard. Beautiful himself.

"Touch me." His voice was deep, gravelly with desire, and she shivered.

Gathering her courage, she placed her hand flat on his chest. His heart beat strong and steady beneath her palm. Filled with curiosity, she used one finger to trace a circle around his flat brown nipple, as he'd done to her to such astonishing effect.

His whole body went rigid.

A wicked thrill raced through her as she remembered all the giggled conversations she'd overheard between the kitchen girls at Castelleon. Things that had sounded disgusting now sounded . . . rather intriguing. She recalled what Vanessa Canozzi had been doing to him in the stables.

Holding her breath at her own daring, Cara trailed her fingers downward and watched in fascination as the muscles of his abdomen twitched in responsive relay. She ran a finger teasingly down the line of hair that led from his navel and he raised his eyebrows, silently daring her to pull away.

He didn't think she'd do it. Well, she'd *never* backed down from a challenge. He should know that about her by now.

She pushed the sheet down and a little shiver ran through her when she saw his naked form. He was magnificent. His member reared up proudly towards his belly, nestled in a mat of curly dark hair. A hum of gratification warmed her at the evidence of his body's reaction. Of course, it probably did this at the sight of *any* naked female, but still, *this* time it was for her, and her alone.

She looked up to find him watching her, gauging her reaction, completely unashamed of his nudity. It was little wonder; if she had a body like his, like some Olympian demigod, she'd probably walk around naked all day long. It was a sin to cover something so beautiful with clothes. He was an animal in its potent prime, as muscled and vital as Saraceno. And tonight he was hers.

Her hand crept lower, but just before she touched him she lifted it away and placed it back in her lap.

He practically growled. "Why did you stop?"

She adopted a prim expression. "I don't even know your full name."

He held her gaze for several heartbeats and Cara rather thought he might be counting to ten. Or praying for the strength not to strangle her. She hoped so. It served him right. He'd tormented her for years. It was only fair that he should suffer a little too.

"Why on earth does that matter?" he asked tersely.

She shrugged. "It just does."

His frustrated exhalation indicated his displeasure as he curled up towards her and kissed her on the lips. "You know my name; Il Diavolo." He gave her another kiss, harder this time. "Kingmaker."Another kiss, more urgent. "Mercenary." Kiss. "Soldier of fortune." Kiss. "I have many names, sweeting. Take your pick."

"You know what I mean," she managed breathlessly. "Your real name."

He lay back down and covered his heart with his palm as if taking a sacred oath. "My name is Alessandro Rafael del Sarto."

It rolled off his tongue like warmed honey from a spoon and Cara nearly laughed at the irony. Of course the devil would have an archangel's name.

She reached out and touched him.

He fisted the sheets and let out an uneven breath as she stroked her fingers from tip to base. She was amazed by the heat, the silky softness of the skin overlaying the hardness beneath.

A muscle twitched in his jaw. He covered her hand with his own, curled her fingers around his shaft and began to move, his fingers enveloping hers. When she caught the rhythm he released her and lay back and she continued alone, stroking up and down. He closed his eyes and his expression was almost tortured. It was clear he was struggling to maintain control. Cara felt a flash of womanly satisfaction.

And then she remembered something else she'd seen in those naughty books he'd given her. Cautiously, she bent her head and touched the very tip of him with her tongue. He nearly jerked off the bed.

She reared back in alarm. "Is that wrong? Did I hurt you?"

He made a strange noise, halfway between a strangled groan and a laugh. "God, no. You're killing me! It's perfect. Carry on."

His words were contradictory but she was encouraged by his response; his body was taut as a bowstring. Filled with a heady sense of power, she bent and feathered slow kisses along the length of him, learning the texture, the taste, barely able to believe what she was doing. The scent of him filled her nose and increased her own desire. Curious, emboldened, she opened her lips and took him into her mouth.

He hissed a curse through his teeth and his hands came up to cradle her head, but he didn't pull her away. His fingers threaded in her hair. Heart thudding in excitement, Cara flicked him playfully with her tongue. His hips bucked. He tasted salty, wonderful. She suppressed a smile of triumph and sucked.

He moved abruptly, catching her by surprise. He pushed her up and away from him, kicked off the remaining sheets, caught her hips and twisted her, following her down and settling himself on top of her.

"Enough!" His voice was strained. He sounded like a man driven to the ends of his endurance.

Cara closed her eyes at the feel of him between her legs. The hard planes of his stomach pressed against hers, his chest warmed her own. The hairs on his legs tickled her thighs. There was no barrier of clothing as there had been in the forest. She could feel him at the opening of her body; huge and hard, slippery and hot against her.

"Last chance to change your mind," he growled.

She met his searing gaze and shook her head. It had always been coming to this, from the first moment she'd seen him, years ago. She wanted it—wanted him—more than anything in the world. She touched his lips with her fingertips. "Don't stop."

His eyes blazed. He rocked his hips and she held his gaze in breathless silence as his body slowly invaded hers. He pressed forward, deeper this time, and she couldn't hide a wince of discomfort.

He stilled.

She tried to squirm away but he stroked her forehead, smoothing back her hair, then kissed the outer corner of her eye. The gentleness of that gesture, even as he was hurting her, was heart-rending.

"Don't be afraid of me," he whispered. "Not you. Let me in."

This was never going to work. She was too small and he was far too big. Tears threatened, and Cara blinked hard. She was *absolutely not* crying. Her body was too hot, too tight. Too everything.

He bent and kissed her lips. "Relax. Stop thinking. Just feel."

And for once in her life, Cara did as she was told.

* * *

ALESSANDRO GLANCED DOWN, giving Cara time to adjust to his body. He was barely inside her and God, it was killing him to hold still when every instinct he possessed was screaming at him to push on, to slide deeper, to find that white-hot bliss he knew he would find in her arms.

His heart was hammering in his chest, his breathing labored. He prided himself on his steely control, but for a moment, watching her climax, he'd nearly lost it. The sight of her—hot, flushed, eyes half closed, sweet body craving his touch, had been exquisite. Even now, the savage part of him was exulting in the fact that he'd given her what no-one else ever had. That she'd chosen *him.*

She gasped as he withdrew a fraction and pushed back in, deeper this time. He dropped his head to her shoulder and nipped her collarbone, just hard enough to make her forget what was going on between her legs, then captured her mouth, coaxing a response until her entire focus was on his lips, his tongue, their shared breath.

Oh, God, she felt so right. Like coming home after a lifetime of wandering. So sweet. And *his*. Finally, indisputably his.

Alessandro buried himself fully inside her, absorbing her gasp with his mouth, inhaling the heady scent of her—of *them*—and held back an incredulous shout of triumph. He—the least-deserving sinner of them all—had somehow, miraculously, found his way into heaven.

* * *

CARA COULDN'T BELIEVE IT. He was inside her. *Inside her!*

The pain receded as he pressed further, stretching, invading, but gently. She stroked her hands over his sides and felt him quiver in response; his muscles bunched and tensed. He moved again and a curl of sheer pleasure shot all the way down to her toes. She let out a surprised breath and waited for him to do it again and when he did she caught a glimmer of the ecstasy he'd given her with his hands. She wriggled, desperate to recapture that elusive shard of lightning.

No wonder people kept doing this! It was . . . extraordinary. She arched upwards as he increased the rhythm, and fought not to cry out with wonder. He rained kisses along her jaw and cheeks, her forehead and eyelids, ardor fraying the edges of his vaunted control. Cara closed her eyes.

I love you, she chanted, a silent litany that matched his every stroke. Her heart ached almost to bursting. She was sobbing for breath, surrounded by the scent of him, the power and incredible heat of his body.

I love you, you monster. I love you.

He made a lost sound and grasped her thigh then pulled her leg upwards and wrapped it around his hip. Cara did the same with her other leg and her eyes widened as the change in angle increased the sensation even more. She met his thrusts with her own, rocking her hips to cradle his body, giving everything, holding nothing back.

More. More. More.

They fit together so perfectly. He found her lips again and kissed her deeply, hungrily, the thrust of his tongue mimicking the thrust of his body.

"Now, sweeting," he moaned.

Cara understood. She wanted it too, that lightning strike, those silver fireworks. She bucked against him, reaching for it blindly.

Her ill-timed movements seemed to free him of the last vestige of control. He surged forward, sliding into her again and again as if he could meld them closer still, closer than this incredible fusion of bodies and souls. He was lost, frenzied, and with a shout he took her with him, hurling them both over the waterfall and into the darkness and bliss. Blinding sweetness filled every corner of her body as Cara came apart like a detonation of black powder.

He dropped his head to her shoulder in panting exhaustion and Cara let out a shaky breath. No wonder women fought to share his bed. The man clearly had some supernatural talent. Perhaps he really *had* made a pact with the devil; sold his soul in exchange for these unearthly skills. She managed an incredulous laugh. If he had, he'd made a good bargain.

As their breathing slowly evened out he rolled to one side, withdrawing from her body but taking her with him. He nested his long frame up against her, chest to chest, and draped a heavy arm over her waist.

She half expected to hear him purr in satisfaction. Her entire body was glowing and tingling; it seemed too much effort to move any part of it. Cara rested her head against his sternum, hardly daring to look up into his face.

"Now what?" she whispered shakily.

His wicked chuckle warmed her heart. "Now we have a rest. And then we do it again."

She tilted her head and looked up at him. "*Again?*"

"Oh yes." His tone was weary, yet teasing. "We have a lot of instruction to pack into a few short hours."

"You mean there's *more?*" She shot him an incredulous look. "More than that?"

His lips brushed hers. "Lots more. I promise."

CHAPTER 34

$\mathcal{I}$n the guttering candlelight, Alessandro watched Cara sleep. She lay on her stomach, the dark cloud of her hair rippling around her, and his fingers twitched, anticipating the feel of it again. One of her arms was thrown out, clutching a pillow, and her pale skin glowed like cream against the blood-red velvet of his bedspread.

His body stirred. He wanted her again, even though he'd made love to her in practically every position depicted in that Oriental picture book he'd given her. No wonder she was exhausted, he thought, arrogantly pleased with himself.

With a glimmer of surprise he realized that he was properly in awe of her. She confounded him, tortured him, twisted him in knots. She was brave and fearless, yet still so innocent, despite what they'd just done. His lips quirked in recollection. He'd almost laughed aloud at her stunned expression when he'd grasped her thighs and turned her so she was sitting on top, astride him.

"What are you doing?" she'd murmured, shocked.

"Ride me. Like a horse."

A look of understanding dawned on her face. "Ohh. So *that's* what Ovid meant!"

His face split into a grin. It had been an unusual experience for him. He couldn't remember when sex had ever been this much *fun.* She'd given herself so joyously, so generously.

So lovingly.

His heart pounded. *I love you.* She'd breathed those three incendiary little words against his shoulder, fevered and frantic. His stupid, scarred heart had seized for an instant—and then soaked it up, even as he told himself not to trust what came out of a woman's mouth at a time like that.

She wasn't in love with him. She was in love with some romantic, fictional version of him. And yet when she looked into his eyes it was as if she could see right down to his shattered, broken soul—and accepted him anyway.

He shook his head. *Impossible.* He did *not* need a woman complicating his life. He'd had to fend for himself since he was twelve years old. He was strong, aloof, utterly self-sufficient. If he ever married it would be to a beautiful simpleton—someone who'd stay in his bed and out of his heart.

Cara turned over in her sleep, rubbing her face against the pillow to get comfortable, sliding her arm across the sheets as if seeking him, and Alessandro let out a slow breath. Somewhere during the past week the real Cara di Montessori had melded with his fictional Cara di Montessori—and then surpassed her in every way. Her untutored caresses had affected him more than the practiced moves of any of his more experienced lovers. They'd been interchangeable; pretty faces, bodies like Vanessa's; pleasant but utterly forgettable.

Cara was was more than just another easy conquest, more than he'd ever imagined. So much more than he deserved.

He settled back down beside her. Reaching out his arm, he gathered her into his body and buried his nose in her hair, relishing the silky texture against his lips. She curled against him as if it were the most natural thing in the world and the thought that had been plaguing him all evening came back to haunt him again: *None of the men who'd offered for her deserved her, either.*

* * *

CARA WOKE in her own bed with the scent of him on her skin.

Cara di Montessori. You've done it now.

Del Sarto had stripped her bare. Not just physically, but emotionally too. And she didn't regret it for a minute. Last night had been the best experience of her life: tender and rough, passionate and thrilling. She'd seen a side of him she'd never imagined, a playful, teasing facet of his personality that she was sure he displayed only rarely and only to a select few. She was absurdly pleased that he'd shown it to her.

She stretched, reveling in the unfamiliar aches in her body. She felt like she'd ridden cross-country for a week. So *this* was what it felt like to be a fallen woman.

Last night hadn't changed anything, of course. She would still leave San Rocco—and he'd be glad to see her go. But at least she had this one sublime experience to hold in her mind forever.

Renata entered the room, carrying yet another gown. "Tired this morning are we?" she said archly.

Cara suppressed a yawn. "I didn't sleep well."

Renata gave her a knowing look but refrained from comment. "My lord's taken the men out on a boar hunt. They're not expected back until this evening."

Cara was both relieved and annoyed. Was this a convenient way of avoiding her? Probably. It only delayed their next encounter, but she welcomed the brief respite. She wasn't quite sure how to act when she saw him next.

A few hours later she studied her reflection in the glass with a critical eye. She *glowed*. Pink tinged her cheeks, her lips were full and rosy, and there was a slight bruise on her shoulder from where he'd teethed her. Flushing, she covered it with the neckline of her dress. For the first time in her life she felt like a real woman; mysterious, feminine and desirable.

The din of the remaining guests increased as she descended the main staircase. They were obviously still enjoying Il Diavolo's hospitality to the hilt. She hovered at the doorway, surveying the room. The hall was overly warm, filled almost to overcrowding.

She'd just spotted del Sarto holding court at the far end of the room when Vanessa Canozzi disengaged herself from a group and approached her through the crowd. Cara suppressed a groan as the woman swept her a disparaging glance from head to toe. Her expression suggested she'd rather step on a dead mouse than endure her presence.

"You didn't escape," she said dully.

Cara shrugged. "His lordship caught me."

A sneer disfigured the woman's beautiful face. "Don't think he brought you back because he's falling for you." Her words slid into Cara's ear like poisoned honey. "He just can't bear to lose anything he thinks of as his. I understand him better than anyone." She gave Cara a pitying glance. "You're just a useful pawn to him. A means to an end."

Across the room, del Sarto turned and frowned when he saw her talking to Vanessa. For someone who claimed he disliked the ways of court, he seemed to have no problem negotiating the crowd. He was completely at ease, master of the situation. Women's eyes followed him; hungry, inviting, flirtatious. They discussed him after he'd passed, giggling behind their fans. Men listened intently to his opinion, bending their heads in deference, straining to catch whatever casual comments he let drop, laughing at his wry comments.

Vanessa's smile was pure bitchery as she glanced over the crowd. "Half the men here are suitors for you, you know. Alessandro sent messengers telling everyone to bring their most eligible menfolk."

"I'm aware of that."

"Then you'll also know it was supposed to be *him* cementing this treaty with marriage to a suitable heiress." Vanessa waved an airy hand. "It wouldn't have stopped us from being lovers, of course. He won't give me up, even when he marries." The gems on her fingers glittered malevolently. "Oh, there's my husband calling me!" She smiled, showing sharp white teeth. She reminded Cara of a stoat, sleek and deadly. "Let me give you one piece of friendly advice, my dear." She patted Cara's arm and it was all she could do not to slap her hand away. "Don't wed an old man. I was fifteen when I married my husband, and he was forty-three. He's good to me—lets me take lovers, so long as I'm discreet—but choose yourself a nice young man, if you get the chance. They're so much easier to manage."

Cara stood trembling for several minutes after Vanessa left, trying to get her emotions under control. Del Sarto appeared at her side.

"What was Vanessa saying to you?"

"Nothing of importance."

He accepted her evasion with a shrug. "I've told the Duke of Parma you've accepted his suit. He's delighted."

Cara's stomach dropped to her toes. What had she expected? That he would suddenly declare his undying love just because she'd given herself to him? No. She was beyond such foolish dreams. This was what she'd wanted, a chance to leave San Rocco. She fought to keep her voice steady. "Where is he? The Duke, I mean?"

"He's making preparations to leave."

"So soon?"

"Tomorrow, at first light."

Her head swam. "He expects me to go with him?"

"No. You'll stay here while I have someone prepare the marriage documents. The Duke will ride ahead to prepare for the wedding. Francesco will escort you to Parma next week."

His voice was casual, devoid of emotion, as if he truly didn't care what she did and Cara swallowed a lump of disappointment. Could this be the same man who'd caressed her body, shown her such glory, such passion? She glanced up at his handsome face and misery churned her stomach. Tears stung her eyes but she wrapped dignity around her like a protective cloak. She would not cry. Pride was all she had left. "That sounds perfect."

* * *

As soon as the last of the guests had retired, Renata swept into Alessandro's bedroom without bothering to knock. Ignoring Francesco, who was already there, she fixed her lord and master with a glare the Gorgons would have been proud of. "Is it true? That Cara's betrothed to the Duke of Parma?"

Alessandro raised his brows. Renata was using her best I'm-old-enough-to-be-your-mother tone, a sure sign that he was in for a lecture. Apparently Cara wasn't the only female in the castle who set little store by his deadly reputation.

"I've found Miss Montessori an admirable husband," he said calmly. "You should be congratulating me."

"For breaking the poor girl's heart?"

"She'll survive."

"She'll be happy enough, being a Duchess," Francesco chipped in.

Renata rounded on him, and poked him in the chest. "*You* can shut up! You don't know a damn thing about women, Francesco Neroni. Never have." She turned back to Alessandro, bristling with irritation. "How can you be so cruel? You've used her, and now you're discarding her."

"I'm often noted for my kindness, am I?"

Renata wasn't fooled. She narrowed her eyes at him. "I've seen the way you look at her." Her gaze turned calculating. "It's not like you to let another man take what you want, Sandro."

THE DEVIL TO PAY

"I don't recall asking for your opinion."

She braced her hands on her hips. "Well, you're getting it, wanted or not. She's not like that Canozzi strumpet. She's a decent, gently-bred girl and you're selling her off to a man twice her age."

"He's a good man."

"He's an *old* man."

Francesco cut in again. "And we all know your thoughts on *that* subject, don't we?"

Alessandro raised his brow in question.

"Two boys of twenty-five are better than one man of fifty, according to Renata here," Francesco explained acidly. "Isn't that right?"

"Right!" Renata snapped. "Still, I expect the Duke will do his husbandly duty, despite his advanced years. He's not blind. Even a wizened old goat like him will want to consummate the marriage. He won't be able to keep his hands off her."

"Better an old man's darling than a young man's fool." Alessandro quipped, even though the thought of anyone but himself touching Cara was unthinkable. Really, he was too cruel, not to tell Renata of his decision, but he couldn't prevent himself from playing devil's advocate. Renata was almost as much fun to tease as Cara. "She'll be well taken care of. It's what her father wanted."

Renata gave a growl of frustration. "Do you honestly think that's what she wants? Safety? A life of luxurious boredom?"

"It's the best thing for her."

"What if by some miracle he *doesn't* touch her? You'll be condemning her to a lifetime of celibacy."

Alessandro shrugged. "She can take a lover, as long as she's discreet. And in a few years she'll be a wealthy widow. She'll be able to marry someone of her own choosing, then. Someone younger."

Over his dead body.

He'd come to his momentous decision last night as he'd held Cara in his arms. Renata was right; he couldn't give her up to another man, however worthy they might be. None of the them could protect her as he could.

Renata threw her arms heavenward. "Oh, Lord, *men*! How can you be so stupid?"

Alessandro treated her to his most insolent stare.

Renata glared back at him like he was a simpleton. "You know what? I'm going with her to Parma. What have I got to stick around *here* for?" She turned on her heel and stormed magnificently from the room.

Francesco let out a long whistle.

Alessandro nodded toward the door. "Aren't you going after her?"

Francesco shrugged. "She's a grown woman. She can do what she likes. I've got no hold over her."

Alessandro poured two goblets of wine and handed one to his friend, who took it, then frowned. "She's right, though. You're not truly sending Cara away with the Duke, are you?"

"No."

Francesco slapped his palm on the table. "I knew it! You have a plan."

"I do. First I'm going to remove the threat of her uncle, as promised. And then I'm going to marry her myself."

Francesco raised his brows and shot him a shrewd look. "To get your hands on Castelleon?"

"And because I owe it to Ercolo's memory to protect her. As you pointed out, none of those other suitors are up to the job. I can't leave her alone and defenseless."

Alessandro wasn't prepared to admit to any other motive for his sudden change of heart. Those were both logical, sensible, *unemotional* reasons.

"But why tell everyone she's accepted the Duke?" Francesco frowned.

"Her uncle has informants here. I've led them to believe that Cara will be leaving tomorrow for Parma."

"You think Lorenzo will attack the convoy?"

"I'm sure of it. Men like him are boringly predictable. His desire to eliminate Cara overrides everything, even his good sense."

"And the Duke's agreed to go along with this deception? He knows he won't be marrying her?"

"He does. He was disappointed—until he heard how much I was willing to pay him for his co-operation. I've told him to expect an attack. And to leave Lorenzo to me."

CHAPTER 35

*C*ara was up and ready to leave at dawn.

She was *not* going to sit around and wait for her betrothed to send for her, like some errant piece of luggage. Another week in the company of del Sarto was more than her bruised heart—and her dented pride—could bear. The hours she'd spent in his bed had been unforgettable, extraordinary, but if she stayed she was afraid she would succumb to the temptation again and again.

She'd just been one more willing body to him, a bit of novelty for his jaded palate. In six months he probably wouldn't even remember her name. To allow herself to become even more deeply entangled with him would be a fatal mistake.

The Duke had brought a large retinue with him. She would sneak down to the stables and hide herself in one of the baggage carts. Then, when they were safely away from San Rocco, she would reveal herself and convince him to take her to Parma rather than return her to Il Diavolo.

She felt guilty for manipulating him; he seemed like a nice man, but—damn it—she didn't *want* a nice man. She wanted del Sarto. The very antithesis of a nice man. She must be insane.

With renewed urgency she strode to the door and turned the handle. It was locked. She twisted the knob again and tugged harder, but it remained stubbornly closed. Anger and disbelief rose in her chest. Del Sarto had locked her in! She stifled a hysterical laugh. Was he suspicious of her easy agreement to marry the Duke? Did he think she'd try to wriggle out of this agreement too? He was right, of course—she had no intention of marrying the Duke. Curse the sneaky devil for knowing her so well!

Cara took a deep breath. She was resourceful. She would *not* be thwarted by the high-handed whim of some self-important, uncaring, contemptuous . . . she wasn't even *thinking* of the cold-hearted beast.

She tried the door that led to his chambers but that, too, was locked and the window provided no escape since the pruning of the chestnut tree outside.

Cara sat down on the bed, throughly irritated. Well, she'd just have to wait until one of the servants came to bid her rise. Presumably del Sarto wasn't going to keep her locked in her chambers until the marriage documents were completed and the Duke sent for her.

The sound of someone trying to open the door made her leap up. Renata's urgent whisper came from the other side of the wood. "My Lady? Why have you locked the door? Are you well?"

"It wasn't me!" Cara hissed back indignantly. "It must have been del Sarto. Do you have a key?"

"One moment."

Renata's muffled footsteps disappeared along the corridor, and a few minutes later Cara heard a grating in the lock. Renata slipped inside and eyed Cara's travel outfit of shirt and breeches without surprise.

"Didn't think you'd want to stay another week with Sandro," she said succinctly. "Are you planning to leave with Parma?"

Cara nodded. "I know I'm supposed to stay here until the marriage settlements are done, but I just can't."

"Then I'm coming with you."

"To Parma? But what about Francesco—?"

The wistful, regretful look on Renata's face spoke volumes. It echoed Cara's sentiments towards del Sarto perfectly.

"Francesco and I?" Renata said finally. "It's complicated. There's attraction between us, true, but I'm too old for him. The man needs children. He should marry some silly young thing and settle down."

Cara made a sound of protest.

"I've been married twice already," Renata said gently. "The first time, we were both eighteen. Marco was killed six months later and I stayed with the army because I had nowhere else to go. I bartered for food, cooked, helped set up the camp. I got plenty more offers of marriage and finally accepted one of the captains. Figured an older man might have more luck staying alive."

She shrugged wryly. "He fell from his horse and broke his neck. After that, I lost my appetite for marriage. So many men needed caring for it seemed pointless to tie myself to just one of them." Her eyes took on a faraway look. "Some of them were so young, away from home for the first time. They needed someone to mother them. Others just wanted the comfort of a soft touch to help them forget the horrors they'd seen. I gave them that. Which I suppose makes me a whore." Her defiant gaze flashed to Cara's. "I don't regret it for a minute."

Cara found she had no words to say. A month ago she'd probably have disapproved, but the events of the past week had made her question her own moral compass. She was hardly as pure as the driven snow herself. Who was she to judge?

Her silence didn't seem to bother Renata. She shook her head as if to clear it of memories. "So, anyway, what's the point in marrying Francesco? He knows I'd sleep with him if he asked.

But he never has. Instead, he treats me like a lady and I can't bear it. I don't deserve it!"

"Everyone deserves to be loved," Cara said softly.

Renata gave a sniff. "When I threatened to go to Parma with you, he didn't even try to stop me."

"Maybe he thought he was being noble?"

"Nobility's just for books," Renata said bitterly. "Unfortunately, other than marriage, there aren't many options open to us women. You can either be a nun, a wife, or a whore."

"Well, I tried being a nun," Cara confessed wryly. "I only lasted a week. It was before my father sent me to St John's. He offered to finance a new altarpiece for the Sisters of Mercy in Siena if they'd take me. I'd only been there six days when everyone was struck down with a mysterious bout of food poisoning. I was sent home to recuperate."

Renata caught the twinkle in her eye and gave a scandalized gasp. "You *poisoned* the *nuns*? Shame on you!"

"I was desperate! And in my defense, I got just as sick as they did because I ate the stew myself to stop any suspicion falling on me. Luckily, by the time I'd recovered, I'd convinced father I wasn't cut out for a nun's life."

"And, let's face it, you'd make a terrible courtesan," Renata sighed. "Don't look so insulted! You've got the looks, but your heart wouldn't be in it." She patted Cara's hand. "There's no shame in sleeping with a man you love." She eyed her closely. "And you do love him, don't you?"

"I don't know who you're talking about."

Renata raised a disbelieving brow.

"Oh, all right," Cara said crossly. "Yes. I do. Not that he deserves it, the heartless pig." She hoisted her meagre bundle of belongings and gestured toward the door. "Are there any guards posted outside?"

Renata shook her head.

"In that case, let's go."

They reached the stables without mishap and took advantage of the hustle and bustle of countless servants preparing for their master's departure. Coaches were being piled high with trunks, horses saddled, last-minute additions thrown onto the carts. Spotting a heavily-laden covered wagon bearing the Duke of Parma's arms on the side, Cara and Renata climbed inside and concealed themselves amongst the assorted trunks and house-hold furnishings the Duke had deemed necessary for his stay.

As they trundled over the cobbled streets and beneath the city gates Cara breathed a wistful sigh. Freedom. At the cost of her heart.

CHAPTER 36

𝒶bbot Andreo Bernotti entered the walls of Torre di San Rocco and uttered a heartfelt prayer of thanks. He was almost seventy; far too old for this sort of thing.

He'd been gallivanting all over the countryside ever since Ercolo had brought his daughter to the hallowed halls of St. John's. From the moment he'd laid eyes on Cara di Montessori, he hadn't had a minute's peace. The girl was like a force of nature, always getting herself into one scrape or another. Andreo smiled fondly in memory. He wouldn't have it any other way. He loved the child, despite her innumerable flaws.

Wishing he had time to appreciate the impressive architecture —this entranceway alone was a masterpiece of the stonemason's art—he dismounted and hobbled stiffly up the steps of the castle, pausing halfway up to catch his breath. A servant greeted him courteously at the top.

"May I help you, Father?"

Andreo wheezed as he mounted the last step. "I must see my Lord del Sarto. Immediately."

"Speak of the devil and he appears," came an ironic voice from the hallway.

Andreo jumped as Il Diavolo himself materialized from a door on the right and bowed low. "What can I do for you, Father?"

Andreo regarded him from beneath his bushy white eyebrows. "Greetings, my lord. I've heard much about you over the years."

"None of it good, I'll wager."

"I prefer to judge for myself," Andreo said calmly. "My Lord Ercolo spoke highly of you. It is a pleasure to finally meet you. I'm Fra Bernotti, Abbot of the monastery of St. John. I've come to see my charge, Cara. I have reason to believe she came here to you?"

"She did indeed."

"Was she injured?"

"Nothing too serious."

The Abbott let out a relieved sigh. "Thank the Lord. When I heard of Ercolo's death and her disappearance I feared the worst." He frowned. "But on my way through the town I heard the most incredible rumor; that she's become engaged to the Duke of Parma!"

"Their betrothal was announced last night."

Andreo's mouth dropped open in surprise. "But Cara? *Engaged*? Are we talking about the same girl?"

Il Diavolo's mouth curled up at one corner. "Irritating little baggage, about this high," he held his flattened palm horizontal at mid-chest height, "—hair like a bird's nest, never stops arguing?"

Andreo eyed him speculatively. "Well, that certainly *sounds* like her." He steadied himself on a nearby hall chair. "You amaze me, my son. Are you *sure*? I would have wagered the entire contents of St. John's coffers that she would never willingly agree to marry anyone. Or abandon her people and her home." He frowned suspiciously. "What have you done to her? Was Ercolo's trust in you misplaced?"

Del Sarto shook his head. "It was not. In fact, the Duke was her own choice."

Andreo shot him a questioning glance. He was about to demand further explanation when a servant interrupted them.

"Apologies, my lord, but Lorenzo di Montessori has been sighted ten leagues from here, heading north."

Del Sarto nodded. "He'll try to intercept the Duke on the Fontana Pass. Tell Captain Neroni to ready the men. We ride immediately."

Andreo frowned in alarm. "What's this? Is Cara riding with the Duke? Is she in danger?

Il Diavolo paused in the act of donning his leather riding gloves. "No, Father. Your charge is safely upstairs, locked in her room for her own safety. She and I made a bargain. I agreed to rid her of Lorenzo—and I am about to do just that."

Andreo crossed himself at the gleam of unholy menace that had appeared in the other man's expression. "What are you planning, del Sarto? Remember, it is a sin to harm another of God's creatures, however deserving they might be. 'Vengeance is mine, sayeth the Lord.'"

The wicked, anticipatory smile that curved del Sarto's mouth was not reassuring. "Sometimes the Lord's not fast enough for my liking, Father."

Andreo gave a resigned sigh. "Hmm. Well, then, I shall pray for your safe return."

Il Diavolo gave a dark laugh. "Save your prayers for Lorenzo." He turned to another servant. "Massimo, tell Signorina Montessori that the Abbot is here, and escort her downstairs." He turned back to the Abbot. "I trust you can make yourself comfortable in my absence, Father?"

Andreo waved him away. "Of course. I shall put my trust in the Almighty."

Del Sarto's eyes glittered with amusement. "Fine words. But I met a Bedouin once who said 'trust in God, but always tie up your camel.' So if it's all the same to you, I'll take my sword, as well as your blessing, to deal with Lorenzo."

Andreo gave a chuckle as Il Diavolo strode to the door. "God speed, my son."

Del Sarto turned abruptly on the threshold. "It's a good thing you're here, Father. When I return, you can officiate at Cara's wedding."

"To the Duke?"

Del Sarto's smile flashed. "Oh no. To me."

CHAPTER 37

*C*ara huddled in the corner of the carriage, sick and tired of being jolted around. She rolled her shoulders. She didn't *feel* like a fallen woman. She felt rather good, in fact. A bit sore in interesting places, maybe, but it was as if her body had been awakened by Alessandro's touch. She felt . . . more. More aware of her clothing touching her body, the linen of her shift rubbing against her stomach and her breasts.

She shifted in her seat, her cheeks heating in memory. *Damn the man.* What had he done to her? He called *her* a witch, but she was the one under his spell. He was like some dark magician, making her feel things that ought to have her in confession fervently praying for absolution—even when he was leagues away.

She banged her head against the side panel of the carriage, relishing the jolt of pain. Maybe it would knock some sense into her.

The Duke rode past, his cloak blowing behind him, and she ducked down to avoid being seen, but he paid her no heed, scanning the road ahead instead.

The carriage wheels hit a rut and she grasped the side. It had been hours since they'd left San Rocco. At first they'd passed through rolling farmland, with rippling fields of wheat and neatly tended rows of vines, but recently the landscape had grown more sparse, the farmsteads more isolated. The lush fields had given way to grazing pastures, and then they'd entered the wooded slopes of some low foothills.

Renata was dozing on a trunk opposite her, huddled under a fur rug. Cara gazed listlessly at the passing trees. She'd never felt so utterly dispirited.

The road became narrower and the trees closer together as they entered some kind of narrow gorge, climbing a path cut into one side. Steep slopes rose on either side and the Duke's men were forced to slow their pace and spread out in single file. The rutted track was barely wide enough for the carriage and Cara peered out, watching as the crumbling edge came increasingly close to the wheels.

They passed a few narrow bridges as they climbed, barely more than rows of wooden planks held together with ropes, and she suppressed a sudden quiver of unease. It was too quiet, too still. There was no birdsong, no chirp of cicadas. Nothing to break the unnatural stillness. Dense forest to one side, deep gorge to the other. *Nowhere to run.*

No sooner had the thought entered her mind than a shout went up from the riders ahead and the cart lurched to a halt. She peered out from between the fabric covering. A single horseman blocked the path ahead and she sucked in a horrified gasp as she recognized the rider.

Renata came awake with a start. "What is it? Why have we stopped? Are we there?"

"It's my uncle!" Cara hissed. *Oh, God. Her father had died in an ambush just like this.* She scanned the carriage for weapons; she had the dagger in her boot, but that was all.

As if to confirm her fears, a group of riders appeared behind Lorenzo and a line of archers came out of the trees, arrows notched in their crossbows. The duke's men formed a protective ring around the coach and horses, drawing their weapons in alarm, but Cara choked back a sob. However well trained they were, the Duke's men were grossly outnumbered. Lorenzo had no mercy. There would be a massacre.

"Perhaps I wasn't clear enough in my request." Lorenzo's voice carried across the clearing. "I'm merely asking for what is mine."

He sounded eminently reasonable, for a madman.

The duke spurred forward. "Your niece is betrothed to me."

"She's promised to my son, Piero. Hand her over and I'll let you and your men go on your way unharmed."

The duke drew his sword. "You murdered her father."

Lorenzo's face darkened. "Step aside, old man."

Cara wanted to scream at the duke for being so foolhardy, even as she appreciated his loyalty. Lorenzo turned his horse and she held her breath, hoping he was leaving, but when he reached the trees he gave a hand signal and his archers released a volley of arrows.

Renata screamed as the rider nearest to them was thrown from his rearing mount, an arrow embedded in his thigh. More arrows thudded into the side of the cart.

Cara thrust her to the floor. "Get down. Whatever you do, do *not* come out after me!"

She leapt out of the cart, dagger drawn, in time to see the duke parry an attack from three of Lorenzo's men. He knocked one to the ground and lunged forward, but was quickly set upon by the others.

"Stop!" She ran forward to help him, but it was too late; he'd already been disarmed. His men lowered their weapons and Cara breathed a grateful prayer that he hadn't been killed. Yet.

Two of Lorenzo's men seized her and marched her forward and the duke gazed at her in horror.

"My Lady! You're supposed to be safe at San Rocco!"

Cara sent him an apologetic glance.

Lorenzo grinned in triumph. "Ah, my niece! Well met. It was foolish of you to run from me."

As if she were an errant schoolgirl caught skipping her lessons.

"Your presence is required at Castelleon."

Cara glared at him.

"I regret to deprive you of your fiancé here, but don't worry. I'm providing you with another." Lorenzo gestured behind him. "Piero!"

Cara watched her cousin's approach through narrowed eyes. He was near her own age, tall and thin, with pale grey eyes, dark hair and pallid skin. His face was twisted in a grimace of distaste. He clearly didn't want to marry her any more than she wanted to marry him. How lowering.

Her uncle shot the young man a glance of acute dislike. "Oh, for God's sake, boy, stop looking like that!"

"My lord!"

Lorenzo frowned at the interruption, but brightened when he saw Renata being dragged from the coach, fists and hair flying. "What do we have here?" He turned to Cara to gauge her reaction. "Your maid?"

Cara blanched at the malevolent glint in his eye. "Let her go."

"And have her run back to San Rocco telling tales? I don't think so." He addressed the soldier holding her. "Kill her."

"No!"

The man ignored Cara's cry of denial but, to her surprise, he looked past Lorenzo to another, pale-haired man for affirmation. The stocky, bearded soldier gave a subtle shake of the head and addressed Lorenzo.

"Leave the woman alone. You have your niece, as we agreed. We don't kill unarmed innocents." He pointed to the duke and his men, being held at sword-point. "They're no threat to you now. Let them leave."

Lorenzo's face turned an unattractive shade of purple. "I'm paying you to do what I tell you!"

Cara blinked. These men must be mercenaries he'd paid to assist him—who apparently still had some shred of honor.

Lorenzo yanked Renata from the soldiers' grip, infuriated by the man's disobedience. She let forth a torrent of abuse and sank her teeth into his forearm.

"Silly bitch!" He backhanded her across the jaw, his face mottled with fury, then grabbed his dagger from his belt and thrust it deep into Renata's stomach.

Cara screamed.

Renata let out a strangled gasp and folded forward like a child's rag doll. Lorenzo pushed her body away from him, watching dispassionately as she crumpled to the ground and lay face down, utterly motionless. He wiped his blade on the front of his tunic.

"Seems I have to do everything myself." His lip curled at the captain's expression of disgust. "What's this? A mercenary who quails at the sight of blood? You're in the wrong profession, my friend."

"You bastard!" Cara's horrified struggles brought his attention back to her. Despite having both arms restrained, she still managed to kick him as he approached. He sidestepped her flailing legs and grabbed her hair.

"Shut up, you little bitch." His breath hissed in her ear. His dagger prodded her ribs. "You're only alive because I suffer it. Don't make the mistake of believing you're indispensable. You'll marry your cousin or end up just like your friend and your sainted father." Signaling to the soldiers to release her, he urged her forward. "Hold them until we're away," he shot at the captain. "Then kill them or not, as you see fit."

He pulled Cara towards the tree line, his wiry strength surprising her. Her scalp stung from his hold on her hair, but she dug her heels into the ground and tried to twist away. She received a stinging blow on the cheek for her efforts. She staggered, barely keeping her feet, as Lorenzo pushed her onwards.

"Think I don't know what you've been up to?" he snarled in her ear. "Spreading your legs for that whoreson del Sarto. Oh, yes, I have my spies. At least the marriage bed won't hold any surprises for you."

He pulled her closer, his rancid breath hot on her face. "You'd better not be breeding that bastard's brat. I want a legitimate heir for Castelleon." He glanced over at his son. "And if Piero there isn't man enough for the job, I'll be delighted to do it for him."

Cara's blood ran cold as she realized what he was suggesting. She cringed away from him in revulsion.

Lorenzo pressed his dagger to her side and prodded her forward—and then stopped dead, staring at the tree line as if seeing the devil himself.

CHAPTER 38

ara blinked. Her ears were ringing from Lorenzo's blow, and she shook her head, certain what she was seeing was an apparition. Her overwrought mind was dreaming up a vision of the one thing she most wanted to see: del Sarto sauntering casually out of the trees.

He looked real enough. Sunlight glinted off his dark hair and flashed on his sword, which was still sheathed. A menacing smile hovered at the corners of his mouth and his eyes glittered with deadly promise.

"You'll pay for that," he said calmly to Lorenzo.

Not a dream.

He came forward with a cocky swagger and was immediately surrounded by soldiers, but he gave their blades a scathing glance and carried on walking toward her and Lorenzo, stopping a few paces away.

"Well, well. Il Diavolo." Lorenzo scanned the tree line as he spoke. "You're just in time to congratulate me. My niece has just agreed to marry my son."

"I have not!" Cara growled.

Del Sarto's gaze didn't even flick to her. His attention was focused on her uncle, as unblinking as a falcon with a rabbit in its sights. "She doesn't sound very keen," he drawled. "And besides, she belongs to me."

Cara's heart gave a funny little flutter.

Lorenzo turned to the mercenary on his left. "What are you waiting for? Disarm him!"

The man shot him a look that clearly said, '*you do it*'.

Del Sarto surprised them all. He unbuckled his sword belt and surrendered his weapon to the nearest soldier.

Cara narrowed her eyes. All those years of warfare must have addled his brain. Admittedly, he could probably still kill all the men around him with his bare hands, but even so, it didn't make any sense. Where were his troops? Francesco? Saraceno?

Lorenzo looked as confused as she felt. He shot a nervous glance at her cousin. "Piero, come on."

Del Sarto took another step forward.

"Stay where you are!" Lorenzo commanded. He whirled Cara round so that her back was pressed against his chest, clamped an arm around her waist, and pressed the tip of his dagger to her throat. "We're going back to that bridge. Don't come any closer or I'll put a knife in her. I mean it!"

Del Sarto's lips quirked. "No, you won't. You don't have the balls for it. You didn't even have the guts to kill your own brother yourself. You got your hirelings to do it for you."

He walked forward, unchecked. The men surrounding him were watching in stupefied fascination, as if he held each one under a spell.

"Seize him!" Nerves raised Lorenzo's voice to a squeak.

Del Sarto turned towards the leader of the mercenaries. "I heard a rumor you were working for this piece of shit, Kaspar. I thought you had better taste."

The commander's mouth broke into a smile which transformed his grim countenance. He grasped del Sarto's outstretched hand and gave a theatrical shrug. "What can I say? A man's got to eat."

Lorenzo gasped. "You *know* each other?"

Del Sarto sent him a mocking smile. "Unfortunately for you, the world of European warfare's rather small. We've fought together several times."

"How's the shoulder?" the mercenary asked.

"Took a while to heal, but it's better now. Whatever this bastard's paying you, I'll double it."

The mercenary nodded amiably. "I've no quarrel with you." He sheathed his sword and his men did the same. Weapons disappeared into scabbards all around the clearing.

Lorenzo hissed in outrage. "You faithless bastards!"

The captain shrugged and turned back to del Sarto. "Want me to stay?"

"No. I'll deal with this. Take your men to San Rocco. I'll meet you there and settle up."

The mercenary gestured towards Cara—who was still in Lorenzo's grasp. "If I'd known she was anything to do with you, I'd have left well alone." He returned del Sarto's sword. "He told me it was a simple kidnap-and-ransom job."

"No harm done." Del Sarto rebuckled the blade around his waist with the ease of long practice and finally turned his mocking gaze on Cara. "Signorina Montessori, may I introduce Kaspar von Silenen, leader of this fine band."

The captain nodded to her briefly, then turned back to del Sarto. "See you back at San Rocco, then. You'd better have some good wine."

Cara felt light-headed. The whole situation was surreal. Both men seemed to have forgotten the fact that she still had *a knife pressed to her throat*. She watched in disbelief as the mercenary band disappeared into the woods as silently as they had arrived.

To everyone's surprise, her cousin spoke up.

"Let us leave, Diavolo, and we'll give you back the girl."

Lorenzo hissed in fury. "Shut up, you little prick! We're not here to negotiate. Get across that bridge."

Piero shrugged, obviously accustomed to such a tone from his father.

Del Sarto gave a low whistle. Francesco, Saraceno, and twenty of his own men emerged from the trees. He drew a dagger from his belt and tossed it from one hand to the other with unnerving accuracy.

Lorenzo cleared his throat. "Stay back or I'll kill her, I swear I will."

He backed up, pulling Cara with him. She had no choice but to go, and she shot del Sarto a pleading glance. Lorenzo's hands were shaking so hard that his blade nicked her skin; she felt a trickle of blood run down her neck.

Del Sarto saw it, and his eyes narrowed. Without taking his eyes off Lorenzo, he addressed Francesco. "See to Renata."

Francesco hurried forward and knelt down next to her body, feeling for a pulse. "She's not dead!" His voice quavered with relief as he stroked Renata's hair back from her face.

"Pity. I thought I'd killed the bitch." Lorenzo slanted another quick glance at his son. "Piero, get over that bridge. Now."

Piero did as he was told. His crossing sent the thin rope bridge swaying back and forth over the gorge. Lorenzo kept Cara tight against his chest, using her as a human shield as he drew them both towards it.

The dry wooden boards creaked as they backed over it and the slightest movement made the whole thing lurch alarmingly. Cara put her hands out to the ropes to steady herself, keeping her eyes fixed on del Sarto. He was coming closer. Could she duck Lorenzo's blade and throw herself into his arms? A quick glance at the dizzying drop below her made her discard that plan. Her stomach heaved. It would be far too easy to topple over the side instead.

"That's it. Slowly." Lorenzo's hot breath by her ear made her stomach pitch even more. "Nearly there."

Del Sarto put his foot onto the bridge as they reached the far side, where three horses were waiting.

"Stay where you are!" Lorenzo shifted his hold on Cara and slashed one of the supporting ropes. It snapped with a twang and the bridge lurched to one side, swinging and bouncing over the precipice.

Del Sarto leapt back, only his unnaturally fast reflexes preventing him from falling, and Lorenzo threw him a triumphant, gloating look across the narrow gap. "Oh dear. It'll never take your weight now. And it's too far to jump, even for the great Diavolo."

Seizing her chance, Cara threw herself sideways and made a grab for the knife, catching Lorenzo's wrist in her hands. He staggered back and shoved her hard against the rock wall. Her head banged against the stone and she loosened her grip, momentarily stunned.

Lorenzo raised his arm to hit her but then dropped the blade with a sudden howl of pain. He stared in disbelief at the dagger protruding from his arm, then back across the chasm at del Sarto, who was already poised to throw another.

The horses, frightened by the noise, pulled free from Piero's hold. One backed up, blocking del Sarto's second shot. Lorenzo released his hold on Cara, grabbed the reins, and hauled himself up into the saddle, staying low as he made a grab for her arm. The sleeve of her dress ripped as she ducked under the horse's belly to evade him and Lorenzo struggled to control his mount on the narrow path. It reared and Cara stumbled, trying to avoid both the pounding hooves and the edge of the ravine. She could barely see anything through the choking cloud of dust kicked up by the horses' hooves.

Lorenzo lunged at her. At first she thought he was trying to pull her up, on to the horse, but then his face creased in a murderous smile. "Little bitch!" he panted madly. "Give my regards to your father!"

He gave her chest a savage shove.

Cara staggered back. With a cry of alarm Piero lunged toward her, his hand outstretched to pull her back from the edge, but nothing could stop her backward momentum. The path disintegrated beneath her feet and suddenly the entire hillside seemed to be moving, a terrifying blur of noise and confusion.

Cara clawed at the rock sliding past in front of her. As she scrabbled blindly for purchase, one of her hands caught a sapling growing out of a crack in the rock and she clutched at it with all her might. Showers of stones fell all around her, bouncing and rolling down the steep slope and into the chasm below. Her shoulder screamed in protest as it supported her entire weight.

The rockslide slowed, leaving a dull rumble like thunder in its wake. Dust hung heavy in the air, and showers of loose scree rained down upon her head, but the worst appeared to be over.

She could barely breathe. She groped around with her free hand but the cliff was so chalky that it crumbled beneath her fingertips. Kicking her legs, she finally gained a foothold on a ledge off to one side. Rocks dug into her stomach and she closed her eyes, panting, coughing, savoring the pain as proof that she was—miraculously—still alive.

She wasn't falling any further down, but she couldn't move from her present position, either. She was completely stuck. She had grit in her eye and she longed to scratch it, but she was barely holding on with her fingers. She turned her head, braving a look downwards for her cousin, and smothered a moan. Piero's body lay only a few feet below her on a rocky outcrop, half-covered in rubble. She couldn't see his face, but the unnatural angle of his limbs told her without a doubt that he was dead. Guilt and nausea racked her; he'd been trying to save her. *Oh, God.*

Her arms began to shake. She swallowed the dust in her mouth and let out a tiny croak.

Pathetic.

She tried again and nearly sobbed with relief when she heard del Sarto calling her name high above her head.

"Cara! Stay there! Don't move."

Despite her dire situation, she was struck by a morbid flash of humor. *Where did he think she was going to go?*

"My lord, take care!" Francesco's voice echoed down.

She risked a glance upwards, but couldn't see anything except for rocky slope and a patch of blue sky. Then the blue disappeared as the underbelly of a black horse sailed overhead.

The madman had jumped the ravine!

The clatter of hooves above her head confirmed it, and moments later del Sarto's grim face appeared over the edge. "Close your eyes," he ordered. "I'm coming down to get you."

He tied a rope around his waist and started backing down the scree slope, dislodging stones as he went. Cara flinched as she was struck by a rock larger than her fist. Swearing, she gripped the branch tighter and squeezed her eyes closed against the dust.

Del Sarto reached her side; his strong arms encircled her waist. "It's all right, sweeting. I've got you."

She managed an incoherent wail and tightened her white-knuckled grip on her twig.

"You'll have to let go of the branch, Cara." He sounded almost amused.

She pried her eyes open. "Don't you dare drop me! I'm too young to die!"

He chuckled. "You're too *stubborn* to die. I won't drop you, I swear. That's it." His voice was gentle, crooning. He spoke to Saraceno with that tone. "Hold on to me."

Cara threw one arm, then the other, around his neck, and held on for dear life. She didn't care if she was choking him. She pressed her face into his shoulder, absorbing the safety of his body. A monster he might be, but she had utter faith in his ability to rescue her.

He gave a shrill whistle and they began to move upwards; he must have tied the other end of the rope to Saraceno. He kept them away from the rock with his legs, holding the rope with one hand and supporting her waist with the other. Cara's ribs felt like they would crack, but better a broken rib or two than a plummet to the bottom.

When they finally reached the top she couldn't seem to let go. Del Sarto dragged her away from the edge and laid her on her back, prying her stiff arms from around his neck. She gazed up at the waving pine branches and scudding clouds as he ran his hands over her body, checking for broken bones with brisk efficiency. He found a cut on her head and scowled as he wiped a streak of blood from her temple. His face was pale and smudged with dirt and he looked unaccountably fierce.

Cara frowned, her thoughts fuzzy and disjointed. "I don't know why you're angry with me," she mumbled. "I didn't throw *myself* off the cliff."

He lifted her, his arms gentle, and she heard a dim cheer from across the ravine.

"I can't jump back over with two," he shouted back to Francesco. "We'll find a lower bridge. Take Renata home and send for the surgeon."

Cara barely registered the conversation. Her head was too heavy. She let it loll back against his arm. Del Sarto glanced down at her, a worried look in his eyes. *That was nice.* He might be a *little* concerned for her.

"Don't you dare faint!" he growled.

She managed an unladylike snort. She *never* fainted. She'd told him that several times. Still, it wouldn't hurt to have a little rest. She was feeling a bit lightheaded and he obviously had things under control. She closed her eyes and sank into the darkness with a grateful sigh.

CHAPTER 39

*C*ara hurt all over—which presumably meant she wasn't dead. Recollection came flooding back. "Oh, God. Renata! The Duke!" She tried to sit up, but found herself seated across del Sarto's lap, on Saraceno's back. His gloved hand pressed her head back to his shoulder.

"They're both fine."

"Truly?"

"Renata's wounded, but she'll live. The Duke's a little shaken, but otherwise unhurt."

* * *

Cara turned her head into his neck as her body began to shake. Alessandro thought she had hiccoughs, and was about to tease her about it, until he realized with a jolt of shock that she was crying. Silently, too proud to make a sound in front of him.

He'd never seen her cry. He'd seen her angry, frustrated, murderous even, but never resorting to tears. His heart, or something in that region of his chest anyway, ached for her. He loosened his arm and to his surprise she didn't use the freedom to pull away. Instead she burrowed closer, ducking her head so it nestled under his chin. Her hot tears trickled down the bare skin of his neck where his shirt was parted and his body, ever unhelpful, responded to her nearness. Even filthy, bloodied, and her crying her eyes out, he still found her attractive. Hell, he'd have to be *dead* not to find her attractive.

He cast around for a topic to divert his attention. "Did I ever tell you about female mercenaries?"

That piqued her interest, as he'd known it would. The shaking stopped. Her head came up. She sniffed.

"I've never heard of any." Her voice was muffled, croaky.

"Of course you haven't. Men don't like to advertise when they're bested by a woman." He felt her smile against his neck and continued. "My favorite's Onorata Rodiana. She started out as an artist. The lord of Cremona commissioned her to paint a fresco, but when she was assaulted by one of his staff she stabbed her attacker and fled, dressed as a man. By the time they called off the search for her, she'd joined a band of condottieri—still in male disguise. She eventually became leader of her own mercenary troupe and excelled at banditry for the next thirty or so years. She died, sword in hand, fighting the Venetians, about forty years ago. Her femininity was only discovered on her death-bed."

Alessandro glanced down at Cara. "Now you have a new heroine to model yourself on."

She gave a watery sniff. "I admire anyone who stands up for themselves and fights their own battles."

He chuckled, relieved. She might be battered and bruised, but her spirit was still intact.

* * *

CARA WAS MORTIFIED that she'd broken down in front of del Sarto. *She never cried.* In fact, she'd often envied Bianca's ability to produce floods of tears—or at least prettily moistened eyes—on demand.

She raised her head reluctantly as he reined in. The light was fading, the forest growing more indistinct around them. The sound of running water came from nearby and there was a strange, salty odor in the air. It was slightly medicinal, but not unpleasant.

"Why have we stopped?"

Del Sarto dismounted, still holding her in his arms. He pushed through the undergrowth and stopped at the edge of a wide pool. Mist swirled and danced over the surface of the water and Cara glanced around in wonder.

"These are the baths of San Casciano—natural hot springs known for their healing properties. You look like you could do with a wash." He smiled as he set her on her feet. "In the daytime it's crowded with travelers. People come from miles around to swim."

He shrugged out of his leather jerkin and let it drop to the floor. "Come on." He peeled his shirt over his head and threw it aside, utterly unselfconscious, tugged off his leather boots, then untied the laces of his breeches.

Cara's strangled squeak earned her a droll glance.

"What? You've seen me naked before." He bent at the waist and stripped off his breeches.

The man was the fastest undresser in the whole of Italy! She caught the barest glimpse of sculpted back and toned backside before he lowered himself into the water. He let out a long sigh and swam to the opposite side of the pool, then turned and shot her a wickedly inviting glance. "Coming in?"

She tried to clear the tantalizing vision of all that naked flesh from her mind, thankful for the encroaching darkness that hid her blushes. "Fine. But only because I'm filthy. Turn around so I can undress."

"I won't peek."

And pigs might fly! Ducking behind a tree, she stripped, wincing as her hair caught on the dried blood at her hairline. She must look an absolute wreck. She poked her head around the tree. "Are your eyes closed?"

"Yes."

She couldn't see him from across the pool. She slipped forward, using her underskirt as a shield, and dipped one toe into the water. It was surprisingly warm, hotter than she took her baths. She dropped the shift and slipped under the surface with a groan of bliss.

"Now that's a view to raise any man's spirits."

"You said you weren't watching!"

White teeth flashed as he chuckled, totally unrepentant. "I keep telling you not to take my word for anything. Mercenary, remember? I take what I can get. Especially when it's free."

Struggling not to smile, Cara ducked beneath the water, luxuriating in the warmth, tasting the slight saltiness on her tongue. Resurfacing, she settled herself as far away from him as possible, given the confines of the pool.

Fingers of mist rose around them. Ferns and mosses crowded round, and the tree canopy above filtered the moonlight into dappled shapes that danced on the water. The whole effect was magical, primeval. It was so quiet, so private; as if they were the only two people in the world, and this the Garden of Eden.

And like Eve, the secretive pull of forbidden attraction was thrumming through Cara's blood.

You should put your clothes back on and go sit on the side.

Ha.

Del Sarto disappeared under the water and she scanned the surface warily, suspecting a trick. Sure enough, he surfaced less than three feet away. Slowly, so slowly she could have moved away, he reached forward and took her hand, turning it over to inspect her palm, which was crisscrossed with scratches and scrapes. He smoothed the pad of his thumb over the lines with a tenderness that made the blood pound in her veins.

His eyes narrowed as he studied the cut on her forehead. "Your uncle's a dead man." He washed the blood from her temple, his gentle touch at odds with hi fierce expression.

"For hurting me?" she croaked.

He nodded and moved closer to place his lips on the cut, so softly it made her want to cry. Cara couldn't move. She was spell-bound by his touch, watching him out of half-closed eyes, accepting his ministrations as if he were her lady's maid. When he lifted his lips from her skin she felt their loss as an ache in her soul.

"Accepting the Duke's proposal was a stupid decision," he murmured.

Her annoyance resurfaced in a rush. "I didn't have much choice, as I recall!"

"You don't want him," he continued as if she hadn't spoken. "You want me."

Cara scowled and he slanted her a simmering glance from under his wet hair. "It's good, honest lust, Cara. Admit it. He can't make you feel like I do."

He leaned closer and her heart rate kicked up another notch, as if she'd been running hard. She could feel her body leaning in to his, as if drawn by some invisible force.

"He doesn't make you burn." His voice was low and wicked. "Whereas I can have you screaming my name in less than five minutes."

"Only in exasperation," she said tartly. The arrogance of the man!

He smiled, smugly confident, and crossed his arms over his chest. The movement made the muscles in his arms bulge and ripples of water slap the exposed part of her chest and Cara bit her lip. Her body felt shivery, leaden. She wanted to put her mouth to his skin and trace those contours with her tongue.

"It's perfectly normal in situations like this. All any soldier wants after a battle is a nice hot bath and a good hard screw."

"How romantic! Excuse me while I swoon."

He ignored her sarcasm. "They're the best things to do to remind yourself you're not dead. The night after a skirmish is always the camp girls' busiest time."

Cara had been with her father's troops long enough to know the truth of that. She'd nearly *died* this afternoon. Life was precious; just look what had happened to her cousin. Why not grab this brief chance at happiness?

The water kept offering tantalizing glimpses of del Sarto's naked form. She crossed her arms over her chest. "Fine. I *desire* you. Happy now?"

"Not even close."

"I'm willing to admit that you might have a point," she conceded. "About not-being-dead."

"That's sporting of you."

"And I haven't thanked you for saving my life," she said, determined to be fair. "So, thank you."

He dipped his head and touched his mouth to the side of her neck. "You're welcome."

His lips left a trail of icy fire in their wake and Cara shivered.

"This is what I imagined doing to you that morning I saw you in the river," he murmured. He feathered a row of tiny kisses along her jaw, sending flurries through her.

Cara tilted her head back to give him better access. "You mean *doused* me in the river."

"Mmm. I dreamed of licking every droplet from your skin." His tongue matched his words and Cara closed her eyes.

"And this." His lips trailed lower, over her throat, her collarbone.

She arched her spine, offering herself shamelessly. His lips closed around her nipple and she stifled a moan as he teethed it gently, then circled the tip with his tongue. Shudders of need raced through her. She speared her fingers through his wet hair and held him hard against her for a breathless instant before she tugged his head up, unable to bear the sweet torture any longer. Their eyes met, clashed.

"What do you want, Cara?" he whispered.

CHAPTER 40

*C*ara knew herself in that moment. She didn't want his sweetness, his practiced courtesies. She wanted him sweaty and earthy, elemental and fierce. She kept her eyes steady on his. "You use passion to forget about your nightmares. I want to forget mine, too."

"It will be my pleasure."

He pulled her towards him, taking them both into the deeper water, and her body bumped against his as he drew her forward for a kiss. They were both hungry, desperate for this affirmation of life. Her tongue met his eagerly, urgently, and he growled into her mouth.

He tasted of rain and desire and she wanted deeper, wilder, more. *More.* She threw everything she had into the kiss; all the fear and frustration and grief of the day. Her tension dissolved with the magic of his touch. Desire bloomed within her, twisting through her blood like poison, insidious and sweet.

She was out of her depth, in more ways than one. She had so much to lose, but at that moment she didn't care. Her body felt weightless in the water and she wound her arms around his neck and clung to him for support, closing her eyes and drowning in sensation. His nakedness, full-length, was shocking and unbelievably arousing.

He pulled back and stroked her wet hair from her cheeks. Steam beaded his face, glimmered silver on his sinfully long eyelashes and Cara took heart from the fact that his hands weren't entirely steady. She might not be able to best him with a sword, but in this arena they could meet as equals. She caught his lower lip between her teeth and tugged it gently, then slid her tongue playfully across it to ease the sting.

His eyes narrowed and her heart thudded in response. *Ah, playing with fire was so much fun!*

"I've created a monster," he murmured.

She sent him a wicked look from under her lashes. "My tutors always said I was an excellent student."

He drew her legs up around his waist and cupped her buttocks in his hands. The hard length of his shaft pressed against her stomach. Cara wriggled experimentally, and he bared his teeth at her with a frustrated growl. But he let her play. She raised herself up and repositioned him between her thighs, exactly where she wanted him, and smiled in satisfaction when he groaned low in his throat. The muscles in his neck and shoulders grew taut as he held her in position.

"Vixen!"

She clasped her hands behind his neck and leaned back in the water. He moved one hand to support her, his fingers spanning her waist, and stroked the other up over the curve of her stomach, between her breasts and along her throat. Cara luxuriated in his touch, arching in pleasure like a cat.

He teased, deliberately pressing himself at the threshold of her body then moving away, so she slid against the smooth, hard ridges of his flat belly instead. The friction was pure torture.

She arched her hips, changing the angle so he was pressed against her, and tightened her thighs around him to hold him in place. She wasn't Cara; she was one of Ovid's wood nymphs, the ones who lived in secret pools and hidden streams. She was a goddess who'd taken human form, unable to resist seducing this handsome mortal despite the punishment it might bring. There was no tomorrow, only now, here; this instant in the dark and heat.

Keeping her eyes locked with his, she pushed herself down, slowly impaling herself on his shaft, claiming him in the most basic way possible, inch by slow, delicious inch. He gasped and she stifled her own cry of exultation. It stung, briefly, and she was glad—she reveled in the heady rush of domination. She might not be able to keep him forever, but for this one perfect moment, he was hers.

He remained still, embedded deep inside her, resting his forehead on her own. His hands clutched her hips and she realized with a fond smile that he was waiting, giving her body time to adjust to his invasion, fighting his own desperate need to move. She shifted a little and he gave a broken chuckle.

"So impatient!"

He lifted her up and pulled out almost to the tip, then pushed forward again. Water sloshed between their bodies and Cara bit her lip at his roughness, his urgency. This was no stately seduction. This was what he'd promised, what she'd wanted; lust and want and mindless need. She bent her head to his shoulder, tasted his warm, slick skin, and savored his growl of reaction.

* * *

ALESSANDRO WAS LOST. He prided himself on being an excellent lover, but his legendary control had abandoned him. Cara was sleek and wet around him, clutching at him like a silken glove. He tried to slow down, but she didn't seem to want that, and it was beyond him, anyway. She wrapped her arms around him and held him even tighter, kissed him with her lips and tongue, lush, deep, as desperate for him as he was for her.

A sense of savage urgency gripped him, remembered dread. For an instant, back at the ravine, seeing her fall over the edge, he'd believed she was dead, that he'd been too late to save her. The twist of impotent rage had been almost too much to bear. Now, with every thrust of his body, he poured out his fury that she'd been hurt, his overwhelming relief that she was alive.

She was so vital, so compelling. So beautiful. The idea of a world without her in it was too bleak, too impossible to consider. He didn't want to live in a world like that. He'd rather die.

He closed his eyes and reveled in her shallow pants as she dug her nails into the skin of his back, scoring him. Those were scars he'd carry with pride, he thought dizzily. Not evidence of a mistake, but of something inescapably right. Something perfect.

In that moment she owned him completely. He, who was mastered by none, had been vanquished by this slip of a girl. He couldn't have stopped if the heavens themselves had opened up and offered him a place.

He leaned back to look at her. She was magnificent; her dark hair thrown back, the tips of it floating on the surface of the water. Her small, perfect breasts jounced upwards with each of his thrusts and her lithe, muscular body fit his to perfection. Her eyes were closed, as if she'd retreated into a world of fantasy.

"Look at me!" he growled as a sudden shard of uncertainty seized him. "Open your eyes and look at me!"

She complied and he captured her gaze, refusing to let her look away. "Know who's taking you, Cara. It's me." He pressed into her again to underline his point. "Not some knight on a white horse. Not some fucking saint. *Me.*"

She held his gaze, unblinking, and the savagery faded from his chest as quickly as it had come. She stroked a lock of hair from his brow with a shaking hand. "I know exactly who you are."

She took his face between her hands, pulled his mouth down to hers, and kissed him.

His defenses crumbled; he was utterly undone. He thrust into her.

"Say my name," he demanded hoarsely. He needed this final pleasure, his name upon her lips. "My name. You've never said it."

"Del Sarto!" she gasped, frowning as she tensed and bit her bottom lip in concentration, craving her own release.

"No. That's not it." He gave another teasing thrust. "My given name, Cara. Say it."

"Sandro!" she practically shouted. "Alessandro!"

"*Yes.*" He reached between their bodies, touched her with his hand, and she exploded with a wild little cry against his neck. The sensation of her body convulsing around him sent him over the edge. With one final drive his own climax claimed him, so hard and fast that he nearly blacked out with pleasure.

Cara collapsed against him, boneless, and his own legs threatened to buckle so they both almost went under. He managed to guide them back to the side of the pool, to shallower water, so at least they wouldn't drown.

Gently, he disentangled their bodies and placed her sideways in his lap. He drew her head down onto his shoulder, stroked her wet hair, and smiled at her complete exhaustion.

His legs were still wobbly when he rose from the water and carried her back to her clothes. Cara stood quietly as he played ladies' maid and dried her. He ignored her dust-soiled and shredded clothes and instead threw his shirt over her head and wrapped her in his cloak.

"Is it always like that?" she mumbled.

He was tempted to lie, but couldn't bring himself to do so. "No."

It had never been like that with anyone else. He'd never felt such heat, such a gut-wrenching need to possess, to claim, to satisfy, with any woman but her.

I know who you are, she'd whispered, with an ache in her voice. Alessandro closed his eyes in despair. She had no idea how true that was. Her clear-eyed gaze saw right down into the darkest corners of his soul. She made him feel stripped bare, defenseless, as he so hated to be. *God help him. They were in for a rough ride.*

He thought she'd demand an explanation for what had happened back at the ravine, but she was asleep before they'd ridden half a league. It wasn't long before the lights of Torre di San Rocco's torches twinkled in the distance.

Alessandro sighed. He had a new plan to put into action. And the woman in his arms was not going to like it one bit.

CHAPTER 41

*C*ara awoke in her own bedchamber at San Rocco. Alone.
Again.

An unfamiliar servant was moving quietly around the room
and she sat up as panicked recollection hit her. "Where's Renata?
Is she well?"

The girl gave a curtsey and a reassuring smile. "She's fine, my
lady, recovering well. She's in the bedchamber down the hall. The
physician's been attending her all night."

"I must go to her."

Dressing swiftly, not even bothering to look in the mirror,
Cara ran along the corridor. She found Renata in bed, apparently
asleep, with one of the doctors she'd met at the hospital at her
bedside. The man smiled in response to her questioning look.

"I've given her a tisane, so she's a little drowsy. The wound
was deep, and she lost a good deal of blood, but the blade missed
all her vital organs. Captain Neroni's efforts in binding it and
getting her here so quickly were invaluable. I don't think there
will be any lasting damage."

Cara took a sniff of the empty cup by the bed. "You used
feverfew? And arnica? What about mandrake?"

The doctor smiled at her interest. "Yes. All those. I added honey and mead to sweeten the mixture." He bowed. "I'll leave you now."

Cara took Renata's hand. Her eyelids fluttered then opened and she managed a weak smile of welcome. "Cara! You're all right!"

"I'm fine! *You're* the one who was stabbed. This is all my fault. If you hadn't been with me, none of this would have happened."

"Stop blaming yourself. I chose to go. And believe me, nothing could have stopped me! I'll be fine in a day or so. I'm tough as old boots. Besides, one good thing has come from all of this; that fool Neroni has finally come to his senses and realized he can't live without me!" Renata chuckled, then winced as the movement pained her.

Cara raised her brows. "Really? What happened?"

"You should have seen him, blustering and swearing. He raced back here like a man possessed, all the while pleading with me to stay awake and threatening me with all sorts of ridiculous punishments if I dared die on him!" Renata smiled in memory. "Apparently I'm incapable of living without the 'steadying influence of a man.' Francesco swore that if I lived, he'd be forced to marry me to stop me getting into any more trouble."

"How noble of him!" Cara grinned.

"I'm sure he thought I'd forget his promise in my delirium. Unfortunately for him, there's no way I'm letting him off the hook now he's finally grown the balls to do something about it!" Renata blushed at her bawdy words and Cara laughed.

"Good for you!"

"Are you truly unhurt?" Renata wrinkled her brow. "That's a fine bruise on your forehead."

Cara put her hand up and winced as she touched the cut. "Lorenzo hit me. And then he pushed me into the ravine. Alessandro rescued me."

Renata raised her brows. "*Alessandro* now, is it?"

Cara flushed. "He *did* save my life."

"So maybe he's not so bad?" Renata ventured.

"Oh, no, he's still the most irritating, overbearing, meddlesome creature that ever lived."

Renata cackled and patted her hands on the covers in delight. "And you're in love with him!"

Cara scowled. "That doesn't mean I *like* him! Or that I want to have anything else to do with him."

"You loooove him!" Renata chanted in a sing-song voice, like a six-year-old child.

Cara crossed her arms. "It will pass. Like a bout of the ague."

"Ha!"

They both looked up as a servant entered. "My lady, my lord wishes to see you. Immediately."

"Off you go," Renata said cheerfully. "Better not keep him waiting."

* * *

CARA ENTERED THE STUDY. Sunlight spilled through the mullioned window and glittered on del Sarto's dark hair, sculpted the harsh angles of his cheekbones. He looked tired. He sat behind the desk with his legs stretched out in front of him like Mephistopheles regarding the newest entrant into hell and she was reminded of all the times she'd been summoned to Abbott Andreo's study to be chastised for some new infringement of the rules. Except this time it wasn't *she* who was in the wrong.

She ignored the seat and hovered behind it instead, using the wood as a protective barrier as she studied his face, searching for some clue to his thoughts. As usual it was impossible to tell what he was thinking.

She squared her shoulders and prepared to do battle. "You used me as bait to draw out my uncle."

"Yes. I had *not* intended for you to be part of the convoy, however. You were supposed to stay here. Safe. I should have remembered your reluctance to follow even the simplest of instructions."

"Was it ever your intention for me to marry him?"

"No." He tilted his head and the corners of his eyes crinkled in amusement at her outraged expression. "Oh, don't pretend you're sorry. I bet you were planning all sorts of schemes to escape the wedding, weren't you? What were you going to do? Blow up his chapel? Steal his horse and escape through the woods?"

Cara's temper simmered at the way he'd tricked her, making her believe she could escape him. He was so sure of himself, so unrepentant. She folded her arms. "So what are you going to do with me now? I suppose it's too much to hope that I'll be allowed to return to Castelleon and be left in peace?"

"Hardly. Your uncle's still alive."

"Surely he's no threat to me now? My cousin is dead. And his mercenaries have been paid off by you."

"You still need my protection. Lorenzo will seek revenge. I guarantee it."

"How convenient for you. But I can't afford any more of your *services*, My Lord Mercenary. I have nothing left to give."

He gave her a long, assessing look. "You have one thing."

She curled her lip. "You've taken my freedom, my honor, and my virginity. What else is left?"

"Your name," he said simply. "You can marry me."

Cara put a hand on the back of the chair to steady herself. "What?"

"I've changed my mind about marriage. None of your suitors are, well, *suitable*." His smile was ironic. "I'm the only one who can provide what you need; experience to defeat your uncle, and troops to protect your home."

Cara sank down into the seat, quite certain her legs would fail her if she remained standing. "You want Castelleon," she said bluntly.

"That's certainly a factor in my decision."

"And you're being hounded to marry. You need an alliance with someone local."

"That's also true," he agreed with irritating calm.

"But I don't want to marry you."

He shot her a pitying glance, as if she were a simpleton. "Of course you don't. Nobody *wants* to get married. At least, no one with any sense. But you don't have a choice, I'm afraid. You need me." His gaze turned molten and Cara felt heat rise up her chest to her face. "And you want me. You can't claim to dislike my advances." He gave a negligent shrug. "Besides, I'm not asking for your agreement. I'm telling you what's going to happen. You have fifteen minutes to get ready and meet me in the chapel, or I'll come and drag you there myself." He stood and stretched, then strolled past her to the door. "And Cara? Don't even think about trying to escape."

Cara gave a cry of impotent fury. She lunged at the desk, picked up the ornamental dagger he used as a letter opener, and flung it at his departing back. She missed. The point embedded itself in the doorframe, shuddering.

He didn't even flinch. "Keep practicing, sweeting!" he chuckled.

CHAPTER 42

*C*ara ran along the gallery, resisting the urge to hit something on the way. The portraits lining the walls smirked at her as she passed and she poked her tongue out at them. It was childish, but it made her feel better.

The high-handed beast! He'd maneuvered her into a corner that even she —the mistress of evasion—could see no way out of.

On the one hand, she'd like nothing better than to marry him, if only to make his life a living hell for the next forty or so years. He might *think* he wanted some vapid, pea-brained socialite, but he'd be bored with someone like that within a week. He'd ship the poor girl off on extended visits to family or on shopping trips abroad and she'd be too stupid to realize she was being neglected. He needed a woman like her to keep him on his toes.

On the other hand, there were hundreds of reasons why marrying him would be a very bad idea. Not least because she was horribly, inescapably, in love with him.

Why had he changed his mind about marriage? She doubted it was because of her non-existent skills at lovemaking. He'd sampled the best Europe had to offer. Her meagre performance could hardly have compared favorably, despite her naïve enthusiasm.

Was it, as he claimed, purely practical? He'd be gaining a gateway to the trade routes for his ships and a tactically important fortified keep in Castelleon. He'd have a hostess and chatelaine for his home, not to mention a regular bed partner whenever he snapped his fingers. She didn't imagine she could hold him off for too long on that front.

But he didn't have to *marry* her to get those things. He could keep her, unwed, until he tired of her.

A tiny, stubbornly romantic part of her soul whispered that he was doing it because he wanted *her*. That a part of him, maybe buried so deep down that even *he* didn't recognize it, acknowledged her as his perfect mate.

Cara shook her head at her own stupidity. A wishful, irrational longing was hardly enough to base the rest of her life on.

* * *

RENATA LISTENED with her mouth agape. "Getting married? Right now?"

Cara nodded and flopped down onto the bed.

Renata struggled to sit up. "But weddings need months of preparation."

"I know! Beatrice d'Este described her sister's wedding to me; they had a procession, a feast, dancing. Fireworks. Her husband even gave her a pure white horse as a wedding present." She scowled. "You know what del Sarto's giving *me*? Fifteen minutes!"

Renata patted her hand. "He won't brook a refusal. I know him. Once he makes up his mind to do something, no force in heaven or hell can stop him."

Cara buried her face in her hands and let out a heartfelt groan.

"Come now, he's not that bad." Renata's tone was cajoling.

"He's rich. Strong. Healthy. Good looking. If I were twenty years younger, I'd have had him myself!"

"You're welcome to him! He's only doing this to get his hands on Castelleon."

Renata chuckled. "Look on the bright side—you'll never want for passion." She slid herself to the edge of the bed and planted her feet on the floor.

Cara stared at her aghast. "What are you doing? You have to stay in bed."

Renata batted away her hands. "And pass up seeing you two married? No chance! Get Neroni up here. He can carry me down to the chapel. You'll need some witnesses anyway."

Cara took a peek out of the window to see if the horse chestnut had miraculously re-grown overnight. It hadn't. She opened the door and sent one of the servants to fetch Francesco.

Renata pointed to a chest by the wall. "Pia sent your new gown up for me to see."

With a growing sense of doom, Cara put the dress on. The fit was perfect; a pale blue silk that clung to her every curve and hollow. Renata beckoned her over and fanned the loose waves of Cara's hair over her shoulders.

"There, lovely. You should always wear it loose like this. Now hand me those flowers." She pinned a few sprigs of jasmine into the strands. The petals gave off a dizzying perfume as Cara turned to study her reflection.

The cut at her hairline looked worse than she'd expected; the area around it was already turning green and purple with bruising. At least she didn't have a black eye for her wedding day, she thought, with sudden gallows humor. That would have clashed terribly with the dress.

Francesco entered, and his expression darkened when he saw Renata sitting up. "What are you doing? Get back into bed, woman!"

Renata chuckled. "I love it when you get all masterful, Neroni!"

"What's all this nonsense about going downstairs?"

"Stop fussing. I want you to carry me to the chapel. Cara and Alessandro are getting married."

Francesco nodded, apparently unsurprised by the news.

Renata beckoned him over. "Come on, you old goat. Pick me up. If you still have the strength, that is."

Francesco's face softened as he looked at her. "I could carry you to the ends of the earth," he said gruffly.

Renata actually blushed.

Their easy banter made Cara's heart clench in wistful longing. They'd be sparring like this for the rest of their lives, feeding off each other's wit, teasing and cherishing at the same time. Despite Francesco's bluster, the gentleness with which he held Renata in his arms was ample evidence of the way he felt about her.

If only she could find the same thing with del Sarto.

CHAPTER 43

hey met her at the entrance to the chapel.

Del Sarto had changed his clothes too; Cara narrowed her eyes. His shoulders were outlined by a close-fitting velvet tunic and a pair of black breeches clung to his long legs with almost indecent faithfulness. Only the startling white of his shirt alleviated the darkness.

He unsheathed his sword and rested it against the wall by the door, in surprising deference to his surroundings, but Cara didn't make the mistake of believing he'd left himself defenseless. He probably had ten more knives secreted about his person. The man was a walking arsenal.

She glanced at the chapel door then back at her tormentor. "Not afraid to enter such a hallowed portal?"

His lips twitched. "Praying I'll get struck down by a bolt of lightning if I set foot on sacred soil? You're not that lucky." He offered his arm.

She ignored it. "Let's get this over with."

"In a hurry, sweeting?"

"Hardly. In fact, if you wanted to wait a while—fifteen or

twenty years, for instance—I'd be more than happy to accommodate you."

His dark eyes flashed. "Oh, you'll *accommodate* me, my lady. Tonight. As my wife."

Cara pushed open the door to avoid answering him and gasped as she recognized the stooped figure waiting at the altar. "Fra Andreo!" She rushed down the narrow aisle and into the embrace of the old man who was as dear to her as her own father had been. "What are you doing here? I'm so glad to see you! How's Castelleon? Is everyone all right? How's Bianca? And Hector?"

The Abbott laughed, holding her back from him at armslength. "One question at a time!" he chided. "Always so impatient! It's good to see you alive and unharmed, my child." He bestowed a benevolent kiss on her forehead. "My lord del Sarto has asked me to perform your marriage ceremony. I think it's an excellent idea."

Cara gasped at her old friend's defection. She'd been certain he'd object on her behalf.

"But I don't *want* to marry him!" she hissed.

Fra Andreo gave her hands a reassuring squeeze and lowered his voice. "This man can protect you, and Castelleon, better than anyone, Cara."

Cara acknowledged the truth of his words, even as her heart cried out in denial. Everything about this situation was *wrong*. Marriage shouldn't be governed by political expediency. She bit her lip as tears threatened. She *would not* cry.

The situation would be funny if it weren't so awful. The cosmos seemed to have saved its cruelest joke for her. Surely a marriage with only *one* of the participants in love was worse than one with no emotion on either side. There wasn't even any hope of future change. Del Sarto might desire her in a physical way, but he'd made it abundantly clear that he was immune—and entirely unreceptive—to any deeper feelings.

THE DEVIL TO PAY

Renata and Francesco had seated themselves in the front row of pews and were watching the byplay with rapt anticipation. Other than that, the chapel was empty.

Interpreting Cara's silence as consent, or at least not downright objection, Abbot Andreo turned to del Sarto. "This really should be done by a notary. I haven't performed a marriage ceremony in years. Not much call for them at the monastery." He chuckled at his own joke, patted his pockets, and withdrew a small leather-bound book. "Better do this properly. First the marriage negotiations." He gave del Sarto an expectant glance. "Any presents for the bride? Jewels? Clothes? Furniture?"

Del Sarto shook his head.

"It is customary to give *something,* my Lord," Andreo prompted. "Such as a bridal belt?" He turned to Cara. "The bridal belt has a fascinating history. It's given in memory of the god Vulcan gifting the cestus—a belt with the power to inspire love— to the goddess Venus. "

"No belt," del Sarto said.

The Abbott leveled him a reproachful look. Cara had been the recipient of that look a hundred times. Even if you *weren't* guilty, you felt as if you were. It apparently worked on del Sarto, too, because he threw up his hands in sudden defeat.

"Oh, fine," he growled. "She can have one if she wants one." He reached to his waist, unfastened his own belt and thrust it at her.

Cara looked down at the offending item as if it were diseased. The leather was worn to a smooth shine and scarred with pale nicks from a lifetime of fighting. The sheathed dagger dragged it down on one side. It was a far cry from the pretty velvet girdle she'd imagined.

She stood still as a statue as del Sarto wrapped his arms around her waist and buckled it. It slid straight down over her hips. Even on the smallest notch it refused to stay up. Losing all patience, he tied the ends in a huge, ungainly knot.

Fra Andreo smiled. "There. Now, I take it neither of you know any reasons why you shouldn't be married?"

Cara drew a deep breath ready to list any number of reasons, but del Sarto forestalled her.

"None whatsoever."

"Anyone else?" The Abbott glanced at the congregation of two, ignoring Cara's squawk of annoyance. "Does anyone here present have any objection?"

Il Diavolo glared over his shoulder. Francesco grinned and opened his mouth, but a glance at his master's face made him change his mind. "No, absolutely not. Perfect couple, those two."

The Abbott smiled beatifically. "Good, good. And you're not already married or betrothed to anyone else are you?"

Cara's heart lightened at this unexpected escape route. "Yes! I'm promised to marry the Duke of Parma!"

Del Sarto swung back around. "No, you're not." He turned to the abbott. "She's not."

The Abbott ignored the venomous glare the bride shot the groom and continued. "Excellent. Now we need to discuss the lady's dowry."

"She brings the keep of Castelleon, its incomes and contents. That's it."

Andreo glanced back at his prayer book, his forehead wrinkling as he struggled to read the small text in the dim light. Then he placed Cara's hand in Il Diavolo's much larger one. Del Sarto's fingers squeezed hers, harder than was comfortable. She tugged, but his grip was firm, inescapable.

"Do you wish to have this woman as your wife, and to love her, honor her, keep her and protect her, in health and in sickness, as a husband should his wife, to keep from all other women except her, as long as your lives shall last?"

Cara raised her eyebrow at the "keep from all other women" part. Let him try to wriggle out of that one.

Del Sarto was watching her, his expression enigmatic. "I do."

"And Cara, the same question is asked of the woman, only instead of the words 'keep him and protect him', you substitute the phrase 'obey and serve'."

That got her attention. "Obey and serve?!"

Del Sarto interrupted again, this time with a faint smile. "She can repeat the man's part, Abbott. That will suffice." Seeing Cara was about to argue further, he lowered his head. His breath feathered the hair by her ear. "It's close enough to the vow of allegiance you've already made. Say it." He tightened his grip. Under the concealment of her dress, she stomped on his instep with her foot and glared at him.

"We *do* need the bride's consent. Do you take him willingly, my dear?" Andreo's eyes were so kind Cara wanted to cry. "Think carefully before you answer. If you *truly* do not wish to wed this man, I can assist you."

Del Sarto frowned at the Abbott, even as he addressed her. "You need me."

"We need active consent, milord." Andreo repeated. "Without coercion. Do you wish to have this man as your husband?"

CHAPTER 44

She could still refuse. It wasn't too late.

Cara closed her eyes. Of course it was too late. She glanced up at the stained-glass window above the altar as if an answer would come to her through the richly colored panes. Beneath Il Diavolo's coat of arms she recognized a passage from the bible; 'The Lord is my rock and my fortress; my strength in whom I will trust; my buckler, and the horn of my salvation.'

Trust del Sarto to commission something warlike, even in a church.

In some distant part of her still-functioning brain she heard herself say, "I do."

"I, Alessandro Rafael del Sarto give my body to you, Cara Elisabetta di Montessori in loyal matrimony."

The Abbott turned to her. "Now you say: 'And I receive it.'"

Her tongue formed the words.

"Do you have a ring?"

Del Sarto removed the thick gold signet ring from his own finger. It slipped easily over her knuckle, still warm from the heat of his skin. Unable to meet his eyes, Cara studied it, for the first time noticing the words engraved on either side of the crest that was his seal. 'Quis est mei ego servo.' *That which is mine, I keep.* Now *she* was his. Would he keep her, as he'd promised?

"Now repeat after me. 'With this ring I thee wed, this gold I thee give, with my body I thee worship.' "

Del Sarto's deep voice repeated the priest's words.

How could it be this simple? How could such a weighty thing —marriage, a lifetime—be done with so few words? Everything had an air of dreamlike unreality, except for the hard press of his arm against her side. His flesh against hers. Cara shivered.

The Abbott beamed, clearly relieved to have got through his part without mishap. "The final stage is the wedding night." He glanced apologetically at Cara. "According to law, the bride's spouse can only collect *half* the dowry until the marriage is consummated." The old man actually blushed.

Del Sarto slanted her a simmering look from under his brows. "Oh, have no fear on that score, Father. Is that it?"

"Well, I believe it's common for a friend of the groom to clap him on the back to fix this moment in his mind for evermore," Andreo said.

"That's my cue!" Francesco strode forward and whacked del Sarto hard on his injured shoulder. "That should do it. You won't forget this day in a hurry!"

Del Sarto pulled Cara towards him, grasped her chin, and claimed her mouth in a kiss that was unashamedly carnal, considering their ecclesiastical surroundings. She hit him on the arm in an attempt to stop the blatant sacrilege, but he ignored her and only broke the kiss when the Abbott slammed his prayer book shut with a disapproving snap.

Del Sarto shot her a brief, smug look.

Francesco stepped forward and cleared his throat. "Since you're in the marrying mood, Father, I'd like you to wed Renata and me."

Renata's screech would have made a fishwife green with envy. "*What,* Neroni?! You can't be serious!"

Francesco glared at her. "I know my own mind, woman. I'm not senile."

"You don't want to marry an invalid!"

"I do. I'm going to take full advantage of your weakened state. You don't have the strength to resist me. Now, do you want to or not?"

Renata gave a long-suffering sigh. "Oh, fine. But only because you've finally worn me down, after years of begging."

Francesco stroked his beard to hide his smile. "Of course."

"I'm a complete mess!" Renata protested, her hands fluttering to her hair. "You could have warned me, you oaf!"

Francesco took her hand in his and his smile was sweet and sure. "Woman, you'd still be beautiful if you were riddled with the plague. Stop making excuses." His smile turned wicked. "Besides, you won't be an invalid forever. I want you back to full health as quickly as possible. Think of me as your motivation to get better."

Renata squealed as he swept her up into his arms and carried her to the altar where the Abbott was waiting.

Cara blinked back tears as they repeated their vows. This was how a real marriage *should be*. A partnership of mutual affection and love. It was almost embarrassing to watch as they gazed into each other's eyes. Renata giggled like a schoolgirl when Francesco shifted his hand to her bottom and gave it a playful squeeze just as the Abbott was finishing his address.

Cara couldn't prevent a dismal little sniff. The contrast to her own union could not have been more marked. She refused to look at the man standing so tall and stiff by her side.

Il Diavolo. Her husband.

What on earth had she done? She'd married the Devil himself.

Ten minutes later del Sarto strode through the castle with Cara's hand firmly clasped in his.

"Where are we going?" she panted, hurrying to keep pace.

"To my chambers."

She didn't pretend to mistake his purpose. "It's the middle of the day!"

He shot her a droll 'as-if-that-matters' look.

"There's no need to do this!" She jerked her wrist in his grasp. "We've already . . . consummated!"

"Not since we've been married. We have to make it official."

"You just want to get legal right to *all* my dowry, not just half!"

Her resistance was getting her nowhere. They mounted the stairs and rounded the corner. The two guards jerked to attention.

"Stand down." Del Sarto thrust open the door to his chamber, pulled her through it, and slammed it shut behind them with his heel.

"If you'll just stop and think for a minute, del Sarto—"

"Alessandro," he corrected tersely. "Use my given name, for God's sake."

"Fine, *Alessandro,* if you'll—"

"On second thought, don't say anything!"

Cara opened her mouth to argue but he pushed her up against the wall, framed her face with his hands, and claimed her lips with his.

His kiss was an enchantment. She fought the pull, even as she felt herself slipping away into the darkness.He tangled his fingers through her hair, undoing Renata's careful styling in his haste. The heady scent of jasmine wound around them both as he crushed the petals beneath his palms.

Desire sparked between them, hot and bright. Tongues of fire raced through her blood. Cara brought her own hands up and bunched his shirt to push him away, but found herself pulling him closer still.

He grasped her shoulders, turned them both, and pushed her back onto the bed, following her down. His urgent roughness sent a thrill of excitement racing through her and the words from the chapel window came back to her; *my rock and my fortress, my strength and my shield*. He was all of those things, and more. She ached with the force of what she was feeling. It was more than lust. More than passion. How could so much love not be reciprocated? How could he kiss her like this and feel nothing? Her heart pounded in anticipation, but sanity demanded an audience. "We need to talk!"

She wriggled out from under him and tried to crawl across the bed but he caught her ankle and flipped her over onto her back again.

"No. Enough talking." He straddled her, his thighs trapping her hips, his hands pinning her wrists above her head.

Cara glared up at him, panting with exertion. "This is no way to behave! Let go of me. If I'm going to be married to you we need to lay out some basic ground rules—"

He dropped a kiss to her collarbone.

"Stop it! You can't just befuddle me with kisses every time you want to avoid an important discussion!"

He pounced on her unintentional admission. "I befuddle you, do I? That's good to know. Let's see if I can do it again."

She scooted away, fending him off with one hand. "It's not too late to admit this was a mistake."

"I don't make mistakes."

"We can still get an annulment."

"Never."

"*Why* did you marry me?"

"It doesn't matter why," he evaded, recapturing her and moving down to teethe her breast through the fabric of her gown. "It's done."

Cara bit her lip to prevent a moan. "Of course it matters!"

His lips were doing wicked things and his hand slid up under her skirts to stroke her naked thigh. Cara clamped her legs together, fighting the surrender that was stealing through her body at his touch.

"Just be quiet and enjoy it," he murmured.

Fury raced in to replace her previous languor. He was *still* manipulating her, counting on her desire to distract her and avoid the discussions they needed to have. Cara made a fist and arched up to hit him, but he dodged the blow with practiced ease. She felt a draught of cold air as he rolled off the bed in one easy movement.

He stood, hands on his hips, and glared down at her. "God, *women*! What's this really about?"

In her anger, Cara snatched at the smallest and least significant of her grievances. "That entire wedding was a farce!"

His brows drew together in a continuous black line. "It was legal. What else did you want?" Bitterness sharpened his tone to one of cutting precision. "Don't tell me! A white horse and flowers and a candle-lit feast?"

"Yes!" She shrieked, incensed by the accuracy of his attack. "What's wrong with that? *Every* woman wants that on her wedding day!"

"It's romantic horseshit and you won't get it from me. You've got what you wanted—my permanent protection for your precious Castelleon."

She sucked in a furious breath. "What I *want* is a husband who sees me as something more than a way of gaining some strategically valuable land!"

Alessandro opened his mouth, but she forged on. White-hot fury pulsed through her veins and made her temples pound. "But what did I get instead? *You!* A barbarian with no feelings, who just takes what he wants with no regard for anyone else!"

"If that were true I'd already be taking *you*, instead of standing here arguing!" he snarled. He took a deep breath, as if struggling for control, then stepped back. A muscle ticked in his jaw, but when he spoke his voice was silken. "It appears we are at stalemate, my lady wife. You want something I can't give. And I want *you* willing, or not at all."

He turned on his heel and strode to the door. The slam of the oak behind him was strong enough to send the chess pieces flying from a nearby table. One rolled across the floor and stopped against the hem of Cara's gown. It was the white knight. The bitter irony didn't escape her; this was the closest she was ever going to get to a white horse as a wedding gift.

Silently, hating the weakness but unable to stop, Cara began to cry. For herself. For the loss of all her stupid dreams. For the mess she'd made of everything. But mainly for the fact that she was hopelessly in love with a complete monster who didn't love her back.

Hooves clattered in the bailey below. Crossing to the window, she watched her new husband gallop out of the castle on Saraceno, fury evident in every taut line of his body.

CHAPTER 45

*F*rancesco caught up with Alessandro after about five miles. "Slow down! You're riding like hell itself is after you!"

"A she-devil, more like. God, that woman is infuriating!"

Francesco grinned. "Whatever happened to the idea of you marrying someone quiet, biddable and stupid, eh?"

Alessandro grunted.

"I tell you what, she'll never bore you." Francesco reined in to match Saraceno's reduced pace.

Alessandro sighed. That was true. No one could ever accuse Cara of being boring. Resourceful, witty, prickly, and exasperating? Yes. But never boring. *Little witch.*

In every aspect of his life he had consummate control, except for two areas; his nightmares and *her*. He could command an entire army with a single curt order, quell an argument with one look. But he had no hope of mastery over her—a twenty-two year old girl. She was both a blessing and a curse, like Achilles' heel.

His enemies would have envied her skills. She knew just how to goad him, just the right little comment or jibe guaranteed to set him grinding his teeth. She left him feeling rubbed up the wrong way, like velvet stroked against the grain. She willfully misunderstood him, deliberately ignored his commands, *enjoyed* flouting his authority. It was vexing, to say the least.

And completely intoxicating.

"You didn't have to marry her," Francesco persisted.

Alessandro glared at him. "None of those other idiots can handle her. I can't afford to let Castelleon fall to someone else. I—"

"—love her!" Francesco finished the sentence with a mighty grin. He slapped Alessandro on the back with a delighted chuckle. "Don't look so cross—it happens to the best of us. Have you told her?"

Alessandro shot him a disgusted look. "Are you mad? Of course not! Once you tell a woman you love her, that's it. You're never master in your own keep again. They hold it over your head, like the sword of Damocles, forevermore."

Francesco grinned, unrepentant. "Fine. Don't tell her. Save your pride. But we're two just-married men, Sandro. I can think of several *far* more enjoyable things I'd rather be doing right now than galloping around the countryside with you. Can we go home?"

Alessandro sighed. Home had always been such an alien concept to him. It hadn't been the underbelly of a Genoese man-of-war, where he'd spent his youth splashing around in the stinking bilge water, ducking oars and low beams, swallowing down the bile of blind panic in his first few military encounters off the Mediterranean coast. It wasn't his familiar campaign tent, either, pitched on a different patch of soil every few weeks as he wound from one confrontation to the next. Nor was it in the echoing, lonely opulence of Torre di San Rocco.

At least, it hadn't been, until *she'd* come.

Alessandro sighed in defeated acknowledgment. His heart had known it years ago. Her father had always known.

Home was wherever Cara was.

What the hell was wrong with him? What was he doing here, running away? He'd never backed down from a challenge in his life and he wasn't about to start now.

Francesco indicated a shabby hostelry on the edge of town. "Come on, I'll buy you a drink, and then we can both get back to our wives."

CARA PACED ACROSS THE BAILEY, cursing the devil she'd just married. Was this going to set the pattern of their entire marriage? Him disappearing at the critical moment? Him refusing to acknowledge any feelings for her except lust?

Abbott Andreo hobbled up and frowned at her mutinous face. "Del Sarto's a complex man," he said, as if this were explanation enough. He held out a folded piece of vellum, sealed with the familiar wax impression of del Sarto's ring; the one she now wore on her fourth finger. "These are your marriage documents. You should read them, my dear."

Cara didn't bother breaking the seal. She tossed them onto a side table instead. "Why bother? They'll simply confirm that my husband is now legal owner of Castelleon. Well, half of it, at least. What else could they—"

A lone rider clattered through the gatehouse, interrupting her diatribe. Dusty and disheveled, he drooped in the saddle, clearly exhausted.

"Ettore?" Cara gasped, recognizing him as one of her men from Castelleon.

The young man practically fell off his horse then sank to his knees in the dust at her feet. "Ettore! What are you doing here? Are you well?"

"My Lady! Thank God you're here! I bring dire news!"

Cara's heart plummeted. "What is it? Has my uncle returned to Castelleon?"

"No. There's been no sign of him since he left a few days ago. But Commander Sansevero sent me with all haste." He accepted a cup of water from one of the servants with a nod of thanks. "A messenger arrived, just after your uncle left. At first he said he'd only deliver his message to Lorenzo himself, but Sansevero persuaded him to leave it in his hands. It was from the French King Charles, milady, thanking your uncle for his forthcoming hospitality."

Cara's blood ran cold as she realized the full extent of her uncle's treachery. He wasn't just a murderer. If he'd allied himself with the French, he was a traitor, too.

Ettore wiped his mouth on his sleeve. "The French are on their way even now. Captain Sansevero begs that you bring Il Diavolo and his men. He says we've no chance of defending Castelleon without his help." The boy made as if to mount the stairs to the castle. "Where is he? I must see him at once!"

"He's not here." Cara flushed. "He's gone . . . hunting. I don't know when he'll return."

"The French will be here at any moment! What shall we do?"

Andreo drew Cara aside so the boy couldn't hear. "We should wait for your husband. I'm sure he won't be much longer—"

"I have no idea where he's gone. He might not be back for days!" Cara snapped.

"He's not likely to miss his own wedding night, whatever you might have argued about," Andreo chuckled, in a tone far too earthy for a sixty-eight year old monk.

Cara flushed. The idea of a wedding night with del Sarto was enough to make her blood warm, although why, when she'd already given herself to him so completely, was a mystery.

Maybe it was because it would finally make their marriage legal.

Inescapable.

"I refuse to wait here while my home is threatened." She turned and addressed Ettore. "I will return with you at once."

Ettore's head sagged onto his knees. "It took me two days to get here. We'll be too late."

"Don't worry. I have a plan."

Abbott Andreo crossed himself. "Dear Lord! Coming from you, those words are enough to strike a chill into an old man's bones."

Cara shot him her most winning smile. It had got her out of countless punishments as a child, and it didn't fail her now. "Are you with me?"

The ancient scholar sighed. "Of course. *Someone* has to make sure you don't do anything too addlebrained. Like get yourself killed," he muttered darkly.

Ten minutes later, having outlined the plan to a wide-eyed Renata, Cara flew down the stairs and called for the sergeant who'd been left in charge in Francesco's absence.

"You've heard that my lord del Sarto and I are wed?"

The soldier gave her a stiff bow. "Of course, my lady. The whole castle knows. Congratulations."

She waved away his felicitations, making sure he got a good look at the signet ring she wore. No harm in invoking del Sarto's authority on her behalf. Marrying the brute had to have *some* compensations. "I must return to Castelleon at once. Please ready fifty of your best men to accompany me immediately."

The man frowned. "But Signorina di Montessori—I mean, Signora del Sarto—he can't have gone far. Let me send one of the men to find him—"

Cara fixed him with a haughty stare. "I have no time to argue. If my lord hears of your tardiness in assisting me he will *not* be pleased—" She let that sentence hang between them for full dramatic effect.

The sergeant blanched at this grim prospect and nodded. "Yes, my lady. At once."

* * *

As the towers of San Rocco disappeared around a bend in the river, Cara tried to shake off the feeling that she was running away. She watched the men she'd 'borrowed' settle themselves, grumbling, in the boat's hull, then turned to check on the other boats that were following.

They made a strange flotilla; she'd commandeered almost every vessel in San Rocco, from fishing boat to trading barge, shamelessly abusing her new position as lady of the keep. News of her marriage had clearly spread through the city like wildfire, because the townsfolk had practically fallen over themselves to offer their boats, however unsuitable, desperate not to offend her and, by proxy, their lord and master.

She slumped onto a wooden strut and glanced at Andreo. "I know what you're about to say. That I should have waited for him. But I have no idea when he'll be back. I *can't* just sit by and let someone destroy my home and hurt the people I love."

Despite her outward show of decisiveness, Cara had no idea whether she'd made the right decision. What would del Sarto think when he returned? Would he follow with the rest of his men, as she'd asked in the quickly-scrawled note she'd left?

A twinge of bitterness crushed her chest. Of course he would come. Castelleon was the reason he'd married her, was it not? Even if he felt no affection for her personally, he wouldn't allow another man take Castelleon. *What's mine I keep.* She turned to study the riverbank as her eyes began to sting.

The Abbott rubbed her back. "There, child, he's not worth your tears."

Cara wiped her nose with her sleeve as unobtrusively as possible. "I'm *not* crying!"

"Really? Your eyes are all red."

"It's the flowers." She swatted at the last few wilted jasmine petals that still clung to her disheveled hair. "Jasmine always makes me sniff."

The Abbott nodded and wisely kept his own counsel.

* * *

ALESSANDRO'S KNUCKLES whitened on the leather reins. Two lines bracketed his mouth. "Say it again? She's *gone back to Castelleon?*"

The pitcher of ale he and Francesco had shared had lowered his temper to a mild simmer. The one after that had mellowed him even further. He'd returned to San Rocco with a rare sense of excitement, anticipating the night ahead, prepared to soothe Cara's objections in the most pleasurable way possible—only to discover that the little witch he'd married had run away—and taken half of his best fighting men with her!

"Ready the rest of the men," he growled.

"Yes, my lord. Are we going after her?"

"Of course we're going after her. And this time I really am going to tan her backside. She's had it coming since she was sixteen years old. I told her father he never spanked her enough when she was a child."

"Are we going by boat?"

Alessandro hated boats. He'd spent the best part of three years on one, and those were some of the worst memories of his entire life. In fact, he'd sworn never to set foot on one again. But he would have done it, for *her*. Unfortunately, time was against them. His stomach clenched at the thought of Cara in danger. "No. She's taken every last thing that floats. We'll take the Fiesole pass."

Francesco raised his bushy brows. "It's a tough ride. Better hope the snows have cleared."

Alessandro shrugged. "The men need a challenge. They've been sitting idle for far too long. Let's go."

CHAPTER 46

Cara swallowed a lump of emotion as the beloved outline of Castelleon appeared on the horizon. She scanned the buildings for traces of damage, but everything appeared just as it had done on the day she'd left.

It seemed like a lifetime ago. She'd been a frightened, innocent child when she'd departed. Now she was the wife of one of the most powerful men in Italy. And innocent no more.

It was hard not to compare the place with Torre di San Rocco. Castelleon was far less imposing. Her critical eye noted all the things that needed improving, things she'd nagged her father about when he was still alive. They were all *her* problems now. Hers and her husband's.

The boat bumped the rocky riverbank and the scrabble of claws interrupted her brooding thoughts. A furry cannonball shot round the corner of a bush and hurled itself at her stomach.

"Hector!" Cara barely held back her tears as her ancient hound threw himself at her in ecstasy, nearly knocking her off her feet. She scratched his ears and buried her face in his wiry fur and he whimpered with delight, his bony tail thumping against her legs. He wasn't the best-looking animal; his wiry fur stuck out in random tufts as though he'd been hit by lightning, but she'd had him from a pup and she loved him dearly.

"My lady!" Giacomo Sansevero, her father's second-in-command, strode forward and gripped her by the arms. "We feared you were dead, like your poor father, God rest his soul!" He kissed her cheeks and glanced expectantly over her shoulder. "Is Il Diavolo with you?"

"He is not."

The commander's face fell.

"He wasn't at San Rocco when I left," Cara said. "But I've brought fifty of his men with me."

She'd decided not to advertise the fact that she'd married the man. It was of no relevance to her present situation and the fewer people who knew about *that* sorry farce the better. She'd sworn Abbott Andreo to secrecy. "Will you accept *my* leadership, as you did my father's?"

Sansevero leveled her an assessing look, and nodded. "Of course, my lady. This way."

They entered the castle walls through the river gate and climbed up the outer walls to the battlements. Cara gazed out at the horizon, staying well back from the dizzying drop.

The city was spread out before them, a riot of color and activity. The cheerful pastel tones of the houses that stepped down to the crescent-shaped harbor seemed incongruous, considering the grave danger they were facing. Vendors hawked their wares in the narrow streets and piazzas, shouting enticements to passers by. Groups of washerwomen gathered by the bridge and workers in the terraces beyond tended the groves of lemon and olive trees that lined up like ranks of gnarled, stooping foot soldiers. Cicadas chirped their steady, thrumming cheep. Everything looked so peaceful.

Cara's stomach knotted with anxiety.

"My Lady, look!" Sansevero pointed out to sea and Cara shielded her eyes against the low-hanging sun. Sure enough, a fleet of ships had appeared on the horizon, growing larger even as she watched. She made a quick tally and her heart sank. So many.

"How long until they're here?"

Sansevero squinted. "Two hours, maybe less. What shall we do?"

Her whole life had been in preparation for this moment, but now it was here she felt like a scared little girl. She swallowed, feeling the weight of responsibility settle heavy on her shoulders.

"This keep has never fallen to invaders, and I'll be damned if it will do so now. Empty the town. Bring everyone inside the bailey. The French will be expecting Lorenzo to welcome them, so take a handful of men and meet them down at the harbor. Then lead them up here."

The old soldier's grey eyes were unflinching. "Should I ready the men for a fight?"

Cara swallowed. "Yes. But I pray it won't come to that. Perhaps I can negotiate."

Her own hopelessness was echoed in the captain's disbelieving look. "They'll have no incentive to leave, once they're here," he said.

"I know. But we'll have the advantage of surprise."

"There'll be too many of them, my lady. If they breech the walls—"

"You think we should surrender *without* a fight?" Cara demanded.

Sansevero shrugged.

Every cell in her body urged her to defend her home, but to do so would risk the slaughter of innocent people. These were townsfolk and laborers, not battle-hardened soldiers like del Sarto's men. Perhaps a bloodless surrender *would* be the wisest course of action? Except there was no guarantee of safety, even then. There was nothing to stop the French from murdering, raping and pillaging once they were in control. Del Sarto had said it himself; no-one played fair in war.

Oh, God, what should she do?

* * *

CARA BOWED her head as she entered the tiny family chapel. A single candle burned on the altar and the air was redolent of incense and flowers. Her steps faltered as she approached the enclave where her mother and, most recently, her father had been laid to rest. An odd sense of peace washed over her as she paused beside the tomb. There they lay, side by side, together now forever.

The sarcophagus itself was a work of art. She smoothed her fingers over the cool marble. Her father had spared no expense for his beloved wife and he'd commissioned the stonemason to carve his own likeness at the same time. Now his recumbent figure lay next to hers, captured looking years younger than the sixty-two he'd been when he'd died; a fit companion for the beautiful woman beside him. They looked so peaceful; hands folded at their waists, heads resting on carved marble pillows.

She wanted this, Cara realized suddenly. A love greater even than death. She bit her lip as guilt and despair gripped her. She'd promised del Sarto 'until death us do part,' too.

Generations of Montessori had been buried here. Hundreds of years of hopes and dreams, struggles and sorrows, successes and defeats. Cara drew strength from their silent presence, the solidity of the history surrounding her. These were her ancestors. They hadn't lived and died just so she could lose it all. She was *not* going to hand their legacy over to some French upstarts, any more than she'd surrender it to her greedy uncle. She would lead by example. And if that meant giving her life to defend her home, so be it.

She pressed a swift kiss to the stone forehead of her father and slipped out of the chapel. The courtyard was a teeming mass of people, all jostling and shouting. Men hurried to don their armor and gather their weapons while women herded children into the safety of the castle itself. Animals flapped and ran around, adding to the general sense of confusion.

Cara went up to her bedroom and removed her own armor from the trunk at the foot of the bed. Father had reluctantly agreed to let her have it made when he'd realized she was serious about accompanying him on crusade. Since traditional metal armor had been too heavy, she'd chosen a leather breastplate instead. It wouldn't withstand a direct arrow hit or stop a well-aimed blade, but it might temper the blow enough to save her life.

A shout echoed from the watchtower as she descended the front steps and her heart skittered in panic. She sprinted up to the outer walls.

"My lady. Soldiers! At the west gate."

"What? I thought we had more time— "

The soldier looked confused. "Not the French, my lady. Il Diavolo."

Cara's hand went to her throat. "*Del Sarto?* Are you *sure?*"

He pointed over the wall. "See for yourself."

She crossed to the parapet. At least two hundred men were approaching, formed in neat, rectangular sections. A standard-bearer held aloft a familiar banner; a flaming torch on a black ground, and her heart missed a beat.

A rider disengaged from the mass and rode towards the gate. A black helmet obscured his face but the tall figure was unmistakable—even if he hadn't been riding Saraceno. He reigned in and waited, infinitely patient, until one of her own men approached him from the gatehouse.

Cara blinked. Was he even real? Maybe she'd summoned him up with her restless longing. It might be possible. Surely such strong desire could have a magic and pull of its own. *How in hell's name had he arrived so quickly?*

She'd taken every spare boat in San Rocco, so he couldn't have come by river, and the overland route took a minimum of two days' hard ride. The man really *was* the devil they called him. Even time and distance bent to his will.

He wore full battle dress. Unlike his men, who wore mail of silvered steel, his armor was a sinister black, from helmet to shield. It was extremely intimidating, even from this distance, as no doubt it was meant to be. Her stomach pitched.

The soldier glanced at her in question. "My lady, shall we open the gates?"

She nodded. "Lower the drawbridge."

CHAPTER 47

a sudden hush descended upon the bailey as the gates were opened to admit Il Diavolo and Cara froze at the top of the steps as she met the coal-black eyes of her husband.

"Well met, my lady wife."

His loud pronouncement met with a ripple of surprised gasps from the assembled crowd. *So much for keeping their marriage quiet.*

"You weren't at San Rocco when I returned, my love."

His tone was polite, his face serenity itself, but there was an edge to his words that gave them bite. Underneath, she was certain, he was furious. "You should have waited for me. You know how much I enjoy a good fight."

He dismounted and approached her, his spurred boots chinking on the cobbles. He moved with the brisk, confident stride of a man comfortable in his own skin, despite his heavy armor. It wasn't black, as she'd first thought; an intricate gold design had been chased over the blackened metal. Scrolls and arabesques licked the contours of his body like tongues of flame. The moving sections overlapped perfectly, like scalloped shells. The workmanship was exquisite.

He was going to enjoy this, making her beg for his help.

Cara cleared her throat, relieved that her voice didn't quaver. "I have need of your skills, my lord."

He raised a cocky eyebrow and he raked her from head to foot. Her face heated at his suggestive scrutiny. Off to the side, some of the women tittered.

"Your military skills," she clarified quickly.

A brief smile twitched his lips, as if he knew just how hot and dark her thoughts were. He spread his arms wide. "I am yours to command, Sweeting. My men—and my own sorry body—are entirely at your disposal."

He took her hand and helped her down the final steps. "You look surprised to see me, my love. Did you think I'd abandon you in your hour of need?" He stepped back and eyed her armor with amusement. "You're not seriously considering attacking them head-on are you?"

Cara scowled. "I suppose you have a better idea?"

He bowed again, somehow managing to make it both graceful and sarcastic. "Of course."

"Am I allowed to know what it is, or shall I try to guess?" She strode past him through the main door of the keep, swept into the great hall. She settled herself in her father's chair on the dais at the far end of the room, hoping it would lend her an air of much-needed authority.

"I need a plan of the keep," he said.

She motioned to Sansevero, who opened a chest in the corner and withdrew a rolled parchment. Del Sarto spread the paper on a nearby table and leaned over to study it and Cara tried to ignore how big and tanned his hands were as they smoothed down the curling corners. Tried to forget how they'd felt on her skin. "What are you looking for?"

He ignored her question. "Do you have any more of your infamous black powder?"

"A little. Why?"

He stood up again and she cursed the instinctive step back she took to avoid touching him. "Go and get it while I have a word with the men."

"I don't like being ordered around in my own castle."

"It won't be yours for much longer, if you keep arguing," he said with irrefutable logic.

Muttering under her breath, Cara hurried to her room and retrieved the paper twists of powder she'd hidden beneath a loose flagstone. Thank God Lorenzo hadn't discovered *them.* She checked the fastenings on her breastplate and secured the vambrace guards on her wrists.

Del Sarto doubtless didn't approve of her breeches and shirt, either, but she was past caring. She checked the knife in her boot and placed another on her belt. If he thought she was going to sit inside while others defended her home, then he didn't know her at all.

The men were bent over the castle plans when she returned. Del Sarto had removed the lower sections of his armor; the cuisses from his thighs and the greaves from his shins, but he still wore his metal breastplate. He was issuing orders, but looked up as she approached.

"Sansevero's going to wait for the French down at the harbor," he said. "He'll lead them up to the keep where your men will be waiting. My men will hide themselves through the town so we can attack them from all sides."

"And what are you going to be doing?"

His smile was infuriatingly enigmatic. He hauled her away from the table, his fingers tight around her wrist. "The question is, what are *we* going to be doing? Which way to the dungeons?"

Cara frowned in confusion, but directed him to the doorway that led down beneath the keep. He started down the steep spiral staircase and Cara followed.

"We should be up on the battlements, overseeing things," she protested at his broad back. "Why do you want to look down here?" She planted her hands on her hips. "No one's been down here for years. Unlike *you*, father never made much use of his dungeons. He punished people with a week in the stocks. What are we doing?"

* * *

ALESSANDRO ALLOWED himself a grin of anticipation as he prowled ahead of her. "We're looking for something," he said, being obtuse just to annoy her.

"If it's your sanity, believe me, it's long gone," she snapped.

He suppressed a chuckle. God, he loved her temper. "It's a tunnel entrance."

"Don't be ridiculous! There's no tunnel here. This is solid stone. A dead-end. I've lived here my entire life. I'd know if there was a tunnel."

Alessandro leaned against the rock wall and waited for her to catch up. The only light was a pale shaft that slanted in between some iron grilles above his head. It illuminated the solid metal bars and the huge locks that secured the entrance to each cell.

He cocked his head, his hearing heightened by his lack of vision. In his mind's eye he could see her, advancing like a wary cat. He grinned again. She thought she was being quiet. She wasn't. If any of his men made such a racket he'd have had them horse-whipped. Signora del Sarto would never make it as one of his elite band. Even his least-trained boot-boy would hear her approach. He'd have to find the time to teach her to creep up on someone in silence.

He caught a faint hint of her perfume as she moved up beside him and cursed as his groin reacted predictably. He never seemed to stop wanting this infuriating woman. Worse, she was the only one he *wanted* to keep him in this perpetual state of yearning. No one else would do. Part of him hated the power she held over him, even as he rejoiced in her nearness.

He pulled her deeper into the darkness, past the rows of cells, and stopped at the farthest wall.

"You've taken too many blows to the head," she hissed. "I know this castle like the back of my hand. And I can categorically state that—what *are* you doing?"

* * *

DEL SARTO WAS FEELING the rock face above his head, dislodging centuries worth of dust and spiders. He set his fingertips to the stone and pried out a small square section. It revealed an iron ring, rusted and grimy with age. With a grunt of satisfaction, he pulled. A dull rumble and the clanking of hidden chains was followed by a cold blast of musty air that swept over them both, blowing Cara's hair back from her face.

A sharp stab of betrayal hit her. A tunnel, here, under her own feet! Tears stung her eyes. Her father might have loved her, but he obviously hadn't *trusted* her. He'd shared this secret with del Sarto, his faithful protégé, but not his own daughter.

Del Sarto ducked into the narrow passageway that had appeared in the rock and Cara followed, curious despite herself. She bumped her head on an overhanging rock and cursed roundly.

He chuckled. "Such ladylike language."

She shivered as they pushed through the darkness. It was like descending into the bowels of hell. So must Persephone must have felt, being kidnapped by Hades, lord of the underworld. Cara frowned, trying to recall the story. Persephone had married *her* monster, too, hadn't she? Had she grown fond of her dark lover? Did she pine for him when they were apart?

Del Sarto had to bend nearly double to fit into the narrow passage; his broad shoulders brushed the walls, raining cobwebs and dirt onto her head. She covered her nose with her palm as the tunnel began to slope steeply downwards and a flurry of panic robbed her of breath as the walls crowded in. She stumbled, barely able to see her own feet, but he put his hand back and caught hers, entwining their fingers.

He was a dark shape in front of her, a shadowy, inhuman form dragging her into the Stygian darkness. For such a large man he was amazingly quiet. And really, he must be part owl, to be able to see so well.

After what seemed an eternity he stopped and Cara cannoned into his back again. His hand left hers and she had a moment's regret for the loss. Rustling and scraping came from in front, and then he pulled her through a tangle of undergrowth and stood upright, stretching his arms in the twilight.

The sun had almost set while they'd been below, but Cara caught the flash of his teeth as he grinned. The idiot was *enjoying* this.

They'd emerged behind the tiny chapel that stood to one side of the harbor. The entrance to the tunnel had been disguised as the back of a shell-decorated grotto where the locals flipped coins into the shallow pool for luck.

Cara wished she had a coin to toss. They needed all the luck they could get.

They were directly above the beach. Del Sarto stepped forward to the edge of the rocks, placed a finger to his lips for quiet, and pointed downwards. Six huge ships were anchored in the bay. As they watched, a rowboat filled with dark shapes headed for the shore. Moonlight glinted off steel helmets and swords. The slap of oars was audible in the quiet night.

Lanterns on the shore showed where Sansevero had already greeted the first boatload of invaders; their torchlit procession began to make its way up the hill towards the keep.

"Your uncle was a fool to believe he could deal with the French," Del Sarto whispered. "They would have waited until he'd opened the gates and then slit his throat."

Cara shuddered. "So now what?"

He pointed to the narrow bridge that linked the harbor and the town. "Do you have enough black powder to take that down?"

She scowled in sudden understanding. "I am not blowing up my own property!"

"You love reducing things to piles of rubble. Just think of the improvements you can make when you rebuild," he hissed back. "I know it's not much of a challenge compared to an *entire monastery*, but we need to cut them off from their ships."

She did some swift mental calculation. "If we destroy one of the central pillar supports it might do enough damage to make it collapse."

He nodded.

They began to scramble down over the uneven rocks. Despite the imminent danger, or perhaps because of it, Cara had never felt so alive, so aware of her surroundings. She could taste the salty spray of the sea, hear the crash of the waves slapping against the rocks. And the man in front of her, leading her into darkness; she realized with a despairing ache that she'd follow him anywhere, wherever he wanted, even down to hell itself.

Staying low, they climbed down one side of the bridge and splashed into the shallow channel of water beneath. Cara lost her footing on the slippery rocks, stumbled, and pitched forward knee-deep into the water with a hushed curse.

Del Sarto grasped her elbow, steadying her. "No swimming today, sweeting!" He released her and stepped under a shadowed archway, holding his hand out for the explosives. She passed him the tiny paper twists, thankful they'd been spared the water.

"Amazing how something so small can be so dangerous," he whispered. She looked up sharply, certain he was teasing her and tried to gauge his expression, but it was hidden in the shadows as he busied himself stuffing the packets into the gaps between the stones. "How do we light it?"

"A rope fuse." She produced a length of hemp twine. "It's a bit short, but it was all I could find. We won't have much time to take cover."

"There is no 'we'. You take shelter behind those rocks. I'll light it."

Cara put her hands on her hips. "It's *my* bridge. If anyone's going to destroy it, it'll be me."

"Stop arguing! This is just one of those times you have to accept that brawn wins the day. I can run faster than you."

"Fine. But you'll have to be quick." Muffled sounds from the beach drew their attention. "There are more men coming!"

She retreated stealthily and ducked behind a rocky outcrop, sending up a brief prayer for those poor souls who might be injured. French invaders or not, they were still people. But this was her home and they *were* the aggressors. And hellfire, she wasn't going to surrender without a fight.

Another group of men thundered across the bridge, streaming up the hill towards the castle. She saw a spark as del Sarto struck the flint, and then he was scrambling up the bank towards her. He dived over the remaining rocks and landed on top of her just as a huge explosion rocked the world around them.

The flash of light was discernible even behind her closed eyelids. *Sweet Lord!* She must have had more powder than she'd thought! The boom echoed round the cliffs and rocks rained down on them from above.

It was like being back on the cliff, with Piero. Cara began to struggle in panic, but del Sarto's body deflected the hail of rubble; he shielded her, his arms bracketing her head, the long length of him pressed over her, around her. She buried her nose into his chest and held on tight.

As the noise faded he pushed himself off her and pulled her up, patting her on the back as she choked on the cloud of dust. "All right?"

Her ears were ringing so loudly she could barely hear what he was saying. "I'm fine," she mouthed, nodding. "Now what?"

"Find the tunnel entrance and get back to the keep."

"Where are you going?"

"To help Francesco." He was already running away from her.

"Wait! I can fight!"

He stopped and turned back, his face stern. "No! For once in your life, just do as you're told!"

"It's my duty, my responsibility!"

He came right back to her and brought his hands to her face, smoothed his thumbs over her cheekbones. The fierceness left his face as an odd, infuriated-yet-tender expression filled his eyes as he looked down at her.

"I need to know you're safe, Cara. Do this for me. Please?"

Please. It was the first time she'd ever heard him say it. He wasn't the sort of man who asked; he gave orders and they were obeyed. He'd probably only said it a few times in his life.

It was hardly a declaration of love, but still, it was *something*, and she was desperate enough to take whatever meagre scraps of affection he threw at her, fool that she was. She nodded. "All right."

He dropped a brief kiss on her hair and stepped back. "Go. I'll see you when it's over." Then he turned and vanished into the night.

CHAPTER 48

*A*s the ringing in Cara's ears receded, the unmistakable noise of metal-on-metal intruded. Shouts of alarm echoed from the keep as the French discovered they'd been deceived. Fire engulfed the bridge; the yawning gap in the centre made passage for those still arriving impossible.

A man ran past Cara toward the beach, shouting in panic as fire licked his clothing. He threw himself down into the surf where he rolled and thrashed to put out the flames. Two stray dogs joined in, yapping in delight, convinced this was a new and exciting game.

Cara took in the scene with a sense of horrified detachment. It was like a vision of hell. Smoke billowed across the harbor, obscuring the town. She held her sleeve to her mouth and staggered toward the nearest building, trying to find the path back up to the chapel, but the acrid smoke distorted everything and made her eyes stream and she couldn't find the way. She slipped between two houses, gasping for breath as another group of soldiers ran by. In the darkness she couldn't tell if they were French troops or her own men.

Frustrated by the smoke, she abandoned the idea of finding

the tunnel entrance and started up one of the narrow alleyways that headed towards the keep instead. The sounds of fighting grew louder as she neared the main square and she gasped as she turned the corner and came face to face with Sansevero and a group of her men engaged with the enemy. Sansevero crossed swords with the nearest Frenchman and their blades struck sparks as they glanced off the edge of the stone fountain. He overpowered the man, but four more ran forward, screaming a battle cry.

Cara didn't hesitate. She snatched the dagger from her boot and hurled it at the nearest Frenchman. He gave a strangled cry and fell to the ground as the blade found its mark.

Sansevero dealt with another man, then glanced around to see who'd saved his life. He shot her an incredulous look. "My lady! You shouldn't be here!" he panted, striking down another man with a savage kick to the knee and a slash of his blade. "Get back to the keep!"

"I'm trying!" Cara croaked, pressing herself back against the wall to avoid another scuffle. Heart pounding, she skirted the fountain then ducked into an alleyway that led up to the castle.

The sounds of fighting echoed from every direction, the noise magnified by the angled streets. She sprinted up the wide, shallow steps but her boots slipped on the worn cobbles and she went down hard onto her hands and knees, cursing.

"Little bitch!"

A figure loomed out of the alleyway to her right and Cara's stomach clenched in dread as she recognized the livid features of her uncle Lorenzo.

His expression was murderous, his clothing filthy and in disarray. She grabbed for the dagger on her belt and cursed as she realized it wasn't there. She must have dropped it when she stumbled. She scanned the ground in front of her, but it was too dark to see where it had gone.

Lorenzo's face was twisted in a rictus of hatred as he advanced towards her. "You killed my son! My only son!"

"*You* killed my father!" She countered, fury overtaking her terror. "Your own brother." She scrambled away, as if retreating from a wild animal. "Piero's death is your fault, too. Your greed led to this, *uncle,* nothing else." Her backside hit the doorstep of a house, stopping her retreat.

Lorenzo's eyes glittered as he realized he had her cornered. "I should have killed you myself, when I first came to Castelleon," he panted. "Recognize this?" He held up a blade so it caught the moonlight and she gasped. Her father's sword.

He had no right to defile it.

"How *dare* you raise that to me! You're not even fit to touch it!"

Rage erupted in her chest and she launched herself at him, heedless of the weapon.

Her sudden attack took him by surprise; she swiped the blade aside with her forearm, protected from the wicked edge by her leather vambrace. The force of her body knocked him off his feet and they both went down in a flurry of limbs. Cara pummeled at his face and head with her fists, heedless of the pain, screaming in fury.

Lorenzo cursed as her knuckles connected with his jaw and his head smashed back against the cobbles. He rolled them both over, yanked her head back, and wrapped his fingers around her throat. Cara clawed at him, gasping for breath, but he was stronger. She flailed around with her hands and connected with a flowerpot that was decorating a doorstep. She smashed it against the side of his head.

Lorenzo howled and loosened his grip. She crawled away, gulping as she tried to catch her breath, but before she could shout for help, he staggered up and delivered a brutal kick to her ribs. Cara collapsed on the cobbles in agony as stars winked in front of her eyes.

He circled her, panting. "Get up, you little whore. I'm not done with you yet."

She didn't want to die like this. Not in some filthy gutter in a dark street, only a few hundred feet from the safety of her own walls. She tried to think, but her brain was thick like wool. She wanted to lie down and never get up.

Something hot was running down her cheek and her left eye was already difficult to open. She could hear rapid panting, the sounds of a frightened animal, and realized they were coming from her.

Lorenzo grabbed the back of her shirt and flung her over on to her back, then dropped down on top of her, spouting a mad litany of obscenities. His wiry body pressed against hers and his knee pushed between her thighs. He tugged at her leather breastplate, but couldn't break the straps that fastened it.

Cara thrashed madly, clawing at his face, but he held her pinned as he fumbled with the front of his breeches, then her own. Her waistband tore with a ripping sound and then she felt his hand clutching at the bare skin of her thigh, her buttock.

Bile rose in her throat and white-hot anger flashed through her as she realized his intent. Rape. She'd rather die. She stopped struggling, feigning exhaustion, which earned her a panting laugh from Lorenzo.

"That's it. Stop fighting. You want it, don't you?"

He brought a filthy hand up to cup her chin. A thin skein of his spittle dripped onto her face as he leaned over her, blocking out the sky. Cara forced herself to stay still, to endure it, even as every muscle was screaming for her to push him away.

"You look just like your mother, you know," he rasped. "Such a beauty. And haughty, just like she was." His thumb stroked her cheek in an obscene caress, smearing blood. Then he bared his teeth in a bitter snarl. "She thought she was too good for me, too. Chose that whoreson brother of mine instead of me."

"He was a hundred times the man you'll ever be!"

Lorenzo's eyes widened in fury. Cara gathered all her strength and kneed him between the legs. He let out a scream of outrage and fell sideways, curling into a ball, his hands clutching his groin. Cara dragged herself up and staggered back down the hill, towards Sansevero and safety.

But Lorenzo wasn't beaten. She could hear him behind her as she stumbled down the steps into the piazza. Her ankle twisted on an uneven cobble and pain shot up her leg.

Oh, God. The square was empty save for the bodies of the men Sansevero had killed. The fight had moved on. Whimpering and gasping in pain, she hobbled over to one of the fallen men and grabbed his sword from the ground just as Lorenzo emerged into the square. He laughed when he saw the blade shaking in her hands, but stepped back when she swung it at his chest.

Cara backed herself up against a wall, using it for both balance and defense. And then a group of Frenchmen entered the square to her left.

There was no way out.

A fatalistic sense of calm washed over her. She wasn't going down without a fight. She was her father's daughter. Il Diavolo's wife. She refused to dishonor either of them.

With a hoarse battle cry she pushed off from the wall and charged at her uncle, bracing herself to receive a fatal blow. It never came. What *did* come was del Sarto, looming out of the darkness like an avenging angel of death.

CHAPTER 49

The French soldiers attacked in unison but del Sarto dispatched them all with chilling efficiency. He ran one through with his sword then twisted the neck of another with a sickening crack before the man could even shout out a warning. Two more rushed him from behind, but he dealt with them too, cutting a lethal swathe directly toward Cara and Lorenzo.

Lorenzo's first blow had landed harmlessly on her breastplate, and he disengaged with a hiss, acknowledging the new player in the game. "Ah, your guard dog. Right on time."

Del Sarto barely flicked Cara a glance, but it was clearly enough for him to notice the damage to her face and neck. "Did he do that?" he asked mildly.

She nodded, gasping for breath.

"All right then." He faced Lorenzo, and his expression hardened. "You're a dead man."

Lorenzo raised his blade in silent challenge. He edged towards Cara again, but del Sarto blocked him, stalking him around the fountain instead, pressing him back.

Cara tried to make herself as small as possible as the two men circled, their intent faces lit by the eerie red light thrown from the burning bridge. When they came together she stifled a moan at the ferocity of the attack. This was no practice bout; it was a fight to the death, brutal and deadly, and both men knew it. The jarring sound of metal-on-metal bounced off the walls and she shrank back, terrified that she might distract them.

Lorenzo was no match for del Sarto's skill but fury and sheer desperation lent him a demonic strength. He threw himself forward time and time again, battering del Sarto's armor, always just managing to dodge a fatal blow, and screaming his fury as he received one shallow nick after another. He hissed and cupped his ear as he received a slash across the cheek.

With a sickening flash of insight Cara realized that Alessandro was toying with her uncle, inflicting pain through a thousand tiny cuts and the unsporting part of her was glad that Lorenzo was being punished. He deserved to suffer. He'd shown no mercy to her father when he'd hacked him down in cold blood.

Lorenzo's panting grunts echoed around the square but del Sarto was frighteningly silent, as though any noise would be a waste of his deadly efficiency. Lorenzo's sword arm was knocked to the side and he pressed forward, trying to head-butt. Alessandro elbowed him in the throat and he staggered back. Lorenzo lowered his blade as he struggled for breath, but recovered at the last second to deflect what should have been a lethal blow. Teeth bared in fury, he spat in del Sarto's face and pressed home his momentary advantage, slashing his blade across his thigh, just below the protection of his breastplate.

Cara screamed as the flesh was sliced open. Blood poured from the gash and Lorenzo hissed in satisfaction, but del Sarto barely gave the wound a second glance. He attacked again, battering Lorenzo back mercilessly.

Lorenzo was flagging. He gave a howl of frustration and swung his blade in a wide arc toward del Sarto's head but he deflected Lorenzo's wrist and slammed it against the wall with a sickening crunch. Lorenzo gave a high-pitched scream and dropped his sword. Alessandro grabbed his hair and pulled his head back, his blade poised to slash his throat.

Cara must have made a sound of protest, because he suddenly stilled and shot her a cold, furious glance over his shoulder.

"One word. One word and I'll kill him," he promised, panting with exertion.

She froze. He was looking to her for a decision. For judgement.

Lorenzo dropped to his knees, sobbing and whimpering, all his previous fight gone. "Oh, God save, niece, have mercy!" he begged. He tried to crawl towards her but del Sarto jerked him back viciously.

Cara shook her head. Lorenzo didn't deserve to live. He'd murdered her father. But could she truly give the signal to end his life?

Del Sarto saw her indecision. With a scornful sound he stepped back, looking disgusted by both Lorenzo's blubbering and, presumably, her weakness. Cara had just opened her mouth to apologize when Lorenzo snatched a dagger from his belt and thrust it hilt-deep into del Sarto's shoulder.

Del Sarto let out a roar of fury. Without conscious thought, Cara snatched her father's sword from the ground and swung it at her uncle. Muscle and flesh gave way beneath the blade in a sickening jolt and she stepped back in horror as Lorenzo's gloating look of triumph faded to one of incredulity. He clutched at the wound with a gasp, then slowly pitched forward onto the floor. A puddle of red pooled beneath him as he writhed, and then stilled.

Cara looked away, sickened. Her stomach heaved and she concentrated on drawing breaths through her mouth. It was no less than Lorenzo deserved. He'd killed her father. Stabbed her husband.

She turned back. The sounds of battle still rang out from the keep above, but del Sarto stood outlined by flame like some ancient god of fire, his sword clenched in his hand. The muscles of his arms were dirty with dust and sweat and blood. As Cara watched, he lowered his head and closed his eyes as if in prayer, then swayed slightly.

Her chest tightened. He was the absolute antithesis of a white knight in shining armor but she didn't care. She'd never been so grateful for his deadly talents. With a sob of relief she collapsed against the wall as her knees gave way. It was over. Finally. Her father was avenged.

Del Sarto turned at her moan and for an instant he stared at her in blank incomprehension; it was the same glazed look he'd had in the forest after reliving his nightmare. And then he seemed to come back to himself—he strode forward and shot her a baleful glance. "I thought I told you to go back to the bloody keep! You could have been killed!"

"I tried!" Cara gasped at the unfairness of the accusation. She struggled up and stumbled towards him, her limbs shaking. "Oh, God! You're hurt. Let me help."

He glanced down and seemed surprised to see Lorenzo's dagger still protruding from his shoulder. He balanced his bloody sword on the edge of the fountain, wrapped both hands around the hilt, and withdrew it with a wince. He tossed it onto the ground with a grimace of distaste. Fresh blood poured from the wound, running in dark rivulets down his arm, staining his white shirtsleeves. He bent to inspect the gash on his thigh. "It's not that bad," he said dispassionately.

Cara made a cry of distress at his cavalier attitude. The wounds were severe. She tore a strip from her already-ripped shirt and bundled it into a pad, then pressed it to his shoulder. Warm wetness spread against her hand as his blood immediately soaked through the fabric. "We have to get back to the castle! Let me bind this up."

He put his hand over hers and pressed down harder, holding the cloth in place and she glanced up into his face. He looked exhausted. Lines of pain were etched around his mouth.

She glanced back at her uncle's body, then quickly away. "Are you sure he's dead?"

A slight quiver of amusement touched his thinned lips, making him more familiar, less remote. "Would you like me to kill him again, just to make sure?"

She shuddered at his morbid humor. "No thank you."

He pushed her hair back, exposing her bruised throat and swollen eye, and his eyes narrowed. "He hurt you. He deserved it." He stroked her cheekbone with his thumb.

Cara leaned in to him, hating the frustratingly solid metal of his chest plate. She wanted to feel him, wanted his arms around her, his strength and comforting solidity. Every fibre of her willed him to gather her into his arms, to kiss her, but the exasperating man refused to co-operate. Instead he pulled away and strode to the edge of the square.

A fierce battle was still raging in the harbor below. A wave of men swarmed like ants over the low wall to the beach and Cara realized that it was the French, being driven back by her men from the keep.

The invaders shouted in dismay when they discovered the bridge was impassable. Some tried to scramble over the rocks to get away, while others braved the smoke and splashed down into the shallow stream. Those on the beach were already fleeing, diving into the boats and rowing back to their ships with all speed. Castelleon's men raced forward to engage the stragglers, and soon the whole beach was a wild melée of scuffles, with swords and curses flying in all directions.

Within minutes it was all over. A large group of the French, realizing the futility of escape, surrendered and were being rounded up at one end of the harbor. Castelleon's men lined the water's edge, jeering and shouting obscenities at the departing invaders and waving their weapons in the air in elation.

Cara hugged her arms around her body. *It was done.* She let her gaze drift over the beating surf and limitless sea. The stars twinkled timelessly, immune to the human drama being enacted far below. Her eyes watered and stung. Her throat hurt. It was the smoke; she wasn't going to cry. Not now it was all over.

She let out a shaky breath. "Thank you."

It seemed such an inadequate thing to say for all that he'd done.

When there was no answer she glanced round and saw del Sarto limping back toward the castle. She hobbled after him as quickly as her own injured ankle would allow. When she reached him she slung her arm around his waist, drew his own arm over her shoulder, and forestalled his rejection with a sharp look. "Don't argue. We both need a little support."

With a growl of defeat he pulled her tighter into his body and together they made their halting way toward the keep.

CHAPTER 50

$\mathcal{B}$y the time they arrived at the castle, flushed and panting from their progress up the hill, the townsfolk were already celebrating. As soon as they got close enough to be seen del Sarto straightened and pulled away from her, trying to hide the extent of his injuries, unwilling to let anyone see him vulnerable. Cara sighed.

She'd never seen the place more crowded, even in her father's time. A huge bonfire had been lit in the central courtyard and people crowded round, toasting the night's victory. Bianca, her old lady's maid, caught sight of her first. She clasped her in a smothering hug, shrieking with relief.

"Cara! My love, you're alive! We thought you'd been taken, or killed. You scared me half to death!" she scolded. "How many times have I told you that proper young women do NOT get involved in fighting!"

This was a familiar theme. Cara had heard it, or a variation of it, almost every day since she'd been old enough to pick up a slingshot. Modest and chaste young ladies did not jump moats, throw daggers, or blow things up. "Yes, Bianca."

Sansevero, bruised and battered, one eye already puffed and

closing, elbowed his way through the crowd and pulled her from Bianca's arms. "Let her go, you old fuss-pot!" He held Cara at arms length and kissed her soundly on both cheeks. "My lady, congratulations! The French are running back to their ships like whipped puppies. We've put the prisoners in the cells. You can decide what to do with them on the morrow, but I say we ransom them back to the French king and fill our coffers."

"How are the men?"

"A few minor injuries, nothing serious. Toni the baker has broken his arm, and Gianni's taken a knock to the head, but he'll be fine by morning. Destroying the bridge was brilliant. They didn't know which way to run! Your father would have been proud, my girl."

"It wasn't all my doing. Del Sarto—" she glanced around and stopped as she realized her husband was nowhere to be seen. Frowning, she allowed herself to be hustled into the great hall and pushed up onto the dais to take the place of honor in her father's chair. A cup of wine was thrust into her hand and she took a sip, listening patiently as each man recounted his own vital part in the battle. Her impatience mounted as she watched the laughing, jubilant faces around her and she forced a tight smile, though her cheeks ached with the effort.

Her temples throbbed. This was what she'd wanted, was it not? Her home had been liberated. Her people were safe. She should have been delighted, but all she wanted was to crawl into bed and sleep for a week. And where was del Sarto, to share the victory with her? It was as much his as it was hers.

She was about to excuse herself when the doors of the hall flew open and he finally deigned to make an appearance. A resounding cheer went up. The crowd parted instinctively to let him through and Cara's pulse quickened as he stalked down the centre of the room towards her.

Once again he reminded her of a wolf. Tall and sleek, all sinew and muscle. He'd changed his bloodstained clothes; gone was his battered black armor—a leather breastplate was buckled over a clean white shirt. He was every inch the soldier, merciless, fierce, commanding the room with his presence alone. Every eye followed his progress as he approached her.

Cara watched him for signs of discomfort, but he moved with long, fluid strides. Only the most observant would notice the slight stiffness in his gait when he put his full weight on his thigh, or the way he held his right shoulder immobile. He was back to being Il Diavolo, a formal, invulnerable stranger.

A wave of sadness swept over her. How good he was at hiding his pain.

He stopped a few feet away from her and she stood, enjoying the extra height the dais granted her. They were almost eye to eye. She clenched her fists against the urge to reach out and stroke the stubble that darkened his cheeks, to smooth away the weariness she saw in his eyes.

"On behalf of Castelleon's inhabitants, I thank you," she said stiffly.

His eyes burned into hers. "I didn't do it for them."

"I know," she said with a sigh. "You have a vested interest in its survival, since half of it is yours."

It would *all* belong to him if they ever consummated their marriage.

He didn't contradict her—which made her spirits sink even more. He regarded her with the same unswerving concentration with which he probably surveyed a battlefield or a besieged keep. She'd seen some of the men cross themselves after receiving the full force of those compelling, mocking eyes and right now she could see why. Del Sarto looked straight into a man's soul, assessed him, and usually found him wanting.

"I'll be leaving for San Rocco at dawn." His expression was unreadable.

Was he expecting her to go with him? Cara lowered her voice so only he could hear. "I want to stay here."

His brows rose.

"Our marriage was a mistake," she whispered quickly, before she lost her nerve. "But it's not too late to remedy it. I want an annulment."

His lips twisted. "Of course it's too late." His voice, unlike hers, echoed round the hall. "You could be carrying my child even now."

Cara felt her face heat in mortification as she realized it could be true. Scandalized gasps and whispers broke out on all sides. He treated her to his most irritating smirk. "No need to be embarrassed, my love. Not after the things we've done together."

His heated gaze could have set a hayrick on fire. A group of townswomen to her right nudged each other in delight. Cara could have scratched his eyes out, witnesses be damned. She'd never been so embarrassed in her life. She clenched her fists at her sides, this time resisting the temptation to do him bodily harm.

"A divorce, then," she said. "I'll write and appeal to the Pope himself—tell him you wed me without my consent."

"You consented," he said darkly. "And Borgia's more likely to congratulate me than to grant you your freedom. He's no paragon himself."

His eyes were shuttered, betraying nothing and for the hundredth time Cara wished she could read him.

"Still, if that's truly what you want, I'll look into it," he said. "I've no desire for a reluctant wife. As I told you before, I want you willing, or not at all."

Her stomach dropped at his words. Wasn't he even going to try to talk her out of it? Did he care so little for her? Maybe he was *glad* she wasn't going with him. He'd probably tired of her already. Was ready to move on to pastures new, now he'd secured Castelleon?

"If that's all, my lady?" Without waiting for her assent, he sketched another effortless bow and strode out of the hall.

Cara clenched her fists so hard that her nails scored crescents into her palms. She wanted to scream, to throw something after him, *anything* to shake his perfect cool composure. But her battered pride refused to call him back. She stood and watched him walk out.

As soon as she could escape the celebrations, she slipped back to her rooms. Not even bothering to undress, she splashed water on her smoke-blackened face and collapsed on the bed. Tired as she was, though, sleep was elusive. Her mind kept conjuring images of her ridiculously heroic, how-dare-he-leave-her? husband. She clutched a pillow to her chest and told herself she wasn't lonely.

She hadn't made the wrong decision. She couldn't go with him. Her place was here. She had everyone in this castle. They loved her. They were safe. That was the important thing.

But Bianca would be curling up next to her husband in their cosy rooms by the kitchen. The soldiers would all be returning to their wives or their sweethearts. Even the stable boys and kitchen girls would be finding their respective partners for the night.

Was her husband eager to console himself in the traditional post-battle way? He could surely find a willing body to help him celebrate his victory if he so desired. Jealousy burned through her like scalding oil. He'd promised to be faithful only to her!

Cara punched the pillow and tortured herself with an image of him with someone else, someone buxom and experienced and agreeable. Someone who wouldn't answer him back, who'd obey him without question. Someone like Julia Canozzi.

She squeezed her eyes shut and willed sleep to come.

CHAPTER 51

*H*e left at daybreak.

Cara watched from the battlements as the ordered rows of men disappeared over the horizon, annoyed at how desperate she was for a glimpse of blackened armor amid the throng. Her heart skipped a beat every time she caught sight of a dark-haired man, then sank in disappointment when he turned out to be too short or too fat or too . . . everything.

Misery twisted her gut. Could a person die from unhappiness? It seemed stupidly dramatic, like something one of Ovid's silly water nymphs might do, but she could have sworn she actually *ached* from loving him. The heart was only a muscle, after all. Surely it could be cut and bruised like any other?

She spent the rest of the morning overseeing the repairs to the keep that needed attention. Then she and Sansevero outlined a host of other improvements they could make with the money from ransoming the French prisoners back to their own king. Cara couldn't summon much excitement about any of it.

Ten days later, she was a shattered wreck. She jumped every time a visitor arrived, still stupidly expecting *him* to walk through the doorway and order her about in his usual high-handed manner.

She *hated* moping. It was all very well for Chrétien de Troye's heroines; they had nothing better to do except languish about and sigh all day. *She* had a keep to run, although it seemed to be doing perfectly well without her, as usual.

She'd avenged her father's death. Castelleon was safe.

It wasn't enough.

She shivered, even though the air was warm. She was cold without del Sarto. Cold and empty and bored. It was galling to realize how much she missed him, even the bossy infuriating bits. Their daily clashes had been exhilarating, something to get out of bed for in the mornings. Getting under his skin had become her favorite occupation.

The days weren't so bad. She kept herself feverishly busy with tasks around the keep, driving everyone insane with her constant meddling. But at night she lay awake in the lonely darkness of her tower room and ached for him.

She'd read, once, about a soldier who'd lost a hand in battle. The man claimed he could still feel the sensations of the missing limb; hot and cold, itching and burning, as if his fingers were still there. She felt the same way about del Sarto. As if an integral part of her were missing. And the empty space where her heart should be still throbbed with pain.

* * *

CARA SAT IN THE SOLAR, staring disconsolately into the fire. The light through the high windows had long since faded to darkness. This room, more than any other in the keep, reminded her of her father. They'd spent most of their evenings here, talking, playing chess, or just reading quietly in each other's company. Her stomach twisted with a knot of longing and loss.

Gathering her wits, she glanced down at the rumpled piece of linen in her hand. She'd been trying to embroider a handkerchief, with scant success. Hector lay curled at her feet like a hairy hearthrug, snoring happily, paws twitching as he dreamed of chasing rabbits in his sleep. Abbott Andreo was seated at her father's desk, engrossed in reading a pile of documents.

Despite the company, Cara felt hollow and abandoned. She'd made such a mess of things. And for what? Pride? Stubbornness? Independence? The silence from Torre di San Rocco had become ominous. Waiting for del Sarto to make his next move was like waiting for the headman's axe to fall.

She scowled down at the stupid flower she was trying to sew. She'd pulled the thread too tight and the whole thing was wrinkled and lopsided. It looked like a wizened prune. She hated embroidery. She stabbed the needle down hard and yelped as she pricked her finger.

The Abbott glanced up as she threw the offending linen away and sucked the tip of her finger. She gestured to the sheaf of papers in front of him. "What are you reading?"

"Your father's will. It was stored at Saint John's for safekeeping. I received it from Brother Giovanni this morning."

"No nasty surprises, I hope? Like another half-uncle?" Cara said, only half joking.

Andreo chuckled. "No. He left Castelleon to you, as promised."

Cara rested her chin on her arm. "It's del Sarto's now." At least, half of it was. They still hadn't officially consummated their marriage. Would they *ever* do so? This entire situation—half-wed, half-not, was insupportable.

Andreo picked up a folded packet from the desk and handed it to her. "This was also in your father's papers. It's addressed to you, my dear."

Cara frowned as she broke the seal and recognized her father's neat, scholarly handwriting. Tears blurred the dark lines as memories of him came flooding back. Would he have been proud of what she'd done? Of how was managing the keep? She prayed so. She'd done her best, overseeing the myriad tasks that needed attention. Despite her husband's dire predictions about her leniency, she'd forced herself to mete out justly severe punishments to a horse thief and a baker accused of cheating his measures. The dungeons had seen some use, after all.

The letter was brief, but it took a few moments for its meaning to sink in. When it did, Cara's heart swelled with gratitude and disbelief. She glanced at the second sheet for confirmation then re-read the lines again. It was as if her father had heard her prayers. Proof of his confidence in her was right here, in her shaking hands.

"Well?" the Abbott asked.

She swallowed a sob and showed him the plan of the castle she held. "There are three different passageways, hidden within the walls. Only to be used in times of *dire* emergency." She lowered her voice, as if in confession. "When Alessandro uncovered that tunnel in the dungeons, I couldn't believe that father hadn't trusted me with the secret. I was so jealous of the friendship they shared, the years they spent fighting together. I always thought father would have preferred Alessandro for his son rather than me as his daughter."

Andreo tsked in disapproval. "How could you have doubted him? Yes, they shared a friendship, and each loved and respected the other, but for all your father's grumbling, he was always so proud of you. He never considered leaving this place to anyone other than yourself."

A great weight lifted off Cara's shoulders, one she hadn't even realized was there. Her heart felt like it would burst with a combination of pride and relief.

"He only wanted you to be happy, my dear. That's why he was always pushing you to get married. He knew you were quite capable of shouldering the responsibilities of ruling alone, but he wanted you to find someone with whom to share the burden—as he'd done with your mother."

Cara lowered her head and stared at her hands, blinking back tears. She'd found someone. Only he didn't want to share *anything* with her, least of all a future.

A commotion in the hallway made them both glance up and her heart leapt as she recognized the visitor being shown into the room. "Francesco! You have news from San Rocco?" She winced inwardly at the eagerness in her voice. She was pathetic.

"My Lady." The old soldier's nod was inscrutable, neither welcoming nor unfriendly. Just professional. He shook out his coat and handed her a folded document.

Her pulse stuttered as she recognized del Sarto's familiar coat of arms, the red wax seal made with the impression of his signet ring she was still stubbornly wearing on her left hand.

"What's this?" she stammered, making no move to take it. "Are we divorced?"

The old man shook his head. "Of course not. You'd need a dispensation from the pope for that."

She almost sagged with relief. "So what—?"

"It's your marriage documents, my lady. You left them at San Rocco. It appears you've never read them."

"I didn't have time." Cara studied his face carefully. "Is he well? My lord, I mean."

"Well enough," Francesco grunted. "If you discount being at death's door for the past week. He took a fever from the wound to his leg." He met her eyes reproachfully, as if the blame could be laid at her feet. "We almost lost him."

Cara's knees buckled and she clutched at the table for support. "He's been ill? Why did no one tell me? Why did no one send for me?"

Francesco leveled her an accusing glare from under his bushy brows. "And what would you have done, my lady? You said you would not return to San Rocco willingly. Would you have rushed to his side with your potions and salves?"

She flinched at his acerbic tone but met his glare. "Yes," she said. "I would have."

He seemed mollified by that. "He doesn't know I'm here," he admitted. "He'd kill me if he knew. He made me swear I wouldn't fetch you."

Her heart sank. "He didn't send you?"

Francesco hesitated, clearly unsure whether to continue, then forged on. "It was *you* he called out for in his fever. Your name he mutters in his sleep." He thrust the folded papers at her again. "Read this. It tells you everything you need to know about your husband, my lady. And what he thinks of you." He turned for the door. "I have to get back before I'm missed. But I could do with a tankard of ale before I go."

Cara belatedly remembered her manners and ushered him into the hallway. "Of course."

"I can find my own way to the kitchens, my lady," Francesco said, stepping past her. "You read that. And then tell me if you want me to take a message back."

Stunned, Cara sank into a chair, broke the seal, and hastily scanned the contents. It was written in del Sarto's own hand; the strokes were bold and forceful, elegant and impatient, just like the man. To her untrained eye it seemed to be the usual assortment of 'in-so-far-as' and 'hereuntoforths'.

Andreo leaned over her shoulder and began to read, too. Presently he chuckled.

"What's wrong?" Cara asked, instantly suspicious.

The Abbott glanced up, a twinkle in his eye. "This is quite unlike any betrothal document I've ever seen."

"What do you mean?"

"Well, marriage agreements generally list all the things that the bride brings to the marriage . . . "

"I know," Cara sighed miserably. "The Sforzas paid the Gonzagas nine thousand ducats when Beatrice got betrothed."

"Precisely." Andreo's grin widened, showing several gaps in his teeth. "But this clearly states that you bring nothing to the marriage except Castelleon. Instead del Sarto's listed all the things that he, as the *bridegroom,* was prepared to give to you on becoming his wife."

Cara frowned. "That can't be right. He only married me to get Castelleon."

Andreo pointed to a paragraph halfway down the page. "He renounces all claim to it. It is to be your property until your death, to keep or dispose of as you will."

Cara stared at him in astonishment. "He's given it to me? Entirely? I can stay here forever?" She narrowed her eyes. "Read it again. Del Sarto never does anything without good reason. What does he want? Mooring rights? A yearly tithe?"

She reread the document with a growing sense of disbelief, searching for some trick, but there was none. He truly renounced all claim to Castelleon and all of its incomes. And in the event of *his* death, everything he owned, including Torre di San Rocco, his fleet, and all his business assets would pass to *her.*

The room spun. "He's giving me everything. In exchange for nothing."

Andreo turned the paper over. "Ah. Look. There's a codicil."

"I knew it!" She squinted at the script. "What does it say?"

"Castelleon is yours *except* in the event of a divorce or an annulment, in which case *he* gets full control."

Her breath caught in her throat. "You mean I have to stay married to him to keep it?"

"It appears so."

"But I don't have to *live* with him?"

"Well, no. But you'll never be free to marry anyone else."

Cara closed her eyes. *She'd never be free of him.* It was both a blessing and a curse. The devious swine was determined to make the rest of her life a misery.

"It doesn't make any sense. What does he gain by writing this?"

Andreo tilted his head. "He doesn't gain anything. He's granting you your freedom, should you want it. But he's also showing that in marrying you, he was getting precisely what he wanted. You. And *only* you."

He studied her, a glimmer of amusement in his pale eyes. "I agree it doesn't make any sense for a soldier or a politician. But it makes perfect sense for a man who's hopelessly in love with his own wife."

Cara stared at him. "He left me. If he truly wanted me, he'd just gallop over here, lay siege to the place, and drag me back to San Rocco by force."

The old man chuckled. "He's a proud warrior. You dented his pride by renouncing him so publicly. I doubt he'll be satisfied with anything less than your unconditional surrender now."

Cara's heart pounded against her ribs. *I want you willing or not at all.* She pressed the heel of her palms against her eyes. "But Castelleon—"

"—will manage perfectly well without you, my dear," Andreo said gently. "Your father wouldn't have wanted you to put it above your own happiness. Appoint a steward to manage it in your absence. Bricks and mortar won't keep you warm at night." His bawdy chuckle was far more suited to Renata than an elderly man of the cloth.

Cara dropped her head into her hands. "Oh, God, I've been so stupid haven't I?"

The Abbott gave a benign nod. "People in love generally are, I believe."

She jumped up. "I have to go with Francesco. Now."

"Of course you do, my dear. And don't worry; absence makes the heart grow fonder. God speed."

CHAPTER 52

his was the third time she'd sneaked into his rooms.

Cara pushed open the door and peered in, expecting to find Alessandro in bed, but the huge mattress was empty. She glanced round warily. A fire had been lit in the grate. An empty bottle and a half-drunk glass of wine stood on a table next to the wing chair.

She registered a presence behind her an instant before she was grabbed around the waist and pulled back against a solid, masculine body. A very *familiar* body. Alessandro's scent enveloped her. She couldn't see his face but she'd recognize him anywhere; in the lowest regions of hell, the blinding whiteness of a snowstorm, the deepest, darkest recesses of her heart. She opened her mouth to speak, but his fingers covered her lips.

"Don't scream!" he whispered roughly at her ear.

"I never scream," she mumbled against his fingers. Her lips tingled at his touch. She wanted to open her mouth and bite him.

He withdrew his hand and stepped back as though the feel of her burned him. "That's what you say about fainting."

She turned and her belly lurched at the sight of him; panic, excitement, despair. He strode across the room, dropped heavily into the chair, and stared moodily into the fire. She smoothed the front of her dress.

"I heard you were ill."

"Come to finish me off, have you?" he growled. "It's a bit late to act the doting wife at my deathbed. You'll have to wait a while to play the merry widow. The doctors say I'll live." He sounded less than thrilled at the prospect.

She studied him by the light of the fire. Despite his protestations, he looked awful. His hair was mussed and untidy. Black stubble darkened his jaw. His tanned face was drawn, the skin tight, with a splash of red over his cheekbones. His shirt lay carelessly open to the waist revealing a bandage binding his shoulder and crossing his chest. The white linen contrasted starkly with his tawny skin. Her heart ached for him.

He turned his head suddenly and his black eyes bored into hers. "Why are you here?"

Goose bumps raised the hairs on her arms at his unwelcoming tone but she stepped forward. This was no time for cowardice. *Temerity is never successful.* She lifted her chin. "I came to ask you why you married me."

His lips curled in a mirthless sneer. "Because I thought you could provide a distraction in bed to keep my nightmares away." He raked her with a bold, suggestive glance and Cara ignored the feverish flush that swept her skin.

She shook her head. "That's not it."

He turned back to the fire. "I wanted someone to run my keep."

She took another step forward. "If that were true you could have done a lot better than someone utterly lacking in feminine accomplishments."

He raised his glass to her in a scornful toast.

"I doubt you're supposed to be drinking that," she said.

He tossed back the contents. "Such a good wife," he mocked. "I should have married someone like Julia Canozzi. She wouldn't have given me half the trouble you have."

That stung. Bastard. Cara stepped closer, so her skirts brushed his knees, determined to break through the barrier of his angry reserve. He still refused to look at her. "I read our marriage documents."

His eyes narrowed. *"Francesco,"* he growled. "I'll strangle that bastard when I see him."

"You've given me Castelleon."

He met her eyes. "So I have. Why do *you* think I married you, then?"

She tilted her head. "Not for my money. I haven't got much."

He grunted in agreement.

"A warped sense of loyalty toward my father, maybe?"

He snorted. "I don't have any loyalty. I keep telling you that."

"Then I don't know why," Cara shrugged. "You're obviously ashamed of me. You married me in secret, after all."

His expression turned thunderous. "Ashamed of you? I declared it to everyone in your whole damn keep, not two weeks ago! You can't get much more public than that. What more did you want?"

Hope tightened her chest. He was no longer distant. He was furious. His voice held all the anger and frustration of a fox run to ground. She reached forward and placed her hand on his rough cheek. He flinched but suffered her touch.

"I'm here. Willingly."

He stilled.

"I've loved you since I was sixteen years old," she said.

His eyes widened, then he jerked his head away and scowled down at the fire again. "You don't know what you're saying. You don't love me. You love the *idea* of me. The Invincible Diavolo." His tone was thick with derision.

She started to speak, but he silenced her with an impatient gesture. "Look at me. It'll take months to walk without a limp. I might never fight again. Half the time I can't even sleep. Find some other poor bastard to win your battles for you. I'm done."

"Do you really think that's all you are to me? A deadly sword-arm?"

He wouldn't look at her. "I'm not a good man like your father was. I'm not one of your courtly heroes. I've done terrible things. Unforgivable things."

The vulnerability in his voice melted her heart. How could he possibly be unsure of himself. Of her?

"I hate flowers," he growled. "I will never, *ever* write you a sonnet."

He seemed determined to make a clean breast of his sins and shortcomings and Cara smiled, even though her eyes were stinging. "I know. You don't have a chivalrous bone in your body. I don't care. I love you."

He closed his eyes and raised his face to the ceiling as if receiving a benediction, or the kiss of rain on his skin. "Stop saying that! I don't deserve you."

"Well, that's true."

That got his attention. His startled gaze snapped to hers.

"You're high-handed, deceitful, and sinfully arrogant. But you're kind to dogs and horses. That counts for something." Cara tried to keep her tone grave but he caught the twinkle in her eyes.

"Are you *laughing* at me?"

"At the fearsome Diavolo? Never. The truth is, I don't think there's another man in Europe who'll put up with me. If *you* don't want me, I'll have to join a nunnery."

His features softened, just slightly. "I don't think they'd take you back. Renata told me about your run-in with the Sisters of Mercy."

"You're probably right." She looked him dead in the eye. "Do you love me?"

"I'd kill for you."

THE DEVIL TO PAY

"That's not an answer. You'd kill for *anyone*, for the right price. Do you love me?"

He avoided her gaze, looking adorably hunted. "I'd die for you," he hedged.

"Do you *love* me?" she persisted. A devilish thread of stubbornness was pushing her to secure the victory that was somehow, miraculously, within her grasp. She knew him. To admit to loving her would be tantamount to admitting a fatal weakness, a dependency on another human being that was entirely foreign to his nature. Which was stupid, but there it was. He was a man. "All or nothing, del Sarto. I want you willing, or not at all."

He scowled at his own words coming back to haunt him. "Yes, I love you, damn it!" He shrugged away from her hand as if she were a leper. "There, are you happy now?"

Cara fought to keep the smile from her voice. "You needn't sound so cross about it."

His face bore an expression of acute disgust. "You think I *like* it?" He must have realized how ridiculous that sounded because he gave a heartfelt sigh. "You want proof? Is that it? Was giving you a castle not enough? Fine, come here, then."

He stood, caught her wrist, and sank to his knees in front of her.

Cara stared at him in astonishment. "What are you doing?"

He enfolded her hands between his own and bowed his head. "I, Alessandro Rafael del Sarto, become your liege man of life and limb and truth and earthly honors, bearing to you against all men that love or move or die, so help me God and the Holy Dame."

319

CHAPTER 53

*C*ara blinked back tears at the sight of Alessandro solemnly pledging allegiance to her, just as she'd done to him on that muddy practice field.

He probably thought he was demeaning himself, but even on the floor he was commanding, enhanced rather than diminished by the gesture. She became acutely aware of the disparity in their sizes. Despite kneeling, his head was still almost level with her shoulder. It was like a lion kneeling to a mouse.

"Don't expect me to do *this* again in public," he growled. "I have to keep some semblance of control. I'll never get any respect if the men realize I'm ruled by a slip of a girl." He slanted her a glance. "I never actually asked you to marry me, did I?"

"It's too late now."

He quirked his brows, not at all repentant. "Always better to ask for forgiveness than permission."

It wasn't much of an apology, but Cara couldn't deny him when he looked at her like that. She sighed. "You're forgiven. Get up, for heaven's sake."

He complied, filling the space before her, shrinking the room. He hadn't let go of her hands. He rolled his thumb over the thick wedding band on her ring finger. "Still wearing this, I see." He tugged at the ribbon she'd wound around it to hold it in place and slid it off her finger. Cara was about to protest when he reached into his shirt. "I have something better for you."

A huge ruby, set on a band of gold, glittered in the firelight, a match for the earrings and necklace he'd already given her. He threaded it onto her finger and met her eyes. "You already have the rest of the set. You might as well have it all."

Cara's heart skipped a beat as he gazed down at her. Her own fallen angel. With dark edges, of course.

"You're so beautiful," he murmured. "Inside and out." He bent and nuzzled her neck, and her pulse leapt in response.

"Do you realize we've never made love in daylight?" he murmured.

"I hadn't really thought about it." His touch was doing ridiculous things to her insides.

"Oh, I have. A lot. I've had six long years to think about it. You have no idea of the places I've dreamed of making love to you. When I was away on campaign I'd lie awake in my tent, listening to the camp get quiet. I'd spend long, cold hours looking up at the trees or the stars, thinking of you."

Cara smiled as his deft fingers began to unlace the front of her bodice.

"It always started out quite innocently. You'd be riding your horse, maybe, with me following at a respectful distance. The wind would be blowing your hair back from your face." He smoothed her hair over her shoulder, matching his words. "But then you'd look back and challenge me to a race."

She was hot and cold all over. "Which I'd win, of course."

"No horse was faster than Saraceno. I'd chase you down and pull you into my arms."

Her skin tingled. His voice was pure sorcery.

"I've had you in every possible way. Fast and furious. Slow

and lazy." He tugged the ribbon from the last eyelet and her bodice fell open. She shrugged her arms out of the sleeves.

"Sometimes I'd take my time undressing you, revealing you inch by inch."

Her skirt collapsed in a whisper of fabric at her feet. She stepped out of it and pulled her shift over her head so she was naked to his gaze. Her nipples beaded in the cool night air.

"Other times I'd barely wait, ripping your clothes off in desperation. I'd take you quickly, savagely, in any number of improbable locations." He stepped back and eyed her naked form with undisguised appreciation, then reached forward and brushed his hands over her breasts.

Need flashed, white-hot. Her knees wobbled. "You've given this quite a bit of thought."

"Hours. Weeks. We've made love in my battlefield tent. Out in the tall grass of a meadow. In the daytime. Under the stars. In France and Italy, Greece, and Spain. Summer and winter. With clothes and without. I let my imagination run riot."

"I can tell. But it's still not daytime now," she felt compelled to point out.

His smile raised her temperature by a few hundred degrees. "It will be, if we take long enough."

She raised an eyebrow in challenge. "Think you can last that long?"

He slanted her a cocky grin. "I'm willing to try." He finally kissed her, hard and full, and her senses reeled with pleasure. "Can you remember any of the tricks from those books I gave you?"

"A few," Cara managed weakly.

"That's good. Because you still owe me a wedding night."

Cara leaned into him, loving his height, his strength, his everything. Her breasts throbbed where they pressed against his shirt and she suddenly couldn't wait to feel his skin against hers. Impatient, she tugged the shirt from his waistband and pushed it off his shoulders, pressing a kiss to his chest as she did so. He lifted his arms to help her but when she dropped the shirt to the floor the bandage fell away with it.

She couldn't prevent a sharp intake of breath at the ugly new scar that disfigured his shoulder. She touched the puckered flesh with her fingertips and he hissed in a breath.

"I'm so sorry," she whispered.

He brought her fingers to his lips. "I'd take a hundred more, if it would keep you safe." He brushed the corner of her mouth with his lips and Cara opened to him on a moan.

He was everything she'd ever dreamed; alternately rough and teasing, demanding and tender. He bit her lips, then soothed them with his tongue, teased her breasts until she was panting and begging for mercy. He drew her down beside him onto the bed and tormented her with his fingers and then again with his mouth, using every one of his formidable skills to take her to the very edge of madness. And when he finally slid inside her, strong and sure, it felt like coming home.

Cara wanted to sing with joy. He was infuriating and challenging and far too overbearing, but he was hers. For a lifetime.

As the last glimmers of ecstasy racked her body she let out a shattered sigh then lay with her head resting on his chest. He slung his arm over her waist and she stroked his wrist, loving the play of muscles under his tawny skin.

"I have a confession to make," he murmured sleepily.

"*Now* what?"

"I lied about the number of marriage proposals I got for you."

"I know the duke of Parma only offered for me because you paid him."

"Not that. I told you eight people asked for your hand, but there were nine."

"Who did you forget?"

"Don Michelotto."

Cara's mouth fell open. "The Borgias' assassin?"

"I think he sensed a kindred spirit. I was tempted to accept on your behalf. The only thing that stopped me was the thought that the poor bastard didn't deserve you."

She pinched his arm. "Charming!"

"I have my moments." He paused, and she sensed him gather himself for his next words. "Are you going to *stay* here this time? With me?"

She nodded. "No more jumping out of windows, I promise. I want to be wherever you are."

He leaned back a fraction to look at her. "You'd really leave Castelleon?"

"I've been thinking about that. Francesco and Renata could run it. They'll care for the people and the land. That's all I ever wanted."

Alessandro rolled her over and kissed her, taking his time. "Just one more promise, then, my lady del Sarto—"

"Mmmm?"

"You'll never try to teach our children alchemy."

Cara smiled as his mouth touched hers again. "Children, eh?"

"It's risky," he murmured, nibbling her lower lip. "Marrying you is the most dangerous thing I've ever done. And I'm including the battle of Fornovo in that assessment. Having children with you might just finish me off."

"I thought you were invincible."

"That's just a myth. What if they inherit your talent for destruction?"

"What if they inherit your brains instead of your brawn?" she countered. "We'll all be doomed."

He slid his palms over her breasts. "It's a risk I'm willing to take."

"How noble!"

"Don't tell anyone. My reputation's already in shreds." He bent his head to her stomach and swirled his tongue around her navel. "We should start practicing now. Let's not forget your woefully advanced age of twenty-two."

HOURS LATER, Cara gazed through the open window as the pale light of dawn touched the sky as Alessandro came to stand behind her. He wrapped his arms around her as she leaned back against him, perfectly content.

A clatter of hooves disturbed the silence in the courtyard below.

"You left in such a hurry I never had time to give you your wedding present," he murmured into her hair.

"I thought Castelleon was my wedding present?"

A stable boy was leading two horses across the cobbles. Cara recognized Saraceno, but her breath caught when she saw the second mount.

"Do you have any *idea* how difficult it is to get a pure-bred white Barbary mare in Europe?" he growled.

"You bought her for me?" She hid a smile by biting her lip. "I hate to break it to you, del Sarto, but that's rather romantic."

He made a sound of acute disgust. "It's not romantic. It's *practical*. Hopefully you'll stop stealing Saraceno if you have your own horse."

"It didn't have to be white, though," she persisted.

He sighed. "No, it didn't. But you wanted a white one. So there it is. The damn thing cost me a king's ransom. *Literally*."

"You should count yourself lucky I didn't ask for a giraffe, like the one in the Medici menagerie."

"That's not why I count myself lucky."

Cara sighed happily.

"What are you thinking?" he asked after a moment.

"Only that my maid, Bianca, was right after all."

He turned her within the confines of his arms. "About what?"

325

"Cook's lemon cake."

He wrinkled his brow in confusion.

"She always insisted the only thing better than cook's lemon cake was making love," Cara explained with a smile. "I think she might be right."

His expression turned wicked. "You only *think*? You're not certain?" He shook his head and brushed his lips across hers. "I wouldn't be much of a husband if you were left in any doubt. Allow me to convince you, my lady. . . for the next fifty or so years."

Cara closed her eyes in delight as her very own knight in tarnished armor set about making his point in the most pleasurable way.

Like what you just read? Find more of Kate's books here:

ABOUT THE AUTHOR

Kate Bateman / K.C. Bateman, is a bestselling author of Regency and Renaissance historical romances, including the Secrets & Spies series, Bow Street Bachelors series, and Ruthless Rivals series. Her books have received multiple Starred Reviews from Publishers Weekly and Library Journal, and her Renaissance romp The Devil To Pay was a 2019 RITA award nominee.

Her books have been translated into multiple languages, including French, Italian, Brazilian, Japanese, German, Romanian, Czech, and Croatian.

When not writing, Kate leads a double life as a fine art appraiser and on-screen antiques expert for several TV shows in the UK. She currently lives in Illinois with a number-loving husband and three inexhaustible children, and regularly returns to her native England 'for research.'

Kate loves to hear from readers. Contact her via her website: www.kcbateman.com and sign up for her newsletter to receive free books, regular updates on new releases, giveaways, and exclusive excerpts.

ALSO BY K. C. BATEMAN

Ruthless Rivals Series:
A Reckless Match
A Daring Pursuit
A Wicked Game

Bow Street Bachelors Series:
This Earl Of Mine
To Catch An Earl
The Princess & The Rogue

Secrets & Spies Series:
To Steal a Heart
A Raven's Heart
A Counterfeit Heart

Italian Renaissance:
The Devil To Pay

Novellas:
The Promise of A Kiss
A Midnight Clear

FOLLOW

Follow Kate online for the latest new releases, giveaways, exclusive sneak peeks, and more!

Join Kate's Facebook reader group: Badasses in Bodices

Sign up for Kate's monthly-ish newsletter via her website for news, exclusive excerpts and giveaways.

Follow Kate Bateman on Bookbub for new releases and sales.

Add Kate's books to your Goodreads lists, or leave a review!

SNEAK PEEK

Read on for a sneak peek of *This Earl Of Mine,*
the first exhilarating historical romance in Kate Bateman's Bow
Street Bachelors Series. . .

THIS EARL OF MINE

$\mathcal{L}$ ondon, March 1816.

THERE WERE WORSE PLACES to find a husband than Newgate Prison.

Of course there were.

It was just that, at present, Georgie couldn't think of any.

"Georgiana Caversteed, this is a terrible idea."

Georgie frowned at her burly companion, Pieter Smit, as the nondescript carriage he'd summoned to convey them to London's most notorious jail rocked to a halt on the cobbled street. The salt-weathered Dutchman always used her full name whenever he disapproved of something she was doing. Which was often.

"Your father would turn in his watery grave if he knew what you were about."

That was undoubtedly true. Until three days ago, enlisting a husband from amongst the ranks of London's most dangerous criminals had not featured prominently on her list of life goals.

But desperate times called for desperate measures. Or, in this case, for a desperate felon about to be hanged. A felon she would marry before the night was through.

Georgie peered out into the rain-drizzled street, then up, up the near-windowless walls. They rose into the mist, five stories high, a vast expanse of brickwork, bleak and unpromising. A church bell tolled somewhere in the darkness, a forlorn clang like a death knell. Her stomach knotted with a grim sense of foreboding.

Was she really going to go through with this? It had seemed a good plan, in the safety of Grosvenor Square. The perfect way to thwart Cousin Josiah once and for all. She stepped from the carriage, ducked her head against the rain, and followed Pieter under a vast arched gate. Her heart hammered at the audacity of what she planned.

They'd taken the same route as condemned prisoners on the way to Tyburn tree, only in reverse. West to east, from the rarefied social strata of Mayfair through gradually rougher and bleaker neighborhoods, Holborn and St. Giles, to this miserable place where the dregs of humanity had been incarcerated. Georgie felt as if she were nearing her own execution.

She shook off the pervasive aura of doom and straightened her spine. This was her choice. However unpalatable the next few minutes might be, the alternative was far worse. Better a temporary marriage to a murderous, unwashed criminal than a lifetime of misery with Josiah.

They crossed the deserted outer courtyard, and Georgie cleared her throat, trying not to inhale the foul-smelling air that seeped from the very pores of the building. "You have it all arranged? They are expecting us?"

Pieter nodded. "Aye. I've greased the wheels with yer blunt, my girl. The proctor and the ordinary are both bent as copper shillings. Used to having their palms greased, those two, the greedy bastards."

Her father's right-hand man had never minced words in front of her, and Georgie appreciated his bluntness. So few people in the ton ever said what they really meant. Pieter's honesty was refreshing. He'd been her father's man for twenty years before she'd even been born. A case of mumps had prevented him from accompanying William Caversteed on his last, fateful voyage, and Georgie had often thought that if Pieter had been with her father, maybe he'd still be alive. Little things like squalls, shipwrecks, and attacks from Barbary pirates would be mere inconveniences to a man like Pieter Smit.

In the five years since Papa's death, Pieter's steadfast loyalty had been dedicated to William's daughters, and Georgie loved the gruff, hulking manservant like a second father. He would see her through this madcap scheme—even if he disapproved.

She tugged the hood of her cloak down to stave off the drizzle. This place was filled with murderers, highwaymen, forgers, and thieves. Poor wretches slated to die, or those "lucky" few whose sentences had been commuted to transportation. Yet in her own way, she was equally desperate.

"You are sure that this man is to be hanged tomorrow?"

Pieter nodded grimly as he rapped on a wooden door. "I am. A low sort he is, by all accounts."

She shouldn't ask, didn't want to know too much about the man whose name she was purchasing. A man whose death would spell her own freedom. She would be wed and widowed within twenty-four hours.

Taking advantage of a condemned man left a sour taste in her mouth, a sense of guilt that her happiness should come from the misfortune of another. But this man would die whether she married him or not. "What are his crimes?"

"Numerous, I'm told. He's a coiner." At her frown, Pieter elaborated. "Someone who forges coins. It's treason, that."

"Oh." That seemed a little harsh. She couldn't imagine what that was like, having no money, forced to make your own. Still,

334

having a fortune was almost as much of a curse as having nothing. She'd endured six years of insincere, lecherous fortune hunters, thanks to her bountiful coffers.

"A smuggler too," Pieter added for good measure. "Stabbed a customs man down in Kent."

She was simply making the best out of a bad situation. This man would surely realize that while there was no hope for himself, at least he could leave this world having provided for whatever family he left behind. Everyone had parents, or siblings, or lovers. Everyone had a price. She, of all people, knew that—she was buying herself a husband. At least this way there was no pretense. Besides, what was the point in having a fortune if you couldn't use it to make yourself happy?

Pieter hammered impatiently on the door again.

"I know you disapprove," Georgie muttered. "But Father would never have wanted me to marry a man who covets my purse more than my person. If you hadn't rescued me the other evening, that's precisely what would have happened. I would have had to wed Josiah to prevent a scandal. I refuse to give control of my life and my fortune to some idiot to mismanage. As a widow, I will be free."

Pieter gave an eloquent sniff.

"You think me heartless," Georgie said. "But can you think of another way?" At his frowning silence, she nodded. "No, me neither."

Heavy footsteps and the jangle of keys finally heralded proof of human life inside. The door scraped open, and the low glare of a lantern illuminated a grotesquely large man in the doorway.

"Mr. Knollys?"

The man gave a brown-toothed grin as he recognized Pieter. "Welcome back, sir. Welcome back." He craned his neck and raised the lantern, trying to catch a glimpse of Georgie. "You brought the lady, then?" His piggy eyes narrowed with curiosity within the folds of his flabby face.

"And the license." Pieter tapped the pocket of his coat.

Knollys nodded and stepped back, allowing them entry. "The ordinary's agreed to perform the service." He turned and began shuffling down the narrow corridor, lantern raised. "Only one small problem." He cocked his head back toward Pieter. "That cove the lady was to marry? Cheated the 'angman, 'e 'as."

Pieter stopped abruptly, and Georgie bumped into his broad back.

"He's dead?" Pieter exclaimed. "Then why are we here? You can damn well return that purse I paid you!"

The man's belly undulated grotesquely as he laughed. It was not a kindly sound. "Now, now. Don't you worry yerself none, me fine lad. That special license don't have no names on it yet, do it? No. We've plenty more like 'im in this place. This way."

The foul stench of the prison increased tenfold as they followed the unpleasant Knollys up some stairs and down a second corridor. Rows of thick wooden doors, each with a square metal hatch and a sliding shutter at eye level lined the walls on either side. Noises emanated from some—inhuman moans, shouts, and foul curses. Others were ominously silent. Georgie pressed her handkerchief to her nose, glad she'd doused it in lavender water.

Knollys waddled to a stop in front of the final door in the row. His eyes glistened with a disquieting amount of glee.

"Found the lady a substitute, I 'ave." He thumped the metal grate with his meaty fist and eyed Georgie's cloaked form with a knowing, suggestive leer that made her feel as though she'd been drenched in cooking fat. She resisted the urge to shudder.

"Wake up, lads!" he bellowed. "There's a lady 'ere needs yer services."

Chapter 2.

BENEDICT WILLIAM HENRY WYLDE, scapegrace second son of the late Earl of Morcott, reluctant war hero, and former scourge of the ton, strained to hear the last words of his cellmate. He bent forward, trying to ignore the stench of the man's blackened teeth and the sickly sweet scent of impending death that wreathed his feverish form.

Silas had been sick for days, courtesy of a festering stab wound in his thigh. The bastard jailers hadn't heeded his pleas for water, bandages, or laudanum. Ben had been trying to decipher the smuggler's ranting for hours. Delirium had loosened the man's tongue, and he'd leaned close, waiting for something useful to slip between those cracked lips, but the words had been frustratingly fragmented. Silas raved about plots and treasons. An Irishman. The emperor. Benedict had been on the verge of shaking the poor bastard when his crew mate let out one last, gasping breath—and died.

"Oh, bloody hell!"

Ben drew back from the hard, straw-filled pallet that stank of piss and death. He'd been so close to getting the information he needed.

Not for the first time, he cursed his friend Alex's uncle, Sir Nathaniel Conant, Chief Magistrate of Bow Street and the man tasked with transforming the way London was policed. Bow Street was the senior magistrate court in the capital, and the "Runners," as they were rather contemptuously known, investigated crimes, followed up leads, served warrants and summons, searched properties for stolen goods, and watched premises where infringements of bylaws or other offenses were suspected.

Conant had approached Ben, Alex, and their friend Seb about a year ago, a few months after their return from fighting Napoleon on the continent. The three of them had just opened the Tricorn Club—the gambling hell they'd pledged to run together while crouched around a smoky campfire in Belgium. Conant had pointed out that their new venture placed them in an ideal position for gathering intelligence on behalf of His Majesty's government, since its members—and their acquaintances—came from all levels of society. He'd also requested their assistance on occasional cases, especially those which bridged the social divide. The three of them not only had entrée into polite society, but thanks to their time in the Rifles, they dealt equally well with those from the lower end of the social spectrum, the "scum of the earth," as Wellington had famously called his own troops.

Conant paid the three of them a modest sum for every mission they undertook, plus extra commission for each bit of new information they brought in. Neither Alex nor Seb needed the money; they were more interested in the challenge to their wits, but Benedict had jumped at the chance of some additional income, even though the work was sometimes—such as now— less than glamorous.

He was in Newgate on Conant's orders, chasing a rumor that someone had been trying to assemble a crew of smugglers to rescue the deposed Emperor Napoleon from the island of St. Helena. Benedict had been ingratiating himself with this band for weeks, posing as a bitter ex-navy gunner, searching for the man behind such a plan. He'd even allowed himself to be seized by customs officials near Gravesend along with half the gang— recently deceased Silas amongst them—in the hopes of discovering more. If he solved this case, he'd receive a reward of five hundred pounds, which could go some way toward helping his brother pay off the mass of debt left by their profligate father.

He'd been in here almost ten days now. The gang's ringleader, a vicious bastard named Hammond, had been hanged yesterday morning. Ben, Silas, and two of the younger gang members had been sentenced to transportation. That was British leniency for you; a nice slow death on a prison ship instead of a quick drop from Tyburn tree.

The prison hulk would be leaving at dawn, but Ben wouldn't be on it. There was no need to hang around now that Silas and Hammond were both dead. He'd get nothing more from them. And the two youngsters, Peters and Fry, were barely in their teens. They knew nothing useful. Conant had arranged for him to "disappear" from the prison hulk before it sailed; its guards were as open to bribery as Knollys.

Several other gang members had escaped the Gravesend raid. Benedict had glimpsed a few familiar faces in the crowd when the magistrate had passed down his sentence. He'd have to chase them down as soon as he was free and see if any of them had been approached for the traitorous mission.

Benedict sighed and slid down the wall until he sat on the filthy floor, his knees bent in front of him. He'd forgotten what it felt like to be clean. He rasped one hand over his stubbled jaw and grimaced—he'd let his beard grow out as a partial disguise. He'd commit murder for a wash and a razor. Even during the worst scrapes in the Peninsular War, and then in France and Belgium, he'd always found time to shave. Alex and Seb, his brothers-in-arms, had mocked him for it mercilessly.

He glanced at the square of rain visible through the tiny barred grate on the outer wall of his cell. Seb and Alex were out there, lucky buggers, playing merry hell with the debutantes, wives, and widows of London with amazing impartiality.

The things he did for king and bloody country.

And cash, of course. Five hundred pounds was nothing to sneeze at.

Tracking down a traitor was admirable. Having to stay celibate and sober because there was neither a woman nor grog to be had in prison was hell. What he wouldn't give for some decent French brandy and a warm, willing wench. Hell, right now he'd settle for some of that watered-down ratafia they served at society balls and a tumble with a barmaid.

A pretty barmaid, of course. His face had always allowed him to be choosy. At least, it did when he was clean-shaven. His own mother probably wouldn't recognize him right now.

Voices and footsteps intruded on his errant fancies as the obsequious voice of Knollys echoed through the stones. A fist slammed into the grate, loud enough to wake the dead, and Benedict glanced over at Silas with morbid humor. Well, almost loud enough.

"Wake up, lads!" Knollys bellowed. "There's a lady 'ere needs yer services."

Benedict's brows rose in the darkness. What the devil?

"Ye promised ten pounds if I'd find 'er a man an' never say nuffink to nobody," he heard Knollys say through the door.

"Are they waiting to hang too?" An older man's voice, that, with a foreign inflection. Dutch, perhaps.

"Nay. Ain't got no more for the gallows. Not since Hammond yesterday." Knollys sounded almost apologetic. "But either one of these'll fit the bill. Off to Van Diemen's Land they are, at first light."

"No, that won't do at all."

Benedict's ears pricked up at the sound of the cultured female voice. She sounded extremely peeved.

"I specifically wanted a condemned man, Mr. Knollys."

"Better come back in a week or so then, milady."

There was a short pause as the two visitors apparently conferred, too low for him to hear.

"I cannot wait another few weeks." The woman sounded resigned. "Very well. Let's see what you have."

Keys grated in the lock and Knollys's quivering belly filled the doorway. Benedict shielded his eyes from the lantern's glare, blinding after the semidarkness of the cell. The glow illuminated Silas's still figure on the bed and Knollys grunted.

"Dead, is 'e?" He sounded neither dismayed nor surprised. "Figured he wouldn't last the week. You'll 'ave to do then, Wylde. Get up."

Benedict pushed himself to his feet with a wince.

"Ain't married, are you, Wylde?" Knollys muttered, low enough not to be heard by those in the corridor.

"Never met the right woman," Benedict drawled, being careful to retain the rough accent of an east coast smuggler he'd adopted. "Still, one lives in 'ope."

Knollys frowned, trying to decide whether Ben was being sarcastic. As usual, he got it wrong. "This lady's 'ere to wed," he grunted finally, gesturing vaguely behind him.

Benedict squinted. Two shapes hovered just outside, partly shielded by the jailer's immense bulk. One of them, the smaller hooded figure, might possibly be female. "What woman comes here to marry?"

Knollys chuckled. "A desperate one, Mr. Wylde."

The avaricious glint in Knollys's eye hinted that he saw the opportunity to take advantage, and Benedict experienced a rush of both anger and protectiveness for the foolish woman, whoever she might be. Probably one of the muslin set, seeking a name for her unborn child. Or some common trollop, hoping her debts would be wiped off with the death of her husband. Except he'd never met a tart who spoke with such a clipped, aristocratic accent.

"You want me to marry some woman I've never met?" Benedict almost laughed in disbelief. "I appreciate the offer, Mr. Knollys, but I'll have to decline. I ain't stepping into the parson's mousetrap for no one."

Knollys took a menacing step forward. "Oh, you'll do it, Wylde, or I'll have Ennis bash your skull in." He glanced over at Silas's corpse. "I can just as easy 'ave 'im dig two graves instead of one."

Ennis was a short, troll-like thug who possessed fewer brains than a sack of potatoes, but he took a malicious and creative pleasure in administering beatings with his heavy wooden cudgel. Benedict's temper rose. He didn't like being threatened. If it weren't for the manacles binding his hands, he'd explain that pertinent fact to Mr. Knollys in no uncertain terms.

Unfortunately, Knollys wasn't a man to take chances. He prodded Benedict with his stick. "Out with ye. And no funny business." His meaty fist cuffed Ben around the head to underscore the point.

Benedict stepped out into the dim passageway and took an appreciative breath. The air was slightly less rancid out here. Of course, it was all a matter of degree.

A broad, grizzled man of around sixty moved to stand protectively in front of the woman, arms crossed and bushy brows lowered. Benedict leaned sideways and tried to make out her features, but the hood of a domino shielded her face. She made a delicious, feminine rustle of silk as she stepped back, though. No rough worsted and cotton for this lady. Interesting.

Knollys prodded him along the passage, and Benedict shook his head to dispel a sense of unreality. Here he was, unshaven, unwashed, less than six hours from freedom, and apparently about to be wed to a perfect stranger. It seemed like yet another cruel joke by fate.

He'd never imagined himself marrying. Not after the disastrous example of his own parents' union. His mother had endured his father's company only long enough to produce the requisite heir and a spare, then removed herself to the gaiety of London. For the next twenty years, she'd entertained a series of lovers in the town house, while his father had remained immured in Herefordshire with a succession of steadily younger live-in mistresses, one of whom had taken it upon herself to introduce a seventeen-year-old Benedict to the mysteries of the female form. It was a pattern of domesticity Benedict had absolutely no desire to repeat.

In truth, he hadn't thought he'd survive the war and live to the ripe old age of twenty-eight. If he had ever been forced to picture his own wedding—under torture, perhaps—he was fairly certain he wouldn't have imagined it taking place in prison. At the very least, he would have had his family and a couple of friends in attendance; his fellow sworn bachelors, Alex and Seb. Some flowers, maybe. A country church.

He'd never envisaged the lady. If three years of warfare had taught him anything, it was that life was too short to tie himself to one woman for the rest of his life. Marriage would be an imprisonment worse than his cell here in Newgate.

They clattered down the stairs and into the tiny chapel where the ordinary, Horace Cotton, was waiting, red-faced and unctuous. Cotton relished his role of resident chaplain; he enjoyed haranguing soon-to-be-dead prisoners with lengthy sermons full of fire and brimstone. No doubt he was being paid handsomely for this evening's work.

Benedict halted in front of the altar—little more than a table covered in a white cloth and two candles—and raised his manacled wrists to Knollys. The jailer sniffed but clearly realized he'd have to unchain him if they were to proceed. He gave Ben a sour, warning look as the irons slipped off, just daring him to try something. Ben shot him a cocky, challenging sneer in return.

How to put a stop to this farce? He had no cash to bribe his way out. A chronic lack of funds was precisely why he'd been working for Bow Street since his return from France, chasing thief-taker's rewards.

Could he write the wrong name on the register, to invalidate the marriage? Probably not. Both Knollys and Cotton knew him as Ben Wylde. Ex-Rifle brigade, penniless, cynical veteran of Waterloo. It wasn't his full name, of course, but it would probably be enough to satisfy the law.

Announcing that his brother happened to be the Earl of Morcott would certainly make matters interesting, but thanks to their father's profligacy, the estate was mortgaged to the hilt. John had even less money than Benedict.

The unpleasant sensation that he'd been neatly backed into a corner made Benedict's neck prickle, as if a French sniper had him in his sights. Still, he'd survived worse. He was a master at getting out of scrapes. Even if he was forced to marry this mystery harridan, there were always alternatives. An annulment, for one.

"Might I at least have the name of the lady to whom I'm about to be joined in holy matrimony?" he drawled.

The manservant scowled at the ironic edge to his tone, but the woman laid a silencing hand on his arm and stepped around him.

"You can indeed, sir." In one smooth movement, she pulled the hood from her head and faced him squarely. "My name is Georgiana Caversteed."

Benedict cursed in every language he knew.

Chapter 3.

GEORGIANA CAVERSTEED? What devil's trick was this?

He knew the name, but he'd never seen the face—until now. God's teeth, every man in London knew the name. The chit was so rich, she might as well have her own bank. She could have her pick of any man in England. What in God's name was she doing in Newgate looking for a husband?

Benedict barely remembered not to bow—an automatic response to being introduced to a lady of quality—and racked his brains to recall what he knew of her family. A cit's daughter. Her father had been in shipping, a merchant, rich as Croesus. He'd died and left the family a fortune.

The younger sister was said to be the beauty of the family, but she must indeed be goddess, because Georgiana Caversteed was strikingly lovely. Her arresting, heart-shaped face held a small straight nose and eyes which, in the candlelight, appeared to be dark grey, the color of wet slate. Her brows were full, her lashes long, and her mouth was soft and a fraction too wide.

A swift heat spread throughout his body, and his heart began to pound.

She regarded him steadily as he made his assessment, neither dipping her head nor coyly fluttering her lashes. Benedict's interest kicked up a notch at her directness, and a twitch in his breeches reminded him with unpleasantly bad timing of his enforced abstinence. This was neither the time nor the place to do anything about that.

They'd never met in the ton. She must have come to town after he'd left for the peninsula three years ago, which would make her around twenty-four. Most women would be considered on the shelf at that age, unmarried after so many social seasons, but with the near-irresistible lure of her fortune and with those dazzling looks, Georgiana Caversteed could be eighty-four and someone would still want her.

And yet here she was.

Benedict kept his expression bland, even as he tried to breathe normally. What on earth had made her take such drastic action? Was the chit daft in the head? He couldn't imagine any situation desperate enough to warrant getting leg-shackled to a man like him.

She moistened her lips with the tip of her tongue—which sent another shot of heat straight to his gut—and fixed him with an imperious glare. "What is your name, sir?" She took a step closer, almost in challenge, in defiance of his unchained hands and undoubtedly menacing demeanor.

He quelled a spurt of admiration for her courage, even if it was ill-advised. His inhaled breath caught a subtle whiff of her perfume. It made his knees weak. He'd forgotten the intoxicating scent of woman and skin. For one foolish moment, he imagined pulling her close and pressing his nose into her hair, just filling his lungs with the divine scent of her. He wanted to drink in her smell. He wanted to see if those lips really were as soft as they looked.

He took an involuntary step toward her but stopped at the low growl of warning from her manservant. Sanity prevailed, and he just remembered to stay in the role of rough smuggler they all expected of him.

"My name? Ben Wylde. At your service."

* * *

HIS VOICE WAS A DEEP RASP, rough from lack of use, and Georgie's stomach did an odd little flip. She needed to take command here, like Father on board one of his ships, but the man facing her was huge, hairy, and thoroughly intimidating.

When she'd glanced around Knollys's rotund form and into the gloomy cell, her first impression of the prisoner had been astonishment at his sheer size. He'd seemed to fill the entire space, all broad shoulders, wide chest, and long legs. She'd been expecting some poor, ragged, cowering scrap of humanity. Not this strapping, unapologetically male creature.

She'd studied his shaggy, overlong hair and splendid proportions from the back as they'd traipsed down the corridor. He stood a good head taller than Knollys, and unlike the jailer's waddling shuffle, this man walked with a long, confident stride, straight-backed and chin high, as if he owned the prison and were simply taking a tour for his pleasure.

Now, in the chapel, she finally saw his face—the parts that weren't covered with a dark bristle of beard—and her skin prickled as she allowed her eyes to rove over him. She pretended she was inspecting a horse or a piece of furniture. Something large and impersonal.

His dark hair was matted and hung around his face almost to his chin. It was hard to tell what color it would be when it was clean. A small wisp of straw stuck out from one side, just above his ear, and she resisted a bizarre feminine urge to reach up and remove it. Dark beard hid the shape of his jaw, but the candle-light caught his slanted cheekbones and cast shadows in the hollows beneath. The skin that she could see—a straight slash of nose, cheeks, and forehead—was unfashionably tanned and emphasized his deep brown eyes.

She'd stepped as close to him as she dared; no doubt he'd smell like a cesspool if she got any nearer, but even so, she was aware of an uncomfortable curl of . . . what? Reluctant attraction? Repelled fascination?

The top of her head only came up to his chin, and his size was, paradoxically, both threatening and reassuring. He was large enough to lean on; she was certain if she raised her hand to his chest, he would be solid and warm. Unmovable. Her heart hammered in alarm. He was huge and unwashed, and yet her body reacted to him in the most disconcerting manner.

His stare was uncomfortably intense. She dropped her eyes, breaking the odd frisson between them, and took a small step backward.

His lawn shirt, open at the neck, was so thin it was almost transparent. His muscled chest and arms were clearly visible through the grimy fabric. His breeches were a nondescript brown, snug at the seams, and delineated the hard ridges of muscles of his lean thighs with unnerving clarity.

Georgie frowned. This was a man in the prime of life. It seemed wrong that he'd been caged like an animal. He exuded such a piratical air of command that she could easily imagine him on the prow of a ship or pacing in front of a group of soldiers, snapping orders.

She found her voice. "Were you in the military, Mr. Wylde?"

That would certainly explain his splendid physique and air of cocky confidence.

His dark brows twitched in what might have been surprise but could equally have been irritation. "I was."

She waited for more, but he did not elaborate. Clearly Mr. Wylde was a man of few words. His story was probably like that of thousands of other soldiers who had returned from the wars and found themselves unable to find honest work. She'd seen them in the streets, ragged and begging. It was England's disgrace that men who'd fought so heroically for their country had been reduced to pursuing a life of crime to survive.

Was the fact that he was not a condemned man truly a problem? Her original plan had been to tell Josiah she'd married a sailor who had put to sea. She would have been a widow, of course, but Josiah would never have known that. Her "absent" husband could have sailed the world indefinitely.

If she married this Wylde fellow, she would not immediately become a widow, but the intended result would be the same. Josiah would not be able to force her into marriage and risk committing bigamy.

Georgie narrowed her eyes at the prisoner. They would be bound together until one or the other of them died, and he looked disconcertingly healthy. Providing he didn't take up heavy drinking or catch a nasty tropical disease, he'd probably outlive her. That could cause problems.

Of course, if he continued his ill-advised occupation, then he'd probably succumb to a knife or a bullet sooner rather than later. Men like him always came to a sticky end; he'd only narrowly escaped the gallows this time. She'd probably be a widow in truth soon enough. But how would she hear of his passing if he were halfway across the world? How would she know when she was free?

She tore her eyes away from the rogue's surprisingly tempting lips and fixed Knollys with a hard stare. "Is there really no one else? I mean, he's so . . .so . . ."

Words failed her. Intimidating? Manly?

Unmanageable.

"No, ma'am. But he won't bother you after tonight."

What alternative did she have? She couldn't wait another few weeks. Her near-miss with Josiah had been the last straw. She'd been lucky to escape with an awful, sloppy kiss and not complete ruination. She sighed. "He'll have to do. Pieter, will you explain the terms of the agreement?"

Pieter nodded. "You'll marry Miss Caversteed tonight, Mr. Wylde. In exchange, you'll receive five hundred pounds to do with as you will."

Georgie waited for the prisoner to look suitably impressed. He did not. One dark eyebrow rose slightly, and the corner of his mobile lips curled in a most irritating way.

"Fat lot of good it'll do me in here," he drawled. "Ain't got time to pop to a bank between now and when they chain me to that floating death trap in the morning."

He had a fair point. "Is there someone else to whom we could send the money?"

His lips twitched again as if at some private joke. "Aye. Send it to Mr. Wolff at number ten St. James's. The Tricorn Club. Compliments of Ben Wylde. He'll appreciate it."

Georgie had no idea who this Mr. Wolff was—probably someone to whom this wretch owed a gambling debt—but she nodded and beckoned Pieter over. He took his cue and unfolded the legal document she'd had drawn up. He flattened it on the table next to the ordinary's pen and ink.

"You must sign this, Mr. Wylde. Ye can read?" he added as an afterthought.

Another twitch of those lips. "As if I'd been educated at Cambridge, sir. But give me the highlights."

"It says you renounce all claim to the lady's fortune, except for the five hundred pounds already agreed. You will make no further financial demands upon her in the future."

"Sounds reasonable."

The prisoner made a show of studying the entire document, or at least pretending to read it, then dipped the pen into the ink. Georgie held her breath.

Papa's will had divided his property equally between his wife and two daughters. To Georgie's mother, he'd left the estate in Lincolnshire. To her sister, Juliet, he'd left the London town house. And to Georgie, his eldest, the one who'd learned the business at his knee, he'd left the fleet of ships with which he'd made his fortune, the warehouses full of spices and silk, and the company ledgers.

His trusted man of business, Edmund Shaw, had done an exemplary job as Georgie's financial guardian for the past few years, but in three weeks' time, she would turn twenty-five and come into full possession of her fortune. And according to English law, as soon as she married, all that would instantly become the property of her husband, to do with as he wished.

That husband would not be Josiah.

Despite her mother's protests that it was vulgar and unlady-like to concern herself with commerce, in the past five years Georgie had purchased two new ships and almost doubled her profits. She loved the challenge of running her own business, the independence. She was damned if she'd give it over to some blithering idiot like Josiah to drink and gamble away.

Which was precisely why she'd had Edmund draw up this detailed document. It stated that all property and capital that was hers before the marriage remained hers. Her husband would receive only a discretionary allowance. To date, she'd received seven offers of marriage, and each time she'd sent her suitor to see Mr. Shaw. Every one of them had balked at signing—proof, if she'd needed it, that they'd only been after her fortune.

She let out a relieved sigh as the prisoner's pen moved confidently over the paper. Ben Wylde's signature was surprisingly neat. Perhaps he'd been a secretary, or written dispatches in the army? She shook her head. It wasn't her job to wonder about him. He was a means to an end, that was all.

He straightened, and his brown eyes were filled with a twinkle of devilry. "There, now. Just one further question, before we get to the vows, Miss Caversteed. Just what do you intend for a wedding night?"

* * *

Want to read more? Check out This Earl Of Mine on your favorite reading platform.

Printed in Great Britain
by Amazon